M000301459

THE LAW OF
SUCCESS

THE LAW OF SUCCESS

SUCCESS

Napoleon Hill

PRABHAT PRAKASHAN
ISO 9001: 2008 Publishers

The content of this book are
in Public Domain.

Published by
PRABHAT PRAKASHAN
4/19 Asaf Ali Road,
New Delhi-110 002 (INDIA)
Tele : +91-11-23289777
e-mail: prabhatbooks@gmail.com

ISBN 978-93-5266-501-3
THE LAW OF SUCCESS
by Napoleon Hill

Edition
2018

© Reserved

Typesetting
Team Prabhat

Dedicated to

A NDREW CARNEGIE Who suggested the writing of the course, and to HENRY FORD Whose astounding achievements form the foundation for practically all of the Six-teen Lessons of the course, and to EDWIN C. BARNES

A business associate of Thomas A. Edison, whose close personal friendship over a period of more than fifteen years served to help the author "carry on" in the face of a great variety of adversities and much temporary defeat met with in organising the course.

WHO said it could not be done? And what great victories has he to his credit which qualify him to judge others accurately?

Acknowledgment

The Author's Acknowledgment of Help Rendered Him in the Writing of This Course.

This course is the result of careful analysis of the life-work of over one hundred men and women who have achieved unusual success in their respective callings.

The author of the course has been more than twenty years in gathering, classifying, testing and organising the Fifteen Laws upon which the course is based. In his labour he has received valuable assistance either in person or by studying the life-work of the following men:

Henry Ford—Edward Bok

Thomas A. Edison—Cyrus H. K. Curtis

Harvey S. Firestone—George W. Perkins

John D. Rockefeller—Henry L. Doherty

Charles M. Schwab—George S. Parker

Woodrow Wilson—Dr. C. O. Henry

Darwin P. Kingsley—General Rufus A. Ayers

Wm. Wrigley, Jr.—Judge Elbert H. Gary

A. D. Lasker—William Howard Taft

E. A. Filene—Dr. Elmer Gates

James J. Hill—John W. Davis

Captain George M. Alex-Samuel Insul Ander (To whom the—F.W. Woolworth author was formerly Judge Daniel T. Wright an assistant) (One of the author's Hugh Chalmers law instructors) Dr. E. W. Strickler—Elbert Hubbard

Edwin C. Barnes—Luther Burbank

Robert L. Taylor—O. H. Harriman

(Fiddling Bob)—John Burroughs

George Eastman—E. H. Harriman

E. M. Statler—Charles P. Steinmetz
Andrew Carnegie—Frank Vanderlip
John Wanamaker—Theodore Roosevelt
Marshall Field—Wm. H. French

Dr. Alexander Graham Bell (To whom the author owes credit for most of Lesson One).

Of the men named, perhaps Henry Ford and Andrew Carnegie should be acknowledged as having contributed most toward the building of this course, for the reason that it was Andrew Carnegie who first suggested the writing of the course and Henry Ford whose life-work supplied much of the material out of which the course was developed.

Some of these men are now deceased, but to those who are still living the author wishes to make here grateful acknowledgment of the service they have rendered, without which this course never could have been written.

The author has studied the majority of these men at close range, in person. With many of them he enjoys, or did enjoy before their death, the privilege of close personal friendship which enabled him to gather from their philosophy facts that would not have been available under other conditions.

The author is grateful for having enjoyed the privilege of enlisting the services of the most powerful men on earth, in the building of The Law of Success course. That privilege has been remuneration enough for the work done, if nothing more were ever received for it.

These men have been the back-bone and the foundation and the skeleton of American business, finance, industry and statesmanship.

The Law of Success course epitomizes the philosophy and the rules of procedure which made each of these men a great power in his chosen field of endeavour. It has been the author's intention to present the course in the plainest and most simple terms available, so it could be mastered by very young men and young women, of the high-school age.

With the exception of the psychological law referred to in Lesson One as the "Master Mind," the author lays no claim to having created anything basically new in this course. What he has done, however, has been to organize old truths and known laws into PRACTICAL,

USABLE FORM, where they may be properly interpreted and applied by the workaday man whose needs call for a philosophy of simplicity.

In passing upon the merits of The Law of Success Judge Elbert H. Gary said: "Two outstanding features connected with the philosophy impress me most. One is the simplicity with which it has been presented, and the other is the fact that its soundness is so obvious to all that it will be immediately accepted."

The student of this course is warned against passing judgment upon it before having read the entire sixteen lessons. This especially applies to this Introduction, in which it has been necessary to include brief reference to subjects of a more or less technical and scientific nature. The reason for this will be obvious after the student has read the entire sixteen lessons.

The student who takes up this course with an open mind, and sees to it that his or her mind remains "open" until the last lesson shall have been read, will be richly rewarded with a broader and more accurate view of life as a whole.

Contents

1

The Master Mind

"You Can Do It if You Believe You Can!"

This is a course on the fundamentals of success. Success is very largely a matter of adjusting one's self to the ever varying and changing environments of life, in a spirit of harmony and poise. Harmony is based upon understanding of the forces constituting one's environment; therefore, this course is in reality a blueprint that may be followed straight to success, because it helps the student to interpret, understand and make the most of these environmental forces of life.

Before you begin reading The Law of Success lessons you should know something of the history of the course. You should know exactly what the course promises to those who follow it until they have assimilated the laws and principles upon which it is based. You should know its limitations as well as its possibilities as an aid in your fight for a place in the world.

From the viewpoint of entertainment The Law of Success course would be a poor second for most any of the monthly periodicals of the 'Snappy Story' variety which may be found upon the newsstands of today.

The course has been created for the serious-minded person who devotes at least a portion of his or her time to the business of succeeding in life. The author of The Law of Success course has not intended to compete with those who write purely for the purpose of entertaining.

The author's aim, in preparing this course, has been of a two-fold nature, namely, first-to help the earnest student find out what are his or her weaknesses, and, secondly-to help create a Definite Plan for bridging those weaknesses.

The most successful men and women on earth have had to correct certain weak spots in their personalities before they began to succeed. The most outstanding of these weaknesses which stand between men and women and success are INTOLERANCE, CUPIDITY, GREED, JEALOUSY, SUSPICION, REVENGE, EGOTISM, CONCEIT, THE TENDENCY TO REAP WHERE THEY HAVE NOT SOWN, and the HABITOF SPENDING MORE THAN THEY EARN. All of these common enemies of mankind, and many more not here mentioned, are covered by The Law of Success course in such a manner that any person of reasonable intelligence may master them but with little effort or inconvenience.

You should know, at the very outset, that The Law of Success course has long since passed through the experimental state; that it already has to its credit a record of achievement that is worthy of serious thought and analysis. You should know, also, that The Law of Success course has been examined and endorsed by some of the most practical minds of this generation.

The Law of Success course was first used as a lecture, and was delivered by its author practically in every city and in many of the smaller localities, throughout the United States, over a period of more than seven years. Perhaps you were one of the many hundreds of thousands of people who heard this lecture.

During these lectures the author had assistants located in the audiences for the purpose of interpreting the reaction of those who heard the lecture, and in this manner he learned exactly what effect it had upon people. As a result of this study and analysis, many changes were made.

The first big victory was gained, for The Law of Success philosophy, when it was used by the author as the basis of a course with which 3,000 men and women were trained as a sales army. The majority of these people were without previous experience, of any sort, in the field of selling. Through this training they were enabled to earn more than One Million Dollars ($1,000,000.00) for themselves and paid the author $30,000.00 for his services, covering a period of approximately six months.

The individuals and small groups of salespeople who have found success through the aid of this course are too numerous to be mentioned in this Introduction, but the number is large and the benefits they derived from the course were definite.

The Law of Success philosophy was brought to the attention of the late Don R. Mellett, former publisher of the Canton (Ohio) Daily News, who formed a partnership with the author of the course and was preparing to resign as publisher of the Canton Daily News and take up the business management of the author's affairs when he was assassinated on July 16, 1926.

Prior to his death Mr. Mellett had made arrangements with judge Elbert H. Gary, who was the then Chairman of the Board of the United States Steel Corporation, to present The Law of Success course to every employee of the Steel Corporation, at a total cost of something like $150,000.00. This plan was halted because of judge Gary's death, but it proves that the author of The Law of Success has produced an educational plan of an enduring nature. Judge Gary was eminently prepared to judge the value of such a course, and the fact that he analysed The Law of Success philosophy and was preparing to invest the huge sum of $150,000.00 in it is proof of the soundness of all that is said in behalf of the course.

You will observe, in this General Introduction to the course, a few technical terms which may not be plain to you. Do not allow this to bother you. Make no attempt at first reading to understand these terms. They will be plain to you after you read the remainder of the course. This entire Introduction is intended only as a background for the other fifteen lessons of the course, and you should read it as such. You will not be examined on this Introduction, but you should read it many times, as you will get from it at each reading a thought or an idea which you did not get on previous readings.

In this Introduction you will find a description of a newly discovered law of psychology which is the very foundation stone of all outstanding personal achievements. This law has been referred to by the author as the 'Master Mind,' meaning a mind that is developed through the harmonious co-operation of two or more people who ally themselves for the purpose of accomplishing any given task.

If you are engaged in the business of selling, you may profitably experiment with this law of the 'Master Mind' in your daily work. It has been found that a group of six or seven salespeople may use the law so effectively that their sales may be increased to unbelievable proportions.

Life Insurance is supposed to be the hardest thing on earth to sell. This ought not to be true, with an established necessity such as life insurance, but it is. Despite this fact, a small group of men working for the Prudential Life Insurance Company, whose sales are mostly small policies, formed a little friendly group for the purpose of experimenting with the law of the 'Master Mind,' with the result that every man in the group wrote more insurance during the first three months of the experiment than he had ever written in an entire year before.

What may be accomplished through the aid of this principle, by any small group of intelligent life-insurance salesmen who have learned how to apply the law of the 'Master Mind' will stagger the imagination of the most highly optimistic and imaginative person.

The same may be said of other groups of salespeople who are engaged in selling merchandise and other more tangible forms of service than life insurance. Bear this in mind as you read this Introduction to The Law of Success course and it is not unreasonable to expect that this Introduction, alone, may give you sufficient understanding of the law to change the entire course of your life.

It is the personalities back of a business which determine the measure of success the business will enjoy. Modify those personalities so they are more pleasing and more attractive to the patrons of the business and the business will thrive. In any of the great cities of the United States one may purchase merchandise of similar nature and price in scores of stores, yet you will find there is always one outstanding store which does more business than any of the others, and the reason for this is that back of that store is a man, or men, who has attended to the personalities of those who come in contact with the public. People buy personalities as much as merchandise, and it is a question if they are not influenced more by the personalities with which they come in contact than they are by the merchandise.

Life insurance has been reduced to such a scientific basis that the cost of insurance does not vary to any great extent, regardless of the company from which one purchases it, yet out of the hundreds of life insurance companies doing business, less than a dozen companies do the bulk of the business of the United States.

Why? Personalities! Ninety-nine people, out of every hundred who purchase life insurance policies, do not know what is in their policies and, what seems more startling, do not seem to care. What they really purchase is the pleasing personality of some man or woman who knows the value of cultivating such a personality.

Your business in life, or at least the most important part of it, is to achieve success. Success, within the meaning of that term as covered by this course on the Fifteen Laws of Success, is "the attainment of your Definite Chief Aim without violating the rights of other people." Regardless of what your major aim in life may be, you will attain it with much less difficulty after you learn how to cultivate a pleasing personality and after you have learned the delicate art of allying yourself with others in a given undertaking without friction or envy.

One of the greatest problems of life, if not, in fact, the greatest, is that of learning the art of harmonious negotiation with others. This course was created for the purpose of teaching people how to negotiate their way through life with harmony and poise, free from the destructive effects of disagreement and friction which bring millions of people to misery, want and failure every year.

With this statement of the purpose of the course, you should be able to approach the lessons with the feeling that a complete transformation is about to take place in your personality.

You cannot enjoy outstanding success in life without power, and you can never enjoy power without sufficient personality to influence other people to cooperate with you in a spirit of harmony. This course shows you step by step, how to develop such a personality.

Lesson by lesson, the following is a statement of that which you may expect to receive from the Fifteen Laws of Success:

I. A DEFINITE CHIEF AIM will teach you how to save the wasted effort which the majority of people expend in trying to find their lifework. This lesson will show you how to-do away forever with aimlessness and fix your heart and hand upon some definite, well conceived purpose as a life-work.—

II. SELF-CONFIDENCE will help you master the six basic fears with which every person is cursed–the fear of Poverty, the fear of Ill Health, the fear of Old Age, the fear of Criticism, the fear of Loss of Love of Someone and the fear of Death. It will teach you the difference between egotism and real self-confidence which is based upon definite, usable knowledge.—

III. HABIT OF SAVING will teach you how to distribute your income systematically so that a definite percentage of it will steadily accumulate, thus forming one of the greatest known sources of personal power. No one may succeed in life without saving money. There is no exception to this rule, and no one may escape it.—

IV. INITIATIVE AND LEADERSHIP will show you how to become a leader instead of a follower in your chosen field of endeavour. It will develop in you the instinct—for leadership which will cause you gradually to gravitate to the top in all undertakings in which you participate.

V. IMAGINATION will stimulate your mind so that you will conceive new ideas and develop new plans which will help you in attaining the object of your Definite Chief Aim. This lesson will teach you how to 'build new houses out of old stones,' so to speak. It will show you how to create new ideas out of old, well known concepts, and how to put old ideas to new uses. This one lesson, alone, is the equivalent of a very practical course in salesmanship, and it is sure to prove a veritable gold mine of knowledge to the person who is in earnest.

VI. ENTHUSIASM will enable you to 'saturate' all with whom you come in contact with interest in you and in your ideas. Enthusiasm is the foundation of a Pleasing Personality, and you must have such a personality in order to influence others to cooperate with you.

VII. SELF-CONTROL is the 'balance wheel' with which you control your enthusiasm and direct it where you wish it to carry you. This lesson will teach you, in a most practical manner, to become 'the master of your fate, the Captain of your Soul.'

VIII. THE HABIT OF DOING MORE THAN PAID FOR is one of the most important lessons of The Law of Success course. It will teach you how to take advantage of the Law of Increasing Returns, which will eventually insure you a return in money far out of proportion to the service you render. No one may become a real leader in any walk of life without practicing the habit of doing more work and better work than that for which he is paid.

IX. PLEASING PERSONALITY is the 'fulcrum' on which you must place the 'crow-bar' of your efforts, and when so placed, with intelligence, it will enable you to remove mountains of obstacles. This one lesson, alone, has made scores of Master Salesmen. It has developed leaders over night. It will teach you how to transform your personality so that you may adapt yourself to any environment, or to any other personality, in such a manner that you may easily dominate.

X. ACCURATE THINKING is one of the important foundation stones of all enduring success. This lesson teaches you how to separate 'facts' from mere 'information.' It teaches you how to organise known facts into two classes: the 'important' and the 'unimportant.' It teaches you how to determine what is an 'important' fact. It teaches you how to build definite working plans, in the pursuit of any calling, out of facts.

XI. CONCENTRATION teaches you how to focus your attention upon one subject at a time until you have worked out practical plans for mastering that subject. It will teach you how to ally yourself with others in such a manner that you may have the use of their entire knowledge to back you up in your own plans and purposes. It will give you a practical working knowledge of the forces around you, and show you how to harness and use these forces in furthering your own interests.

XII. CO-OPERATION will teach you the value of team-work in all you do. In this lesson you will be taught how to apply the law of the 'Master Mind' described in this Introduction and in Lesson Two of this course. This lesson will show you how to co-ordinate your own efforts with those of others, in such a manner that friction, jealousy, strife, envy and cupidity will be eliminated. You will learn how to make use of all that other people have learned about the work in which you are engaged.

XIII. PROFITING BY FAILURE will teach you how to make stepping stones out of all of your past and future mistakes and failures. It will teach you the difference between 'failure' and 'temporary defeat,' a difference which is very great and very important. It will teach you how to profit by your own failures and by the failures of other people.

XIV. TOLERANCE will teach you how to avoid the disastrous effects of racial and religious prejudices which mean defeat for millions of people who permit themselves to become entangled in foolish argument over these subjects, thereby poisoning their own minds and closing the door to reason and investigation. This lesson is the twin sister of the one on ACCURATE THOUGHT, for the reason that no one may become an Accurate Thinker without practicing tolerance. Intolerance closes the book of Knowledge and writes on the cover, 'Finis! I have learned it all!" Intolerance makes enemies of those who should be friends. It destroys opportunity and fills the mind with doubt, mistrust and prejudice.

XV. PRACTICING THE GOLDEN RULE will teach you how to make use of this great universal law of human conduct in such a manner that you may easily get harmonious co-operation from any individual or group of individuals. Lack of understanding of the law upon which the Golden Rule philosophy is based is one of the major causes of failure of millions of people who remain in misery, poverty and want all their lives. This lesson has nothing whatsoever to do with religion in any form, nor with sectarianism, nor have any of the other lessons of this course on The Law of Success.

When you have mastered these Fifteen Laws and made them your own, as you may do within a period of from fifteen to thirty weeks, you will be ready to develop sufficient personal power to insure the attainment of your Definite Chief Aim.

The purpose of these Fifteen Laws is to develop or help you organise all the knowledge you have, and all you acquire in the future, so you may turn this knowledge into POWER.

You should read The Law of Success course with a note-book by your side, for you will observe that ideas will begin to 'flash' into your mind as you read, as to ways and means of using these laws in advancing your own interests.

You should also begin teaching these laws to those in whom you are most interested, as it is a well known fact that the more one tries to teach a subject the more he learns about that subject. A man who has a family of young boys and girls may so indelibly fix these Fifteen Laws of Success in their minds that this teaching will change the entire course of their lives. The man with a family should interest his wife in studying this course with him, for reasons which will be plain before you complete reading this Introduction.

POWER is one of the three basic objects of human endeavour.

POWER is of two classes-that which is developed through co-ordination of natural physical laws, and that which is developed by organising and classifying KNOWLEDGE.

POWER growing out of organised knowledge is the more important because it places in man's possession a tool with which he may transform, redirect and to some extent harness and use the other form of power.

The object of this reading course is to mark the route by which the student may safely travel in gathering such facts as he may wish to weave into his fabric of KNOWLEDGE.

There are two major methods of gathering knowledge, namely, by studying, classifying and assimilating facts which have been organised by other people, and through one's own process of gathering, organising and classifying facts, generally called 'personal experience.'

This lesson deals mainly with the ways and means of studying the facts and data gathered and classified by other people.

The state of advancement known as 'civilisation' is but the measure of knowledge which the race has accumulated. This knowledge is of two classes-mental and physical.

Among the useful knowledge organised by man, he has discovered and catalogued the eighty-odd physical elements of which all material forms in the universe consist.

By study and analysis and accurate measurements man has discovered the 'bigness' of the material side of the universe as represented by planets, suns and stars, some of which are known to be over ten million times as large as the little earth on which he lives.

On the other hand, man has discovered the 'littleness' of the physical forms which constitute the universe by reducing the eighty-odd physical elements to molecules, atoms, and, finally, to the smallest particle, the electron. An electron cannot be seen; it is but a centre of force consisting of a positive or a negative. The electron is the beginning of everything of a physical nature.

MOLECULES, ATOMS AND ELECTRONS: To understand both the detail and the perspective of the process through which knowledge is gathered, organised and classified, it seems essential for the student to begin with the smallest and simplest particles of physical matter, because these are the A B C's with which Nature has constructed the entire frame-work of the physical portion of the universe.

The molecule consists of atoms, which are said to be little invisible particles of matter revolving continuously with the speed of lightning, on exactly the same principle that the earth revolves around the sun.

These little particles of matter known as atoms, which revolve in one continuous circuit, in the molecule, are said to be made up of electrons, the smallest particles of physical matter. As already stated, the electron is nothing but two forms of force. The electron is uniform, of but one class, size and nature; thus in a grain of sand or a drop of water the entire principle upon which the whole universe operates is duplicated.

How marvellous! How stupendous! You may gather some slight idea of the magnitude of it all the next time you eat a meal, by remembering that every article of food you eat, the plate on which you eat it, the tableware and the table itself are, in final analysis, but a collection of ELECTRONS.

In the world of physical matter, whether one is looking at the largest star that floats through the heavens or the smallest grain of sand to be found on earth, the object under observation is but an organised collection of molecules, atoms and electrons revolving around one another at inconceivable speed.

Every particle of physical matter is in a continuous state of highly agitated motion. Nothing is ever still, although nearly all physical matter may appear, to the physical eye, to be motionless. There is no 'solid' physical matter. The hardest piece of steel is but an organised mass of revolving molecules, atoms and electrons. Moreover, the electrons in a piece of steel are of the same nature, and move at the same rate of speed as the electrons in gold, silver, brass or pewter.

The eighty-odd forms of physical matter appear to be different from one another, and they are different, don't be afraid of a little opposition. Remember that the 'Kite' of Success generally rises AGAINST the wind of Adversity-not with it] because they are made up of different combinations of atoms (although the electrons in these atoms are always the same, except that some electrons are positive and some are negative, meaning that some carry a positive charge of electrification while others carry a negative charge).

Through the science of chemistry, matter may be broken up into atoms which are, within themselves, unchangeable. The eighty-odd elements are created through and by reason of combining and changing of the positions of the atoms. To illustrate the modus operandi of chemistry through which this change of atomic position is wrought, in terms of modern science:

"Add four electrons (two positive and two negative) to the hydrogen atom, and you have the element lithium; knock out of the lithium atom (composed of three positive and three negative electrons) one positive and one negative electron, and you have one atom of helium (composed of two positive and two negative electrons).

Thus it may be seen that the eighty-odd physical elements of the universe differ from one another only in the number of electrons composing their atoms, and the number and arrangement of those atoms in the molecules of each element.

As an illustration, an atom of mercury contains eighty positive charges (electrons) in its nucleus, and eighty negative outlying charges (electrons). If the chemist were to expel two of its positive electrons it would instantly become the metal known as platinum. If the chemist could then go a step further and take from it a negative ('planetary') electron, the mercury atom would then have lost two positive electrons and one negative; that is, one positive charge on the whole; hence it would retain seventy-nine positive charges in the nucleus and seventy-nine outlying negative electrons, thereby becoming GOLD!

The formula through which this electronic change might be produced has been the object of diligent search by the alchemists all down the ages, and by the modern chemists of today.

It is a fact known to every chemist that literally tens of thousands of synthetic substances may be composed out of only four kinds of atoms, viz.: hydrogen, oxygen, nitrogen and carbon.

"Differences in the number of electrons in atoms confer upon them qualitative (chemical) differences, though all atoms of any one element are chemically alike. Differences in the number and special arrangement of these atoms (in groups of molecules) constitute both physical and chemical differences in substances, i.e., in compounds. Quite different substances are produced by combinations of precisely the same kinds of atoms, but in different proportions.

"Take from a molecule of certain substances one single atom, and they may be changed from a compound necessary to life and growth into a deadly poison. Phosphorus is an element, and thus contains but one kind of atoms; but some phosphorus is yellow and some is red, varying with the special distribution of the atoms in the molecules composing the phosphorus."

It may be stated as a literal truth that the atom is the universal particle with which Nature builds all material forms, from a grain of sand to the largest star that floats through space. The atom is Nature's 'building block' out of which she erects an oak tree or a pine, a rock of sandstone or granite, a mouse or an elephant.

Some of the ablest thinkers have reasoned that the earth on which we live, and every material particle on the earth, began with two atoms which attached themselves to each other, and through hundreds of millions of years of flight through space, kept contacting and accumulating other atoms until, step by step, the earth was formed. This, they point out, would account for the various and differing strata of the earth's substances, such as the coal beds, the iron ore deposits, the gold and silver deposits, the copper deposits, etc.

They reason that, as the earth whirled through space, it contacted groups of various kinds of nebulae, or atoms, which it promptly appropriated, through the law of magnetic attraction. There is much to be seen, in the earth's surface composition, to support this theory, although there may be no positive evidence of its soundness.

These facts concerning the smallest analyzable particles of matter have been briefly referred to as a starting point from which we shall undertake to ascertain how to develop and apply the law of POWER.

It has been noticed that all matter is in a constant state of vibration or motion; that the molecule is made up of rapidly moving particles called atoms, which, in turn, are made up of rapidly moving particles called electrons.

THE VIBRATING FLUID OF MATTER: In every particle of matter there is an invisible 'fluid' or force which causes the atoms to circle around one another at an inconceivable rate of speed.

This 'fluid' is a form of energy which has never been analysed. Thus far it has baffled the entire scientific world. By many scientists it is believed to be the same energy as that which we call electricity. Others prefer to call it vibration. It is believed by some investigators that the rate of speed with which this force (call it whatever you will) moves determines to a large extent the nature of the outward visible appearance of the physical objects of the universe.

One rate of vibration of this 'fluid energy' causes what is known as sound. The human ear can detect only the sound which is produced through from 32,000 to 38,000 vibrations per second.

As the rate of vibrations per second increases above that which we call sound they begin to manifest themselves in the form of heat. Heat begins with about 1,500,000 vibrations per second.

Still higher up the scale vibrations begin to register in the form of light. 3,000,000 vibrations per second create violet light. Above this number vibration sheds ultra-violet rays (which are invisible to the naked eye) and other invisible radiations.

And, still higher up the scale-just how high no one at present seems to know-vibrations create the power with which man THINKS.

It is the belief of the author that the 'fluid' portion of all vibration, out of which grow all known forms of energy, is universal in nature; that the 'fluid' portion of sound is the same as the 'fluid' portion of light, the difference in effect between sound and light being only a difference in rate of vibration, also that the 'fluid' portion of thought is exactly the same as that in sound, heat and light, excepting the number of vibrations per second.

Just as there is but one form of physical matter, of which the earth and all the other planets-suns and stars-are composed-the electron-so is there but one form of 'fluid' energy, which causes all matter to remain in a constant state of rapid motion.

AIR AND ETHER: The vast space between the suns, moons, stars and other planets of the universe is filled with a form of energy known as ether. It is this author's belief that the 'fluid' energy which keeps all particles of matter in motion is the same as the universal 'fluid' known as ether which fills all the space of the universe. Within a certain distance of the earth's surface, estimated by some to be about fifty miles, there exists what is called air, which is a gaseous substance composed of oxygen and nitrogen. Air is a conductor of sound vibrations, but a non-conductor of light and the higher vibrations, which are carried by the ether. The ether is a conductor of all vibrations from sound to thought.

Air is a localised substance which performs, in the main, the service of feeding all animal and plant life with oxygen and nitrogen, without which neither could exist. Nitrogen is one of the chief necessities of plant life and oxygen one of the mainstays of animal life. Near the top of very high mountains the air becomes very light, because it contains but little nitrogen, which is the reason why plant life cannot exist there. On the other hand, the 'light' air found in render more service than that for which you are paid and you will soon be paid for more than you render. The law of 'Increasing Returns' takes care of this high altitudes consists largely of oxygen, which is the chief reason why tubercular patients are sent to high altitudes.

Even this brief statement concerning molecules, atoms, electrons, air, ether and the like, may be heavy reading to the student, but, as will be seen shortly, this introduction plays an essential part as the foundation of this lesson.

Do not become discouraged if the description of this foundation appears to have none of the thrilling effects of a modern tale of fiction. You are seriously engaged in finding out what are your available powers and how to organise and apply these powers. To complete this discovery successfully you must combine determination, persistency and a well defined DESIRE to gather and organise knowledge.

The late Dr. Alexander Graham Bell, inventor of the long distance telephone and one of the accepted authorities on the subject of vibration, is here introduced in support of this author's theories concerning the subject of vibration:

"Suppose you have the power to make an iron rod vibrate with any desired frequency in a dark room. At first, when vibrating slowly, its movement will be indicated by only one sense, that of touch. As soon as the vibrations increase, a low sound will emanate from it and it will appeal to two senses.

"At about 32,000 vibrations to the second the sound will be loud and shrill, but at 40,000 vibrations it will be silent and the movements of the rod will not be perceived by touch. Its movements will be perceived by no ordinary human sense.

"From this point up to about 1,500,000 vibrations per second, we have no sense that can appreciate any effect of the intervening vibrations. After that stage is reached, movement is indicated first by the sense of temperature and then, when the rod becomes red hot, by the sense of sight. At 3,000,000 it sheds violet light. Above that it sheds ultra-violet rays and other invisible radiations, some of which can be perceived by instruments and employed by us.

"Now it has occurred to me that there must be a great deal to be learned about the effect of those vibrations in the great gap where the ordinary human senses are unable to hear, see or feel the movement. The power to send wireless messages by ether vibrations lies in that gap, but the gap is so great that it seems there must be much more. You must make machines practically to supply new senses, as the wireless instruments do.

"Can it be said, when you think of that great gap, that there are not many forms of vibrations that may give us results as wonderful as, or even more wonderful than, the wireless waves? It seems to me that in this gap lie the vibrations which we have assumed to be given off by our brains and nerve cells when we think. But then, again, they may be higher up, in the scale beyond the vibrations that produce the ultra-violet rays. (AUTHOR'S NOTE: The last sentence suggests the theory held by this author.)

"Do we need a wire to carry these vibrations? Will they not pass through the ether without a wire, just as the wireless waves do? How will they be perceived by the recipient? Will he hear a series of signals or will he find that another man's thoughts have entered into his brain?

"We may indulge in some speculations based on what we know of the wireless waves, which, as I have said, are all we can recognise of a vast series of vibrations which theoretically must exist. If the thought waves are similar to the wireless waves, they must pass from the brain and flow endlessly around the world and the universe. The body and the skull and other solid obstacles would form no obstruction to their passage, as they pass through the ether which surrounds the molecules of every substance, no matter how solid and dense.

"You ask if there would not be constant interference and confusion if other people's thoughts were flowing through our brains and setting up thoughts in them that did not originate with ourselves?

"How do you know that other men's thoughts are not interfering with yours now? I have noticed a good many phenomena of mind disturbances that I have never been able to explain. For instance, there is the inspiration or the discouragement that a speaker feels in addressing an audience. I have experienced this many times in my life and have never been able to define exactly the physical causes of it.

"Many recent scientific discoveries, in my opinion, point to a day not far distant perhaps, when men will read one another's thoughts, when thoughts will be conveyed directly from brain to brain without intervention of speech, writing or any of the present known methods of communication.

"It is not unreasonable to look forward to a time when we shall see without eyes, hear without ears and talk without tongues.

"Briefly, the hypothesis that mind can communicate directly with mind rests on the theory that thought or vital force is a form of electrical disturbance, that it can be taken up by induction and transmitted to a distance either through a wire or simply through the all-pervading ether, as in the case of wireless telegraph waves.

"There are many analogies which suggest that thought is of the nature of an electrical disturbance. A nerve, which is of the same substance as the brain, is an excellent conductor of the electric current. When we first passed an electrical current through the nerves of a dead man we were shocked and amazed to see him sit up and move. The electrified nerves produced contraction of the muscles very much as in life.

"The nerves appear to act upon the muscles very much as the electric current acts upon an electromagnet. The current magnetizes a bar of iron placed at right angles to it, and the nerves produce, through the intangible current of vital force that flows through them, contraction of the muscular fibbers that are arranged at right angles to them.

"It would be possible to cite many reasons why thought and vital force may be regarded as of the same nature as electricity. The electric current is held to be a wave motion of the ether, the hypothetical substance that fills all space and pervades all substances. We believe that there must be ether because without it the electric current could not pass through a vacuum, or sunlight through space. It is reasonable to believe that only a wave motion of a similar character can produce the phenomena of thought and vital force. We may assume that the brain cells act as a battery and that the current produced flows along the nerves.

"But does it end there? Does it not pass out of the body in waves which flow around the world unperceived by our senses, just as the wireless waves passed unperceived before Hertz and others discovered their existence?"

EVERY MIND BOTH A BROADCASTING AND A RECEIVING STATION: This author has proved, times too numerous to enumerate, to his own satisfaction at least, that every human brain is both a broadcasting and a receiving station for vibrations of thought frequency.

If this theory should turn out to be a fact, and methods of reasonable control should be established, imagine the part it would play in the gathering, classifying and organising of knowledge. The possibility, much less the probability, of such a reality, staggers the mind of man!

Thomas Paine was one of the great minds of the American Revolutionary Period. To him more, perhaps, than to any other one person, we owe both the beginning and the happy ending of the Revolution, for it was his keen mind that both helped in drawing up the Declaration of Independence and in persuading the signers of that document to translate it into terms of reality.

In speaking of the source of his great storehouse of knowledge, Paine thus described it:

"Any person, who has made observations on the every failure is a blessing in disguise, providing it teaches some needed lesson one could not have learned without it. Most so-called Failures are only temporary defeats state of progress of the human mind, by observing his own, cannot but have observed that there are two distinct classes of what are called Thoughts: those that we produce in ourselves by reflection and the act of thinking, and those that bolt into the mind of their own accord. I have always made it a rule to treat these voluntary visitors with civility, taking care to examine, as well as I was able, if they were worth entertaining; and it is from them I have acquired almost all the knowledge that I have. As to the learning that any person gains from school education, it serves only like a small capital, to put him in the way of beginning learning for himself afterwards. Every person of learning is finally his own teacher, the reason for which is, that principles cannot be impressed upon the memory; their place of mental residence is the understanding, and they are never so lasting as when they begin by conception."

In the foregoing words Paine, the great American patriot and philosopher, described an experience which at one time or another is the experience of every person. Who is there so unfortunate as not to have received positive evidence that thoughts and even complete ideas will 'pop' into the mind from outside sources?

What means of conveyance is there for such visitors except the ether? Ether fills the boundless space of the universe. It is the medium of conveyance for all known forms of vibration such as sound, light and heat. Why should it not be, also, the medium of conveyance of the vibration of Thought?

Every mind, or brain, is directly' connected with every other brain by means of the ether. Every thought released by any brain may be instantly picked up and interpreted by all other brains that are 'en rapport' with the sending brain. This author is as sure of this fact as he is that the chemical formula H2O will produce water. Imagine, if you can, what a part this principle plays in every walk of life.

Nor is the probability of ether being a conveyor of thought from mind to mind the most astounding of its performances. It is the belief of this author that every thought vibration released by any brain is picked up by the ether and kept in motion in circuitous wave lengths corresponding in length to the intensity of the energy used in their release; that these vibrations remain in motion forever; that they are one of the two sources from which thoughts which 'pop' into one's mind emanate, the other source being direct and, immediate contact through the ether with the brain releasing the thought vibration. Thus it will be seen that if this theory is a fact the boundless space of the whole universe is now and will continue to become literally a mental library wherein may be found all the thoughts released by mankind.

The author is here laying the foundation for one of the most important hypotheses enumerated in the lesson Self-confidence, a fact which the student should keep in mind as he approaches that lesson.

This is a lesson on Organised Knowledge. Most of the useful knowledge to which the human race has become heir has been preserved and accurately recorded in Nature's Bible. By turning back the pages of this unalterable Bible man has read the story of; the terrific struggle through and out of which the present civilisation has grown. The pages of this Bible are made up of the physical elements of which this earth and the other planets consist, and of the ether which fills all space.

By turning back the pages written on stone and covered near the surface of this earth on which he lives, man has uncovered the bones, skeletons, footprints and other unmistakable evidence of the history of animal life on this earth, planted there for his enlightenment and guidance by the hand of Mother Nature throughout unbelievable periods of time. The evidence is plain and unmistakable. The great stone pages of Nature's Bible found on this earth and the endless pages of that Bible represented by the ether wherein all past human thought has been recorded, constitute an authentic source of communication between the Creator and man. This Bible was begun before man had reached the thinking stage; indeed, before man had reached the amoeba (one-cell animal) stage of development.

This Bible is above and beyond the power of man to alter. Moreover, it tells its story not in the ancient dead languages or hieroglyphics of half savage races, but in universal language which all who have eyes may read. Nature's Bible, from which we have derived all the knowledge that is worth knowing, is one that no man may alter or in any manner tamper with.

The most marvellous discovery yet made by man is that of the recently discovered radio principle, which operates through the aid of ether, an important portion of Nature's Bible. Imagine the ether picking up the ordinary vibration of sound, and transforming that vibration from audio-frequency into radio-frequency, carrying it to a properly attuned receiving station and surprise no one that such a force could gather up the vibration of thought and keep that vibration in motion forever.

The established and known fact of instantaneous transmission of sound, through the agency of the ether, by means of the modern radio apparatus, removes the theory of transmission of thought vibration from mind to mind from the possible to the probable.

THE MASTER MIND: We come, now, to the next step in the description of the ways and means by which one may gather, classify and organise useful knowledge, through harmonious alliance of two or more minds, out of which grows a Master Mind.

The term 'Master Mind' is abstract, and has no counterpart in the field of known facts, except to a small number of people who have made a careful study of the effect of one mind upon other minds.

This author has searched in vain through all the textbooks and essays available on the subject of the human mind, but nowhere has been found even the slightest reference to the principle here described as the 'Master Mind.' The term first came to the attention of the author through an interview with Andrew Carnegie, in the manner described in Lesson Two.

CHEMISTRY OF THE MIND: It is this author's belief that the mind is made up of the same universal 'fluid' energy as that which constitutes the ether which fills the universe. It is a fact as well known to the layman as to the man of scientific investigation, that some minds clash the moment they come in contact with each other, while other minds show a natural affinity for each other. Between the two extremes of natural antagonism and natural affinity growing out of the meeting or contacting of minds there is a wide range of possibility for varying reactions of mind upon mind.

Some minds are so naturally adapted to each other that 'love at first sight' is the inevitable outcome of the contact. Who has not known of such an experience? In other cases minds are so antagonistic that violent mutual dislike shows itself at first meeting. These results occur without a word being spoken, and without the slightest signs of any of the usual causes for love and hate acting as a stimulus.

It is quite probable that the 'mind' is made up of a fluid or substance or energy, call it what you will, similar to (if not in fact the same substance as) the ether. When two minds come close enough to each other to form a contact, the mixing of the units of this 'mind stuff' (let us call it the electrons of the ether) sets up a chemical reaction and starts vibrations which affect the two individuals pleasantly or unpleasantly.

The effect of the meeting of two minds is obvious to even the most casual observer. Every effect must have a cause! What could be more reasonable than to suspect that the cause of the change in mental attitude between two minds which have just come in close contact is none other than the disturbance of the electrons or units of each mind in the process of rearranging themselves in the new field created by the contact?

For the purpose of establishing this lesson upon a sound foundation we have gone a long way toward success by admitting that the meeting or coming in close contact of two minds sets up in each of those minds a certain noticeable 'effect' or state of mind quite different from the one existing immediately prior to the contact. While it is desirable it is not essential to know what is the 'cause' of this reaction of mind upon mind. That the reaction takes place, in every instance, is a known fact which gives us a starting point from which we may show what is meant by the term 'Master Mind.'

A Master Mind may be created through the bringing together or blending, in a spirit of perfect harmony, of two or more minds.

out of this harmonious blending the chemistry of the mind creates a third mind which may be appropriated and used by one or all of the individual minds. This Master Mind will remain available as long as the friendly, harmonious alliance between the individual minds exists. It will disintegrate and all evidence of its former existence will disappear the moment the friendly alliance is broken.

This principle of mind chemistry is the basis and cause for practically all the so-called 'soul-mate' and 'eternal triangle' cases, so many of which unfortunately find their way into the divorce courts and meet with popular ridicule from ignorant and uneducated people who manufacture vulgarity and scandal out of one of the greatest of Nature's laws.

The entire civilised world knows that the first two or three years of association after marriage are often marked by much disagreement, of a more or less petty nature. These are the years of 'adjustment.' If the marriage survives them it is more than apt to become a permanent alliance. These facts no experienced married person will deny. Again we see the 'effect' without understanding the 'cause.'

While there are other contributing causes, yet, in the main, lack of harmony during these early years of marriage is due to the slowness of the chemistry of the minds in blending harmoniously. Stated differently, the electrons or units of the energy called the mind are often neither extremely friendly nor antagonistic upon first contact; but, through constant association they gradually adapt themselves in harmony, except in rare cases where association has the opposite effect of leading, eventually, to open hostility between these units.

It is a well known fact that after a man and a woman have lived together for ten to fifteen years they become practically indispensable to each other, even though there may not be the slightest evidence of the state of mind called love. Moreover, this association and relationship sexually not only develops a natural, affinity between the two minds, but it actually causes the two people to take on a similar facial expression' and to resemble each other closely in many other marked ways. Any competent analyst of human nature can easily go into a crowd of strange people' and pick out the wife after having been introduced to her husband. The expression of the eyes, the contour of the faces and the tone of the voices of people who have long been associated in marriage, become similar to a marked degree.

So marked is the effect of the chemistry of the human mind that any experienced public speaker may quickly interpret the manner in which his statements are accepted by his audience. Antagonism in the mind of but one person in an audience of one thousand may be readily detected by the speaker who has learned how to 'feel' and register the effects of antagonism. Moreover, the public speaker can make these interpretations without observing or in any manner being influenced by the expression on the faces of those in his audience. On account of this fact an audience may cause a speaker to rise to great heights of oratory, or heckle him into failure, without making a sound or denoting a single expression of satisfaction or dissatisfaction through the features of the face.

All 'Master Salesmen' know the moment the 'psychological time for closing' has arrived; not by what the prospective buyer says, but from the effect of the chemistry of his mind as interpreted or 'felt' by the salesman. Words often belie the intentions of those speaking them but a correct interpretation of the chemistry of the mind leaves no loophole for such a possibility. Every able salesman knows that the majority of buyers have the habit of affecting a negative attitude almost to the very climax of a sale.

Every able lawyer has developed a sixth sense whereby he is enabled to 'feel' his way through the most artfully selected words of the clever witness who is lying, and correctly interpret that which is in the witness's mind, through the chemistry of the mind. Many lawyers have developed this ability without knowing the real source of it; they possess the technique without the scientific understanding upon which it is based. Many salesmen have done the same thing.

One who is gifted in the art of correctly the chemistry of the minds of others may, figuratively speaking, walk in at the front door of the mansion of a given mind and leisurely explore the entire building, noting all its details, walking out again with a complete picture of the interior of the building, without the owner of the building so much as knowing that he has entertained a visitor. It will be observed, in the lesson Accurate Thinking, that this principle may be put to a very practical use (having reference to the principle of the chemistry of the mind). The principle is referred to merely as an approach to the major principles of this lesson.

Enough has already been stated to introduce the principle of mind chemistry, and to prove, with the aid of the student's own every-day experiences and casual observations that the moment two minds come within close range of each other a noticeable mental change takes place in both, sometimes registering in the nature of antagonism and at other times registering in the nature of friendliness. Every mind has what might be termed an electric field. The nature of this field varies, depending upon the 'mood' of the individual mind back of it, and upon the nature of the chemistry of the mind creating the 'field.'

It is believed by this author that the normal or natural condition of the chemistry of any individual mind is the result of his physical heredity plus the nature of thoughts which have dominated that mind; that every mind is continuously changing to the extent that the individual's philosophy and general habits of thought change the chemistry of his or her mind. These principles the author BELIEVES to be true. That any individual may voluntarily change the chemistry of his or her mind so that it will either attractor repel all with whom it comes in contact is a KNOWN FACT! Stated in another manner, any person may assume a mental attitude which will attract and please others or repel and antagonize them, and this without the aid of words or facial expression or other form of bodily movement or demean our.

Go back, now, to the definition of a 'Master Mind'-a mind which grows out of the blending and coordination of two or more minds, IN A spirit of PERFECT HARMONY, and you will catch the full significance of the word 'harmony' as it is here used. Two minds will not blend nor can they be coordinated unless the element of perfect harmony is present, wherein lies the secret of success or failure of practically all business and social partnerships.

Every sales manager and every military commander and every leader in any other walk of life understands the necessity of an 'esprit de corps'-a spirit of common understanding and co-operation-in the attainment of success. This mass spirit of harmony of purpose is obtained through discipline, voluntary or forced, of such a nature that the individual minds become blended into a 'Master Mind,' by which is meant that the chemistry of the individual minds is modified in such a manner that these minds blend and function as one.

The methods through which this blending process takes place are as numerous as the individuals engaged in the various forms of leadership. Every leader has his or her own method of coordinating the minds of the followers. One will use force. Another uses persuasion. One will play upon the fear of penalties while another plays upon rewards, in order to reduce the individual minds of a given group of people to where they may be blended into a mass mind. The student will not have to search deeply into history of statesmanship, politics, business or finance, to discover the technique employed by the leaders in these fields in the process of blending the minds of individuals into a mass mind.

The really great leaders of the world, however, have been provided by Nature with a combination of mind chemistry favourable as a nucleus of attraction for other minds. Napoleon was a notable example of a man possessing the magnetic type of mind which had a very decided tendency to attract all minds with which it came in contact. Soldiers followed Napoleon to certain death without flinching, because of the impelling or attracting nature of his personality, and that personality was nothing more nor less than the chemistry of his mind.

No group of minds can be blended into a Master Mind if one of the individuals of that group possesses one of these extremely negative, repellent minds. The negative and positive minds will not blend in the sense here described as a Master Mind. Lack of knowledge of this fact has brought many an otherwise able leader to defeat.

Any able leader who understands this principle of mind chemistry may temporarily blend the minds of practically any group of people, so that it will represent a mass mind, but the composition will disintegrate almost the very moment the leader's presence is removed from the group. The most successful life-insurance sales organisations and other sales forces meet once a week, or more often, for the purpose of what?

For the purpose of merging the individual minds into a master mind which—will, for a limited number of Days,serve as a stimulus to the individual minds!

It may be, and generally is, true that the leaders of these groups do not understand what actually takes place in these meetings, which are usually called 'pep meetings.' The routine of such meetings is usually given over to talks by the leader and other members of the group, and occasionally from someone outside of the group, meanwhile the minds of the individuals are contacting and recharging one another.

The brain of a human being may be compared to an electric battery in that it will become exhausted or run down, causing the owner of it to feel despondent, discouraged and lacking in 'pep.' Who is so fortunate as never to have had such a feeling? The human brain, when in this depleted condition, must be recharged, and the manner in which this is done is through contact with a more vital mind or minds. The great leaders understand the necessity of this 'recharging' process, and, moreover, they understand how to accomplish this result. This knowledge is the main feature which distinguishes a leader from a follower!

Fortunate is the person who understands this principle sufficiently well to keep his or her brain vitalized or 'recharged' by periodically contacting it with a more vital mind. Sexual contact is one of the most effective of the stimuli through which a mind may be recharged, providing the contact is intelligently made, between man and woman who have genuine affection for each other. Any other sort of sexual relationship is a devitalize of the mind. Any competent practitioner of Psycho-therapeutics can 'recharge' a brain within a few minutes.

Before passing away from the brief reference made to sexual contact as a means of revitalizing a depleted mind it seems appropriate to call attention to the fact that all of the great leaders, in whatever walks of life they have arisen, have been and are people of highly sexed natures. (The word 'sex' is not an indecent word. You'll find it in all the dictionaries.)

There is a growing tendency upon the part of the best informed physicians and other health practitioners, to accept the theory that all diseases begin when the brain of the individual is in a depleted or devitalized state. Stated in another way, it is a known fact that a person who has a perfectly vitalized brain is practically, if not entirely, immune from all manner of disease.

Every intelligent health practitioner, of whatever school or type, knows that 'Nature' or the mind cures disease in every instance where a cure is affected. Medicines, faith, laying on of hands, chiropractic, osteopathy and all other forms of outside stimulant are nothing more than artificial aids to NATURE, or, to state it correctly, mere methods of setting the chemistry of the mind into motion to the end that it readjusts the cells and tissues of the body, revitalizes the brain and otherwise causes the human machine to function normally.

The most orthodox practitioner will admit the truth, of this statement.

What, then, may be the possibilities of the future developments in the field of mind chemistry?

Through the principle of harmonious blending of minds perfect health may be enjoyed. Through the aid of this same principle sufficient power may be developed to solve the problem of economic pressure which constantly presses upon every individual.

We may judge the future possibilities of mind chemistry by taking inventory of its past achievements, keeping in mind the fact that these achievements have been largely the result of accidental discovery and of chance groupings of minds. We are approaching the time when the professoriate of the universities will teach mind chemistry the same as other subjects are now taught. Meanwhile, study and experimentation in connection with this subject open vistas of possibility for the individual student.

MIND CHEMISTRY AND ECONOMIC, POWER: That mind chemistry may be appropriately applied to the workaday affairs of the economic and, commercial world is a demonstrable fact.

Through the blending of two or more minds, in a spirit of PERFECT HARMONY, the principle of mind chemistry may be made to develop sufficient power to enable the individuals whose minds have been thus blended to perform seemingly superhuman feats. Power is the force with which man achieves success in any undertaking. Power, in unlimited quantities, may, be enjoyed by any group of men, or men and women, who possess the wisdom with which to submerge their own personalities and their own immediate individual interests, through the blending of their minds in a spirit of perfect harmony.

Observe, profitably, the frequency with which the word 'harmony' appears throughout this Introduction! There can be no development of a 'Master Mind' where this element of PERFECT HARMONY does not exist. The individual units of the mind will not blend with the individual units of another mind UNTIL THE Two minds have been aroused and warmed, as it were, with a spirit of perfect harmony of purpose. The moment two minds begin to take divergent roads of interest the individual units of each mind separate, and the third element, known as a 'MASTER MIND,' which grew out of the friendly or harmonious alliance, will disintegrate.

We come, now, to the study of some well known men who have accumulated great power (also great fortunes) through the application of mind chemistry.

Let us begin our study with three men who are known to be men of great achievement in their respective fields of economic, business and professional endeavour.

Their names are Henry Ford, Thomas A. Edison and Harvey S. Firestone.

Of the three Henry Ford is, by far, the most POWERFUL, having reference to economic and financial power. Mr. Ford is the most powerful man now living on earth. Many who have studied Mr. Ford believe him to be the most powerful man who ever lived. As far as is known Mr. Ford is the only man now living, or who ever lived, with sufficient power to outwit the money trust of the United States. Mr. Ford gathers millions of dollars with as great ease as a child fills its bucket with sand when playing on the beach. It has been said, by those who were in position to know, that Mr. Ford, if he needed it, could send out the call for money and gather in a billion dollars (a thousand million dollars) and have it available for use within one week. No one who knows of Ford's achievements doubts this. Those who know him well know that he could do it with no more effort than the average man expends in raising the money with which to pay a month's house rent. He could get this money, if he needed it, through the intelligent application of the principles on which this course is based.

While Mr. Ford's new automobile was in the process of perfection, in 1927, it is said that he received advance orders, with cash payments, for more than 375,000 cars. At an estimated price of $600.00 per car this would amount to $225,000,000.00 which he received before a single car was delivered. Such is the power of confidence in Ford's ability.

Mr. Edison, as everyone knows, is a philosopher, scientist and inventor. He is, perhaps, the keenest Bible student on earth; a student of Nature's Bible, however, and not of the myriads of man-made Bibles. Mr. Edison has such a keen insight into Mother Nature's Bible that he has harnessed and combined, for the good of mankind, more of Nature's laws than any other person now living or who ever lived. It was he who brought together the point of a needle and a piece of revolving wax, in such a way that the vibration of the human voice may be recorded and reproduced through the modern talking machine.

(And it may be Edison who will eventually enable man to pick up and correctly interpret the vibrations of thought which are now recorded in the boundless universe of ether, just as he has enabled man to record and reproduce the spoken word.)

It was Edison who first harnessed the lightning and made it serve as a light for man's use, through the aid of the incandescent electric light bulb.

It was Edison who gave the world the modern moving picture.

These are but a few of his outstanding achievements. These modern 'miracles' which he has performed (not by trickery, under the sham preteens of superhuman power, but in the very midst of the bright light of science) transcend all of the so-called 'miracles' described in the man-made books of fiction.

Mr. Firestone is the moving spirit in the great Firestone Tire industry, in Akron, Ohio. His industrial achievements are so well known wherever automobiles are used that no special comment on them seems necessary.

All three of these men began their careers, business and professional, without capital and with but little-schooling of that type usually referred to as 'education.'

All three men are now well educated. All three are wealthy. All three are powerful. Now let us inquire into the source of their wealth and power. Thus far we have been dealing only with effect; the true philosopher wishes to understand the cause of a given effect.

It is a matter of general knowledge that Mr. Ford, Mr. Edison and Mr. Firestone are close personal friends, and have been so for many years; that in former years they were in the habit of going away to the woods once a year for a period of rest, meditation and recuperation.

But it is not generally known-it is a grave doubt if these three men themselves know it-that there exists between the three men a bond of harmony which has caused their minds to become blended into a 'Master Mind' which is the real source of the power of each. This mass mind, growing out of the co-ordination of the individual minds of Ford, Edison and Firestone, has enabled these men to 'tune in' on forces (and sources of knowledge) with which most men are to no extent familiar.

If the student doubts either the principle or the effects here described, let him remember that more than half the theory here set forth is a known fact. For example, it is known that these three men have great power. It is known that they are wealthy. It is known that they began without capital and with but little schooling. It is known that they form periodic mind contacts. It is known that they are harmonious and friendly. It is known that their achievements are so outstanding as to make it impossible to compare these achievements with those of other men in their respective fields of activity.

All these 'effects' are known to practically every school-boy in the civilised world, therefore there can be no dispute as far as effects are concerned.

Of one fact connected with the cause of the achievements of Edison, Ford and Firestone we may be sure, namely, that these achievements were in no way based upon trickery, deceit, the 'supernatural' or so-called "revelations" or any other form of unnatural law. These men do not possess a stock of legerdemain. They work with natural laws; laws which, for the most part, are well known to all economists and leaders in the field of science, with the possible exception of the law upon which chemistry of the mind is based. As yet chemistry of the mind is not sufficiently developed to be classed, by scientific men, in their catalogue of known laws.

A 'Master Mind' may be created by any group of people who will co-ordinate their minds, in a spirit of perfect harmony. The group may consist of any number from two upward. Best results appear available from the blending of six or seven minds.

It has been suggested that Jesus Christ discovered how to make use of the principle of mind chemistry, and that His seemingly miraculous performances grew out of the power He developed through the blending of the minds of His twelve disciples. It has been pointed out that when one of the disciples (Judas Iscariot) broke faith the 'Master Mind' immediately disintegrated and Jesus met with the supreme catastrophe of His life.

When two or more people harmonize their minds and produce the effect known as a 'Master Mind', each person in the group becomes vested with the power to contact with and gather knowledge through the 'subconscious' minds of all the other members of the group. This power becomes immediately noticeable, having the effect of stimulating the mind to a higher rate of vibration, and otherwise evidencing itself in the form of a more vivid imagination and the consciousness of what appears to be a sixth sense. It is through this sixth sense that new ideas will 'flash' into the mind. These ideas take on the nature and form of the subject dominating the mind of the individual. If the entire group has met for the purpose of discussing a given subject, ideas concerning that subject will come pouring into the minds of all present, as if an outside influence were dictating them. The minds of those participating in the 'Master Mind' become as magnets, attracting ideas and thought stimuli of the most highly organised and practical nature, from no one knows where!

The process of mind-blending here described as a 'Master Mind' may be likened to the act of one who connects many electric batteries to a single transmission wire, thereby 'stepping up' the power flowing over that line. Each battery added increases the power passing over that line by the amount of energy the battery carries. Just so in the case of blending individual minds into a 'Master Mind.' Each mind, through the principle of mind chemistry, stimulates all the other minds in the group, until the mind energy thus becomes so great that it penetrates to and connects with the universal energy known as ether, which, in turn, touches every atom of the entire universe.

The modern radio apparatus substantiates, to a considerable extent, the theory here expounded. Powerful sending or broadcasting stations must be erected through which the vibration of sound is 'stepped up' before it can be picked up by the much higher vibrating energy of the ether and carried in all directions. A 'Master Mind' made up of many individual minds, so blended that they produce a strong vibrating energy, constitutes almost an exact counterpart of the radio broadcasting station.

Every public speaker has felt the influence of mind chemistry, for it is a well-known fact that as soon as the individual minds of an audience become 'en rapport' (attuned to the rate of vibration of the mind of the speaker) with the speaker, there is a noticeable increase of enthusiasm in the speaker's mind, and he often rises to heights of oratory which surprise all, including himself.

The first five to ten minutes of the average speech are devoted to what is known as 'warming up.' By this is meant the process through which the minds of the speaker and his audience are becoming blended in a spirit of PERFECT HARMONY.

Every speaker knows what happens when this state of 'perfect harmony' fails to materialize upon part of his audience.

The seemingly supernatural phenomena occurring in spiritualistic meetings are the result of the reaction, upon one another, of the minds in the group. These phenomena seldom begin to manifest themselves under ten to twenty minutes after the group is formed, for the reason that this is about the time required for the minds-in the group to become harmonized or blended.

The 'messages' received by members of a spiritualistic group probably come from one of two sources, or from both, namely:

First: From the vast storehouse of the subconscious mind of some member of the group; or

Second:—From the universal storehouse of—the ether, in which, it is more than probable, all thought vibration is preserved.

Neither any known natural law nor human reason supports the theory of communication with individuals who have died.

It is a known fact that any individual may explore the store of knowledge in another's mind, through this principle of mind chemistry, and it seems reasonable to suppose that this power may be extended to include contact with whatever vibrations are available in the ether, if there are any.

The theory that all the higher and more refined vibrations, such as those growing out of thought, are preserved in the ether grows out of the known fact that neither matter nor energy (the two known elements of the universe) may be either created or destroyed. It is reasonable to suppose that all vibrations which have been 'stepped up' sufficiently to be picked up and absorbed in the ether, will go on forever. The lower vibrations, which do not blend with or otherwise contact the ether, probably live a natural life and die out.

All the so-called geniuses probably gained their reputations because, by mere chance or otherwise, they formed alliances with other minds which enabled them to 'step up' their own mind vibrations to where they were enabled to contact the vast Temple of Knowledge recorded and filed in the ether of the universe. All of the great geniuses, as far as this author has been enabled to gather the facts, were highly sexed people. The fact that sexual contact is the greatest known mind stimulant lends color to the theory herein described.

Inquiring further into the source of economic power, as manifested by the achievements of men in the field of business, let us study the case of the Chicago group known as the 'Big Six,' consisting of Wm. Wrigley, Jr., who owns the chewing gum business bearing his name, and whose individual income is said to be more than Fifteen Million Dollars a year; John R. Thompson, who operates the chain of lunch rooms bearing his name; Mr. Lasker, who owns the Lord & Thomas Advertising Agency; Mr. McCullough, who owns the Parmalee Express Company, the largest transfer business in America; and Mr. Ritchie and Mr. Hertz, who own the Yellow Taxicab business.

A reliable financial reporting company has estimated the yearly income of these six men at upwards of Twenty-five Million Dollars ($25,000,000.00), or an average of more than Four Million Dollars a year per man.

Analysis of the entire group of six men discloses the fact that not one of them had any special educational advantages; that all began without capital or extensive credit; that their financial achievement has been due to their own individual plans, and not to any fortunate turn of the wheel of chance.

Many years ago these six men formed a friendly alliance, meeting at stated periods for the purpose of assisting one another with ideas and suggestions in their various and sundry lines of business endeavour.

With the exception of Hertz and Ritchie none of the six men were in any manner associated in a legal Partnership. These meetings were strictly for the purpose of co-operating on the give and take basis of assisting one another with ideas and suggestions, and occasionally by endorsing notes and other securities to assist some member of the group who had met with an emergency making such help necessary.

It is said that each of the individuals belonging to this Big Six group is a millionaire many times over. As a rule there is nothing worthy of special comment on behalf of a man who does nothing more than accumulate a few million dollars. However, there is something connected with the financial success of this particular group of men that is well worth comment, study, analysis and even emulation, and that 'something' is the fact that they have learned how to coordinate their individual minds by blending them in a spirit of perfect harmony, thereby creating a 'Master Mind' that unlocks, to each individual of the group, doors which are closed to most of the human race.

The United States Steel Corporation is one of the strongest and most powerful industrial organisations in the world. The Idea out of which this great industrial giant grew was born in the mind of Elbert H. Gary, a more or less commonplace small-town lawyer who was born and reared in a small Illinois town near Chicago.

Mr. Gary surrounded himself with a group of men whose minds he successfully blended in a spirit of perfect harmony, thereby creating the 'Master Mind' which is the moving spirit of the great United States Steel Corporation.

Search where you will, wherever you find an outstanding success in business, finance, industry or in any of the professions, you may be sure that back of the success is some individual who has applied the principle of mind chemistry, out of which a 'Master Mind' has been created. These outstanding successes often appear to be the handiwork of but one person, but search closely and the other individuals whose minds have been coordinated with his own may be found. Remember that two or more persons may operate the principle of mind chemistry so as to create a 'Master Mind.'

Power (man-power) is organised knowledge, expressed through intelligent efforts!

No effort can be said to be Organised unless the individuals engaged in the effort co-ordinate their knowledge and energy in a spirit of perfect harmony. Lack of such harmonious co-ordination of effort is the main cause of practically every business failure.

An interesting experiment was conducted by this author, in collaboration with the students of a well known college. Each student was requested to write an essay on "How and Why Henry Ford Became Wealthy."

Each student was required to describe, as a part of his or her essay, what was believed to be the nature of Ford's real assets, of what these assets consisted in detail.

The majority of the students gathered financial statements and inventories of the Ford assets and used these as the basis of their estimates of Ford's wealth.

Included in these 'sources of Ford's wealth' were such as cash in banks, raw and finished materials in stock, real estate and buildings, good-will, estimated at from ten to twenty-five per cent of the value of the material assets.

YOU cannot become a power in your community nor achieve enduring success in any worthy undertaking until you become big enough to blame yourself for your own mistakes and reverses.

One student out of the entire group of several hundred answered as follows:

"Henry Ford's assets consist, in the main, of two items, viz.: (1) Working capital and raw and finished materials; (2) The knowledge, gained from experience, of Henry Ford, himself, and the co-operation of a well trained organisation which understands how to apply this knowledge to best advantage from the Ford viewpoint. It is impossible to estimate, with anything approximating correctness, the actual dollars and cents value of either of these two groups of assets, but it is my opinion that their relative values are:

"The organised knowledge of the Ford Organisation...75%

The value of cash and physical assets of every nature, including raw and finished materials...25%

This author is of the opinion that this statement was not compiled by the young man whose name was signed to it, without the assistance of some very analytical and experienced mind or minds.

Unquestionably the biggest asset that Henry Ford has is his own brain. Next to this would come the brains of his immediate circle of associates, for it has been through co-ordination of these that the physical assets which he controls were accumulated.

Destroy every plant the Ford Motor Company owns: every piece of machinery; every atom of raw or finished material, every finished automobile, and every dollar on deposit in any bank, and Ford would still be the most powerful man, economically, on earth. The brains which have built the Ford business could duplicate it again in short order. Capital is always available, in unlimited quantities, to such brains as Ford's.

Ford is the most powerful man on earth (economically) because he has the keenest and most practical conception of the principle of Organised KNOWLEDGE of any man on earth, as far as this author has the means of knowing.

Despite Ford's great power and financial success, it may be that he has blundered often in the application of the principles through which he accumulated this power. There is but little doubt that Ford's methods of mind co-ordination have often been crude; they must needs have been in the earlier days of this experience, before he gained the wisdom of application that would naturally go with maturity of years.

Neither can there be much doubt that Ford's application of the principle of mind chemistry was, at least at the start, the result of a chance alliance with other minds, particularly the mind of Edison. It is more than probable that Mr. Ford's remarkable insight into the laws of nature was first begun as the result of his friendly alliance with his own wife long before he ever met either Mr. Edison or Mr. Firestone. Many a man who never knows the real source of his success is made by his wife, through application of the 'Master Mind' principle. Mrs. Ford is a most remarkably intelligent woman, and this author has reason to believe that it was her mind, blended with Mr. Ford's, which gave him his first real start toward power.

It may be mentioned, without in any way depriving Ford of any honour or glory, that in his earlier days of experience he had to combat the powerful enemies of illiteracy and ignorance to a greater extent than did either Edison or Firestone, both of whom were gifted by natural heredity with a most fortunate aptitude for acquiring and applying knowledge. Ford had to hew this talent out of the rough, raw timbers of his hereditary estate.

Within an inconceivably short period of time Ford has mastered three of the most stubborn enemies of mankind and transformed them into assets constituting the very foundation of his success.

These enemies are: Ignorance, illiteracy and poverty!

Any man who can stay the hand of these three savage forces, much less harness and use them to good account, is well worth close study by the less fortunate individuals.

This is an age of INDUSTRIAL POWER in which we are living!

The source of all this POWER is Organised EFFORT. Not only has the management of industrial enterprises efficiently organised individual workers, but, in many instances, mergers of industry have been effected in such a manner and to the end that these combinations (as in the case of the United States Steel Corporation, for example) have accumulated practically unlimited power.

One may hardly glance at the news of a day's events without seeing a report of some business, industrial or financial merger, bringing under one management enormous resources and thus creating great power.

One day it is a group of banks; another day it is a chain of railroads; the next day it is a combination of steel plants, all merging for the purpose of developing power through highly organised and coordinated effort.

Knowledge, general in nature and unorganised, is not POWER; it is only potential power-the material out of which real power may be developed. Any modern library contains an unorganised record of all the knowledge of value to which the present stage of civilisation is heir, but this knowledge is not power because it is not organised.

Every form of energy and every species of animal or plant life, to survive, must be organised. The oversized animals whose bones have filled Nature's bone-yard through extinction have left mute but certain evidence that non-organisation means annihilation.

From the electron-the smallest particle of matter-to the largest star in the universe: these and every material thing in between these two extremes offer proof positive that one of Nature's first laws is that of ORGANISATION. Fortunate is the individual who recognises the importance of this law and makes it his business to familiarize himself with the various ways in which the law may be applied to advantage.

The astute business man has not only recognised the importance of the law of organised effort, but he has made this law the warp and the woof of his POWER.

Without any knowledge, whatsoever, of the principle of mind chemistry, or that such a principle exists, many men have accumulated great power by merely organising the knowledge they possessed.

The majority of all who have discovered the principle of mind chemistry and developed that principle into a 'Master Mind' have stumbled upon this knowledge by the merest of accident; often failing to recognise the real nature of their discovery or to understand the source of their power.

This author is of the opinion that all living persons who at the present time are consciously making use of the principle of mind chemistry in developing power through the blending of minds, may be counted on the fingers of the two hands, with, perhaps, several fingers left to spare.

If this estimate is even approximately true the student will readily see that there is but slight danger of the field of mind chemistry practice becoming overcrowded.

It is a well known fact that one of the most difficult tasks that any business man must perform is that of inducing those who are associated with him to coordinate their efforts in a spirit of harmony. To induce continuous co-operation between a group of workers, in any undertaking, is next to impossible. Only the most efficient leaders can accomplish this highly desired object, but once in a great while such a leader will rise above the horizon in the field of industry, business or finance, and then the world hears of a Henry Ford, Thomas A. Edison, John D. Rockefeller, Sr., E.H. Harri man or James J. Hill.

Power and success are practically synonymous terms!

One grows out of the other; therefore, any person who has the knowledge and the ability to develop power, through the principle of harmonious co-ordination of effort between individual minds, or in any other manner, may be successful in any reasonable undertaking that is possible of successful termination.

It must not be assumed that a 'Master Mind' will immediately spring, mushroom fashion, out of every group of minds which make preteens of co-ordination in a spirit of HARMONY!

Harmony, in the real sense of meaning of the word, is as rare among groups of people as is genuine Christianity among those who proclaim themselves Christians.

Harmony is the nucleus around which the state of mind known as 'Master Mind' must be developed. Without this element of harmony there can be no 'Master Mind,' a truth which cannot be repeated too often.

Woodrow Wilson had in mind the development of a 'Master Mind,' to be composed of groups of minds representing the civilised nations of the world, in his proposal for establishing the League of Nations. Wilson's conception was the most far-reaching humanitarian idea ever created in the mind of man, because it dealt with a principle which embraces sufficient power to establish a real Brotherhood of Man on earth. The League of Nations, or some similar blending of international minds, in a spirit of harmony, is sure to become a reality.

The time when such unity of minds will take place will be measured largely by the time required for the great universities and

NON-SECTARIAN institutions of learning to supplant ignorance and superstition with understanding and wisdom. This time is rapidly approaching.

THE PSYCHOLOGY OF THE REVIVAL MEETING: The old religious orgy known as the 'revival' offers a favourable opportunity to study the principle of mind chemistry known as 'Master Mind.'

It will be observed that music plays no small part in bringing about the harmony essential to the blending of a group of minds in a revival meeting. Without music the revival meeting would be a tame affair.

During revival services the leader of the meeting has no difficulty in creating harmony in the minds of his devotees, but it is a well known fact that this state of harmony lasts no longer than the presence of the leader, after which the 'Master Mind' he has temporarily created disintegrates.

By arousing the emotional nature of his followers the revivalist has no difficulty, under the proper stage setting and with the embellishment of the right sort of music, in creating a 'Master Mind' which becomes noticeable to all who come in contact with it. The very air becomes charged with a positive, pleasing influence which changes the entire chemistry of all minds present.

The revivalist calls this energy 'the spirit of the Lord.'

This author, through experiments conducted with a group of scientific investigators and laymen (who were unaware of the nature of the experiment), has created the same state of mind and the same positive atmosphere without calling it the spirit of the Lord.

On many occasions this author has witnessed the creation of the same positive atmosphere in a group of men and women engaged in the business of salesmanship, without calling it the spirit of the Lord.

The author helped conduct a school of salesmanship for Harrison Parker, founder of the Co-operative Society, of Chicago, and, by the use of the same principle of mind chemistry which the revivalist calls the spirit of the Lord, so transformed the nature of a group of 3,000 men and women (all of whom were without former sales experience) that they sold more than $10,000,000.00 worth of securities in less than nine months, and earned more than $1,000,000 for themselves.

It was found that the average person who joined this school would reach the zenith of his or her selling power within one week, after which it was necessary to revitalize the individual's brain through a group sales meeting. These sales meetings were conducted on very much the same order as are the modern revival meetings of the religionist, with much the same stage equipment, including music and 'high-powered' speakers who exhorted the salespeople in very much the same manner as does the modern religious revivalist.

Call it religion, psychology, mind chemistry or anything you please (they are all based upon the same principle), but there is nothing more certain than the fact that wherever a group of minds are brought into contact, in a spirit of PERFECT HARMONY, each mind in the group becomes immediately supplemented and re-enforced by a noticeable energy called a 'Master Mind.'

For all this writer professes to know this uncharted energy may be the spirit of the Lord, but it operates just as favourably when called by any other name.

The human brain and nervous system constitute a piece of intricate machinery which but few, if any, understand. When controlled and properly directed this piece of machinery can be made to perform wonders of achievement and if not controlled it will perform wonders fantastic and phantom-like in nature, as may be seen by examining the inmates of any insane asylum.

The human brain has direct connection with a continuous influx of energy from which man derives his power to think. The brain receives this energy, mixes it with the energy created by the food taken into the body, and distributes it to every portion of the body, through the aid of the blood and the nervous system. It thus becomes what we call life.

From what source this outside energy comes no one seems to know; all we know about it is that we must have it or die. It seems reasonable to suppose that this energy is none other than that which we call ether, and that it flows into the body along with the oxygen from the air, as we breathe.

Every normal human body possesses a first-class chemical laboratory and a stock of chemicals sufficient to carry on the business of breaking up, assimilating and properly mixing and compounding the food we take into the body, preparatory to distributing it to wherever it is needed as a body builder.

Ample tests have been made, both with man and beast, to prove that the energy known as the mind plays an important part in this chemical operation of compounding and transforming food into the required substances to build and keep the body in repair.

It is known that worry, excitement or fear will interfere with the digestive process, and in extreme cases stop this process altogether, resulting in illness or death. It is obvious, then, that the mind enters into the chemistry of food digestion and distribution.

It is believed by many eminent authorities, although it may never have been scientifically proved, that the energy known as mind or thought may become contaminated with negative or 'unsociable' units to such an extent that the whole nervous system is thrown out of working order, digestion is interfered with and various and sundry forms of disease will manifest themselves. Financial difficulties and unrequited love affairs head the list of causes of such mind disturbances.

A negative environment such as that existing where some member of the family is constantly 'nagging,' will interfere with the chemistry of the mind to such an extent that the individual will lose ambition and gradually sink into oblivion. It is because of this fact that the old saying that a man's wife may either 'make' or 'break' him is literally true. In a subsequent lesson a whole chapter on this subject is addressed to the wives of men.

Any high-school student knows that certain food combinations will, if taken into the stomach, result in indigestion, violent pain and even death. Good health depends, in part at least, upon a food combination that 'harmonizes.' But harmony of food combinations is not sufficient to insure good health; there must be harmony, also, between the units of energy known as the mind.

A man is half whipped the minute he begins to feel sorry for himself, or to spin an alibi with which he would explain away his defects.

"Harmony "seems to be one of Nature's laws, without which there can be no such thing as Organised ENERGY, or life in any form whatsoever.

The health of the body as well as the mind is literally built around, out of and upon the principle of HARMONY! The energy known as life begins to disintegrate and death approaches when the organs of the body stop working in harmony.

The moment harmony ceases at the source of any form of organised energy (power) the units of that energy are thrown into a chaotic state of disorder and the power is rendered neutral or passive.

Harmony is also the nucleus around which the principle of mind chemistry known as a 'Master Mind' develops power. Destroy this harmony and you destroy the power growing out of the coordinated effort of a group of individual minds.

This truth has been stated, re-stated and presented in every manner which the author could conceive, with unending repetition, for the reason that unless the student grasps this principle and learns to apply it this lesson is useless.

Success in life, no matter what one may call success, is very largely a matter of adaptation to environment in such a manner that there is harmony between the individual and his environment. The palace of a king becomes as a hovel of a peasant if harmony does not abound within its walls. Conversely stated, the hut of a peasant may be made to yield more happiness than that of the mansion of the rich man, if harmony obtains in the former and not in the latter.

Without perfect harmony the science of astronomy would be as useless as the 'bones of a saint,' because the stars and planets would clash with one another, and all would be in a state of chaos and disorder.

Without the law of harmony an acorn might grow into a heterogeneous tree consisting of the wood of the oak, poplar, maple and what not.

Without the law of harmony the blood might deposit the food which grows finger nails on the scalp where hair is supposed to grow, and thus create a horny growth which might easily be mistaken, by the superstitious, to signify man's relationship to a certain imaginary gentleman with horns, often referred to by the more primitive type.

Without the law of harmony there can be no organisation of knowledge, for what, may one ask, is organised knowledge except the harmony of facts and truths and natural laws?

The moment discord begins to creep in at the front door harmony edges out at the back door, so to speak, whether the application is made to a business partnership or the orderly movement of the planets of the heavens.

If the student gathers the impression that the author is laying undue stress upon the importance of HARMONY, let it be remembered that lack of harmony is the first, and often the last and only, cause of FAILURE!

There can be no poetry nor music nor oratory worthy of notice without the presence of harmony.

Good architecture is largely a matter of harmony. Without harmony a house is nothing but a mass of building material, more or less a monstrosity.

Sound business management plants the very sinews of its existence in harmony.

Every well dressed man or woman is a living picture and a moving example of harmony.

With all these workaday illustrations of the important part which harmony plays in the affairs of the world-nay, in the operation of the entire universe-how could any intelligent person leave harmony out of his 'Definite Aim' in life? As well have no 'definite aim' as to omit harmony as the chief stone of its foundation.

The human body is a complex organisation of organs, glands, blood vessels, nerves, brain cells, muscles, etc. The mind energy which stimulates to action and co-ordinates the efforts of the component parts of the body is also a plurality of ever-varying and changing energies. From birth until death there is continuous struggle, often assuming the nature of open combat, between the forces of the mind. For example, the life-long struggle between the motivating forces and desires of the human mind, which takes place between the impulses of right and wrong, is well known to everyone.

Every human being possesses at least two distinct mind powers or personalities, and as many as six distinct personalities have been discovered in one person. One of man's most delicate tasks is that of harmonizing these mind forces so that they may be organised and directed toward the orderly attainment of a given objective. Without this element of harmony no individual can become an accurate thinker.

It is no wonder that leaders in business and industrial enterprises, as well as those in politics and other fields of endeavour, find it so difficult to organise groups of people so they will function in the attainment of a given objective, without friction. Each individual human being possesses forces, within himself, which are hard to harmonize, even when he is placed in the environment most favourable to harmony. If the chemistry of the individual's mind is such that the units of his mind cannot be easily harmonized, think how much more difficult it must be to harmonize a group of minds so they will function as one, in an orderly manner, through what is known as a 'Master Mind.'

The leader who successfully develops and directs the energies of a 'Master Mind' must possess tact, patience, persistence, self-confidence, intimate knowledge of mind chemistry and the ability to adapt himself (in a state of perfect poise and harmony) to quickly changing circumstances, without showing the least sign of annoyance.

How many are there who can measure up to this requirement?

The successful leader must possess the ability to change the color of his mind, chameleon-like, to fit every circumstance that arises in connection with the object of his leadership. Moreover, he must possess the ability to change from one mood to another without showing the slightest signs of anger or lack of self-control. The successful leader must understand the Fifteen Laws of Success and be able to put into practice any combination of these Fifteen Laws whenever occasion demands.

Without this ability no leader can be powerful, and without power no leader can long endure.

THE MEANING OF EDUCATION: There has long been a general misconception of the meaning of the word 'educate.' The dictionaries have not aided in the elimination of this misunderstanding, because they have defined the word 'educate' as an act of imparting knowledge.

The word educate has its roots in the Latin word educo, which means to develop FROM WITHIN; to educe; to draw out; to grow through the law of USE.

Nature hates idleness in all its forms. She gives continuous life only to those elements which are in use. Tie up an arm, or any other portion of the body, taking it out of use, and the idle part will soon atrophy and become lifeless. Reverse the order, give an arm more than normal use, such as that engaged in by the blacksmith who wields a heavy hammer all day long, and that arm (developed from within) grows strong.

Power grows out of Organised KNOWLEDGE, but, mind you, it 'grows out of it' through application and use!

A man may become a walking encyclopaedia of knowledge without possessing any power of value. This knowledge becomes power only to the extent that it is organised, classified and put into action. Some of the best educated men the world has known possessed much less general knowledge than some who have been known as fools, the difference between the two being that the former put what knowledge they Possessed into use while the latter made no such application.

An 'educated' person is one who knows how to acquire everything he needs in the attainment of his main Purpose in life, without violating the rights of his fellow men. It might be a surprise to many so-called men of 'learning' to know that they come nowhere near qualification as men of 'education.' It might also be a great surprise to many who believe they suffer from lack of 'learning' to know that they are well 'educated.'

The successful lawyer is not necessarily the one who memorises the greatest number of principles of law. On the contrary, the successful lawyer is the one who knows where to find a principle of law, plus a variety of opinions supporting that principle which fit the immediate needs of a given case.

In other words, the successful lawyer is he who knows where to find the law he wants when he needs it.

This principle applies, with equal force, to the affairs of industry and business.

Henry Ford had but little elementary schooling, yet he is one of the best 'educated' men in the world because he has acquired the ability so to combine natural and economic laws, to say nothing of the minds of men, that he has the power to get anything of a material nature he wants.

Some years ago during the world war Mr. Ford brought suit against the Chicago Tribune, charging that newspaper with libellous publication of statements concerning him, one of which was the statement that Ford was an 'ignoramus,' an ignorant pacifist, etc.

When the suit came up for trial the attorneys for the Tribune undertook to prove, by Ford himself, that their statement was true; that he was ignorant, and with this object in view they catechized and cross-examined him on all manner of subjects.

One question they asked was:

"How many soldiers did the British send over to subdue the rebellion in the Colonies in 1776?"

With a dry grin on his face Ford nonchalantly replied:

"I do not know just how many, but I have heard that it was a lot more than ever went back."

Loud laughter from Court, jury, court-room spectators, and even from the frustrated lawyer who had asked the question.

This line of interrogation was continued for an hour or more, Ford keeping perfectly calm the meanwhile. Finally, however, he had permitted the 'smart Aleck' lawyers to play with him until he was tired of it, and in reply to a question which was particularly obnoxious and insulting, Ford straightened himself up, pointed his finger at the questioning lawyer and replied:

"If I should really wish to answer the foolish question you have just asked, or any of the others you have been asking, let me remind you that I have a row of electric push-buttons hanging over my desk and by placing my finger on the right button I could call in men who could give me the correct answer to all the questions you have asked and to many that you have not the intelligence either to ask or answer. Now, will you kindly tell me why I should bother about filling my mind with a lot of useless details in order to answer every fool question that anyone may ask, when I have able men all about me who can supply me with all the facts I want when I call for them?"

This answer is quoted from memory, but it substantially relates Ford's answer.

There was silence in the court-room. The questioning attorney's under jaw dropped down, his eyes opened widely; the judge leaned forward from the bench and gazed in Mr. Ford's direction; many of the jury awoke and looked around as if they had heard an explosion (which they actually had).

A prominent clergyman who was present in the court-room at the time said, later, that the scene reminded him of that which must have existed when Jesus Christ was on trial before Pontius Pilate, just after He had given His famous reply to Pilate's question, 'What is truth?'

In the vernacular of the day, Ford's reply knocked the questioner cold.

Up to the time of that reply the lawyer had been enjoying considerable fun at what he believed to be Ford's expense, by adroitly displaying his (the lawyer's) sample case of general knowledge and comparing it with what he inferred to be Ford's ignorance as to many events and subjects.

But that answer spoiled the lawyer's fun !

It also proved once more (to all who had the intelligence to accept the proof) that true education means mind development; not merely the gathering and classifying of knowledge.

Ford could not, in all probability, have named the capitals of all the States of the United States, but he could have and in fact had gathered the 'capital' with which to 'turn many wheels' within every State in the Union.

Education-let us not forget this-consists of the power with which to get everything one needs when he needs it, without violating the rights of his fellow men. Ford comes well within that definition, and for the reason which the author has here tried to make plain, by relating the foregoing incident connected with the simple Ford philosophy.

There are many men of 'learning' who could easily entangle Ford, theoretically, with a maze of questions none of which he, personally, could answer. But Ford could turn right around and wage a battle in industry, or finance that would exterminate those same men, with all of their knowledge and all of their wisdom.

Ford could not go into his chemical laboratory and separate water into its component atoms of hydrogen and oxygen and then re-combine these atoms in their former order, but he knows how to surround himself with chemists who can do this for him if he wants it done. The man who can intelligently use the knowledge possessed by another is as much or more a man of education as the person who merely has the knowledge but does not know what to do with it.

The president of a well known college inherited a large tract of very poor land. This land had no timber of commercial value, no minerals or other valuable appurtenances, therefore it was nothing but a source of expense to him, for he had to pay taxes on it. The State built a highway through the land. An 'uneducated' man who was driving his automobile over this road observed that this poor land was on top of a mountain which commanded a wonderful view for many miles in all directions. He (the ignorant one) also observed that the land was covered with a growth of small pines and other saplings. He bought fifty acres of the land for $10.00 an acre. Near the public highway he built a unique log house to which he attached a large dining room. Near the house he put in a gasoline filling station. He built a dozen single-room log houses along the road, these he rented out to tourists at $3.00 a night, each. The dining room, gasoline filling station and log houses brought him a net income of $15,000.00 the first year. The next year he extended his plan by adding fifty more log houses, of three rooms each, which he now rents out as summer country homes to people in a near-by city, at a rental of $150.00 each for the season.

The building material cost him nothing, for it grew on his land in abundance (that same land which the college president believed to be worthless).

Moreover, the unique and unusual appearance of the log bungalows served as an advertisement of the plan, whereas many would have considered it a real calamity had they been compelled to build out of such crude materials.

Less than five miles from the location of these log houses this same man purchased an old worked-out farm of 150 acres, for $25.00 an acre, a price which the seller believed to be extremely high.

By building a dam, one hundred feet in length, the purchaser of this old farm turned a stream of water into a lake that covered fifteen acres of the land, stocked the lake with fish, then sold the farm off in building lots to people who wanted summering places around the lake. The total profit realised from this simple transaction was more than $25,000.00, and the time required for its consummation was one summer.

Yet this man of vision and imagination was not 'educated' in the orthodox meaning of that term.

Let us keep in mind the fact that it is through these simple illustrations of the use of organised knowledge that one may become educated and powerful.

In speaking of the transaction here related, the college president who sold the fifty acres of worthless (?) land for $500.00 said:

"Just think of it! That man, whom most of us might call ignorant, mixed his ignorance with fifty acres of worthless land and made the combination yield more yearly than I earn from five years of application of so-called education."

There is an opportunity, if not scores of them, in every State in America, to make use of the idea here described. From now on make it your business to study the lay of all land you see that is similar to that described in this lesson, and you may find a suitable place for developing a similar money-making enterprise. The idea is particularly adaptable in localities where bathing beaches are few, as people naturally like such conveniences.

The automobile has caused a great system of public highways to be built throughout the United States. On practically every one of these highways there is a suitable spot for a 'Cabin City' for tourists which can be turned into a regular money-making mint by the man with the IMAGINATION and SELF-CONFIDENCE to do it.

There are opportunities to make money all around you. This course was designed to help you 'see' these opportunities, and to inform you how to make the most of them after you discover them.

Who can profit most by The Law of Success philosophy?

RAILROAD OFFICIALS who want a better spirit of co-operation between their trainmen and the public they serve.

SALARIED PEOPLE who wish to increase their earning power and market their services to better advantage.

SALESPEOPLE who wish to become masters in their chosen field. The Law of Success philosophy covers every known law of selling, and includes many features not included in any other course.

INDUSTRIAL PLANT MANAGERS who understand the value of greater harmony among their employees.

RAILROAD EMPLOYEES who wish to establish records of efficiency which will lead to more responsible positions, with greater pay.

MERCHANTS who wish to extend their business by adding new customers. The Law of Success philosophy will help any merchant increase his business by teaching him how to make a walking advertisement of every customer who comes into his store.

AUTOMOBILE AGENTS who wish to increase the selling power of their salesmen. A large part of The Law of Success course was developed from the lifework and experience of the greatest automobile salesman living, and it is therefore of unusual help to the Sales Manager who is directing the efforts of Automobile Salesmen.

LIFE INSURANCE AGENTS who wish to add new policy-holders and increase the insurance on present policy-holders. One Life Insurance Salesman, in Ohio, sold a Fifty Thousand Dollar policy to one of the officials of the Central Steel Company, as the result of butone reading of the lesson on 'Profiting by Failures.' This same salesman has become one of the star men of the New York Life Insurance Company's staff, as the result of his training in the Fifteen Laws of Success.

SCHOOL TEACHERS who wish to advance to the top in their present occupation, or who are looking for an opportunity to enter the more profitable field of business as a life-work.

STUDENTS, both College and High School, who are undecided as to what field of endeavour they wish to enter as a life-work. The Law of Success course covers a complete Personal Analysis service which helps the student of the philosophy to determine the work for which he or she is best fitted.

BANKERS who wish to extend their business through better and more courteous methods of serving their clients.

BANK CLERKS who are ambitious to prepare themselves for executive positions in the field of banking, or in some commercial or industrial field.

PHYSICIANS and DENTISTS who wish to extend their practice without violating the ethics of their profession by direct advertising. A prominent physician has said that The Law of Success course is worth $1,000.00 to any professional man or woman whose professional ethics prevent direct advertising.

PROMOTERS who wish to develop new and heretofore unworked combinations in business or industry.

The principle described in this Introductory Lesson is said to have made a small fortune for a man who used it as the basis of a real estate promotion.

REAL ESTATE MEN who wish new methods for promoting sales. This Introductory Lesson contains a description of an entirely new real-estate promotion plan which is sure to make fortunes for many who will put it to use. This plan may be put into operation in practically every State. Moreover, it may be employed by men who never promoted an enterprise.

FARMERS who wish to discover new methods of marketing their products so as to give them greater net returns, and those who own lands suitable for subdivision promotion under the plan referred to at the end of this Introductory Lesson. Thousands of farmers have 'gold mines' in the land they own which is not suitable for cultivation, which could be used for recreation and resort purposes, on a highly profitable basis.

STENOGRAPHERS and BOOKKEEPERS who are looking for a practical plan to promote themselves into higher and better paying positions. The Law of Success course is said to be the best course ever written on the subject of marketing personal services.

PRINTERS who want a larger volume of business and more efficient production as the result of better cooperation among their own employees.

DAY LABORERS who have the ambition to advance into more responsible positions, in work that has greater responsibilities and consequently offers more pay.

LAWYERS who wish to extend their clientele through dignified, ethical methods which will bring them to the attention, in a favourable way, of a greater number of people who need legal services.

BUSINESS EXECUTIVES who wish to expand their present business, or who wish to handle their present volume with less expense, as the result of greater co-operation between their employees.

LAUNDRY OWNERS who wish to extend their business by teaching their drivers how to serve more courteously and efficiently.

LIFE INSURANCE GENERAL AGENTS who wish bigger and more efficient sales organisations.

CHAIN STORE MANAGERS who want a greater volume of business as the result of more efficient individual sales efforts.

MARRIED PEOPLE who are unhappy, and therefore unsuccessful, because of lack of harmony and cooperation in the home.

To all described in the foregoing classification The Law of Success philosophy offers both DEFINITE and SPEEDY aid.

Summary of Introductory Lesson

The purpose of this summary is to aid the student in mastering the central idea around which the lesson has been developed. This idea is represented by the term 'Master Mind' which has been described in great detail throughout the lesson.

All new ideas, and especially those of an abstract nature, find lodgement in the human mind only after much repetition, a well known truth which accounts for the re-statement, in this summary, of the principle known as the 'Master Mind.'

A 'Master Mind' may be developed by a friendly alliance, in a spirit of harmony of purpose, between two or more minds.

This is an appropriate place at which to explain that out of every alliance of minds, whether in a spirit of harmony or not, there is developed another mind which affects all participating in the alliance. No two or more minds ever met without creating, out of the contact, another mind, but not always is this invisible creation a 'Master Mind.'

There may be, and altogether too often there is, developed out of the meeting of two or more minds a negative power which is just the opposite to a 'Master Mind.'

There are certain minds which, as has already been stated throughout this lesson, cannot be made to blend in a spirit of harmony. This principle has its comparable analogy in chemistry, reference to which may enable the student to grasp more clearly the principle here referred to.

For example, the chemical formula H2 O (meaning the combining of two atoms of hydrogen with one atom of oxygen) changes these two elements into water. One atom of hydrogen and one atom of oxygen will not produce water; moreover, they cannot be made to associate themselves in harmony!

There are many known elements which, when combined, are immediately transformed from harmless into deadly poisonous substances. Stated differently, many well known poisonous elements are neutralised and rendered harmless when combined with certain other elements.

Just as the combining of certain elements changes their entire nature, the combining of certain minds changes the nature of those minds, producing either a certain degree of what has been called a 'Master Mind,' or its opposite, which is highly destructive.

Any man who has found his mother-in-law to be incompatible has experienced the negative application of the principle known as a 'Master Mind.' For some reason as yet unknown to investigators in the field of mind behaviour, the majority of mothers-in-law appear to affect their daughters' husbands in a highly negative manner, the meeting of their minds with those of their sons-in-law creating a highly antagonistic influence instead of a 'Master Mind.'

This fact is too well known as a truth to make extended comment necessary.

Some minds will not be harmonized and cannot be blended into a 'Master Mind,' a fact which all leaders of men will do well to remember. It is the leader's responsibility so to group his men that those who have been placed at the most strategic points in his organisation are made up of individuals whose minds CAN and WILL BE blended in a spirit of friendliness and harmony.

Ability so to group men is the chief outstanding quality of leadership. In Lesson Two of this course the student will discover that this ability was the main source of both the power and fortune accumulated by the late Andrew Carnegie.

Knowing nothing whatsoever of the technical end of the steel business, Carnegie so combined and grouped the men of which his 'Master Mind' was composed that he built the most successful steel industry known to the world during his life-time.

Henry Ford's gigantic success may be traced to the successful application of this selfsame principle. With all the self-reliance a man could have, Ford, nevertheless, did not depend upon himself for the knowledge necessary in the successful development of his industries.

Like Carnegie, he surrounded himself with men who supplied the knowledge which he, himself, did not and could not possess.

Moreover, Ford picked men who could and did harmonize in group effort.

The most effective alliances, which have resulted in the creation of the principle known as the 'Master Mind,' have been those developed out of the blending of the minds of men and women. The reason for this is the fact that the minds of male and female will more readily blend in harmony than will the minds of males. Also, the added stimulus of sexual contact often enters into the development of a 'Master Mind' between a man and a woman.

It is a well known fact that the male of the species is keener and more alert for 'the chase,' let the goal or object of the chase be what it may, when inspired and urged on by a female.

This human trait begins to manifest itself in the male at the age of puberty, and continues throughout his life. The first evidence of it may be observed in athletics, where boys are playing before an audience made up of females.

Remove the women from the audience and the game known as football would soon become a very tame affair. A boy will throw himself into a football game with almost superhuman effort when he knows that the girl of his choice is observing him from the grandstand.

And that same boy will throw himself into the game of accumulating money with the same enthusiasm when inspired and urged on by the woman of his choice; especially if that woman knows how to stimulate his mind with her own, through the law of the 'Master Mind.'

On the other hand, that same woman may, through a negative application of the law of the 'Master Mind' (nagging, jealousy, selfishness, greed, vanity), drag this man down to sure defeat!

The late Elbert Hubbard understood the principle here described so well that when he discovered that the incompatibility between himself and his first wife was dragging him down to sure defeat he ran the gamut of public opinion by divorcing her and marrying the woman who is said to have been the main source of his inspiration.

Note very man would have had the courage to defy public opinion, as Hubbard did, but who is wise enough to say that his action was not for the best interest of all concerned?

A man's chief business in life is to succeed!

The road to success may be, and generally is, obstructed by many influences which must be removed before the goal can be reached. One of the most detrimental of these obstacles is that of unfortunate alliance with minds which do not harmonize. In such cases the alliance must be broken or the end is sure to be defeat and failure.

The man who has mastered the six basic fears, one of which is the Fear of Criticism, will have no hesitancy in taking what may seem to the more convention-bound type of mind to be drastic action when he finds himself circumscribed and bound down by antagonistic alliances, no matter of what nature or with whom they may be.

It is a million times better to meet and face criticism than to be dragged down to failure and oblivion on account of alliances which are not harmonious, whether the alliances be of a business or social nature.

To be perfectly frank, the author is here justifying divorce, when the conditions surrounding marriage are such that harmony cannot prevail. This is not intended to convey the belief that lack of harmony may not be removed through other methods than that of divorce; for there are instances where the cause of antagonism may be removed and harmony established without taking the extreme step of divorce.

While it is true that some minds will not blend in a spirit of harmony, and cannot be forced or induced to do so, because of the chemical nature of the individuals' brains, do not be too ready to charge the other party to your alliance with all the responsibility of lack of harmony remember, the trouble may be with your own brain!

Remember, also, that a mind which cannot and will not harmonize with one person or persons may harmonize perfectly with other types of minds. Discovery of this truth has resulted in radical changes in methods of employing men. It is no longer customary to discharge a man because he does not fit in the position for which he was originally hired. The discriminating leader endeavours to place such a man in some other position, where, it has been proved more than once, misfits may become valuable men.

The student of this course should be sure that the principle described as the 'Master Mind' is thoroughly understood before proceeding with the remaining lessons of the course. The reason for this is the fact that practically the entire course is closely associated with this law of mind operation.

If you are not sure that you understand this law, communicate with the author of the course and secure further explanation by asking such questions as you may wish concerning points in connection with which you believe you need further information.

You cannot spend too much time in serious thought and contemplation in connection with the law of the 'Master Mind,' for the reason that when you have mastered this law and have learned how to apply it new worlds of opportunity will open to you.

This Introductory Lesson, while not really intended as a separate lesson of The Law of Success course, contains sufficient data to enable the student who has an aptitude for selling to become a Master Salesman.

Any sales organisation may make effective use of the law of the 'Master Mind' by grouping the salesmen in groups of two or more people who will ally themselves in a spirit of friendly co-operation and apply this law as suggested in this lesson.

An agent for a well known make of automobile, who employs twelve salesmen, has grouped his organisation in six groups of two men each, with the object of applying the law of the 'Master Mind,' with the result that all the salesmen have established new high sales records.

This same organisation has created what it calls the 'One-A-Week Club,' meaning that each man belonging to the Club has averaged the sale of one car a week since the Club was organised.

The results of this effort have been surprising to all!

Each man belonging to the Club was provided with a list of 100 prospective purchasers of automobiles. Each salesman sends one postal card a week to each of his 100 prospective purchasers, and makes personal calls on at least ten of these each day.

Each postal card is confined to the description of butone advantage of the automobile the salesman is selling, and asks for a personal interview.

Interviews have increased rapidly, as have, also, sales!

The agent who employs these salesmen has offered an extra cash bonus to each salesman who earns the right to membership in the 'One-A-Week Club' by averaging one car a week.

The plan has injected new vitality into the entire organisation. Moreover, the results of the plan are showing in the weekly sales record of each salesman.

A similar plan could be adopted very effectively by Life Insurance Agencies. Any enterprising General Agent might easily double or even triple the volume of his business, with the same number of salesmen, through the use of this plan.

Practically no changes whatsoever would need to be made in the method of use of the plan. The Club might be called the 'Policy-A-Week Club,' meaning that each member pledged himself to sell at least one policy, of an agreed minimum amount, each week.

The student of this course who has mastered the second lesson, and understands how to apply the fundamentals of that lesson (A Definite Chief Aim) will be able to make much more effective use of the plan here described.

It is not suggested or intended that any student shall undertake to apply the principles of this lesson, which is merely an Introductory Lesson, until he has mastered at least the next five lessons of The Law of Success course.

The main purpose of this Introductory Lesson is to state some of the principles upon which the course is founded. These principles are more accurately described, and the student is taught in a very definite manner how to apply them, in the individual lessons of the course.

The automobile sales organisation referred to in this summary meets at luncheon once a week. One hour and a half is devoted to luncheon and to the discussion of ways and means of applying the principles of this course. This gives each man an opportunity to profit by the ideas of all the other members of the organisation.

Two tables are set for the luncheon.

Atone table all who have earned the right to membership in the One-A-Week Club are seated. At the other table, which is serviced with tin ware instead of china, all who did not earn the right to membership in the Club are seated. These, needless to say, become the object of considerable good-natured chiding from the more fortunate members seated at the other table.

It is possible to make an almost endless variety of adaptations of this plan, both in the field of automobile salesmanship and in other fields of selling.

The justification for its use is that it pays!

It pays not only the leader or manager of the organisation, but every member of the sales force as well.

This plan has been briefly described for the purpose of showing the student of this course how to make practical application of the principles outlined in this course.

The final acid test of any theory or rule or principle is that it will ACTUALLY WORK! The law of the 'Master Mind' has been proved sound because it WORKS.

If you understand this law you are now ready to proceed with Lesson Two, in which you will be further and much more deeply initiated in the application of the principles described in this Introductory Lesson.

A winner never quits, and a quitter never wins!

NOTICE

Study this chart carefully and compare the ratings of these ten men before grading yourself, in the two columns at the right.

Henry Ford Benjamin Franklin George Washington Theodore Roosevelt Abraham Lincoln Woodrow Wilson— William h Taft Napoleon Bonaparte Calvin Coolidge Jesse James

Grade yourself in these two columns, before and after completing The Law of Success course.

BEFORE AFTER

THE FIFTEEN LAWS OF SUCCESS

I.	Definite Chief Aim	100	100	100	100	100
		100	100	100	100	-
II.	Self-Confidence	100	80	90	100	75
		80	50	100	60	75
III.	Habit of Saving	100	100	75	50	20
		40	30	40	100	-
IV.	Initiative & Leadership	100	60	100	100	60
		90	20	100	25	90
V.	Imagination	90	90	80	80	70
		80	65	90	50	60
VI.	Enthusiasm	75	80	90	100	60
		90	50	80	50	80
VII.	Self-Control	100	90	50	75	95
		75	80	40	100	50
VIII.	Habit of Doing More Than Paid For	100	100	100	100	100
		100	100	100	100	-
IX.	Pleasing Personality	50	90	80	80	80
		75	90	100	40	50
X.	Accurate Thinking	90	80	75	60	90
		80	80	90	70	20
XI.	Concentration	100	100	100	100	100
		100	100	100	100	75
XII.	Cooperation	75	100	100	50	90
		40	100	50	60	50
XIII.	Profiting by Failure	100	90	75	60	80
		60	60	40	40	-
XIV.	Tolerance	90	100	80	75	100
		70	100	10	75	-
XV.	Plasticising Golden Rule	100	100	100	100	100
		100	100	-	100	-
	GENERAL AVERAGE	91	90	86	82	81
		79	75	70	71	37

The ten men who have been analysed, in the above chart, are well known throughout the world. Eight of these are known to be successful, while two are generally considered to have been failures. The failures are Jesse James and Napoleon Bonaparte. They have been analysed for comparison. Carefully observe where these two men have been graded zero and you will see why they failed. A grading of zero on any one of the Fifteen Laws of Success is sufficient to cause failure, even though all other grades are high.

Notice that all the successful men grade 100% on a Definite Chief Aim. This is a prerequisite to success, in all cases, without exception. If you wish to conduct an interesting experiment replace the above ten names with the names of ten people whom you know, five of whom are successful and five of whom are failures, and grade each of them. When you are through, GRADE YOURSELF, taking care to see that you really know what are your weaknesses.

Your Six Most Dangerous Enemies

An After-the-Lesson Visit With the Author

The Six Spectres are labelled: Fear of Poverty, Fear of Death, Fear of Ill-Health, Fear of the Loss of Love, Fear of Old Age, Fear of Criticism.

Every person on earth is afraid of something. Most fears are inherited. In this essay you may study the six basic fears which do the most damage. Your fears must be mastered before you can win in any worth-while undertaking in life. Find out how many of the six fears are bothering you, but more important than this, determine, also how to conquer these fears

IN this picture you have the opportunity to study our six worst enemies.

These enemies are not beautiful. The artist who drew this picture did not paint the six characters as ugly as they really are. If he had, no one would have believed him.

As you read about these ugly characters analyse yourself and find out which of them does YOU the most damage!

The purpose of this essay is to help the readers of this course throw off these deadly enemies. Observe that the six characters are at your back, where you cannot conveniently see them.

Every human being on this earth is bound down to some extent by one or more of these unseen FEARS. The first step to be taken in killing off these enemies is to find out where and how you acquired them.

They got their grip upon you through two forms of heredity. One is known as physical heredity, to which Darwin devoted so much study. The other is known as social heredity, through which the fears, superstitions and beliefs of men who lived during the dark ages have been passed on from one generation to another.

Let us study, first, the part that physical heredity has played in creating these six BASIC FEARS. Starting at the beginning, we find that Nature has been a cruel builder. From the lowest form of life to the highest, Nature has permitted the stronger to prey upon the weaker forms of animal life.

The fish prey upon the worms and insects, eating them bodily. Birds prey upon the fish. Higher forms of animal life prey upon the birds, and upon one another, all the way up the line to man. And, man preys upon all the other lower forms of animal life, and upon MAN!

The whole story of evolution is one unbroken chain of evidence of cruelty and destruction of the weaker by the stronger. No wonder the weaker forms of animal life have learned to FEAR the stronger. The Fear consciousness is born in every living animal.

So much for the FEAR instinct that came to us through physical heredity. Now let us examine social heredity, and find out what part it has played in our make-up. The term 'social heredity' has reference to everything that we are taught, everything we learn or gather from observation and experience with other living beings.

Lay aside any prejudices and fixed opinions you may have formed, at least temporarily, and you may know the truth about your Six Worst Enemies, starting with:

THE FEAR OF POVERTY! It requires courage to tell the truth about the history of this enemy of mankind, and still greater courage to hear the truth after it has been told. The Fear of Poverty grows out of man's habit of preying upon his fellow men, economically. The animals which have instinct, but no power to THINK, prey upon one another physically. Man, with his superior sense of intuition, and his more powerful weapon of THOUGHT, does not eat his fellow man bodily; he gets more pleasure from eating him FINANCIALLY.

So great an offender is man, in this respect, that nearly every state and nation has been obliged to pass laws, scores of laws, to protect the weak from the strong. Every blue-sky law is indisputable evidence of man's nature to prey upon his weaker brother economically.

The second of the Six Basic Fears with which man is bound down is:

THE FEAR OF OLD AGE! This Fear grows out of two major causes. First, the thought that old Age may bring with it POVERTY. Secondly, from false and cruel sectarian teachings which have been so well mixed with fire and brimstone that every human being learned to Fear Old Age because it meant the approach of another and, perhaps, a more horrible world than this.

The third of the Six Basic Fears is:

THE FEAR OF ILL HEALTH: This Fear is born of both physical and social heredity. From birth until death there is eternal warfare within every physical body; warfare between groups of cells, one group being known as the friendly builders of the body, and the other as the destroyers, or 'disease germs.' The seed of Fear is born in the physical body, to begin with, as the result of Nature's cruel plan of permitting the stronger forms of cell life to prey upon the weaker. Social heredity has played its part through lack of cleanliness and knowledge of sanitation. Also, through the law of suggestion cleverly manipulated by those who profited by ILL HEALTH.

The fourth of the Six Basic Fears is:

THE FEAR OF LOSS OF LOVE OF SOMEONE: This Fear fills the asylums with the insanely jealous, for jealousy is nothing but a form of insanity. It also fills the divorce courts and causes murders and other forms of cruel punishment. It is a holdover, handed down through social heredity, from the stone age when man preyed upon his fellow man by stealing his mate by physical force. The method, but not the practice, has now changed to some extent. Instead of physical force man now steals his fellow man's mate with pretty colourful ribbons and fast motor cars and bootleg whisky, and sparkling rocks and stately mansions.

Man is improving. He now 'entices' where once he 'drove.'

The fifth of the Six Basic Fears is:

THE FEAR OF CRITICISM: Just how and where man got this Fear is difficult to determine, but it is certain that he has it. But for this Fear men would not become bald-headed. Bald heads come from tightly fitting hat-bands, which cutoff the circulation from the roots of the hair. Women seldom are bald because they wear loose fitting hats. But for Fear of Criticism man would lay aside his hat and keep his hair.

The makers of clothing have not been slow to capitalize this Basic Fear of mankind. Every season the styles change, because the clothes makers know that few people have the courage to wear a garment that is one season out of step with what 'They are all wearing.' If you doubt this (you gentlemen) start down the street with last year's narrow-brimmed straw hat on, when this year's style calls for the broad brim. Or (you ladies), take a walk down the street on Easter morning with last year's hat on. Observe how uncomfortable you are, thanks to your unseen enemy, the FEAR OF CRITICISM.

The sixth, and last of the Six Basic Fears is the most dreaded of them all. It is called:

THE FEAR OF DEATH! For tens of thousands of years man has been asking the still unanswered questions-'WHENCE?' and 'WHITHER?' The more crafty of the race have not been slow to offer the answer to this eternal question, 'Where did I come from and where am I going after Death?' 'Come into my tent,' says one leader, 'and you may go to Heaven after Death.' Heaven was then pictured as a wonderful city whose streets were lined with gold and studded with precious stones. 'Remain out of my tent and you may go straight to hell.' Hell was then pictured as a blazing furnace where the poor victim might have the misery of burning forever in brimstone.

No wonder mankind FEARS DEATH!

Take another look at the picture at the beginning of this essay and determine, if you can, which of the Six Basic Fears is doing you the greatest damage. An enemy discovered is an enemy half whipped.

Thanks to the schools and colleges man is slowly discovering these Six Enemies. The most effective tool with which to fight them is Organised KNOWLEDGE. Ignorance and Fear are twin sisters. They are generally found together.

But for IGNORANCE and SUPERSTITION the Six Basic Fears would disappear from man's nature in one generation. In every public library may be found the remedy for these six enemies of mankind, providing you know what books to read.

Begin by reading The Science of Power, by Benjamin Kidd, and you will have broken the strangle hold of most of your Six Basic Fears. Follow this by reading Emerson's essay on Compensation.

Then select some good book on auto-suggestion (self-suggestion) and inform yourself on the principle through which your beliefs of today become the realities of tomorrow. Mind In the Making, by Robinson, will give you a good start toward understanding your own mind.

Through the principle of social heredity the IGNORANCE and SUPERSTITION of the dark ages have been passed on to you. But, you are living in a modern age. On every hand you may see evidence that every EFFECT has a natural CAUSE. Begin, now, to study effects by their causes and soon you will emancipate your mind from the burden of the Six Basic Fears.

Begin by studying men who have accumulated great wealth, and find out the CAUSE of their achievements. Henry Ford is a good subject to start with. Within the short period of twenty-five years he has whipped POVERTY and made himself the most powerful man on earth. There was no luck or chance or accident back of his achievement. It grew out of his careful observation of certain principles which are as available to you as they were to him.

Henry Ford is not bound down by the Six Basic Fears; make no mistake about this.

If you feel that you are too far away from Ford to study him accurately, then begin by selecting two people whom you know close at hand; one representing your idea of FAILURE and the other corresponding to your idea of SUCCESS. Find out what made one a failure and the other a success. Get the real FACTS. In the process of gathering these facts you will have taught yourself a great lesson on CAUSE and EFFECT.

Nothing ever just 'happens.' Everything, from the lowest animal form that creeps on the earth or swims in the seas, on up to man, is the effect of Nature's evolutionary process. Evolution is 'orderly change.' No 'miracles' are connected with this orderly change.

Not only do the physical shapes and colors of animals undergo slow, orderly change from one generation to another, but the mind of man is also undergoing constant change. Herein lies your hope for improvement. You have the power to force your mind through a process of rather quick change. In a single month of properly directed self-suggestion you may place your foot upon the neck of every one of your Six Basic Fears. In twelve months of persistent effort you may drive the entire herd into the corner where it will never again do you any serious injury.

You will resemble, tomorrow, the DOMINATING THOUGHTS that you keep alive in your mind today! Plant in your mind the seed of DETERMINATION to whip your Six Basic Fears and the battle will have been half won then and there. Keep this intention in your mind and it will slowly push your Six Worst Enemies out of sight, as they exist nowhere except in your own mind.

The man who is powerful FEARS nothing; not even God. The POWERFUL man loves God, but FEARS Him never! Enduring power never grows out of FEAR. Any power that is built upon FEAR is bound to crumble and disintegrate. Understand this great truth and you will never be so unfortunate as to try to raise yourself to power through the FEARS of other people who may owe you temporary allegiance.

> Man is of soul and body formed for deeds
> Of high resolve; on fancy's boldest wing
> To soar unwearied, fearlessly to turn
> The keenest pangs to peacefulness, and taste
> The joys which mingled sense and spirit yield;
> Or he is formed for abjectness and woe,
> To grovel on the dunghill of his fears,
> To shrink at every sound, to quench the flame
> Of natural love in sensualist, to know
> That hour as blest when on his worthless days
> The frozen hand of death shall set its seal,
> Yet fear the cure, though hating the disease.
> The one is man that shall hereafter be,
> The other, man as vice has made him now.

—SHELLEY

□

2

Self-Confidence

"You Can Do It if You Believe You Can!"

Before approaching the fundamental principles upon which this lesson is founded it will be of benefit to you to keep in mind the fact that it is practical-that it brings you the discoveries of more than twenty-five years of research-that it has the approval of the leading scientific men and women of the world who have tested every principle involved.

Scepticism is the deadly enemy of progress and self-development. You might as well lay this book aside and stop right here as to approach this lesson with the feeling that it was written by some long-haired theorist who had never tested the principles upon which the lesson is based.

Surely this is no age for the sceptic, because it is an age in which we have seen more of Nature's laws uncovered and harnessed than had been discovered in all past history of the human race. Within three decades we have witnessed the mastery of the air; we have explored the ocean; we have all but annihilated distances on the earth; we have harnessed the lightning and made it turn the wheels of industry; we have made seven blades of grass grow where but one grew before; we have instantaneous communication between the nations of the world. Truly, this is an age of illumination and enfoldment, but we have as yet barely scratched the surface of knowledge. However, when we shall have unlocked the gate that leads to the secret power which is stored up within us it will bring us knowledge that will make all past discoveries pale into oblivion by comparison.

Thought is the most highly organised form of energy known to man, and this is an age of experimentation and research that is sure to bring us into greater understanding of that mysterious force called thought, which reposes within us. We have already found out enough about the human mind to know that a man may throw off the accumulated effects of a thousand generations of fear, through the aid of the principle of Auto-suggestion. We have already discovered the fact that fear is the chief reason for poverty and failure and misery that takes on a thousand different forms. We have already discovered the fact that the man who masters fear may march on to successful achievement in practically any undertaking, despite all efforts to defeat him.

The development of self-confidence starts with the elimination of this demon called fear, which sits upon a man's shoulder and whispers into his ear, "You can't do it-you are afraid to try-you are afraid of public opinion-you are afraid that you will fail-you are afraid you have not the ability."

This fear demon is getting in to close quarters.

Science has found a deadly weapon with which to put it to flight, and this lesson on self-confidence has brought you this weapon for use in your battle with the world-old enemy of progress, fear.

THE SIX BASIC FEARS OF MANKIND: Every person falls heir to the influence of six basic fears. Under these six fears may be listed the lesser fears. The six basic or major fears are here enumerated and the sources from which they are believed to have grown are described.

The six basic fears are:

a. The fear of Poverty
b. The fear of Old Age
c. The fear of Criticism
d. The fear of Loss of Love of Someone.
e. The fear of Ill Health
f. The fear of Death.

Study the list, then take inventory of your own fears and ascertain under which of the six headings you can classify them.

Every human being who has reached the age of understanding is bound down, to some extent, by one or more of these six basic fears. As the first step in the elimination of these six evils let us examine the sources from whence we inherited them.

Physical and Social Heredity

All that man is, both physically and mentally, he came by through two forms of heredity. One is known as physical heredity and the other is called social heredity.

Through the law of physical heredity man has slowly evolved from the amoeba (a single-cell animal form), through stages of development corresponding to all the known animal forms now on this earth, including those which are known to have existed but which are now extinct.

Every generation through which man has passed has added to his nature something of the traits, habits and physical appearance of that generation. Man's physical inheritance, therefore, is a heterogeneous collection of many habits and physical forms.

There seems little, if any, doubt that while the six basic fears of man could not have been inherited through physical heredity (these six basic fears being mental states of mind and therefore not capable of transmission through physical heredity), it is obvious that through physical heredity a most favourable lodging place for these six fears has been provided.

For example, it is a well known fact that the whole process of physical evolution is based upon death, destruction, pain and cruelty; that the elements of the soil of the earth find transportation, in their upward climb through evolution, based upon the death of one form of life in order that another and higher form may subsist. All vegetation lives by 'eating' the elements of the soil and the elements of the air. All forms of animal life live by 'eating' some other and weaker form, or some form of vegetation.

The cells of all vegetation have a very high order of intelligence. The cells of all animal life likewise have a very high order of intelligence.

Undoubtedly the animal cells of a fish have learned, out of bitter experience, that the group of animal cells known as a fish hawk are to be greatly feared.

By reason of the fact that many animal forms (including that of most men) live by eating the smaller and weaker animals, the 'cell intelligence' of these animals which enter into and become a part of man brings with it the FEAR growing out of their experience in having been eaten alive.

This theory may seem to be far-fetched, and in fact it may not be true, but it is at least a logical theory if it is nothing more. The author makes no particular point of this theory, nor does he insist that it accounts for any of the six basic fears. There is another, and a much better explanation of the source of these fears, which we will proceed to examine, beginning with a description of social heredity.

By far the most important part of man's make-up comes to him through the law of social heredity, this term having reference to the methods by which one generation imposes upon the minds of the generation under its immediate control the superstitions, beliefs, legends and ideas which it, in turn, inherited from the generation preceding.

The term 'social heredity' should be understood to mean any and all sources through which a person acquires knowledge, such as schooling of religious and all other natures; reading, word of mouth conversation, storytelling and all manner of thought inspiration coming from what is generally accepted as one's 'personal experiences.'

Through the operation of the law of social heredity anyone having control of the mind of a child may, through intense teaching, plant in that child's mind any idea, whether false or true, in such a manner that the child accepts it as true and it becomes as much a part of the child's personality as any cell or organ of its physical body (and just as hard to change in its nature).

It is through the law of social heredity that the religionist plants in the child mind dogmas and creeds and religious ceremonies too numerous to describe, holding those ideas before that mind until the mind accepts them and forever seals them as a part of its irrevocable belief.

The mind of a child which has not come into the age of general understanding, during an average period covering, let us say, the first two years of its life, is plastic, open, clean and free. Any idea planted in such a mind by one in whom the child has confidence takes root and grows, so to speak, in such a manner that it never can be eradicated or wiped out, no matter how opposed to logic or reason that idea may be.

Many religionists claim that they can so deeply implant the tenets of their religion in the mind of a child that there never can be room in that mind for any other religion, either in whole or in part. The claims are not greatly overdrawn.

With this explanation of the manner in which the law of social heredity operates the student will be ready to examine the sources from which man inherits the six basic fears. Moreover, any student (except those who have not yet grown big enough to examine truth that steps upon the 'pet corns' of their own superstitions) may check the soundness of the principle of social heredity as it is here applied to the six basic fears, without going outside of his or her own personal experiences.

Fortunately, practically the entire—mass of evidence submitted in this lesson is of such a nature that all who sincerely seek the truth may ascertain, for themselves, whether the evidence is sound or not.

For the moment at least, lay aside your prejudices and preconceived ideas (you may always go back and pick them up again, you know) while we study the origin and nature of man's Six Worst Enemies, the six basic fears, beginning with:

THE FEAR OF POVERTY: It requires courage to tell the truth about the origin of this fear, and still greater courage, perhaps, to accept the truth after it has been told. The fear of poverty grew out of man's inherited tendency to prey upon his fellow man economically. Nearly all forms of lower animals have instinct but appear not to have the power to reason and think; therefore, they prey upon one another physically. Man, with his superior sense of intuition, thought and reason, does not eat his fellow men bodily; he gets more satisfaction out of eating them FINANCIALLY!

Of all the ages of the world of which we know anything, the age in which we live seems to be the age of money worship. A man is considered less than the dust of the earth unless he can display a fat bank account. Nothing brings man so much suffering and humiliation as does POVERTY. No wonder man FEARS poverty. Through a long line of inherited experiences with the man-animal man has learned, for certain, that this animal cannot always be trusted where matters of money and other evidences of earthly possessions are concerned.

Many marriages have their beginning (and oftentimes their ending) solely on the basis of the wealth possessed by one or both of the contracting parties.

It is no wonder that the divorce courts are busy! 'Society' could quite properly be spelled 'Society,' because it is inseparably associated with the dollar mark. So eager is man to possess wealth that he will acquire it in whatever manner he can; through legal methods, if possible, through other methods if necessary.

The fear of poverty is a terrible thing!

A man may commit murder, engage in robbery, rape and all other manner of violation of the rights of others and still regain a high station in the minds of his fellow men, PROVIDING always that he does not lose his wealth. Poverty, therefore, is a crime-an unforgivable sin, as it were.

No wonder man fears it!

Every statute book in the world bears evidence that the fear of poverty is one of the six basic fears of mankind, for in every such book of laws may be found various and sundry laws intended to protect the weak from the strong. To spend time trying to prove either that the fear of poverty is one of man's inherited fears, or that this fear has its origin in man's nature to cheat his fellow man, would be similar to trying to prove that three times two are six. Obviously no man would ever fear poverty if he had any grounds for trusting his fellow men, for there is food and shelter and raiment and luxury of every nature sufficient for the needs of every person on earth, and all these blessings would be enjoyed by every person except for the swinish habit that man has of trying to push all the other 'swine' out of the trough, even after he has all and more than he needs.

The second of the six basic fears with which man is bound is:

THE FEAR OF OLD AGE: In the main this fear grows out of two sources. First, the thought that old Age may bring with it POVERTY. Secondly, and by far the most common source of origin, from false and cruel sectarian teachings which have been so well mixed with 'fire and brimstone' and with 'purgatories' and other bogies that human beings have learned to fear Old Age because it meant the approach of another, and possibly a much more HORRIBLE, world than this one which is known to be bad enough.

In the basic fear of Old Age man has two very sound reasons for his apprehension: the one growing out of distrust of his fellow men who may seize whatever worldly goods he may possess, and the other arising from the terrible pictures of the world to come which were deeply planted in his mind, through the law of social heredity, long before he came into possession of that mind.

Is it any wonder that man fears the approach of Old Age?

The third of the six basic fears is:

THE FEAR OF CRITICISM: Just how man acquired this basic fear it would be hard, if not impossible, definitely to determine, but one thing is certain, he has it in well developed form.

Some believe that this fear made its appearance in the mind of man about the time that politics came into existence. Others believe its source can be traced no further than the first meeting of an organisation of females known as a "Woman's Club.' Still another school of humorists charges the origin to the contents of the Holy Bible, whose pages abound with some very vitriolic and violent forms of criticism. If the latter claim is correct, and those who believe literally all they find in the Bible are not mistaken, then God is responsible for man's inherent fear of Criticism, because God caused the Bible to be written.

This author, being neither a humorist nor a 'prophet,' but just an ordinary workaday type of person, is inclined to attribute the basic fear of Criticism to that part of man's inherited nature which prompts him not only to take away his fellow man's goods and wares, but to justify his action by CRITICISM of his fellow man's character.

The fear of Criticism takes on many different forms, the majority of which are petty and trivial in nature, even to the extent of being childish in the extreme.

Bald-headed men, for example, are bald for no other reason than their fear of Criticism. Heads become bald because of the protection of hats with tight fitting bands which cutoff the circulation at the roots of the hair. Men wear hats, not because they actually need them for the sake of comfort, but mainly because 'everybody's doing it,' and the individual falls in line and does it also, lest some other individual CRITICISE him.

Women seldom have bald heads, or even thin hair, because they wear hats that are loose, the only purpose of which is to make an appearance.

But it must not be imagined that women are free from the fear of Criticism associated with hats. If any woman claims to be superior to man with reference to this fear, ask her to walk down the street wearing a hat that is one or two seasons out of style!

IN every soul there has been deposited the seed of a great future, but that seed will never germinate, much less grow to maturity, except through the rendering of useful service.

The makers of all manner of clothing have not been slow to capitalize this basic fear of Criticism with which all mankind is cursed. Every season, it will be observed, the 'styles' in many articles of wearing apparel change. Who establishes the 'styles'? Certainly not the purchaser of clothes, but the manufacturer of clothes. Why does he change the styles so often? Obviously this change is made so that the manufacturer can sell more clothes.

For the same reason the manufacturers of automobiles (with a few rare and very sensible exceptions) change styles every season.

The manufacturer of clothing knows how the man-animal fears to wear a garment which is one season out of step with 'that which they are all wearing now.'

Is this not true? Does not your own experience back it up?

We have been describing the manner in which people behave under the influence of the fear of Criticism as applied to the small and petty things of life. Let us now examine human behaviour under this fear when it affects people in connection with the more important matters connected with human intercourse. Take, for example, practically any person who has reached the age of 'mental maturity' (from thirty-five to forty-five years of age, as a general average), and if you could read his or her mind you would find in that mind a very decided disbelief of and rebellion against most of the fables taught by the majority of the religionists.

Powerful and mighty is the fear of CRITICISM! The time was, and not so very long ago at that, when the word 'infidel' meant ruin to whomsoever it was applied. It is seen, therefore, that man's fear of CRITICISM is not without ample cause for its existence.

The fourth basic fear is that of:

THE FEAR OF LOSS OF LOVE OF SOMEONE: The source from which this fear originated needs but little description, for it is obvious that it grew out of man's nature to steal his fellow man's mate; or at least to take liberties with her, unknown to her rightful 'lord' and master. By nature all men are polygamous, the statement of a truth which will, of course, bring denials from those who are either too old to function in a normal way sexually, or have, from some other cause, lost the contents of certain glands which are responsible for man's tendency toward the plurality of the opposite sex.

There can be but little doubt that jealousy and all other similar forms of more or less mild dementia praecox (insanity) grew out of man's inherited fear of the Loss of Love of Someone.

Of all the 'sane fools' studied by this author, that represented by a man who has become jealous of some woman, or that of a woman who has become jealous of some man, is the oddest and strangest. The author, fortunately, never had but one case of personal experience with this form of insanity, but from that experience he learned enough to justify him in stating that the fear of the Loss of Love of Someone is one of the most painful, if not in fact the most painful, of all the six basic fears. And it seems reasonable to add that this fear plays more havoc with the human mind than do any of the other six basic fears, often leading to the more violent forms of permanent insanity. The fifth basic fear is that of:

THE FEAR OF ILL HEALTH: This fear has its origin, to considerable extent also, in the same sources from which the fears of Poverty and Old Age are derived.

The fear of Ill Health must needs be closely associated with both Poverty and Old Age, because it also leads toward the border line of 'terrible worlds' of which man knows not, but of which he has heard some discomforting stories.

The author strongly suspects that those engaged in the business of selling good health methods have had considerable to do with keeping the fear of Ill Health alive in the human mind.

For longer than the record of the human race can be relied upon, the world has known of various and sundry forms of therapy and health purveyors. If a man gains his living from keeping people in good health it seems but natural that he would use every means at his command for persuading people that they needed his services. Thus, in time, it might be that people would inherit a fear of Ill Health.

The sixth and last of the six basic fears is that of: THE FEAR OF DEATH: To many this is the worst of all the six basic fears, and the reason why it is so regarded becomes obvious to even the casual student of psychology.

The terrible pangs of fear associated with DEATH may be charged directly to religious fanaticism, the source which is more responsible for it than are all other sources combined.

So-called 'heathen' are not as much afraid of DEATH as are the 'civilised,' especially that portion of the civilised population which has come under the influence of theology.

For hundreds of millions of years man has been asking the still unanswered (and, it may be, the unanswerable) questions, 'WHENCE?' and 'WHITHER?' 'Where did I come from and where am I going after death?'

The more cunning and crafty, as well as the honest but credulous, of the race have not been slow to offer the answer to these questions. In fact the answering of these questions has become one of the so-called 'learned' professions, despite the fact that but little learning is required to enter this profession.

Witness, now, the major source of origin of the fear of DEATH!

"Come into my tent, embrace my faith, accept my dogmas (and pay my salary) and I will give you a ticket that will admit you straightway into heaven when you die," says the leader of one form of sectarianism. 'Remain out of my tent,' says this same leader, "and you will go direct to hell, where you will burn throughout eternity."

While, in fad, the self-appointed leader may not be able to provide safe-conduct into heaven nor, by lack of such provision, allow the unfortunate seeker after truth to descend into hell, the possibility of the latter seems so terrible that it lays hold of the mind and creates that fear of fears, the fear of DEATH!

In truth no man knows, and no man has ever known, what heaven or hell is like, or if such places exist, and this very lack of definite knowledge opens the door of the human mind to the charlatan to enter and control that mind with his stock of legerdemain and various brands of trickery, deceit and fraud.

The truth is this-nothing less and nothing more-That NO MAN KNOWS NOR HAS ANY MAN EVER KNOWN WHERE WE COME FROM AT BIRTH OR WHERE WE GO AT DEATH. Any person claiming otherwise is either deceiving himself or he is a conscious impostor who makes it a business to live without rendering service of value, through play upon the credulity of humanity.

Be it said, in their behalf, however, the majority of those engaged in 'selling tickets into heaven' actually believe not only that they know where heaven exists, but that their creeds and formulas will give safe passage to all who embrace them.

This belief may be summed up in one word-CREDULITY!

Religious leaders, generally, make the broad, sweeping claim that the present civilisation owes its existence to the work done by the churches. This author, as far as he is personally concerned, is willing to grant their claims to be correct, if, at the same time he be permitted to add that even if this claim be true the theologians haven't a great deal of which to brag.

But, it is not-cannot be-true that civilisation has grown out of the efforts of the organised churches and creeds, if by the term 'civilisation' is meant the uncovering of the natural laws and the many inventions to which the world is the present heir.

If the theologians wish to claim that part of civilisation which has to do with man's conduct toward his fellow man they are perfectly welcome to YOU are fortunate if you have learned the difference between temporary defeat and failure; more fortunate still, if you have learned the truth that the very seed of success is dormant in every defeat that you experience it, as far as this author is concerned; but, on the other hand, if they presume to gobble up the credit for all the scientific discovery of mankind the author begs leave to offer vigorous protest.

It is hardly sufficient to state that—social heredity is the method through which man gathers all knowledge that reaches him through the five senses. It is more to the point to state HOW social heredity works, in as many different applications as will give the student a comprehensive understanding of that law.

Let us begin with some of the lower forms of animal life and examine the manner in which they are affected by the law of social heredity.

Shortly after this author began to examine the major sources from which men gather the knowledge which makes them what they are, some thirty-odd years ago, he discovered the nest of a ruffed grouse. The nest was so located that the mother bird could be seen from a considerable distance when she was on the nest. With the aid of a pair of field glasses the bird was closely watched until the young birds were hatched out. It happened that the regular daily observation was made but a few hours after the young birds came out of the shell. Desiring to know what would happen, the author approached the nest. The mother bird remained nearby until the intruder was within ten or twelve feet of her, then she disarranged her feathers, stretched one wing over her leg and went hobbling away, making a preteens of being crippled. Being somewhat familiar with the tricks of mother birds, the author did not follow, but, instead, went to the nest to take a look at the little ones. Without the slightest signs of fear they turned their eyes toward him, moving their heads first one way and then another. He reached down and picked one of them up. With no signs of fear it stood in the palm of his hand. He laid the bird back in the nest and went away to a safe distance to give the mother bird a chance to return.

The wait was short. Very soon she began cautiously to edge her way back toward the nest until she was within a few feet of it, when she spread her wings and ran as fast as she could, uttering, meanwhile, a series of sounds similar to those of a hen when she has found some morsel of food and wishes to call her brood to partake of it.

She gathered the little birds around and continued to quiver in a highly excited manner, shaking her wings and ruffling her feathers. One could almost hear her words as she gave the little birds their first lesson in self-defence, through the law of SOCIAL HEREDITY:

"You silly little creatures! Do you not know that men are your enemies? Shame on you for allowing that man to pick you up in his hands. It's a wonder he didn't carry you off and eat you alive! The next time you see a man approaching make yourselves scarce. Lie down on the ground, run under leaves, go anywhere to get out of sight, and remain out of sight until the enemy is well on his way."

The little birds stood around and listened to the lecture with intense interest. After the mother bird had quieted down the author again started to approach the nest. When within twenty fetor so of the guarded household the mother bird again started to lead him in the other direction by crumpling up her wing and hobbling along as if she were crippled. He looked at the nest, but the glance was in vain. The little birds were nowhere to be found! They had learned rapidly to avoid their natural enemy, thanks to their natural instinct.

Again the author retreated, awaited until the mother bird had reassembled her household, then came out to visit them, but with similar results. When he approached the spot where he last saw the mother bird not the slightest signs of the little fellows were to be found.

When a small boy the—author captured a young crow and made a pet of it. The bird became quite well satisfied with its domestic surroundings and learned to perform many tricks requiring considerable intelligence. After the bird was big enough to fly it was permitted to go wherever it pleased. Sometimes it would be gone for many hours, but it always returned home before dark.

One day some wild crows became involved in a fight with an owl in a field near the house where the pet crow lived. As soon as the pet heard the 'caw, caw, caw' of its wild relatives it flew up on top of the house, and with signs of great agitation, walked from one end of the house to the other. Finally it took wing and flew in the direction of the 'battle.' The author followed to see what would happen. In a few minutes he came up with the pet. It was sitting on the lower branches of a tree and two wild crows were sitting on a limb just above, chattering and walking back and forth, acting very much in the same fashion that angry parents behave toward their offspring when chastising them.

As the author approached, the two wild crows flew away, one of them circling around the tree a few times, meanwhile letting out a terrible flow of most abusive language, which, no doubt, was directed at its foolish relative who hadn't enough sense to fly while the flying was good.

The pet was called, but it paid no attention. That evening it returned home, but would not come near the house. It sat on a high limb of an apple tree and talked in crow language for about ten minutes, saying, no doubt, that it had decided to go back to the wild life of its fellows, then flew away and did not return until two days later, when it came back and did some more talking in crow language, keeping at a safe distance meanwhile. It then went away and never returned.

Social heredity had rob bed the author of a fine pet!

The only consolation he got from the loss of his crow was the thought that it had shown fine sportsmanship by coming back and giving notice of its intention to depart. Many farm hands had left the farm without going to the trouble of this formality.

It is a well known fact that a fox will prey upon all manner of fowl and small animals with the exception of the skunk. No reason need be stated as to why Mr. Skunk enjoys immunity. A fox may tackle a skunk once, but never twice! For this reason a skunk hide, when nailed to a chicken roost, will keep all but the very young and inexperienced foxes at a safe distance.

The door of a skunk, once experienced, is never to be forgotten. No other smell even remotely resembles it. It is nowhere recorded that any mother fox ever taught her young how to detect and keep away from the familiar smell of a skunk, but all who are informed on 'fox lore' know that foxes and skunks never seek lodgement in the same cave.

But one lesson is sufficient to teach the fox all it cares to know about skunks. Through the law of social heredity, operating via the sense of smell, one lesson serves for an entire life-time.

A bullfrog can be caught on a fish-hook by attaching a small piece of red cloth or any other small red object to the hook and dangling it in front of the frog's nose. That is, Mr. Frog may be caught in this manner, provided he is hooked the first time he snaps at the bait, but if he is poorly hooked and makes a get-away, or if he feels the point of the hook when he bites at the bait but is not caught, he will never make the same mistake again. The author spent many hours in stealthy attempt to hook a particularly desirable specimen which had snapped and missed, before learning that but one lesson in social heredity is enough to teach even a humble 'croaker' that bits of red flannel are things to be let alone.

The author once owned a very fine male Airedale dog which caused no end of annoyance by his habit of coming home with a young chicken in his mouth.

IS it not strange that we fear most that which never happens? That we destroy our initiative by the fear of defeat, when in reality, defeat is a most useful tonic and should be accepted as such.

Each time the chicken was taken away from the dog and he was soundly switched, but to no avail; he continued in his liking for fowl.

For the purpose of saving the dog, if possible, and as an experiment with social heredity, this dog was taken to the farm of a neighbour who had a hen and some newly hatched chickens. The hen was placed in the barn and the dog was turned in with her. As soon as everyone was out of sight the dog slowly edged up toward the hen, sniffed the air in her direction a time or two (to make sure she was the kind of meat for which he was looking), then made a dive toward her. Meanwhile Mrs. Hen had been doing some 'surveying' on her own account, for she met Mr. Dog more than halfway; moreover, she met him with such a surprise of wings and claws as he had never before experienced. The first round was clearly the hen's. But a nice fat bird, reckoned the dog, was not to slip between his paws so easily; therefore he backed away a short distance, then charged again. This time Mrs. Hen lit upon his back, drove her claws into his skin and made effective use of her sharp bill! Mr. Dog retreated to his comer, looking for all the world as if he were listening for someone to ring the bell and call the fight off until he got his bearings. But Mrs. Hen craved no time for deliberation; she had her adversary on the run and showed that she knew the value of the offensive by keeping him on the run.

One could almost understand her words as she flogged the poor Airedale from one corner to another, keeping up a series of rapid-fire sounds which for all the world resembled the remonstrations of an angry mother who had been called upon to defend her offspring from an attack by older boys.

The Airedale was a poor soldier! After running around the barn from corner to corner for about two minutes he spread himself on the ground as flat as he could and did his best to protect his eyes with his paws. Mrs. Hen seemed to be making a special attempt to peck out his eyes.

The owner of the hen then stepped in and retrieved her-or, more accurately stating it, he retrieved the dog-which in no way appeared to meet with the dog's disapproval.

The next day a chicken was placed in the cellar where the dog slept. As soon as he saw the bird he tucked his tail between his legs and ran for a corner! He never again attempted to catch a chicken. One lesson in social heredity, via the sense of 'touch,' was sufficient to teach him that while chicken-chasing may offer some enjoyment, it is also fraught with much hazard.

All these illustrations, with the exception of the first, describe the process of gathering knowledge through direct experience. Observe the marked difference between knowledge gathered by direct experience and that which is gathered through the training of the young by the old, as in the case of the ruffed grouse and her young.

The most impressive lessons are those learned by the young from the old, through highly collared or emotionalized methods of teaching. When the mother grouse spread her wings, stood her feathers on end, shook herself like a man suffering with the palsy and chattered to her young in a highly excited manner, she planted the fear of man in their hearts in a manner which they were never to forget.

The term 'social heredity,' as used in connection with this lesson, has particular reference to all methods through which a child is taught any idea, dogma, creed, religion or system of ethical conduct, by its parents or those who may have authority over it, before reaching the age at which it may reason and reflect upon such teaching in its own way; estimating the age of such reasoning power at, let us say, seven to twelve years.

There are myriads of forms of fear, but none are more deadly than the fear of poverty and old age. We drive our bodies as if they were slaves because we are so afraid of poverty that we wish to hoard money for– w h a t-old age! This common form of fear drives us so hard that we overwork our bodies and bring on the very thing we are struggling to avoid.

What a tragedy to watch a man drive himself when he begins to arrive along about the forty-year mile post of life-the age at which he is just beginning to mature mentally. At forty a man is just entering the age in which he is able to see and understand and assimilate the handwriting of Nature, as it appears in the forests and flowing brooks and faces of men and little children, yet this devil fear drives him so hard that he becomes blinded and lost in the entanglement of a maze of conflicting desires. The principle of organised effort is lost sight of, and instead of laying hold of Nature's forces which are in evidence all around him, and permitting those forces to carry him to the heights of great achievement, he defies them and they become forces of destruction.

Perhaps none of these great forces of Nature are more available for man's enfoldment than is the principle of Auto-suggestion, but ignorance of this force is leading the majority of the human race to apply it so that it acts as a hindrance and not as a help.

Let us here enumerate the facts which show just how this misapplication of a great force of Nature takes place:

Here is a man who meets with some disappointment; a friend proves false, or a neighbour seems indifferent. Forthwith he decides (through self-suggestion) all men are untrustworthy and all neighbours unappreciative. These thoughts so deeply imbed themselves in his subconscious mind that they color his whole attitude toward others. Go back, now, to what was said in Lesson Two, about the dominating thoughts of a man's mind attracting people whose thoughts are similar.

Apply the Law of Attraction and you will soon see and understand why the unbeliever attracts other unbelievers.

Reverse the Principle:

Here is a man who sees nothing but the best there is in all whom he meets. If his neighbours seem indifferent he takes no notice of that fact, for he makes it his business to fill his mind with dominating thoughts of optimism and good cheer and faith in others. If people speak to him harshly he speaks back in tones of softness. Through the operation of this same eternal Law of Attraction he draws to himself the attention of people whose attitude toward life and whose dominating thoughts harmonize with his own. Tracing the principle a step further:

Here is a man who has been well schooled and has the ability to render the world some needed service. Somewhere, sometime, he has heard it said that modesty is a great virtue and that to push himself to the front of the stage in the game of life savours of egotism. He quietly slips in at the back door and takes a seat at the rear while other players in the game of life boldly step to the front. He remains in the back row because he fears 'what they will say.'

Public opinion, or that which he believes to be public opinion, has him pushed to the rear and the world hears but little of him. His schooling counts for naught because he is afraid to let the world know that he has had it. He is constantly suggesting to himself (thus using the great force of Auto-suggestion to his own detriment) that he should remain in the background lest he be criticized, as if criticism would do him any damage or defeat his purpose.

Here is another man who was born of poor parents. Since the first day that he can remember he has seen evidence of poverty. He has heard talk of poverty. He has felt the icy hand of poverty on his shoulders and it has so impressed him that he fixes it in his mind as a curse to which he must submit. Quite unconsciously he permits himself to fall victim of the belief 'once poor always poor" until that belief becomes the dominating thought of his mind. He resembles a horse that has been harnessed and broken until it forgets that it has the potential power with which to throw off that harness. Auto-suggestion is rapidly relegating him to the back of the stage of life.

Your work and mine are peculiarly akin; I am helping the laws of Nature create more perfect specimens of vegetation, while you are using those same laws, through The Law of Success philosophy, to create more perfect specimens of thinkers.

—Luther Burbank

Finally he becomes a quitter. Ambition is gone. Opportunity comes his way no longer, or if it does he has not the vision to see it. He has accepted his FATE! It is a well established fact that the faculties of the mind, like the limbs of the body, atrophy and wither away if not used. Self-confidence is no exception. It develops when used but disappears if not used.

One of the chief disadvantages of inherited wealth is the fact that it too often leads to inaction and loss of Self-confidence. Some years ago a baby boy was born to Mrs. E. B. McLean, in the city of Washington. His inheritance was said to be around a hundred million dollars. When this baby was taken for an airing in its carriage it was surrounded by nurses and assistant nurses and detectives and other servants whose duty was to see that no harm befell it. As the years passed by this same vigilance was kept up. This child did not have to dress himself; he had servants who did that. Servants watched over him while he slept and while he was at play. He was not permitted to do anything that a servant could do for him. He had grown to the age of ten years. One day he was playing in the yard and noticed that the back gate had been left open. In all of his life he had never been outside of that gate alone, and naturally that was just the thing that he wished to do. During a moment when the servants were not looking he dashed out at the gate, and was run down and killed by an automobile before he reached the middle of the street.

He had used his servants' eyes until his own no longer served him as they might have done had he learned to rely upon them.

Twenty years ago the man whom I served as secretary sent his two sons away to school. One of them went to the University of Virginia and the other to a college in New York. Each month it was a part of my task to make out a check for $100.00 for each of these boys. This was their 'pin money,' to be spent as they wished. How profitably I remember the way I envied those boys as I made out those checks each month. I often wondered why the hand of fate bore me into the world in poverty. I could look ahead and see how these boys would rise to the high stations in life while I remained a humble clerk.

In due time the boys returned home with their 'sheep-skins.' Their father was a wealthy man who owned banks and railroads and coal mines and other property of great value. Good positions were waiting for the boys in their father's employ.

But, twenty years of time can play cruel tricks on those who have never had to struggle. Perhaps a better way to state this truth would be that time gives those who have never had to struggle a chance to play cruel tricks on themselves! At any rate, these two boys brought home from school other things besides their sheep-skins. They came back with well developed capacities for strong drink-capacities which 'they developed because the hundred dollars which each of them received each month made it unnecessary for them to struggle.

Theirs is a long and sad story, the details of which will not interest you, but you will be interested in their 'finis' As this lesson is being written I have on my desk a copy of the newspaper published in the town where these boys lived. Their father has been bankrupted and his costly mansion, where the boys were born, has been placed on the block for sale. One of the boys died of delirium tremens and the other one is in an insane asylum.

Not all rich men's sons turn out so unfortunately, but the fact remains, nevertheless, that inaction leads to atrophy and this, in turn, leads to loss of ambition and self-confidence, and without these essential qualities a man will be carried through life on the wings of uncertainty, just as a dry leaf may be carried here and there on the bosom of the stray winds.

Far from being a disadvantage, struggle is a decided advantage, because it develops those qualities which would forever lie dormant without it. Many a man has found his place in the world because of having been forced to struggle for existence early in life. Lack of knowledge of the advantages accruing from struggle has prompted many a parent to say, 'I had to work hard when I was young, but I shall see to it that my children have an easy time!' Poor foolish creatures. An 'easy' time usually turns out to be a greater handicap than the average young man or woman can survive. There are worse things in this world than being forced to work in early life. Forced idleness is far worse than forced labour. Being forced to work, and forced to do your best, will breed in you temperance and self-control and strength of will and content and a hundred other virtues which the idle will never know.

Not only does lack of the necessity for struggle lead to weakness of ambition and will-power, but, what is more dangerous still, it sets up in a person's mind a state of lethargy that leads to the loss of Self-confidence. The person who has quit struggling because effort is no longer necessary is literally applying the principle of Auto-suggestion in undermining his own power of Self-confidence. Such a person will finally drift into a frame of mind in which he will actually look with more or less contempt upon the person who is forced to carry on.

The human mind, if you will pardon repetition, may be likened to an electric battery. It may be positive or it may be negative. Self-confidence is the quality with which the mind is re-charged and made positive.

Let us apply this line of reasoning to salesmanship and see what part Self-confidence plays in this great field of endeavour. One of the greatest salesmen this country has ever seen was once a clerk in a newspaper office.

It will be worth your while to analyse the method through which he gained his title as 'the world's leading salesman.'

He was a timid young man with a more or less retiring sort of nature. He was one of those who believe it best to slip in by the back door and take a seat at the rear of the stage of life. One evening he heard a lecture on the subject of this lesson, Self-confidence, and that lecture so impressed him that he left the lecture hall with a firm determination to pull himself out of the rut into which he had drifted.

He went to the Business Manager of the paper and asked for a position as solicitor of advertising and was put to work on a commission basis. Everyone in the office expected to see him fail, as this sort of salesmanship calls for the most positive type of sales ability. He went to his room and made out a list of a certain type of merchants on whom he intended to call. One would think that he would naturally have made up his list of the names of those whom he believed he could sell with the least effort, but he did nothing of the sort. He placed on his list only the names of the merchants on whom other advertising solicitors had called without making a sale. His list consisted of only twelve names. Before he made a single call he went out to the city park, took out his list of twelve names, read it over a hundred times, saying to himself as he did so, "You will purchase advertising space from me before the end of the month."

Then he began to make his calls. The first day he closed sales with three of the twelve 'impossibilities.' During the remainder of the week he made sales to two others. By the end of the month he had opened advertising accounts with all but one of the merchants that he had on the list. For the ensuing month he made no sales, for the reason that he made no calls exception this one obstinate merchant. Every morning when the store opened he was on hand to interview this merchant and every morning the merchant said 'No.' The merchant knew he was not going to buy advertising space, but this young man didn't know it. When the merchant said No the young man did not hear it, but kept right on coming. On the last day of the month, after having told this persistent young man No for thirty consecutive times, the merchant said:

"Look here, young man, you have wasted a whole month trying to sell me; now, what I would like to know is this-why have you wasted your time?"

"Wasted my time nothing," heretorted; "I have been going to school and you have been my teacher. Now I know all the arguments that a merchant can bring up for not buying, and besides that I have been drilling myself in Self-confidence."

Then the merchant said: "I will make a little confession of my own. I, too, have been going to school, and you have been my teacher. You have taught me a lesson in persistence that is worth money to me, and to show you my appreciation I am going to pay my tuition fee by giving you an order for advertising space."

And that was the way in which the Philadelphia North American's best advertising account was brought in. Likewise, it marked the beginning of a reputation that has made that same young man a millionaire.

He succeeded because he deliberately charged his own mind with sufficient Self-confidence to make that mind an irresistible force. When he sat down to make up that list of twelve names he did something that ninety-nine people out of a hundred would not have done-he selected the names of those whom he believed it would be hard to sell, because he understood that out of the resistance he would meet with in trying to sell them would come strength and Self-confidence. He was one of the very few people who understand that all rivers and some men are crooked because of following the line of least resistance.

I am going to digress and here break the line of thought for a moment while recording a word of advice to the wives of men. Remember, these lines are intended only for wives, and husbands are not expected to read that which is here set down.

From having analysed more than 16,000 people, the majority of whom were married men, I have learned something that may be of value to wives. Let me state my thought in these words:

You have it within your power to send your husband away to his work or his business or his profession each day with a feeling of Self-confidence that will carry him successfully over the rough spots of the day and bring him home again, at night, smiling and happy. One of my acquaintances of former years married a woman who had a set of false teeth. One day his wife dropped her teeth and broke the plate. The husband picked up the pieces and began examining them. He showed such interest in them that his wife said:

"You could make a set of teeth like those if you made up your mind to do it."

This man was a farmer whose ambitions had never carried him beyond the bounds of his little farm until his wife made that remark. She walked over and laid her hand on his shoulder and encouraged him to try his hand at dentistry. She finally coaxed him to make the start, and today he is one of the most prominent and successful dentists in the state of Virginia. I know him well, for he is my father!

No one can foretell the possibilities of achievement available to the man whose wife stands at his back and urges him on to bigger and better endeavour, for it is a well known fact that a woman can arouse a man so that he will perform almost superhuman feats. It is your right and your duty to encourage your husband and urge him on in worthy undertakings until he shall have found his place in the world. You can induce him to put forth greater effort than can any other person in the world. Make him believe that nothing within reason is beyond his power of achievement and you will have rendered him a service that will go a long way toward helping him win in the battle of life.

One of the most successful men in his line in America gives entire credit for his success to his wife. When they were first married she wrote a creed which he signed and placed over his desk. This is a copy of the creed:

I believe in myself. I believe in those who work with me. I believe in my employer. I believe in my friends. I believe in my family. I believe that God will lend me everything I need with which to succeed if I do my best to earn it through faithful and honest service. I believe in prayer and I will never close my eyes in sleep without praying for divine guidance to the end that I will be patient with other people and tolerant with those who do not believe as I do. I believe that success is the result of intelligent effort and does not depend upon luck or sharp practices or double-crossing friends, fellow men or my employer. I believe I will get out of life exactly what I put into it, therefore I will be careful to conduct myself toward others as I would want them to act toward me. I will not slander those whom I do not like. I will not slight my work no matter what I may see others doing. I will render the best service of which I am capable because I have pledged myself to succeed in life and I know that success is always the result of conscientious and efficient effort. Finally, I will forgive those who offend me because I realise that I shall sometimes offend others and I will need their forgiveness.

Signed ....

The woman who wrote this creed was a practical psychologist of the first order. With the influence and guidance of such a woman as a helpmate any man could achieve noteworthy success.

Analyse this creed and you will notice how freely the personal pronoun is used. It starts off with the affirmation of Self-confidence, which is perfectly proper. No man could make this creed his own without developing the positive attitude that would attract to him people who would aid him in his struggle for success.

This would be a splendid creed for every salesman to adopt. It might not hurt your chances for success if you adopted it. Mere adoption, however, is not enough. You must practice it! Read it over and over until you know it by heart. Then repeat it at least once a day until you have literally transformed it into your mental make-up. Keep a copy of it before you as a daily reminder of your pledge to practice it. By doing so you will be making efficient use of the principle of

Auto-suggestion as a means of developing Self-confidence. Never mind what anyone may say about your procedure. Just remember that it is your business to succeed, and this creed, if mastered and applied, will go a long way toward helping you.

You learned in Lesson Two that any idea you firmly fix in your subconscious mind, by repeated affirmation, automatically becomes a plan or blueprint which an unseen power uses in directing your efforts toward the attainment of the objective named-in the plan.

You have also learned that the principle through which you may fix any idea you choose in your mind is called Auto-suggestion, which simply means a suggestion that you give to your own mind. It was this principle of Auto-suggestion that Emerson had in mind when he wrote:

"Nothing can bring you peace but yourself!"

You might well remember that No thing can bring you success but yourself. Of course you will need the co-operation of others if you aim to attain success of a far-reaching nature, but you will never get that cooperation unless you vitalize your mind with the positive attitude of Self-confidence.

Perhaps you have wondered why a few men advance to highly paid positions while others all around them, who have as much training and who seemingly perform as much work, do not get ahead. Select any two people of these two types that you choose, and study them, and the reason why one advances and the other stands still will be quite obvious to you. You will find that the one who advances believes in himself. You will find that he backs this belief with such dynamic, aggressive action that he lets others know that he believes in himself. You will also notice that this Self-confidence is contagious; it is impelling; it is persuasive; it attracts others.

IF you want a thing done well, call on some busy person to do it. Busy people are generally the most painstaking and thorough in all they do.

You will also find that the one who does not advance shows clearly, by the look on his face, by the posture of his body, by the lack of briskness in his step, by the uncertainty with which he speaks, that he lacks Self-confidence. No one is going to pay much attention to the person who has no confidence in himself.

He does not attract others because his mind is a negative force that repels rather than attracts.

In no other field of endeavour does Self-confidence or the lack of it play such an important part as in the field of salesmanship, and you do not need to be a character analyst to determine, the moment you meet him, whether a salesman possesses this quality of Self-confidence. If he has it the signs of its influence are written all over him. He inspires you with confidence in him and in the goods he is selling the moment he speaks.

We come, now, to the point at, which you are ready to take hold of the principle of Auto-suggestion and make direct use of it in developing yourself into a positive and dynamic and self-reliant person. You are instructed to copy the following formula, sign it and commit it to memory:

Self-Confidence Formula

First: I know that I have the ability to achieve the object of my definite purpose, therefore I demand of myself persistent, aggressive and continuous action toward its attainment.

Second: I realise that the dominating thoughts of my mind eventually reproduce themselves in outward, bodily action, and gradually transform themselves into physical reality, therefore I will concentrate my mind for thirty minutes daily upon the task of thinking of the person I intend to be, by creating a mental picture of this person and then transforming that picture into reality through practical service.

Third: I know that through the principle of Auto-suggestion, any desire that I persistently hold in my mind will eventually seek expression through some practical means of realizing it, therefore I shall devote ten minutes daily to demanding of myself the development of the factors named in the sixteen lessons of this Reading Course on The Law of Success.

Fourth: I have clearly mapped out and written down a description of my definite purpose in life, for the coming five years. I have set a price on my services for each of these five years; a price that I intend to earn and receive, through strict application of the principle of efficient, satisfactory service which I will render in advance.

Fifth: I fully realise that no wealth or position can long endure unless built upon truth and justice, therefore I will engage in no transaction which does not benefit all whom it affects. 1 will succeed by attracting to me the forces I wish to use, and the co-operation of other people. I will induce others to serve me because I will first serve them. I will eliminate hatred, envy, jealousy, selfishness and cynicism by developing love for all humanity, because I know that a negative attitude toward others can never bring me success. I will cause others to believe in me because I will believe in them and in myself.

I will sign my name to this formula, commit it to memory and repeat it aloud once a day with full faith that it will gradually influence my entire life so that I will become a successful and happy worker in my chosen field of endeavour.

Signed.........

Before you sign your name to this formula make sure that you intend to carry out its instructions. Back of this formula lies a law that no man can explain. The psychologists refer to this law as Auto-suggestion and let it go at that, but you should bear in mind one point about which there is no uncertainty, and that is the fact that whatever this law is it actually works!

Another point to be kept in mind is the fact that, just as electricity will turn the wheels of industry and serve mankind in a million other ways, or snuff out life if wrongly applied, so will this principle of Auto-suggestion lead you up the mountain-side of peace and prosperity, or down into the valley of misery and poverty, according to the application you make of it. If you fill your mind with doubt and unbelief in your ability to achieve, then the principle of Auto-suggestion takes this spirit of unbelief and sets it up in your subconscious mind as your dominating thought and slowly but surely draws you into the whirlpool of failure. But, if you fill your mind with radiant Self-confidence, the principle of Auto-suggestion takes this belief and sets it up as your dominating thought and helps you master the obstacles that fall in your way until you reach the mountain-top of success.

The Power of Habit

Having, myself, experienced all the difficulties that stand in the road of those who lack the understanding to make practical application of this great principle of Auto-suggestion, let me take you a short way into the principle of habit, through the aid of which you may easily apply the principle of Auto-suggestion in any direction and for any purpose whatsoever.

Habit grows out of environment; out of doing the same thing or thinking the same thoughts or repeating the same words over and over again. Habit may be likened to the groove on a phonograph record, while the human mind may be likened to the needle that fits into that groove. When any habit has been well formed, through repetition of thought or action, the mind has a tendency to attach itself to and follow the course of that habit as closely as the phonograph needle follows the groove in the wax record.

Habit is created by repeatedly directing one or more of the five senses of seeing, hearing, smelling, tasting and feeling, in a given direction. It is through this repetition principle that the injurious drug habit is formed. It is through this same principle that the desire for intoxicating drink is formed into a habit.

After habit has been well established it will automatically control and direct our bodily activity, wherein may be found a thought that can be transformed into a powerful factor in the development of Self-confidence. The thought is this: Voluntarily, and by force if necessary, direct your efforts and your thoughts along a desired line until you have formed the habit that will lay hold of you and continue, voluntarily, to direct your efforts along the same line.

The object in writing out and repeating the Self-confidence formula is to form the habit of making belief in yourself the dominating thought of your mind until that thought has been thoroughly imbedded in your subconscious mind, through the principle of habit.

You learned to write by repeatedly directing the muscles of your arm and hand over certain outlines known as letters, until finally you formed the habit of tracing these outlines. Now you write with ease and rapidity, without tracing each letter slowly. Writing has become a habit with you.

The principle of habit will lay hold of the faculties of your mind just the same as it will influence the physical muscles of your body, as you can easily prove by mastering and applying this lesson on Self-confidence. Any statement that you repeatedly make to yourself, or any desire that you deeply plant in your mind through repeated statement, will eventually seek expression through your physical, outward bodily efforts. The principle of habit is the very foundation upon which this lesson on Self-confidence is built, and if you will understand and follow the directions laid down in this lesson you will soon know more about the law of habit, from first-hand knowledge, than could be taught you by a thousand such lessons as this.

You have but little conception of the possibilities which lie sleeping within you, awaiting but the awakening hand of vision to arouse you, and you will never have a better conception of those possibilities unless you develop sufficient Self-confidence to lift you above the commonplace influences of your present environment.

The human mind is a marvellous, mysterious piece of machinery, a factor which I was reminded a few months ago when I picked up Emerson's Essays and re-read his essay on Spiritual Laws. A strange thing happened. I saw in that essay, which I had read scores of times previously, much that I had never noticed before. I saw more in this essay than I had seen during previous readings because the enfoldment of my mind since the last reading had prepared me to interpret more.

The human mind is constantly unfolding, like the petals of a flower, until it reaches the maximum of development. What this maximum is, where it ends, or whether it ends at all or not, are unanswerable questions, but the degree of enfoldment seems to vary according to the nature of the individual and the degree to which he keeps his mind at work. A mind that is forced or coaxed into analytical thought every day seems to keep on unfolding and developing greater powers of interpretation.

Down in Louisville, Kentucky, lives Mr. Lee Cook, a man who has practically no legs and has to wheel himself around on a cart. In spite of the fact that Mr. Cook has been without legs since birth, he is the owner of a great industry and a millionaire through his own efforts. He has proved that a man can get along very well without legs if he has a well developed Self-confidence.

In the city of New York one may see a strong able-bodied and able-headed young man, without legs, rolling himself down Fifth Avenue every afternoon, with cap in hand, begging for a living. His head is perhaps as sound and as able to think as the average.

This young man could duplicate anything that Mr. Cook, of Louisville, has done, if he thought of himself as Mr. Cook thinks of himself.

Henry Ford owns more millions of dollars than he will ever need or use. Not so many years ago, he was working as a labourer in a machine shop, with but little schooling and without capital. Scores of other men, some of them with better organised brains than his, worked near him. Ford threw off the poverty consciousness, developed confidence in himself, thought of success and attained it. Those who worked around him could have done as well had they thought as he did.

Milo C. Jones, of Wisconsin, was stricken down with paralysis a few years ago. So bad was the stroke that he could not turn himself in bed or move a muscle of his body. His physical body was useless, but there was nothing wrong with his brain, so it began to function in earnest, probably for the first time in its existence. Lying flat on his back in bed, Mr. Jones made that brain create a definite purpose. That purpose was prosaic and humble enough in nature, but it was definite and it was a purpose, something that he had never known before.

His definite purpose was to make pork sausage. Calling his family around him he told of his plans and began directing them in carrying the plans into action. With nothing to aid him except a sound mind and plenty of Self-confidence, Milo C. Jones spread the name and reputation of 'Little Pig Sausage' all over the United States, and accumulated a fortune besides.

All this was accomplished after paralysis had made it impossible for him to work with his hands. Where thought prevails power may be found! Henry Ford has made millions of dollars and is still making millions of dollars each year because he believed in Henry Ford and transformed that belief into a definite purpose and backed that purpose with a definite plan. The other machinists who worked along with Ford, during the early days of his career, versioned nothing but a weekly pay envelope and that was all they ever got. They demanded nothing out of the ordinary of themselves. If you want to get more be sure to demand more of yourself. Notice that this demand is to be made on yourself!

There comes to mind a well-known poem whose author expressed a great psychological truth:

If you think you are beaten, you are;

If you think you dare not, you don't; If you like to win, but you think you can't,

It is almost certain you won't.

If you think you'll lose you've lost,
For out of the world we find
Success begins with a fellow's will–
It's all in the state of mind.
If you think you are outclassed, you are-You've got to think high to rise.
You've got to be sure of yourself before You can ever win a prize.
Life's battles don't always go
To the stronger or faster man;
But soon or late the man who wins
Is the man who thinks he can.

It can do no harm if you commit this poem to memory and use it as a part of your working equipment in the development of Self-confidence.

Somewhere in your make-up there is a 'subtle something' which, if it were aroused by the proper outside influence, would carry you to heights of achievement such as you have never before anticipated. Just as a master player can take hold of a violin and cause that instrument to pour forth the most beautiful and entrancing strains of music, so is there some outside influence that can lay hold of your mind and cause you to go forth into the field of your chosen endeavour and play a glorious symphony of success. No man knows what hidden forces lie dormant within you. You, yourself, do not know your capacity for achievement, and you never will know until you come in contact with that particular stimulus which arouses you to greater action and extends your vision, develops your Self-confidence and moves you with a deeper desire to achieve.

It is not unreasonable to expect that some statement, some idea or some stimulating word of this Reading Course on The Law of Success will serve as the needed stimulus that will re-shape your destiny and re-direct your thoughts and energies along a pathway that will lead you, finally, to your coveted goal of life. It is strange, but true, that the most important turning-points of life often come at the most unexpected times and in the most unexpected ways. I have in mind a typical example of how some of the seemingly unimportant experiences of life often turn out to be the most important of all, and I am relating this ease because it shows, also, what a man can accomplish when he awakens to a full understanding of the value of Self-confidence. The incident to which I refer happened in the city of Chicago, while I was engaged in the work of character analysis. One day a tramp presented himself at my office and asked for an interview. As I looked up from my work and greeted him he said, "I have come to see the man who wrote this little book," as he removed from his pocket a copy of a book entitled Self-confidence, which I had written many years previously. "It must have been the hand of fate," he continued, "that slipped this book into my pocket yesterday afternoon, because I was about ready to go out there and punch a hole in Lake Michigan. I had about come to the conclusion that everything and everybody, including God, had it in for me until I read this book, and it gave me a new viewpoint and brought me the courage and the hope that sustained me through the night. I made up my mind that if I could see the man who wrote this book he could help me get on my feet again. Now, I am here and I would like to know what you can do for a man like me."

While he was speaking I had been studying him from head to foot, and I am frank to admit that down deep in my heart I did not believe there was anything I could do for him, but I did not wish to tell him so. The glassy stare in his eyes, the lines of discouragement in his face, the posture of his body, the ten days' growth of beard on his face, the nervous manner about this man all conveyed to me the impression that he was hopeless, but I did not have the heart to tell him so, therefore I asked him to sit down and tell me his whole story. I asked him to be perfectly frank and tell me, as nearly as possible, just what had brought him down to the ragged edge of life. I promised him that after I had heard his entire story I would then tell him whether or not I could be of service to him. He related his story, in lengthy detail, the sum and substance of which was this: He had invested his entire fortune in a small manufacturing business. When the world war began in 1914, it was impossible for him to get the raw materials necessary in the operation of his factory, and he therefore failed. The loss of his money broke his heart and so disturbed his mind that he left his wife and children and became a tramp. He had actually brooded over his loss until he had reached the point at which he was contemplating suicide.

After he had finished his story, I said to him: "I have listened to you with a great deal of interest, and I wish that there was something which I could do to help you, but there is absolutely nothing."

He became as pale as he will be when he is laid away in a coffin, and settled back in his chair and dropped his chin on his chest as much as to say, 'That settles it.' I waited for a few seconds, then said:

"While there is nothing that I can do for you, there is a man in this building to whom I will introduce you, if you wish, who can help you regain your lost fortune and put you back on your feet again." These words had barely fallen from my lips when he jumped up, grabbed me by the hands and said, 'For God's sake lead me to this man.'

It was encouraging to note that he had asked this 'for God's sake.' This indicated that there was still a spark of hope within his breast, so I took him by the arm and led him out into the laboratory where my psychological tests in character analysis were conducted, and stood with him in front of what looked to be a curtain over a door. I pulled the curtain aside and uncovered a tall looking-glass in which he saw himself from head to foot. Pointing my finger at the glass I said:

"There stands the man to whom I promised to introduce you. There is the only man in this world who can put you back on your feet again, and unless you sit down and become acquainted with that man, as you never became acquainted with him before, you might just as well go on over and `punch a hole' in Lake Michigan, because you will be of no value to yourself or to the world until you know this man better."

He stepped over to the glass, rubbed his hands over his bearded face, studied himself from head to foot for a few moments, then stepped back, dropped his head and began to weep. I knew that the lesson had been driven home, so I led him back to the elevator and sent him away. I never expected to see him again, and I doubted that the lesson would be sufficient to help him regain his place in the world, because he seemed to be too far gone for redemption. He seemed to be not only down, but almost out.

A few days later I met this man on the street. His transformation had been so complete that I hardly recognised him. He was walking briskly, with his head tilted back. That old, shifting, nervous posture of his body was gone. He was dressed in new clothes from head to foot. He looked prosperous and he felt prosperous. He stopped me and related what had happened to bring about his rapid transformation from a state of abject failure to one of hope and promise.

"I was just on my way to your office," he explained, "to bring you the good news. I went out the very day that I was in your office, a down-and-out tramp, and despite my appearance I sold myself at a salary of $3,000.00 a year. Think of it, man, three thousand dollars a year! And my employer advanced me money enough with which to buy some new clothes, as you can see for yourself. He also advanced me some money to send home to my family, and I am once more on the road to success. It seems like a dream when I think that only a few days ago I had lost hope and faith and courage, and was actually contemplating suicide.

"I was coming to tell you that one of these days, when you are least expecting me, I will pay you another visit, and when I do. I will be a successful man. I will bring with me a check, signed in blank and made payable to you, and you may fill in the amount because you have saved me from myself by introducing me to myself-that self which I never knew until you stood me in front of that looking-glass and pointed out the real me."

As that man turned and departed in the crowded streets of Chicago I saw, for the first time in my life, what strength and power and possibility lie hidden in the mind of the man who has never discovered the value of Self-reliance. Then and there I made up my mind that I, too, would stand in front of that same looking-glass and point an accusing finger at myself for not having discovered the lesson which I had helped another to learn. I did stand before that same looking-glass, and as I did so I then and there fixed in my mind, as my definite purpose in life, the determination to help men and women discover the forces that lie sleeping within them. The book you hold in your hands is evidence that my definite purpose is being carried out.

The man whose story I have related is now the president of one of the largest and most successful concerns of its kind in America, with a business that extends from coast to coast and from Canada to Mexico.

A short while after the incident just related, a woman came to my office for personal analysis. She was then a teacher in the Chicago public schools. I gave her an analysis chart and asked her to fill it out. She had been at work on the chart but a few minutes when she came back to my desk, handed back the chart and said, "I do not believe I will fill this out." I asked her why she had decided not to fill out the chart and she replied: "To be perfectly frank with you, one of the questions in this chart put me to thinking and I now know what is wrong with me, therefore I feel it unnecessary to pay you a fee to analyse me." With that the woman went away and I did not hear from her for two years. She went to New York City, became a writer of advertising copy for one of the largest agencies in the country and her income at the time she wrote me was $10,000.00 a year.

This woman sent me a check to cover the cost of my analysis fee, because she felt that the fee had been earned, even though I did not render her the service that I usually render my clients. It is impossible for anyone to foretell what seemingly insignificant incident may lead to an important turning-point in one's career, but there is no denying the fact that these 'turning-points' may be more readily recognised by those who have well-rounded-out confidence in themselves.

One of the irreparable losses to the human race lies in the lack of knowledge that there is a definite method through which Self-confidence can be developed in any person of average intelligence. What an immeasurable loss to civilisation that young men and women are not taught this known method of developing Self-confidence before they complete their schooling, for no one who lacks faith in himself is really educated in the proper sense of the term.

Oh, what glory and satisfaction would be the happy heritage of the man or woman who could pull aside the curtain of fear that hangs over the human race and shuts out the sunlight of understanding that Self-confidence brings, wherever it is in evidence.

Where fear controls, noteworthy achievement becomes an impossibility, a fact which brings to mind the definition of fear, as stated by a great philosopher:

"Fear is the dungeon of the mind into which it runs and hides and seeks seclusion. Fear brings on superstition and superstition is the dagger with which hypocrisy assassinates the soul."

In front of the typewriter on which I am writing the manuscripts for this Reading Course hangs a sign with the following wording, in big letters:

"Day by day in every way I am becoming more successful."

A sceptic who read that sign asked if I really believed 'that stuff' and I replied, "Of course not. All it ever did for me was to help me get out of the coal mines, where I started as a labourer, and find a place in the world in which I am serving upwards of 100,000 people, in whose minds I am planting the same positive thought that this sign brings out; therefore, why should I believe in it?"

As this man started to leave he said: "Well, perhaps there is something to this sort of philosophy, after all, for I have always been afraid that I would be a failure, and so far my fears have been thoroughly realised."

You are condemning yourself to poverty, misery and failure, or you are driving yourself on toward the heights of great achievement, solely by the thoughts you think. If you demand success of yourself and back up this demand with intelligent action you are sure to win. Bear in mind, though, that there is a difference between demanding success and just merely wishing for it. You should find out what this difference is, and take advantage of it.

Do you remember what the Bible says (look it up, somewhere in the book of Matthew) about those who have faith as a grain of mustard seed? Go at the task of developing Self-confidence with at least that much faith if not more. Never mind 'what they will say' because you might as well know that 'they' will be of little aid to you in your climb up the mountain-side of life toward the object of your d e finite purpose. You have within you all the power you need with which to get whatever you want or need in this world, and about the best way to avail yourself of this power is to believe in yourself.

'Know thyself, man; know thyself.'

This has been the advice of the philosophers all down the ages. When you really know yourself you will know that there is nothing foolish about hanging a sign in front of you that reads like this: "Day by day in every way I am becoming more successful," with due apologies to the Frenchman who made this motto popular. I am not afraid to place this sort of suggestion in front of my desk, and, what is more to the point, I am not afraid to believe that it will influence me so that I will become a more positive and aggressive human being.

More than twenty-five years ago I learned my first lesson in Self-confidence building. One night I was sitting before an open fire-place, listening to a conversation between some older men, on the subject of Capital and Labour. Without invitation I joined in the conversation and said something about employers and employees settling their differences on the Golden Rule basis. My remarks attracted the attention of one of the men, who turned to me, with a look of surprise on his face and said:

"Why, you are a bright boy, and if you would go out and get a schooling you would make your mark in the world."

Those remarks fell on 'fertile' ears, even though that was the first time anyone had ever told me that I was bright, or that I might accomplish anything worthwhile in life. The remark put me to thinking, and the more I allowed my mind to dwell upon that thought the more certain I became that the remark had back of it a possibility.

It might be truthfully stated that whatever service I am rendering the world and whatever good I accomplish, should be credited to that off-hand remark.

Suggestions such as this are often powerful, and none the less so when they are deliberate and self-expressed. Go back, now, to the Self-confidence formula and master it, for it will lead you into the 'power-house' of your own mind, where you will tap a force that can be made to carry you to the very top of the Ladder of Success.

Others will believe in you only when you believe in yourself. They will 'tune in' on your thoughts and feel toward you just as you feel toward yourself. The law of mental telepathy takes care of this. You are continuously broadcasting *hat you think of yourself, and if you have no faith in yourself others will pick up the vibrations of your thoughts and mistake them for their own. Once understand the law of mental telepathy and you will know why Self-confidence is the second of the Fifteen Laws of Success.

You should be cautioned, however, to learn the difference between Self-confidence, which is based upon sound knowledge of what you know and what you can do, and egotism, which is only based upon what you wish you knew or could do. Learn the difference between these two terms or you will make yourself bore some, ridiculous and annoying to people of culture and understanding. Self-confidence is something which should never be proclaimed or announced except through intelligent performance of constructive deeds.

If you have Self-confidence those around you will discover this fact. Let them make the discovery. They will feel proud of their alertness in having made the discovery, and you will be free from the suspicion of egotism. Opportunity never stalks the person with a highly developed state of egotism, but brick-bats and ugly remarks do. Opportunity forms affinities much more easily and quickly with Self-confidence than it does with egotism. Self-praise is never a proper measure of self-reliance. Bear this in mind and let your Self-confidence speak only through the tongue of constructive service rendered without fuss or flurry.

Self-confidence is the product of knowledge. Know yourself, know how much you know (and how little), why you know it, and how you are going to use it. 'Four-flushers' come to grief, therefore, do not pretend to know more than you actually do know. There's no use of preteens, because any educated person will measure you quite accurately after hearing you speak for three minutes. What you really are will speak so loudly that what you 'claim' you are will not be heard.

If you heed this warning the last four pages of this one lesson may mark one of the most important turning-points of your life.

Believe in yourself, but do not tell the world what you can do-SHOW IT!

You are now ready for Lesson Four, which will take you the next step up the Ladder of Success.

DISCONTENTMENT : An After-the-Lesson Visit With the Author

The marker stands at the Entrance Gate of Life and writes 'Poor Fool' on the brow of the wise man and 'Poor Sinner' on the brow of the saint.

The supreme mystery of the universe is life! We come here without our consent, from whence we know not! We go away without our consent, whither, we know not!

We are eternally trying to solve this great riddle of 'LIFE,' and, for what purpose and to what end?

That we are placed on this earth for a definite reason there can be no doubt by any thinker. May it not be possible that the power which placed us here will know what to do with us when we pass on beyond the Great Divide?

Would it not be a good plan to give the Creator who placed us here on earth, credit for having enough intelligence to know what to do with us after we pass on; or, should we assume the intelligence and the ability to control the future life in our own way? May it not be possible that we can co-operate with the Creator very intelligently by assuming to control our conduct on this earth to the end that we may be decent to one another and do all the good we can in all the ways we can during this life, leaving the hereafter to one who probably knows, better than we, what is best for us?

THE artist has told a powerful story in the picture at the top of this page.

From birth until death the mind is always reaching out for that which it does not possess.

The little child, playing with its toys on the floor, sees another child with a different sort of toy and immediately tries to lay hands on that toy.

The female child (grown tall) believes the other woman's clothes more becoming than her own and sets out to duplicate them.

The male child (grown tall) sees another man with a bigger collection of railroads or banks or merchandise and says to himself: 'How fortunate! How fortunate! How can I separate him from his belongings?'

F. W. Woolworth, the Five and Ten Cent Store king, stood on Fifth Avenue in New York City and gazed upward at the tall Metropolitan Building and said: "How wonderful! I will build one much taller." The crowning achievement of his life was measured by the Woolworth Building. That building stands as a temporary symbol of man's nature to excel the handiwork of other men.

A MONUMENT TO THE Vanity of man, with but little else to justify its existence!

The little ragged newsboy on the street stands, with wide-open mouth, and envies the business man as he alights from his automobile at the curb and starts into his office. "How happy I would be," the newsboy says to himself, 'if I owned a Lizzie.' And, the business man seated at his desk inside, thinks how happy he would be if he could add another million dollars to his already over swollen bank roll.

The grass is always sweeter on the other side of the fence, says the jackass, as he stretches his neck in the attempt to get to it.

Turn a crowd of boys into an apple orchard and they will pass by the nice mellow apples on the ground. The red, juicy ones hanging dangerously high in the top of the tree look much more tempting, and up the tree they will go.

The married man takes a sheepish glance at the daintily dressed ladies on the street and thinks how fortunate he would be if his wife were as pretty as they. Perhaps she is much prettier, but he misses that beauty because-well, because 'the grass is always greener on the other side of the fence.' Most divorce cases grow out of man's tendency to climb the fence into the other fellow's pastures.

Happiness is always just around the bend; always in sight but just out of reach. Life is never complete, no matter what we have or how much of it we possess. One thing calls for something else to go with it.

Milady buys a pretty hat. She must have a gown to match it. That calls for new shoes and hose and gloves, and other accessories that run into a big bill far beyond her husband's means.

Man longs for a home-just a plain little house setting off in the edge of the woods. He builds it, but it is not complete; he must have shrubbery and flowers and landscaping to go with it. Still it is not complete; he must have a beautiful fence around it, with a gravelled driveway.

That calls for a motor car and a garage in which to house it.

All these little touches have been added, but to no avail! The place is now too small. He must have a house with more rooms. The Ford Coupe must be replaced by a Cadillac sedan, so there will be room for company in the cross country tours.

On and on the story goes, ad infinitum!

The young man receives a salary sufficient to keep him and his family fairly comfortable. Then comes a promotion and an advance in salary of a thousand dollars a year. Does he lay the extra thousand dollars away in the savings account and continue living as before? He does nothing of the sort. Immediately he must trade the old car in for a new one. A porch must be added to the house. The wife needs a new wardrobe. The table must be set with better food and more of it. (Pity his poor, groaning stomach.) At the end of the year is he better off with the increase? He is nothing of the sort! The more he gets the more he wants, and the rule applies to the man with millions the same as to the man with but a few thousands.

The young man selects the girl of his choice, believing he cannot live without her. After he gets her he is not sure that he can live with her. If a man remains a bachelor he wonders why he is so stupid as to deprive himself of the joys of married life. If he marries he wonders how she happened to catch him off guard long enough to 'harpoon' him.

And the god of Destiny cries out 'O fool, 0 fool! You are damned if you DO and you are damned if you DON'T.'

At every crossroad of Life the imps of Discontentment stand in the shadows of the back-ground, with a grin of mockery on their faces, crying out "Take the road of your own choice! We will get you in the end!"

At last man becomes disillusioned and begins to learn that Happiness and Contentment are not of this world. Then begins the search for the pass-word that will open the door to him in some world of which he knows not. Surely there must be Happiness on the other side of the Great Divide. In desperation his tired, care-worn heart turns to religion for hope and encouragement.

But, his troubles are not over; they are just starting!

"Come into our tent and accept our creed," says one sect, "and you may go straight to heaven after death." Poor man hesitates, looks and listens. Then he hears the call of another brand of religion whose leader says:

"Stay out of the other camp or you'll go straight to hell! They only sprinkle water on your head, but we push you all the way under, thereby insuring you safe passage into the Land of Promise."

In the midst of sectarian claims and counter-claims Poor man becomes undecided. Not knowing whether to turn this way or that, he wonders which brand of religion offers the safest passage-way, until Hope vanishes.

"Myself when young did eagerly frequent Doctor and Saint and heard great argument About it and about; but evermore came out by the same door where in I went."

Always seeking but never finding-thus might be described man's struggle for Happiness and Contentment. He tries one religion after another, finally joining the 'Big Church' which the world has named the 'Damned.' His mind becomes an eternal question mark, searching hither and yon for an answer to the questions-'Whence and Whither?'

"The worldly hope men set their Hearts upon

Turns Ashes-or it prospers; and anon,

Like Snow upon the Desert's Dusty Face
Lighting a little Hour or two is gone."

Life is an everlasting question-mark!

That which we want most is always in the embryonic distance of the future. Our power to acquire is always a decade or so behind our power to DESIRE!

And, if we catch up with the thing we want we no longer want it!

Fortunate is the young woman who learns this great truth and keeps her lover always guessing, always on the defensive lest he may lose her.

Our favourite author is a hero and a genius until we meet him in person and learn the sad truth that, after all, he is only a man. "How often must we learn this lesson? Men cease to interest us when we find their limitations. The only sin is limitation. As soon as you once come up with a man's limitations, it is all over with him."

—EMERSON

How beautiful the mountain yonder in the distance; but, the moment we draw near it we find it to be nothing but a wretched collection of rocks and dirt and trees.

Out of this truth grew the oft-repeated adage "Familiarity breeds contempt."

Beauty and Happiness and Contentment are states of mind. They can never be enjoyed except through vision of the afar. The most beautiful painting of Rembrandt becomes a mere smudge of daubed paint if we come too near it.

Destroy the Hope of unfinished dreams in man's heart and he is finished.

The moment a man ceases to cherish the vision of future achievement he is through. Nature has built man so that his greatest and only lasting Happiness is that which he feels in the pursuit of some yet unattained object. Anticipation is sweeter than realisation. That which is at hand does not satisfy. The only enduring satisfaction is that which comes to the Person who keeps alive in his heart the HOPE of future achievement. When that hope dies write FINIS across the human heart.

Life's greatest inconsistency is the fact that most of that which we believe is not true. Russel Conwell wrote the most popular lecture ever delivered in the English language. He called it 'Acres of Diamonds.' The central idea of the lecture was the statement that one need not seek opportunity in the distance; that opportunity may be found in the vicinity of one's birth. Perhaps! but, how many believe it?

Opportunity may be found wherever one really looks for it, and nowhere else! To most men the picking looks better on the other side of the fence. How futile to urge one to try out one's luck in the little home-town when it is man's nature to look for opportunity in some other locality.

Do not worry because the grass looks sweeter on the other side of the fence. Nature intended it so. Thus does she allure us and groom us for the life-long task of GROWTH THROUGH STRUGGLE.

□

3

Imagination

"You Can Do It if You Believe You Can!"

Imagination is the workshop of the human mind wherein old ideas and established facts may be reassembled into new combinations and put to new uses. The modern dictionary defines imagination as follows:

"The act of constructive intellect in grouping the materials of knowledge or thought into new, original and rational systems; the constructive or creative faculty; embracing poetic, artistic, philosophic, scientific and ethical imagination.

"The picturing power of the mind; the formation of mental images, pictures, or mental representation of objects or ideas, particularly of objects of sense perception and of mathematical reasoning! also the reproduction and combination, usually with more or less irrational or abnormal modification, of the images or ideas of memory or recalled facts of experience."

Imagination has been called the creative power of the soul, but this is somewhat abstract and goes more deeply into the meaning than is necessary from the viewpoint of a student of this course who wishes to use the course only as a means of attaining material or monetary advantages in life.

If you have mastered and thoroughly understood the preceding lessons of this Reading Course you know that the materials out of which you built your d e finite chief aim were assembled and combined in your imagination. You also know that self-confidence and initiative and leadership must be created in your imagination before they can become a reality, for it is in the workshop of your imagination that you will put the principle of Auto-suggestion into operation in creating these necessary qualities.

This lesson on imagination might be called the 'hub' of this Reading Course, because every lesson of the course leads to this lesson and makes use of the principle upon which it is based, just as all the telephone wires lead to the exchange office for their source of power. You will never have a definite purpose in life, you will never have self-confidence, you will never have initiative and leadership unless you first create these qualities in your imagination and see yourself in possession of them.

Just as the oak tree develops from the germ that lies in the acorn, and the bird develops from the germ that lies asleep in the egg, so will your material achievements grow out of the organised plans that you create in your imagination. First comes the thought; then, organisation of that thought into ideas and plans; then transformation of those plans into reality. The beginning, as you will observe, is in your imagination.

The imagination is both interpretative and creative in nature. It can examine facts, concepts and ideas, and it can create new combinations and plans out of these.

Through its interpretative capacity the imagination has one power not generally attributed to it; namely, the power to register vibrations and thought waves that are put into motion from outside sources, just as the radio-receiving apparatus picks up the vibrations of sound. The principle through which this interpretative capacity of the imagination functions is called telepathy; the communication of thought from one mind to another, at long or short distances, without the aid of physical or mechanical appliances, in the manner explained in the Introductory Lesson of this course.

Telepathy is an important factor to a student who is preparing to make effective use of imagination, for the reason that this telepathic capacity of the imagination is constantly picking up thought waves and vibrations of every description. So-called 'snap-judgment' and 'hunches,' which prompt one to form an opinion or decide upon a course of action that is not in harmony with logic and reason, are usually the result of stray thought waves that have registered in the imagination.

The recently developed radio apparatus has enabled us to understand that the elements of the ether are so sensitive and alive that all manner of sound waves are constantly flying here and there with lightning-like speed. You have only to understand the modern radio outfit to understand, also, the principle of telepathy. So well has this principle been established, through psychological research, that we have abundance of proof that two minds which are properly attuned and in harmony with each other may send and receive thought at long distances without the aid of mechanical apparatus of any sort. Rarely have two minds become so well attuned that unbroken chains of thought could be registered in this manner, but there is evidence sufficient to establish the fact that parts of organised thought have been picked up.

That you may understand how closely interwoven are the fifteen factors upon which this Reading Course is based, consider, for example, what happens when a salesman who lacks confidence in himself, and in his goods, walks in to see a prospective buyer. Whether the prospective buyer is conscious of it or not, his imagination immediately 'senses' that lack of confidence in the salesman's mind. The salesman's own thought s are actually undermining his efforts. This will explain, from another angle, why self-confidence is one of the most important factors entering into the great struggle for success.

The principle of telepathy and the law of attraction, through which like attracts like, explain many a failure. If the mind has a tendency to attract from the ether those thought vibrations which harmonize with the dominating thoughts of a given mind, you can easily understand why a negative mind that dwells upon failure and lacks the vitalizing force of self-confidence would not attract a positive mind that is dominated by thoughts of success.

Perhaps these explanations are somewhat abstract to the student who has not made any particular study of the functioning processes of the mind, but it seems necessary to inject them into this lesson as a means of enabling the student to understand and make practical use of the subject of this lesson. The imagination is too often regarded merely as an indefinite, untraceable, indescribable something that does nothing but create fiction. It is this popular disregard of the powers of the imagination that has made necessary these more or less abstract references to one of the most important subjects of this course. Not only is the subject of imagination an important factor in this course; but, it is one of the most interesting subjects, as you will observe when you begin to see how it affects all that you do toward the achievement of your definite chief aim.

You will see how important is the subject of imagination when you stop to realise that it is the only thing in the world over which you have absolute control. Others may deprive you of your material wealth and cheat you in a thousand ways, but no man can deprive you of the control and use of your imagination. Men may deal with you unfairly, as men often do; they may deprive you of your liberty, but they cannot take from you the privilege of using your imagination as you wish.

The most inspiring poem in all literature was written by Leigh Hunt, while he was a poverty-stricken prisoner in an English prison, where he had been unjustly confined because of his advanced views on politics. This poem is entitled Abou Ben Adhem, and it is here re-printed as a reminder that one of the great things a man may do, in his own imagination, is to forgive those who have dealt unjustly with him:

Abou Ben Adhem (may his tribe increase)
Awoke one night from a deep dream of peace,
And saw within the moonlight of his room,
Making it rich and like a lily in bloom,
An angel writing in a book of gold,
Exceeding peace had made Ben Adhem bold,
And to the presence in the room he said:
"What writest thou?"-the vision raised its head,
And, with a look made of all sweet accord,
Answered, "The names of those who love the Lord."
"And is mine one?" said Abou. "Nay, not so,"
Replied the angel,-Abou spoke more low,
But cheerily still; and said, "I pray thee, then,
Write me as one that loves his fellow men."
The angel wrote, and vanished.
The next night It came again, with a great wakening light,
And showed the names whom love of God had blessed, And, lo!
Ben Adhem's name led all the rest!

Civilisation, itself, owes its existence to such men as Leigh Hunt, in whose fertile imagination s have been pictured the higher and nobler standards of human relationship. Abou Ben Adhem is a poem that will never die, thanks to this man who pictured in his imagination the hope of an ideal that is constructive.

The major trouble with this world today lies in our lack of understanding of the power of imagination, for if we understood this great power we could use it as a weapon with which to wipe out poverty and misery and injustice and persecution, and this could be done in a single generation. This is a rather broad statement, and no one understands better than the author of this course how useless such a statement would be if the principle upon which it is founded were not explained in terms of the most practical, workaday nature; therefore, let us proceed to describe what is meant.

To make this description understandable we must accept as a reality the principle of telepathy, through the operation of which every thought we release is registering itself in the minds of other people. We need devote no time to proving that telepathy is a reality, for the reason that this lesson on imagination cannot be of the slightest value to the student who has not sufficiently informed himself to understand and accept telepathy as an established principle. We will take it for granted that you are one who accepts and understands this principle.

You have often heard of 'mob psychology,' which is nothing more nor less than some strong, dominating idea that has been created in the mind of one or more persons and registers itself in the minds of other persons, through the principle of telepathy. So strong is the power of mob psychology that two men fighting in the street will often start a 'free-for-all' fight in which by standards will engage each other in battle without even knowing what they are fighting about, or with whom they are fighting.

On armistice day, 1918, we had evidence in abundance to prove the reality of the principle of telepathy, on a scale such as the world had never before witnessed. I remember, distinctly, the impression made on my mind on that eventful day. So strong was this impression that it awakened me at about 3:00 o'clock in the morning, just as effectively as if someone had aroused me by physical force. As I sat up in bed I knew that something out of the ordinary had happened, and so strange and impelling was the effect of this experience that I got up, dressed myself and went out in the streets of Chicago, where I was met by thousands of others who had felt the touch of the same influence. Everyone was asking: 'What has happened?'

What had happened was this:

Millions of men had received instructions to cease fighting, and their combined joy set into motion a thought wave that swept the entire world and made itself felt in every normal mind that was capable of registering this thought wave. Perhaps never in the history of the world had so many millions of people thought of the same thing, in the same manner, at the same time. For once in the history of the world everybody felt something in common, and the effect of this harmonized thought was the world-wide 'mob psychology' that we witnessed on armistice day. In connection with this statement it will be helpful if you recall what was said about the method of creating a 'Master Mind,' through the harmony of thought of two or more persons, in the Introductory Lesson of this course.

We will bring the application of this principle a little nearer home by showing how it may be made to make or break the harmonious working relationship of a business or industry. You may not have satisfied yourself that it was the harmony of thought of millions of soldiers that registered in the minds of the, people of the world and caused the 'mob' psychological condition that was everywhere in evidence on armistice day, but you will need no proof that a disgruntled person always disturbs everyone with whom he comes in contact. It is a well established fact that one such person in a place of employment will disrupt the entire organisation. The time is almost at hand when neither the workers nor the employers will tolerate the typical 'grouch' inside of a place of employment, for the reason that his state of mind registers itself in the minds of those about him, resulting in distrust, suspicion and lack of harmony. The time is near at hand when the workers in a place of employment will no more tolerate one of their own rank and file who is a typical 'grouch' than they would a poisonous snake.

Apply the principle in another way: Place among a group of workers one person whose personality is of the positive, optimistic type, and who makes it his business to sow the seeds of harmony around the place where he works, and his influence will reflect itself in every person who works with him.

If every business is 'the extended shadow of one man' as Emerson stated, then it behoves that one man to reflect a shadow of confidence and good cheer and optimism and harmony, that these qualities may, in turn, reflect themselves in all who are connected with the business.

In passing to the next step in our application of the power of imagination in the attainment of success we will cite some of the most recent and modern examples of its use in the accumulation of material wealth and the perfection of some of the leading inventions of the world.

In approaching this next step it should be borne ill mind that 'there is nothing new under the sun.' Lift, on this earth may be likened to a great kaleidoscope before which the scenes and facts and material substances are ever shifting and changing, and all any man can do is to take these facts and substances and re-arrange them in new combinations.

The process through which this is done is called imagination.

We have stated that the imagination is both interpretative and creative in its nature. It can receive impressions or ideas and out of these it can form new combinations.

As our first illustration of the power of imagination in modern business achievement, we will take the case of Clarence Saunders, who organised the Piggy-Wiggly system of self-help grocery stores.

Saunders was a grocery clerk in a small southern retail store. One day he was standing in a line, with a tin tray in his hands, waiting his turn to secure food in a cafeteria. He had never earned more than $20.00 a week before that time, and no one had ever noticed anything about him that indicated unusual ability, but something took place in his mind, as he stood in that line of waiting people, that put his imagination to work. With the aid of his imagination he lifted that 'self-help' idea out of the cafeteria in which he found it (not creating anything new, merely shifting an old idea into a new use) and set it down in a grocery store. In an instant the Piggy-Wiggly chain-store grocery plan had been created and Clarence Saunders the twenty-dollar-a-week grocery clerk rapidly became the million-dollar chain-store grocery man of America.

Where, in that transaction, do you see the slightest indication of a performance that you could not duplicate?

IT will make a big difference to you whether you are a person with a message or a person with a grievance.

Analyse this transaction and measure it by the previous lessons of this course and you will see that Clarence Saunders created a very definite purpose. He supported this purpose with sufficient self-confidence to cause him to take the initiative to transform it into reality. His imagination was the workshop in which these three factors, definite purpose, self-confidence and initiative were brought together and made to supply the momentum for the first step in the organisation of the Piggy-Wiggly plan.

Thus are great ideas changed into realities.

When Thomas A. Edison invented the incandescent electric light bulb he merely brought together two old, well known principles and associated them in a new combination. Mr. Edison and practically all others who were informed on the subject of electricity, knew that a light could be produced by heating a small wire with electricity, but the difficult problem was to do this without burning the wire in two. In his experimental research Mr. Edison tried out every conceivable sort of wire, hoping to find some substance that would withstand the tremendous heat to which it had to be subjected before a light could be produced.

His invention was half completed, but it was of no practical value until he could find the missing link that would supply the other half. After thousands of tests and much combining of old ideas in his imagination, Edison finally found this missing link. In his study of physics he had learned, as all other students of this subject learn, that there can be no combustion without the presence of oxygen. He of course knew that the difficulty with his electric light apparatus was the lack of a method through which to control the heat. When it occurred to him that there could be no combustion where there was no oxygen he placed the little wire of his electric light apparatus inside of a glass globe, shutout all the oxygen, and lo! the mighty incandescent light was a reality.

When the sun goes down tonight you step to the wall, press a button and bring it back again, a performance that would have mystified the people of a few generations ago, and yet there is no mystery back of your act. Thanks to the use of Edison's imagination, you have simply brought together two principles both of which were in existence since the beginning of time.

No one who knew him intimately ever accredited Andrew Carnegie with unusual ability, or the power of genius, except in one respect, and that was his ability to select men who could and would co-operate in a spirit of harmony, in carrying out his wishes. But what additional ability did he need in the accumulation of his millions of dollars?

Any man who understands the principle of organised effort, as Carnegie understood it, and knows enough about men to be able to select just those types that are needed in the performance of a given task, could duplicate all that Carnegie accomplished.

Carnegie was a man of imagination. He first created a definite purpose and then surrounded himself with men who had 'the training and the vision and the capacity necessary for the transformation of that purpose into reality. Carnegie did not always create his own plans for the attainment of his definite purpose. He made it his business to know what he wanted, then found the men who could create plans through which to procure it. And that was not only imagination, it was genius of the highest order.

But it should be made clear that men of Mr. Carnegie's type are not the only ones who can make profitable use of imagination. This great power is as available to the beginner in business as it is to the man who has 'arrived.'

One morning Charles M. Schwab's private car was backed on the side-track at his Bethlehem Steel plant. As he alighted from his car he was met by a young man stenographer who announced that he had come to make sure that any letters or telegrams Mr. Schwab might wish to write would be taken care of promptly. No one told this young man to be on hand, but he had enough imagination to see that his being there would not hurt his chances of advancement. From that day on, this young man was 'marked' for promotion. Mr. Schwab singled him out for promotion because he had done that which any of the dozen or so other stenographers in the employ of the Bethlehem Steel Company might have done, but didn't. Today this same man is the president of one of the largest drug concerns in the world and has all of this world's goods and wares that he wants and much more than he needs.

A few years ago I received a letter from a young man who had just finished Business College, and who wanted to secure employment in my office. With his letter he sent a crisp ten-dollar bill that had never been folded. The letter read as follows:

"I have just finished a commercial course in a first-class business college and I want a position in your office because I realise how much it would be worth to a young man, just starting out on his business career, to have the privilege of working under the direction of a man like you.

"If the enclosed ten-dollar bill is sufficient to pay for the time you would spend in giving me my first week's instructions I want you to accept it. I will work the first month without pay and you may set my wages after that at whatever I prove to be worth.

"I want this job more than I ever wanted anything in my life and I am willing to make any reasonable sacrifice to get it. Very cordially,"

This young man got his chance in my office. His imagination gained for him the opportunity that he wanted, and before his first month had expired the president of a life insurance company who heard of this incident offered the young man a private secretary-ship at a substantial salary. He is today an official of one of the largest life insurance companies in the world.

Some years ago a young man wrote to Thomas A. Edison for a position. For some reason Mr. Edison did not reply. By no means discouraged on this account the young man made up his mind that he would not only get a reply from Mr. Edison, but what was more important still, he would actually secure the position he sought. He lived a long distance from West Orange, New Jersey, where the Edison industries are located, and he did not have the money with which to pay his railroad fare. But he did have imagination. He went to West Orange in a freight car, got his interview, told his story in person and got the job he sought.

Today this same man lives in Bradentown, Florida. He has retired from active business, having made all the money he needs. His name, in case you wish to confirm my statements, is Edwin C. Barnes.

By using his imagination, Mr. Barnes saw the advantage of close association with a man like Thomas A. Edison. He saw that such an association would give him the opportunity to study Mr. Edison, and at the same time it would bring him in contact with Mr. Edison's friends, who are among the most influential people of the world.

These are but a few cases in connection with which I have personally observed how men have climbed to high places in the world and accumulated wealth in abundance by making practical use of their imagination.

Theodore Roosevelt engraved his name on the tablets of time by one single act during his tenure of office as President of the United States, and after all else that he did while in that office will have been forgotten this one transaction will record him in history as a man of imagination.

He started the steam shovels to work on the Panama Canal.

Every President, from Washington on up to Roosevelt, could have started the canal and it would have been completed, but it seemed such a colossal undertaking that it required not only imagination but daring courage as well. Roosevelt had both, and the people of the United States have the canal.

At the age of forty-the age at which the average man begins to think he is too old to start anything new-James J. Hill was still sitting at the telegraph key, at a salary of $30.00 per month. He had no capital.

He had no influential friends with capital, but he did have that which is more powerful than either-imagination.

In his mind's eye he saw a great railway system that would penetrate the undeveloped northwest and unite the Atlantic and Pacific oceans. So vivid was his imagination that he made others see the advantages of such a railway system, and from there on the story is familiar enough to every school-boy. I would emphasize the part of the story that most people never mention-that Hill's Great Northern Railway system became a reality in his own imagination first. The railroad was built with steel rails and wooden cross ties, just as other railroads are built, and these things were paid for with capital that was secured in very much the same manner that capital for all railroads is secured, but if you want the real story of James J. Hill's success you must go back to that little country railway station where he worked at $30.00 a month and there pick up the little threads that he wove into a mighty railroad, with materials no more visible than the thoughts which he organised in his imagination.

What a mighty power is imagination, the workshop of the soul, in which thought s are woven into railroads and skyscrapers and mills and factories and all manner of material wealth.

"I hold it true that thoughts are things;
They're endowed with bodies and breath and wings;
And that we send them forth to fill
The world with good results or ill.
That which we call our secret thought
Speeds forth to earth's remotest spot,
Leaving its blessings or its woes,
Like tracks behind it as it goes.
We build our future, thought by thought,
For good or ill, yet know it not,
Yet so the universe was wrought.
Thought is another name for fate;
Choose, then, thy destiny and wait,
For love brings love and hate brings hate."

If your imagination is the mirror of your soul, then you have a perfect right to stand before that mirror and see yourself as you wish to be. You have the right to see reflected in that magic mirror the mansion you intend to own, the factory you intend to manage, the bank of which you intend to be president, the station in life you intend to occupy. Your imagination belongs to you! Use it! The more you use it the more efficiently it will serve you.

At the east end of the great Brooklyn Bridge, in New York City, an old man conducts a cobbler shop. When the engineers began driving stakes and marking the foundation place for that great steel structure this man shook his head and said 'It can't be done!'

Now he looks out from his dingy little shoe-repair shop, shakes his head and asks himself: 'How did they do it?'

He saw the bridge grow before his very eyes and still he lacks the imagination to analyse that which he saw. The engineer who planned the bridge saw it a reality long before a single shovel of dirt had been removed for the foundation stones. The bridge became a reality in his imagination because he had trained that imagination to weave new combinations out of old ideas.

Through recent experiments in the department of electricity one of our great educational institutions of America has discovered how to put flowers to sleep and wake them up again, with electric 'sunlight.' This discovery makes possible the growth of vegetables and flowers without the aid of sunshine. In a few more years the city dweller will be raising a crop of vegetables on his back porch, with the aid of a few boxes of dirt and a few electric lights, with some new vegetable maturing every month of the year.

This new discovery, plus a little imagination, plus Luther Burbank's discoveries in the field of horticulture, and lo! the city dweller will not only grow vegetables all the year around, within the confines of his back porch, but he will grow bigger vegetables than any which the modern gardener grows in the open sunlight.

In one of the cities on the coast of California all of the land that was suitable for building lots had been developed and put into use. On one side of the city there were some steep hills that could not be used for building purposes, and on the other side the land was unsuitable for buildings because it was so low that the back-water covered it once a day.

A man of imagination came to this city. Men of imagination usually have keen minds, and this man was no exception. The first day of his arrival he saw the possibilities for making money out of real estate. He secured an option on those hills that were unsuitable for use because of their steepness. He also secured an option on the ground that was unsuitable for use because of the back-water that covered it daily. He secured these options at a very low price because the ground was supposed to be without substantial value.

With the use of a few tons of explosives he turned those steep hills into loose dirt. With the aid of a few tractors and some road scrapers he levelled the ground down and turned it into beautiful building lots, and with the aid of a few mules and carts he dumped the surplus dirt on the low ground and raised it above the water level, thereby turning it into beautiful building lots.

He made a substantial fortune, for what?

For removing some dirt from where it was not needed to where it was needed! For mixing some useless dirt with imagination!

The people of that little city gave this man credit for being a genius; and he was-the same sort of genius that any one of them could have been had he used his imagination as this man used his.

In the field of chemistry it is possible to mix two or more chemical ingredients in such proportions that the mere act of mixing gives each of the ingredients a tremendous amount of energy that it did not possess. It is also possible to mix certain chemical ingredients in such proportions that all the ingredients of the combination take on an entirely different nature, as in the case of H2 O, which is a mixture of two parts hydrogen and one part oxygen, creating water.

Chemistry is not the only field in which a combination of various physical materials can be so assembled that each takes on a greater value, or the result is a product entirely foreign in nature to that of its component parts. The man who blew up those useless hills of dirt and stone and removed the surplus from where it was not needed over to the low-land, where it was needed, gave that dirt and stone a value that it did not have before.

A ton of pig-iron is worth but little. Add to that pig-iron carbon, silicon, manganese, sulphur and phosphorus, in the right proportions, and you have transformed it into steel, which is of much greater value. Add still other substances, in the right proportion, including some skilled labour, and that same ton of steel is transformed into watch-springs worth a small fortune. But, in all these transformation processes the one ingredient that is worth most is the one that has no material form-imagination!

Here lie great piles of loose brick, lumber, nails and glass. In its present form it is worse than useless for it is a nuisance and an eye-sore. But mix it with the architect's imagination and add some skilled labour and lo! it becomes a beautiful mansion worth a king's ransom.

On one of the great highways between New York and Philadelphia stood an old ramshackle, time-worn barn, worth less than fifty dollars. With the aid of a little lumber and some cement, plus imagination, this old barn has been turned into a beautiful automobile supply station that earns a small fortune for the man who supplied the imagination.

Across the street from my office is a little print-shop that earns coffee and rolls for its owner and his helper, but no more. Less than a dozen blocks away stands one of the most modern printing plants in the world, whose owner spends most of his time travelling and has far more wealth than he will ever use.

I know I am here. I know I had nothing to do with my coming, and I shall have but little, if anything, to do with my going, therefore I will not worry because worries are of no avail.

Twenty-two years ago those two printers were in business together.

The one who owns the big print-shop had the good judgment to ally himself with a man who mixed imagination with printing. This man of imagination is a writer of advertisements and he keeps the printing plant with which he is associated supplied with more business than it can handle by analyzing its clients' business, creating attractive advertising features and supplying the necessary printed material with which to make these—features of service. This—plant receives top-notch—prices for its printing—because the imagination mixed with that printing produces a product that most printers cannot supply.

In the city of Chicago the level of a certain boulevard was raised, which spoiled a row of beautiful residences because the side-walk was raised to the level of the second story windows. While the property owners were bemoaning their ill-fortune a man of imagination came along, purchased the property for a 'song,' converted the second stories into business property, and now enjoys a handsome income from his rentals.

As you read these lines please keep in mind all that was stated in the beginning of this lesson; especially the fact that the greatest and most profitable thing you can do with your imagination is the act of rearranging old ideas in new combinations.

If you properly use your imagination it will help you convert your failures and mistakes into assets of priceless value; it will lead you to discovery of a truth known only to those who use their imagination; namely, that the greatest reverses and misfortunes of life often open the door to golden opportunities.

One of the finest and most highly paid engravers in the United States was formerly a mail-carrier. One day he was fortunate enough to be on a street car that met with an accident and had one of his legs cutoff. The street railway company paid him $5,000.00 for his leg. With this money he paid his way through school and became an engraver. The product of his hands, plus his imagination, is worth much more than he could earn with his legs, as a mail-carrier. He discovered that he had imagination when it became necessary to re-direct his efforts, as a result of the street car accident.

You will never know what is your capacity for achievement until you learn how to mix your efforts with imagination. The products of your hands, minus imagination, will yield you but a small return, but those selfsame hands, when properly guided by imagination, can be made to earn you all the material wealth you can use.

There are two ways in which you can profit by imagination. You can develop this faculty in your own mind, or you can ally yourself with those who have already developed it. Andrew Carnegie did both. He not only made use of his own fertile imagination, but he gathered around him a group of other men who also possessed this essential quality, for his definite purpose in life called for specialists whose imagination ran in numerous directions. In that group of men that constituted Mr. Carnegie's 'Master Mind' were men whose imagination s were confined to the field of chemistry. He had other men in the group whose imagination s were confined to finances. He had still others whose imagination s were confined to salesmanship, one of whom was Charles M. Schwab, who is said to have been the most able salesman on Mr. Carnegie's staff.

If you feel that your own imagination is inadequate you should form an alliance with someone whose imagination is sufficiently developed to supply your deficiency. There are various forms of alliance. For example, there is the alliance of marriage and the alliance of a business partnership and the alliance of friendship and the alliance of employer and employee. Not all men have the capacity to serve their own best interests as employers, and those who haven't this capacity may profit by allying themselves with men of imagination who have such capacity.

It is said that Mr. Carnegie made more millionaires of his employees than any other employer in the steel business. Among these was Charles M. Schwab, who displayed evidence of the soundest sort of imagination by his good judgment in allying himself with Mr. Carnegie. It is no disgrace to serve in the capacity of employee. To the contrary, it often proves to be the most profitable side of an alliance since not all men are fitted to assume the responsibility of directing other men.

Perhaps there is no field of endeavour in which imagination plays such an important part as it does in salesmanship. The master salesman sees the merits of the goods he sells or the service he is rendering, in his own imagination, and if he fails to do so he will not make the sale.

A few years ago a sale was made which is said to have been the most far-reaching and important sale of its kind ever made. The object of the sale was not merchandise, but the freedom of a man who was confined in the Ohio penitentiary and the development of a prison reform system that promises a sweeping change in the method of dealing with unfortunate men and women who have become entangled in the meshes of the law.

That you may observe just how imagination plays the leading part in salesmanship I will analyse this sale for you, with due apologies for personal references, which cannot be avoided without destroying much of the value of the illustration.

A few years ago I was invited to speak before the inmates of the Ohio penitentiary. When I stepped upon the platform I saw in the audience before me a man whom I had known as a successful business man, more than ten years previously. That man was B_, whose pardon I later secured, and the story of whose release has been spread upon the front page of practically every newspaper in the United States. Perhaps you will recall it.

After I had completed my address I interviewed Mr. B_ and found out that he had been sentenced for forgery, for a period of twenty years. After he had told me his story I said:

'I will have you out of here in less than sixty days!'

With a forced smile he replied: "I admire your spirit but question your judgment. Why, do you know that at least twenty influential men have tried every means at their command to get me released, without success? It can't be done!"

I suppose it was that last remark-It can't be done-that challenged me to show him that it could be done. I returned to New York City and requested my wife to pack her trunks and get ready for an indefinite stay in the city of Columbus, where the Ohio penitentiary is located.

I had a definite purpose in mind! That purpose was to get B_ out of the Ohio penitentiary. Not only did I have in mind securing his release, but I intended to do it in such a way that his release would erase from his breast the scarlet letter of 'convict' and at the same time reflect credit upon all who helped to bring about his release.

Not once did I doubt that I would bring about his release, for no salesman can make a sale if he doubts that he can do it. My wife and I returned to Columbus and took up permanent headquarters.

The next day I called on the governor of Ohio and stated the object of my visit in about these words:

"Governor: I have come to ask you to release B_ from the Ohio penitentiary. I have sound reason for asking his release and I hope you will give him his freedom atone, but I have come prepared to stay until he is released, no matter how long that may be.

"During his imprisonment B_has inaugurated a system of correspondence instruction in the Ohio penitentiary, as you of course know. He has influenced 1729 of the 2518 prisoners of the Ohio penitentiary to take up courses of instruction. He has managed to beg sufficient textbooks and lesson materials with which to keep these men at work on their lessons, and has done this without a penny of expense to the state of Ohio. The warden and the chaplain of the penitentiary tell me that he has carefully observed the prison rules. Surely a man who can influence 1729 men to turn their efforts toward self-betterment cannot be a very bad sort of fellow.

"I have come to ask you to release B_ because I wish to place him at the head of a prison school that will give the 160,000 inmates of the other penitentiaries of the United States a chance to profit by his influence. I am prepared to assume full responsibility for his conduct after his release.

"That is my case, but, before you give me your answer, I want you to know that I am not unmindful of the fact that your enemies will probably criticize you if you release him; in fact if you release him it may cost you many votes if you run for office again."

With his fist clinched and his broad jaw set firmly Governor Vic Donahue of Ohio said:

"If that is what you want with B_ I will release him if it costs me five thousand votes. However, before I sign the pardon I want you to see the Clemency Board and secure its favourable recommendation. I want you also to secure the favourable recommendation of the warden and the chaplain of the Ohio penitentiary. You know a governor is amenable to the Court of Public Opinion, and these gentlemen are the representatives of that Court."

The sale had been made! and the whole transaction had required less than five minutes.

The next day I returned to the governor's office, accompanied by the chaplain of the Ohio penitentiary, and notified the governor that the Clemency Board, the Warden and the Chaplain all joined in recommending the release. Three days later the pardon was signed and B walked through the big iron gates, a free man.

I have cited the details to show you that there was nothing difficult about the transaction. The groundwork for the release had all been prepared before I came upon the scene. B_ had done that, by his good conduct and the service he had rendered those 1729 prisoners. When he created the world's first prison correspondence school system he created the key that unlocked the prison doors for himself.

Why, then, had the others who asked for his release failed to secure it?

They failed because they used no imagination! Perhaps they asked the governor for B_'s release on the ground that his parents were prominent people, or on the ground that he was a college graduate and not a bad sort of fellow. They failed to supply the governor of Ohio with a sufficient motive to justify him in granting a pardon, for had this not been so he would undoubtedly have released B_ long before I came upon the scene and asked for his release.

Before I went to see the governor I went over all the facts and in my own imagination I saw myself in the governor's place and made up my mind what sort of a presentation would appeal most strongly to me if I were in reality in his place.

When I asked for B_'s release I did so in the name of the 160,000 unfortunate men and women inmates of the prisons of the United States who would enjoy the benefits of the correspondence school system that he had created. I said nothing about his prominent parents. I said nothing about my friendship with him during former years. I said nothing about his being a deserving fellow. All these matters might have been used as sound reasons for his release, but they seemed insignificant when compared with the bigger and sounder reason that his release would be of help to 160,000 other people who would feel the influence of his correspondence school system after his release.

When the governor of Ohio came to a decision I doubt not that B_ was of secondary importance as far as his decision was concerned. The governor no doubt saw a possible benefit, not to B_ alone, but to 160,000 other men and women who needed the influence that B_ could supply, if released.

And that was imagination!

It was also salesmanship! In speaking of the incident after it was over, one of the men who had worked diligently for more than a year in trying to secure B_'s freedom, asked:

"How did you do it?"

And I replied: "It was the easiest task I ever performed, because most of the work had been done before I took hold of it. In fact I didn't do it B_ did it himself."

This man looked at me in bewilderment. He did not see that which I am here trying to make clear; namely, that practically all difficult tasks are easily performed if one approaches them from the right angle. There were two important factors entering B_'s release. The first was the fact that he had supplied the material for a good case before I took it in charge; and the second was the fact that before I called on the governor of Ohio I so completely convinced myself that I had a right to ask for B_'s release that I had no difficulty in presenting my case effectively.

Go back to what was stated in the beginning of this lesson, on the subject of telepathy, and apply it to this case. The governor could tell, long before I had stated my mission, that I knew I had a good case. If my brain did not telegraph this thought to his brain, then the look of self-confidence in my eyes and the positive tone of my voice made obvious my belief in the merits of my case.

Again I apologize for these personal references with the explanation that I have used them only because the whole of America was familiar with the B_ case that I have described. I disclaim all credit for the small part I played in the case, for I did nothing except use my imagination as an assembly room in which to piece together the factors out of which the sale was made. I did nothing except that which any salesman of imagination could have done.

It requires considerable courage to prompt one to use the personal pronoun as freely as it has been used in relating the facts connected with this case, but justification lies in the value of application of the principle of imagination to a case with which nearly everybody is familiar.

I cannot recall an incident in my entire life in connection with which the soundness of the fifteen factors that enter into this Reading Course was more clearly manifested than it was in securing the release of B_.

It is but another link in a long chain of evidence that proves to my entire satisfaction the power of imagination as a factor in salesmanship. There are endless millions of approaches to every problem, but there is only one best approach. Find this one best approach and your problem is easily solved. No matter how much merit your goods may have, there are millions of wrong ways in which to offer them. Your imagination will assist you in finding the right way.

In your search for the right way in which to offer your merchandise or your services, remember this peculiar traitor mankind:

Men will grant favours that you request for the benefit of a third person when they would not grant them if requested for your benefit.

Compare this statement with the fact that I asked the governor of Ohio to release B_, not as a favour to me, and not as a favour to B_, but, for the benefit of 160,000 unfortunate inmates of the prisons of America.

Salesmen of imagination always offer their wares in such terminology that the advantages of those wares to the prospective purchaser are obvious. It is seldom that any man makes a purchase of merchandise or renders another a favour just to accommodate the salesman. It is a prominent traitor human nature that prompts us all to do that which advances our own interests. This is a cold, indisputable fact, claims of the idealist to the contrary notwithstanding.

To be perfectly plain, men are selfish!

To understand the truth is to understand how to present your case, whether you are asking for the release of a man from prison or offering for sale some commodity. In your own imagination so plan your presentation of your case that the strongest and most impelling advantages to the buyer are made plain.

This is imagination!

I never see a person trying to disclose the scarlet letter on another's breast that I do not wonder if he doesn't carry some mark of disgrace which would have ruined him had he been overtaken by justice.

A farmer moved to the city, taking with him his well trained shepherd dog. He soon found that the dog was out of place in the city, so he decided to 'get rid of him.' (Note the words in quotation.) Taking the dog with him he went out into the country and rapped on the door of a farm-house. A man came hobbling to the door, on crutches. The man with the dog greeted the man in the house in these words

"You wouldn't care to buy a fine shepherd dog, that I wish to get rid of, would you?"

The man on crutches replied, 'No!' and closed the door.

The man with the dog called at half a dozen other farm-houses, asking the same question, and received the same answer. He made up his mind that no one wanted the dog and returned to the city. That evening he was telling of his misfortune, to a man of imagination. The man heard how the owner of the dog had tried in vain to 'get rid of him.'

'Let me dispose of the dog for you,' said the man of imagination. The owner was willing. The next morning the man of imagination took the dog out into the country and stopped at the first farm-house at which the owner of the dog had called the day before. The same old man hobbled out on crutches and answered the knock at the door.

The man of imagination greeted him in this fashion:

"I see you are all crippled with rheumatism. What you need is a fine dog to run errands for you. I have a dog here that has been trained to bring home the cows, drive away wild animals, herd the sheep and perform other useful services. You may have this dog for a hundred dollars."

'All right,' said the crippled man, 'I'll take him!' That, too, was imagination!

No one wants a dog that someone else wants to 'get rid of,' but most anyone would like to own a dog that would herd sheep and bring home the cows and perform other useful services.

The dog was the same one that the crippled buyer had refused the day before, but the man who sold the dog was not the man who had tried to 'get rid of him.' If you use your imagination you will know that no one wants anything that someone else is trying to 'get rid of.'

Remember that which was said about the Law of Attraction through the operation of which 'like attracts like.' If you look and act the part of a failure you will attract nothing but failures.

Whatever your life-work may be, it calls for the use of imagination.

Niagara Falls was nothing but a great mass of roaring water until a man of imagination harnessed it and converted the wasted energy into electric current that now turns the wheels of industry. Before this man of imagination came along millions of people had seen and heard— those roaring falls, but lacked the imagination to harness them.

The first Rotary Club of the world was born in the—fertile— imagination of—Paul Harris,—of Chicago, who saw in this child of his brain an effective means of cultivating prospective clients and the extension of his law practice. The ethics of the legal profession forbid advertising in the usual way, but Paul Harris' imagination found a way to extend his law practice without advertising in the usual way.

If the winds of Fortune are temporarily blowing against you, remember that you can harness them and make them carry you toward your definite purpose, through the use of your imagination. A kite rises against the wind-not with it!

Dr. Frank Crane was a struggling 'third-rate' preacher until the starvation wages of the clergy forced him to use his imagination. Now he earns upward of a hundred thousand dollars a year for an hour's work a day, writing essays.

Bud Fisher once worked for a mere pittance, but he now earns seventy-five thousand dollars a year by making folks grin, with his Mutt and Jeff comic strip. No art goes into his drawings, therefore he must be selling his imagination.

Woolworth was a poorly paid clerk in a retail store-poorly paid, perhaps, because he had not yet found out that he had imagination. Before he died he built the tallest office building in the world and girdled the United States with Five and Ten Cent Stores, through the use of his imagination.

You will observe, by analyzing these illustrations, that a close study of human nature played an important part in the achievements mentioned. To make profitable use of your imagination you must make it give you a keen insight into the motives that cause men to do or refrain from doing a given act. If your imagination leads you to understand how quickly people grant your requests when those requests appeal to their self-interest, you can have practically anything you go after.

I saw my wife make a very clever sale to our baby not long ago. The baby was pounding the top of our mahogany library table with a spoon. When my wife reached for the spoon the baby refused to give it up, but being a woman of imagination she offered the baby a nice stick of red candy; he dropped the spoon immediately and cantered his attention on the more desirable object.

That was imagination! It was also salesmanship. She won her point without using force.

I was riding in an automobile with a friend who was driving beyond the speed limit. An officer rode up on a motorcycle and told my friend he was under arrest for speeding. The friend smiled pleasantly at the officer and said: 'I'm sorry to have brought you out in all this rain, but I wanted to make the ten o'clock train with my friend here, and I was hitting it up around thirty-five miles an hour.'

'No, you were only going twenty-eight miles an hour,' replied the officer, 'and as long as you are so nice about it I will let you off this time if you will watch yourself hereafter.'

And that, too, was imagination! Even a traffic cop will listen to reason when approached in the right manner, but woe unto the motorist who tries to bully the cop into believing his speedometer was not registering properly.

There is one form of imagination against which I would caution you. It is the brand which prompts some people to imagine that they can get something for nothing, or that they can force themselves ahead in the world without observing the rights of others. There are more than 160,000 prisoners in the penal institutions of the United States, practically every one of whom is in prison because he imagined he could play the game of life without observing the rights of his fellow men.

There is a man in the Ohio penitentiary who has served more than thirty-five years of time for forgery, and the largest amount he ever got from his misapplication of imagination on was twelve dollars.

There are a few people who direct their imagination s in the vain attempt to work out a way to show what happens when "an immovable body comes in contact with an irresistible force," but these types belong in the psychopathic hospitals.

There is also another form of misapplied imagination ; namely, that of the young boy or girl who knows more about life than his or her 'Dad.' But this form is subject to modification with time. My own boys have taught me many things that my 'Dad' tried, in vain, to teach me when I was their age.

Time and imagination (which is often but the product of time) teach us many things, but nothing of more importance than this:

That all men are much alike in many ways.

If you would know what your customer is thinking, Mr. Salesman, study yourself and find out what you would be thinking if you were in your customer's place.

Study yourself, find out what are the motives which actuate you in the performance of certain deeds and cause you to refrain from performing other deeds, and you will have gone far toward perfecting yourself in the accurate use of imagination.

The detective's biggest asset is imagination. The first question he asks, when called in to solve a crime is: 'What was the motive?' If he can find out the motive he can usually find the perpetrator of the crime.

A man who had lost a horse posted a reward of five dollars for its return. Several days later a boy who was supposed to have been 'weak-minded' came leading the horse home and claimed the reward. The owner was curious to know how the boy found the horse. "How did you ever think where to look for the horse?" he asked, and the boy replied, "Well, I just thought where I would have gone if I had been a horse and went there, and he had." Not so bad for a 'weak-minded' fellow. Some who are not accused of being weak-minded go all the way through life without displaying as much evidence of imagination as did this boy.

If you want to know what the other fellow will do, use your imagination, put yourself in his place and find out what you would have done. That's imagination.

Every person should be somewhat of a dreamer. Every business needs the dreamer. Every industry and every profession needs him. But, the dreamer must be, also, a doer; or else he must form an alliance with someone who can and does translate dreams into reality.

The greatest nation upon the face of this earth was conceived, born and nurtured through the early days of its childhood, as the result of imagination in the minds of men who combined dreams with acttion!

Your mind is capable of creating many new and useful combinations of old ideas, but the most important thing it can create is a definite chief aim that will give you that which you most desire.

Your definite chief aim can be speedily translated into reality after you have fashioned it in the cradle of your imagination. If you have faithfully followed the instructions set down for your guidance in Lesson Two you are now well on the road toward success, because you know what it is that you want, and you have a plan for getting that which you want.

The battle for the achievement of success is half won when one knows definitely what is wanted. The battle is all over except the 'shouting' when one knows what is wanted and has made up his mind to get it, whatever the price may be.

The selection of a definite chief aim calls for the use of both imagination and decision! The power of decision grows with use. Prompt decision in forcing the imagination to create a definite chief aim renders more powerful the capacity to reach decisions in other matters.

Adversities and temporary defeat are generally blessings in disguise, for the reason that they force one to use both imagination and decision. This is why a man usually makes a better fight when his back is to the wall and he knows there is no retreat. He then reaches the decision to fight instead of running.

The imagination is never quite so active as it is when one faces some emergency calling for quick and definite decision and action.

In these moments of emergency men have reached decisions, built plans, used their imagination in such a manner that they became known as geniuses. Many a genius has been born out of the necessity for unusual stimulation of the imagination, as the result of some trying experience which forced quick thought and prompt decision.

It is a well-known fact that the only manner in which an over pampered boy or girl may be made to become useful is by forcing him or her to become self-sustaining. This calls for the exercise of both imagination and decision, neither of which would be used except out of necessity.

The Reverend P. W. Welshimer is the pastor of a church in Canton, Ohio, where he has been located for nearly a quarter of a century. Ordinarily pastors do not remain at the head of one church for so great a length of time, and Reverend Welshimer would have been no exception to this rule if he had not mixed imagination with his pastoral duties.

Three years constitute the usual time that one pastor may remain in a given pastorate without wearing out his welcome.

The church of which Reverend Welshimer is the leader has a sunday school of over 5,000 members-the largest membership enjoyed by any church in the United States.

No pastor could have remained at the head of one church for a quarter of a century, with the full consent of his followers, and have built up a Sunday School of this size, without employing the Laws of Initiative and Leadership, a Definite Chief Aim, Self-confidence and imagination.

The author of this course made it his business to study the methods employed by Reverend Welshimer, and they are here described for the benefit of the students of this philosophy.

It is a well known fact that church factions, jealousy, etc., often lead to disagreements which make a change in leaders essential. Reverend Welshimer has steered around this common obstacle by a unique application of the Law of Imagination. When a new member comes into his church he immediately assigns a DEFINITE task to that member-one that suits the temperament, training and business qualifications of the individual, as nearly as possible-and, to use the minister's own words, he "keeps each member so busy pulling for the church that there is no time left for kicking or disagreeing with other members."

Not a bad policy for application in the field of business, or in any other field. The old saying that "idle hands are the devil's best tools" is more than a mere play upon words, for it is true.

Give any man something to do that he likes to do, and keep him busy doing it, and he will not be apt to degenerate into a disorganising force. If any member of the Sunday School misses attendance twice in succession a committee from the church calls to find out the reason for the failure to attend. There is a 'committee' job for practically every member of the church. In this way Reverend Welshimer delegates to the members, themselves, the responsibility of rounding up the delinquents and keeping them interested in church affairs. He is an organiser of the highest type. His efforts have attracted the attention of business men throughout the country, and times too numerous to be mentioned he has been offered positions, at fancy salaries, by banks, steel plants, business houses, etc., that recognised in him a real Leader.

In the basement of the church Reverend Welshimer operates a first-class printing plant where he publishes, weekly, a very creditable church paper that goes to all the members. The production and distribution of this paper is another source of employment which keeps the church members out of mischief, as practically all of them take some sort of an active interest in it. The paper is devoted exclusively to the affairs of the church as a whole, and those of the individual members. It is read by each member, line by line, because there is always a chance that each member's name may be mentioned in the news locals.

The church has a well trained choir and an orchestra that would be a credit to some of the largest theatres. Here Reverend Welshimer serves the double purpose of supplying entertainment and at the same time keeping the more 'temperamental' members who are artists employed so they, also, remain out of mischief, incidentally giving them a chance to do that which they like best.

The late Dr. Harper, who was formerly president of the University of Chicago, was one of the most efficient college presidents of his time. He had a penchant for raising funds in large amounts. It was he who induced John D. Rockefeller to contribute millions of dollars to the support of the University of Chicago.

It may be helpful to the student of this philosophy to study Dr. Harper's technique, because he was a Leader of the highest order. Moreover, I have his own word for it that his leadership was never a matter of chance or accident, but always the result of carefully planned procedure.

The following incident will serve to show just how Dr. Harper made use of imagination in raising money in large sums:

He—needed—an—extra—million—dollars—for—the construction of a new building. Taking inventory of the wealthy men of Chicago to whom he might turn for this large sum, he decided upon two men, each of whom was a millionaire, and both were bitter enemies.

One of these men was, at that time, the head of the Chicago Street Railway system. Choosing the noon hour, when the office force and this man's secretary, in particular, would be apt to be out at lunch, Dr. Harper nonchalantly strolled into the office, and, finding no one on guard at the outer door, walked into the office of his intended 'victim,' whom he surprised by his appearance unannounced.

'My name is Harper,' said the doctor, "and I am presidentof the University of Chicago. Pardon my intrusion, but I found no one in the outer office (which was no mere accident) so I took the liberty of walking on in.

"I have thought of you and your street railway system many times. You have built up a wonderful system, and I understand that you have made lots of money for your efforts. I never think of you, however, without its occurring to me that one of these days you will be passing out into the Great Unknown, and after you are gone there will be nothing left as a monument to your name, because others will take over your money, and money has a way of losing its identity very quickly, as soon as it changes hands.

"I have often thought of offering you the opportunity to perpetuate your name by permitting you to build a new Hall out on the University grounds, and naming it after you. I would have offered you this opportunity long ago had it not been for the fact that one of the members of our Board wishes the honour to go to Mr. X_ (the street car head's enemy). Personally, however, I have always favoured you and I still favour you, and if I have your permission to do so I am going to try to swing the opposition over to you.

"I have not come to ask for any decision today, however, as I was just passing and thought it a good time to drop in and meet you. Think the matter over and if you wish to talk to me about it again, telephone me at your leisure.

"Good day, sir! I am happy to have had this opportunity of meeting you."

With this he bowed himself out without giving the head of the street car company a chance to say either yes or no. In fact the street car man had very little chance to do any talking. Dr. Harper did the talking. That was as he planned it to be. He went into the office merely to plant the seed, believing that it would germinate and spring into life in due time.

His belief was not without foundation. He had hardly returned to his office at the University when the telephone rang. The street car man was on the other end of the wire. He asked for an appointment with Dr. Harper, which was granted, and the two met in Dr. Harper's office the next morning, and the check for a million dollars was in Dr. Harper's hands an hour later.

Despite the fact that Dr. Harper was a small, rather insignificant-looking man it was said of him that "he had a way about him that enabled him to get everything he went after."

And as to this 'way' that he was reputed to have had-what was it?

It was nothing more nor less than his understanding of the power of Imagination. Suppose he had gone to the office of the street car head and asked for an appointment. Sufficient time would have elapsed between the time he called and the time when he would have actually seen his man, to have enabled the latter to anticipate the reason for his call, and also to formulate a good, logical excuse for saying, 'No!'

Suppose, again, he had opened his interview with the street car man something like this:

"The University is badly in need of funds and I have come to you to ask your help. You have made lots of money and you owe something to the community in which you have made it. (Which, perhaps, was true.) If you will give us a million dollars we will place your name on a new Hall that we wish to build."

What might have been the result?

In the first place, there would have been no motive suggested that was sufficiently appealing to sway the mind of the street car man. While it may have been true that he "owed something to the community from which he had made a fortune," he probably would not have admitted that fact. In the second place, he would have enjoyed the position of being on the offensive instead of the defensive side of the proposal.

But Dr. Harper, shrewd in the use of Imagination as he was, provided for just such contingencies by the way he stated his case. First, he placed the street car man on the defensive by informing him that it was not certain that he (Dr. Harper) could get the permission of his Board to accept the money and name the Hall after the street car man. In the second place, he intensified the desire of the street car man to have his name on that building because of the thought that his enemy and competitor might get the honour if it got away from him.

Moreover (and this was no accident, either), Dr. Harper had made a powerful appeal to one of the most common of all human weaknesses by showing this street car man how to perpetuate his own name.

All of which required a practical application of the Law of Imagination.

Dr. Harper was a Master Salesman. When he asked men for money he always paved the way for success by planting in the mind of the man of whom he asked it a good sound reason why the money should be given; a reason which emphasized some advantage accruing to the man as the result of the gift. Often this would take on the form of a business advantage. Again it would take on the nature of an appeal to that part of man's nature which prompts him to wish to perpetuate his name so it will live after him. But, always, the request for money was carried out according to a plan that had been carefully thought out, embellished and smoothed down with the use of Imagination.

While The Law of Success philosophy was in the embryonic stage, long before it had been organised into a systematic course of instruction and reduced to textbooks, the author was lecturing on this philosophy in a small town in Illinois.

One of the members of the audience was a young life insurance salesman who had but recently taken up that line of work. After hearing what was said on the subject of Imagination he began to apply what he had heard to his own problem of selling life insurance. Something was said, during the lecture, about the value of allied effort, through which men may enjoy greater success by co-operative effort, through a working arrangement under which each 'boosts' the interests of the other.

Taking this suggestion as his cue, the young man in question immediately formulated a plan whereby he gained the co-operation of a group of business men who were in no way connected with the insurance business.

Going to the leading grocer in his town he made arrangements with that grocer to give a thousand dollar insurance policy to every customer purchasing no less than fifty dollars' worth of groceries each month. He then made it a part of his business to inform people of this arrangement and brought in many new customers. The grocery man had a large neatly lettered card placed in his store, informing his customers of this offer of free insurance, thus helping himself by offering all his customers an inducement to do all their trading in the grocery line with him.

This young life insurance man then went to the leading gasoline filling station owner in the town and made arrangements with him to insure all customers who purchased all their gasoline, oil and other motor supplies from him.

Next he went to the leading restaurant in the town and made a similar arrangement with the owner. Incidentally, this alliance proved to be quite profitable to the restaurant man, who promptly began an advertising campaign in which he stated that his food was so pure, wholesome and good that all who ate at his place regularly would be apt to live much longer, therefore he would insure the life of each regular customer for $1,000.00.

The life insurance salesman then made arrangements with a local builder and real estate man to insure the life of each person buying property from him, for an amount sufficient to pay off the balance due on the property in case the purchaser died before payments were completed.

The young man in question is now the General Agent for one of the largest life insurance companies in the United States, with headquarters in one of the largest cities in Ohio, and his income now averages well above $25,000.00 a year.

The turning-point in his life came when he discovered how he might make practical use of the Law of Imagination.

There is no patent on his plan. It may be duplicated over and over again by other life insurance men who know the value of imagination. Just now, if I were engaged in selling life insurance, I think I should make use of this plan by allying myself with a group of automobile distributors in each of several cities, thus enabling them to sell more automobiles and at the same time providing for the sale of a large amount of life insurance, through their efforts.

Financial success is not difficult to achieve after one learn show to make practical use of creative imagination. Someone with sufficient initiative and leadership, and the necessary imagination, will duplicate the fortunes being made each year by the owners of Five and Ten Cent Stores, by developing a system of marketing the same sort of goods now sold in these stores, with the aid of vending machines. This will save a fortune in clerk hire, insure against theft, and cut down the overhead of store operation in many other ways. Such a system can be conducted just as successfully as food can be dispensed with the aid of automatic vending machines.

The seed of the idea has been here sown. It is yours for the taking!

Someone with an inventive turn of the mind is going to make a fortune and at the same time save thousands of lives each year, by perfecting an automatic railroad crossing 'control' that will reduce the number of automobile accidents on crossings.

The system, when perfected, will work somewhat after this fashion: A hundred yards or so before reaching the railroad crossing the automobile will cross a platform somewhat on the order of a large scale platform used for weighing heavy objects, and the weight of the automobile will lower a gate and ring a gong. This will force the automobile to slow down. After the lapse of one minute the gate will again rise and the car may continue on its way. Meanwhile, there will have been plenty of time for observation of the track in both directions, to make sure that no trains are approaching.

Imagination, plus some mechanical skill, will give the motorist this much needed safe-guard, and make the man who perfects the system all the money he needs and much more besides.

Some inventor who understands the value of imagination and has a working knowledge of the radio principle, may make a fortune by perfecting a burglar alarm system that will signal police headquarters and at the same time switch on lights and ring a gong in the place about to be burglarized, with the aid of apparatus similar to that now used for broadcasting.

Any farmer with enough imagination to create a plan, plus the use of a list of all automobile licenses issued in his state, may easily work up a clientele of motorists who will come to his farm and purchase all the vegetables he can produce and all the chickens he can raise, thus saving him the expense of hauling his products to the city. By contracting with each motorist for the season the farmer may accurately estimate the amount of produce he should provide. The advantage to the motorist, accruing under the arrangement, is that he will be sure of direct-from-the-farm produce, at less cost than he could purchase it from local dealers.

The roadside gasoline filling station owner can make effective use of imagination by placing a lunch stand near his filling station, and then doing some attractive advertising along the road in each direction, calling attention to his 'barbecue,' 'home-made sandwiches' or whatever else he may wish to specialize on. The lunch stand will cause the motorists to stop, and many of them will purchase gasoline before starting on their way again.

These are simple suggestions, involving no particular amount of complication in connection with their use, yet it is just such uses of imagination that bring financial success.

The Piggly-Wiggly self-help store plan, which made millions of dollars for its originator, was a very simple idea which anyone could have adopted, yet consider able imagination was required to put the idea to work in a practical sort of way.

The more simple and easily adapted to a need an idea is, the greater is its value, as no one is looking for ideas which are involved with great detail or in any manner complicated.

Imagination is the most important factor entering into the art of selling. The Master Salesman is always one who makes systematic use of imagination. The outstanding merchant relies upon imagination for the ideas which make his business excel.

Imagination may be used effectively in the sale of even the smallest articles of merchandise, such as ties, shirts, hosiery, etc. Let us proceed to examine just how this may be done.

I walked into one of the best known haberdasheries in the city of Philadelphia, for the purpose of put chasing some shirts and ties.

As I approached the tie counter a young man stepped forward and inquired:

'Is there something you want?'

Now if I had been the man behind the counter I would not have asked that question. He ought to have known, by the fact that I had approached the tie counter, that I wanted to look at ties.

I picked up two or three times from the counter, examined them briefly, then laid down all but one light blue which somewhat appealed to me. Finally I laid this one down, also, and began to look through the remainder of the assortment.

The young man behind the counter then had a happy idea. Picking up a gaudy-looking yellow tie he wound it around his fingers to show how it would look when tied, and asked:

'Isn't this a beauty?'

Now I hate yellow ties, and the salesman made no particular hit with me by suggesting that a gaudy yellow tie is pretty. If I had been in that salesman's place I would have picked up the blue tie for which I had shown a decided preference, and I would have wound it around my fingers so as to bring out its appearance after being tied. I would have known what my customer wanted by watching the kinds of ties that he picked up and examined. Moreover, I would have known the particular tie that he liked best by the time he held it in his hands. A man will not stand by a counter and fondle a piece of merchandise which he does not like. If given the opportunity, any customer will give the alert salesman a clue as to the particular merchandise which should be stressed in an effort to make a sale.

I then moved over to the shirt counter. Here I was met by an elderly gentleman who asked:

'Is there something I can do for you today?' Well, I thought to myself that if he ever did anything for me it would have to be today, as I might never come back to that particular store again. I told him I wanted to look at shirts, and described the style and color of shirt that I wanted.

The old gentleman made quite a hit with me when he replied by saying:

THE man who is afraid to give credit to those who help him do a piece of creditable work is so small that opportunity will pass by without seeing him some day.

'I am sorry, sir, but they are not wearing that style this season, so we are not showing it."

I said I knew 'they' were not wearing the style for which I had asked, and for that very reason, among others, I was going to wear it providing I could find it in stock.

If there is anything which nettles a man-especially that type of man who knows exactly what he wants and describes it the moment he walks into the store-it is to be told that 'they are not wearing it this season.'

Such a statement is an insult to a man's intelligence, or to what he thinks is his intelligence, and in most cases it is fatal to a sale. If I were selling goods I might think what I pleased about a customer's taste, but I surely would not be so lacking intact and diplomacy as to tell the customer that I thought he didn't know his business. Rather I would prefer to manage tactfully to show him what I believed to be more appropriate merchandise than that for which he had called, if what he wanted was not in stock.

One of the most famous and highly paid writers in the world has built his fame and fortune on the sole discovery that it is profitable to write about that which people already know and with which they are already in accord. The same rule might as well apply to the sale of merchandise.

The old gentleman finally pulled down some shirt boxes and began laying out shirts which were not even similar to the shirt for which I had asked. I told him that none of these suited, and as I started to walk out he asked if I would like to look at some nice suspenders.

Imagine it! To begin with I do not wear suspenders, and, furthermore, there was nothing about my manner or bearing to indicate that I might like to look at suspenders.

It is proper for a salesman to try to interest a customer in wares for which he makes no inquiry, but judgment should be used and care taken to offer something which the salesman has reason to believe the customer may want.

I walked out of the store without having bought either shirts or ties, and feeling somewhat resentful because I had been so grossly misjudged as to my tastes for colors and styles.

A little further down the street I went into a small, one-man shop which had shirts and ties on display in the window.

Here I was handled differently!

The man behind the counter asked no unnecessary or stereotyped questions. He took one glance at me as I entered the door, sized me up quite accurately and greeted me with a very pleasant "Good morning, sir!'

He then inquired, 'Which shall I show you first, shirts or ties?' I said I would look at the shirts first. He then glanced at the style of shirt I was wearing asked my size, and began laying out shirts of the very type and color for which I was searching, without my saying another word. He laid out six different styles and watched to see which I would pick up first. I looked at each shirt, in turn, and laid them all back on the counter, but the salesman observed that I examined one of the shirts a little more closely than the others, and that I held it a little longer. No sooner had I laid this shirt down than the salesman picked it up and began to explain how it was made. He then went to the tie counter and came back with three very beautiful blue ties, of the very type for which I had been looking, tied each and held it in front of the shirt, calling attention to the perfect harmony between the colors of the ties and the shirt.

Before I had been in the store five minutes I had purchased three shirts and three ties, and was on my way with the package under my arm, feeling that here was a store to which I would return when I needed more shirts and ties.

I learned, afterwards, that the merchant who owns the little shop where I made these purchases pays a monthly rental of $500.00 for the small store, and makes a handsome income from the sale of nothing but shirts, ties and collars. He would have to go out of business, with a fixed charge of $500.00 a month for rent, if it were not for his knowledge of human nature which enables him to make a very high percentage of sales to all who come into his store.

I have often observed women when they were trying on hats, and have wondered why salespeople did not read the prospective buyer's mind by watching her manner of handling the hats.

A woman goes into a store and asks to be shown some hats. The salesperson starts bringing out hats and the prospective buyer starts trying them on. If a hat suits her, even in the slightest sort of way, she will keep it on a few seconds, or a few minutes, but if she does not like it she will pull it right off her head the moment the salesperson takes her hands off the hat.

Finally, when the customer is shown a hat that she likes she will begin to announce that fact, in terms which no well-informed salesperson will fail to understand, by arranging her hair under the hat, or pulling it down on her head to just the angle which she likes best, and by looking at the hat from the rear, with the aid of a hand-mirror. The signs of admiration are unmistakable. Finally, the customer will remove the hat from her head, and begin to look at it closely; then she may lay it aside and permit another hat to be tried on her, in which event the clever salesperson will lay aside the hat just removed, and at the opportune time she will bring it back and ask the customer to try it on again.

By careful observation of the customer's likes and dislikes a clever saleswoman may often sell as many as three or four hats to the same customer, at one sitting, by merely watching what appeals to the customer and then concentrating upon the sale of that.

The same rule applies in the sale of other merchandise. The customer will, if closely observed, clearly indicate what is wanted, and, if the clue is followed, very rarely will a customer walk out without buying.

I believe it a conservative estimate when I say that fully seventy-five per cent of the 'walk-outs,' as the non-purchasing customers are called, are due to lack of tactful showing of merchandise.

Last Fall I went into a hat store to purchase a felt hat. It was a busy Saturday afternoon and I was approached by a young 'extra' rush-hour salesman who had not yet learned how to size people up at a glance. For no good reason whatsoever the young man pulled down a brown derby and handed it to me, or rather tried to hand it to me. I thought he was trying to be funny, and refused to take the hat into my hands, saying to him, in an attempt to return his compliment and be funny in turn, 'Do you tell bed-time stories also?' He looked at me in surprise, but didn't take the cue which I had offered him.

If I had not observed the young man more closely than he had observed me, and sized him up as an earnest but inexperienced 'extra,' I would have been highly insulted, for if there is anything I hate it is a derby of any sort, much less a brown derby.

One of the regular salesmen happened to see what was going on, walked over and snatched the brown derby out of the young man's hands, and, with a smile on his face intended as a sort of sop to me, said, 'What the hell are you trying to show this gentleman, anyway?'

That spoiled my fun, and the salesman who had immediately recognised me as a gentleman sold me the first hat he brought out.

The customer generally feels complimented when a salesman takes the time to study the customer's personality and lay out merchandise suited to that personality.

I went into one of the largest men's clothing stores in New York City, a few years ago, and asked for a suit, describing exactly what was wanted, but not mentioning price. The young man, who purported to be a salesman, said he did not believe they carried such a suit, but I happened to see exactly what I wanted hanging on a model, and called his attention to the suit. He then made a hit with me by saying, 'Oh, that one over there? That's a high-priced suit!'

His reply amused me; it also angered me, so I inquired of the young man what he saw about me which indicated that I did not come in to purchase a high-priced suit? With embarrassment he tried to explain, but his explanations were as bad as the original offense, and I started toward the door, muttering something to myself about 'dumb-bells.' Before I reached the door I was met by another salesman who had sensed by the way I walked and the expression on my face that I was none too well pleased.

With tact well worth remembering, this salesman engaged me in conversation while I unburdened my woes and then managed to get me to go back with him and look at the suit. Before I left the store I purchased the suit I came in to look at, and two others which I had not intended purchasing.

That was the difference between a salesman and one who drove customers away. Moreover, I later introduced two of my friends to this same salesman and he made sizable sales to each of them.

I was once walking down Michigan Boulevard, in Chicago, when my eye was attracted to a beautiful gray suit in the window of a men's store. I had no notion of buying the suit, but I was curious to know the price, so I opened the door, and, without entering, merely pushed my head inside and asked the first man I saw how much the suit in the window was.

Then followed one of the cleverest bits of sales manoeuvring I have ever observed. The salesman knew he could not sell me the suit unless I came into the store, so he said, 'Will you not step inside, sir, while I find out the price of the suit?'

Of course he knew the price, all the time, but that was his way of disarming me of the thought that he intended trying to sell me the suit. Of course I had to be as polite as the salesman, so I said, 'Certainly,' and walked inside.

The salesman said, 'Step right this way, sir, and I will get the information for you.'

In less than two minutes I found myself standing in front of a case, with my coat off, getting ready to try on a coat like the one I had observed in the window.

After I was in the coat, which happened to fit almost perfectly (which was no accident, thanks to the accurate eyes of an observing salesman) my attention was called to the nice, smooth touch of the material. I rubbed my hand up and down the arm of the coat, as I had seen the salesman do while describing the material, and, sure enough, it was a very fine piece of material. By this time I had again asked the price, and when I was told that the suit was only fifty dollars I was agreeably surprised, because I had been led to believe that it might have been priced much higher. However, when I first saw the suit in the window my guess was that it was priced at about thirty-five dollars, and I doubt that I would have paid that much for it had I not fallen into the hands of a man who knew how to show the suit to best advantage. If the first coat tried on me had been about two sizes too large, or a size too small, I doubt that any sale would have been made, despite the fact that all ready-to-wear suits sold in the better stores are altered to fit the customer.

I bought that suit 'on the impulse of the moment,' as the psychologist would say, and I am not the only man who buys goods on that same sort of impulse. A single slip on the part of the salesman would have lost him the sale of that suit. If he had replied, 'Fifty dollars,' when I asked the price I would have said, 'Thank you,' and have gone my way without looking at the suit.

Later in the season I purchased two more suits from this same salesman, and if I now lived in Chicago the chances are that I would buy still other suits from him, because he always showed me suits that were in keeping with my personality.

The Marshall Field store, in Chicago, gets more for merchandise than does any other store of its kind in the country. Moreover, people knowingly pay more at this store, and feel better satisfied than if they bought the merchandise at another store for less money.

Why is this?

Well, there are many reasons, among them the fact that anything purchased at the Field store which is not entirely satisfactory may be returned and exchanged for other merchandise, or the purchase price may be refunded, just as the customer wishes.

An implied guarantee goes with every article sold in the Field store.

Another reason why people will pay more at the Field store is the fact that the merchandise is displayed and shown to better advantage than it is at most other stores. The Field window-displays are truly works of art, no less than if they were created for the sake of art alone, and not merely to sell merchandise. The same is true of the goods displayed in the store. There is harmony and proper grouping of merchandise throughout the Field establishment, and this creates an 'atmosphere' that is more-much more-than merely an imaginary one.

Still another reason why the Field store can get more for merchandise than most other merchants is due to the careful selection and supervision of salespeople. One would seldom find a person employed in the Field store whom one would not be willing to accept as a social equal, or as a neighbour. Not a few men have made the acquaintance of girls in the Field store who later became their wives.

Merchandise purchased in the Field store is packed or wrapped more artistically than is common in other stores, which is still another reason why people go out of their way and pay higher prices to trade there.

While we are on the subject of artistic wrapping of merchandise I wish to relate the experience of a friend of mine which will not fail to convey a very definite meaning to those engaged in the business of selling, as it shows how imagination may be used even in wrapping merchandise.

This friend had a very fine silver cigarette case which he had carried for years, and of which he was very proud because it was a gift from his wife.

Constant usage had banged the case up rather badly. It had been bent, dented, the hinges warped, etc., until he decided to take it to Caldwell the jeweller, in Philadelphia, to be repaired. He left the case and asked them to send it to his office when it was ready.

About two weeks later a splendid-looking new delivery wagon with the Caldwell name on it drew up in front of his office, and a nice-looking young man in a neat uniform stepped out with a package that was artistically wrapped and tied with a ribbon tape string.

The package happened to be delivered to my friend on his birthday, and, having forgotten about leaving the cigarette case to be repaired, and observing the beauty and size of the package that was handed to him, he naturally imagined that someone had sent him a birthday present.

His secretary and other workers in his office gathered around his desk to watch him open up his 'present.' He cut the ribbon and removed the outer covering. Under this was a covering of tissue paper, fastened with beautiful gold seals bearing the Caldwell initials and trademark. This paper was removed and behold! a most beautiful plush-lined box met his eyes. The box was opened, and, after removing the tissue paper packing, there was a cigarette case which he recognised, after careful examination, as the one he had left to be repaired, but it did not look like the same case, thanks to the imagination of the Caldwell manager.

Every dent had been carefully straightened out. The hinges had been trued and the case had been polished and cleaned so it shone as it did when it was first purchased.

Simultaneously a prolonged 'Oo-o-o-o-o-o-Oh!' of admiration came from the onlookers, including the owner of the cigarette case.

And the bill! Oh, it was a plenty, and yet the price charged for the repair did not seem too high. As a matter of fact everything that entered into the transaction from the packing of the case, with the fine tissue paper cover, the gold seals, the ribbon tape string, the delivery of the package by a neatly uniformed boy, from a well appointed new delivery wagon, was based upon carefully calculated psychology which laid the foundation for a high price for the repair.

People, generally, do not complain of high prices, providing the 'service' or embellishment of the merchandise is such as to pave the way for high prices. What people do complain of, and rightly so, is high prices and 'sloppy' service.

To me there was a great lesson in this cigarette case incident, and I think there is a lesson in it for any person who makes a business of selling any sort of merchandise.

The goods you are selling may actually be worth all you are asking for them, but if you do not carefully study the subjects of advantageous display and artistic packing you may be accused of overcharging your customers.

On Broad Street, in the city of Philadelphia, there is a fruit shop where those who patronize the store are met at the door by a man in uniform who opens the door for them. He does nothing else but merely open the door, but he does it with a smile (even though it be a carefully studied and rehearsed smile) which makes the customer feel welcome even before he gets inside of the store. This fruit merchant specializes on specially prepared baskets of fruit. Just outside the store is a big blackboard on which are listed the sailing dates of the various ocean liners leaving New York City. This merchant caters to people who wish baskets of fruit delivered on board departing boats on which friends are sailing. If a man's sweetheart, or perhaps his wife or a very dear friend, happens to be sailing on a certain date he naturally wants the basket of fruit he purchases for her to be embellished with frills and 'trimmings.' Moreover, he is not necessarily looking for something 'cheap' or even inexpensive.

All of which the fruit merchant capitalizes! He gets from $10.00 to $25.00 for a basket of fruit which one could purchase just around the corner, not more than a block away, for from $3.00 to $7.50, with the exception that the latter would not be embellished with the seventy-five cents' worth of frills which the former contains.

This merchant's store is a small affair, no larger than the average small fruit-stand store, but he pays, a rent of at least $15,000.00 a year for the place and makes more money than half a hundred ordinary fruit stands combined, merely because he knows how to display and deliver his wares so they appeal to the vanity of the buyers. This is but another proof of the value of imagination.

The American people-and this means all of them, not merely the so-called rich-are the most extravagant spenders on earth, but they insist on 'class' when it comes to appearances such as wrapping and delivery and other embellishments which add no real value to the merchandise they buy. The merchant who understands this, and has learned how to mix IMAGINATION with his merchandise, may reap a rich harvest in return for his knowledge.

And a great many are doing it, too.

The salesman who understands the psychology of proper display, wrapping and delivery of merchandise, and who knows how to show his wares to fit the whims and characteristics of his customers, can make ordinary merchandise bring fancy prices, and what is more important still, he can do so and still retain the patronage of his customers more readily than if he sold the same merchandise without the 'studied' appeal and the artistic wrapping and delivery service.

In a 'cheap' restaurant, where coffee is served in heavy, thick cups and the silverware is tarnished or dirty, a ham sandwich is only a ham sandwich, and if the restaurant keeper gets fifteen cents for it he is doing well; but just across the street, where the coffee is served in dainty thin cups, on neatly covered tables, by neatly dressed young women, a much smaller ham sandwich will bring a quarter, to say nothing of the cost of the tip to the waitress. The only difference in the sandwiches is merely in appearances; the ham comes from the same butcher and the bread from the same baker, whether purchased from the former or the latter restaurant. The difference in price is very considerable, but the difference in the merchandise is not a difference of either quality or quantity so much as it is of 'atmosphere,' or appearances.

People love to buy 'appearance' or atmosphere! which is merely a more refined way of saying that which P. T. Barnum said about 'one being born every minute.'

It is no overstatement of fact to say that a master of sales psychology could go into the average merchant's store, where the stock of goods was worth, let us say, $50,000.00, and at very slight additional expense make the stock bring $60,000.00 to $75,000.00. He would do nothing except coach the salespeople on the proper showing of the merchandise, after having purchased a small amount of more suitable fixtures, perhaps, and re-packed the merchandise in more suitable coverings and boxes.

A man's shirt, packed one to the box, in the right sort of a box, with a piece of ribbon and a sheet of, tissue paper added for embellishment, can be made to bring a dollar or a dollar and a half more than the same shirt would bring without the more artistic packing. I know this is true, and I have proved it more times than I can recall, to convince some sceptical merchant who had not studied the effect of 'proper displays.'

Conversely stated, I have proved, many times, that, the finest shirt made cannot be sold for half its value if it is removed from its box and placed on a bargain counter, with inferior looking shirts, both of which examples prove that people do not know what they are buying- that they go more by appearances than they do by actual analysis of the merchandise they purchase.

This is noticeably true in the purchase of automobiles. The American people want, and DEMAND, style in the appearance of automobiles. What is under the hood or in the rear axle they do not know and really do not care, as long as the car looks the part.

Henry Ford required nearly twenty years of experience to learn the truth of the statement just made, and even then, despite all of his analytical ability, he only acknowledged the truth when forced to do so by his competitors. If it were not true that people buy 'appearances' more than they buy 'reality' Ford never would have created his new automobile. That car is the finest sort of example of a psychologist who appeals to the tendency which people have to purchase 'appearance,' although, of course, it must be admitted that in this particular example the real value of the car actually exists.

□

4

Enthusiasm

"You Can Do It if You Believe You Can!"

Enthusiasm is a state of mind that inspires and arouses one to put a c t ion into the task at hand. It does more than this-it is contagious, and vitally affects not only the enthusiast, but all with whom he comes in contact.

Enthusiasm bears the same relationship to a human being that steam does to the locomotive-it is the vital moving force that impels action. The greatest leaders of men are those who know how to inspire enthusiasm in their followers. Enthusiasm is the most important factor entering into salesmanship. It is, by far, the most vital factor that enters into public speaking.

If you wish to understand the difference between a man who is enthusiastic and one who is not, compare Billy Sunday with the average man of his profession. The finest sermon ever delivered would fall upon deaf ears if it were not backed with enthusiasm by the speaker.

How Enthusiasm Will Affect You

Mix enthusiasm with your work and it will not seem hard or monotonous. Enthusiasm will so energize your entire body that you can get along with less than half the usual amount of sleep and at the same time it will enable you to perform from two to three times as much work as you usually perform in a given period, without fatigue.

For many years I have done most of my writing at night. One night, while I was enthusiastically at work over my typewriter, I looked out of the window of my study, just across the square from the Metropolitan tower, in New York City, and saw what seemed to be the most peculiar reflection of the moon on the tower. It was of a silvery gray shade, such as I had never seen before. Upon closer inspection I found that the reflection was that of the early morning sun and not that of the moon. It was daylight! I had been at work all night, but I was so engrossed in my work that the night had passed as though it were but an hour. I worked at my task all that day and all the following night without stopping, except for a small amount of light food.

Two nights and one day without sleep, and with but little food, without the slightest evidence of fatigue, would not have been possible had I not kept my body energized with Enthusiasm over the work at hand.

Enthusiasm is not merely a figure of speech; it is a vital force that you can harness and use with profit. Without it you would resemble an electric battery without electricity.

Enthusiasm is the vital force with which you recharge your body and develop a dynamic personality. Some people are blessed with natural enthusiasm, while others must acquire it. The procedure through which it may be developed is simple. It begins by the doing of the work or rendering of the service which one likes best. If you should be so situated that you cannot conveniently engage in the work which you like best, for the time being, then you can proceed along another line very effectively by adopting a definite chief aim that contemplates your engaging in that particular work at some future time.

Lack of capital and many other circumstances over which you have no immediate control may force you to engage in work which you do not like, but no one can stop you from determining in your own mind what your definite chief aim in life shall be, nor can anyone stop you from planning ways and means for translating this aim into reality, nor can anyone stop you from mixing enthusiasm with your plans.

Happiness, the final object of all human effort, is a state of mind that can be maintained only through the hope of future achievement. Happiness lies always in the future and never in the past. The happy person is the one who dreams of heights of achievement that are yet unattained. The home you intend to own, the money you intend to earn and place in the bank, the trip you intend to take when you can afford it, the' Position in life you intend to fill when you have prepared yourself, and the preparation, itself-these are the things that produce happiness. Likewise, these are the materials out of which your definite chief aim is formed; these are the things over which you may become enthusiastic, no matter what your present station in life may be.

More than twenty years ago I became enthusiastic over an idea. When the idea first took form in my mind I was unprepared to take even the first step toward its transformation into reality. But I nursed it in my mind-I became enthusiastic over it as I looked ahead, in my imagination, and saw the time when I would be prepared to make it a reality.

The idea was this: I wanted to become the editor of a magazine, based upon the Golden Rule, through which I could inspire people to keep up courage and deal with one another squarely.

Finally my chance came! and, on armistice day, 1918, I wrote the first editorial for what was to become the material realisation of a hope that had lain dormant in my mind for nearly a score of years.

With enthusiasm I poured into that editorial the emotions which I had been developing in my heart over a period of more than twenty years. My dream had come true. My editorship of a national magazine had become a reality.

As I have stated, this editorial was written with enthusiasm. I took it to a man of my acquaintance and with enthusiasm I read it to him. The editorial ended in these words: "At last my twenty-year-old dream is about to come true. It takes money, and a lot of it, to publish a national magazine, and I haven't the slightest idea where I am going to get this essential factor, but this is worrying me not at all because I know I am going to get it somewhere!" As I wrote those lines, I mixed enthusiasm and faith with them.

I had hardly finished reading this editorial when the man to whom I read it-the first and only person to whom I had shown it-said:

"I can tell you where you are going to get the money, for I am going to supply it."

And he did!

Yes, enthusiasm is a vital force; so vital, in fact, that no man who has it highly developed can begin even to approximate his power of achievement.

Before passing to the next step in this lesson, I wish to repeat and to emphasize the fact that you may develop enthusiasm over your definite chief aim in life, no matter whether you are in position to achieve that purpose at this time or not. You may be a long way from realisation of your definite chief aim, but if you will kindle the fire of enthusiasm in your heart, and keep it burning, before very long the obstacles that now stand in the way of your attainment of that purpose will melt away as if by the force of magic, and you will find yourself in possession of power that you did not know you possessed.

How Your Enthusiasm Will Affect others

We come, now, to the discussion of one of the most important subjects of this Reading Course, namely, suggestion.

In the preceding lessons we have discussed the subject of Auto-suggestion, which is self-suggestion. You saw, in Lesson Three, what an important part

Auto-suggestion played.

Suggestion is the principle through which your words and your acts and even your state of mind influence others. That you may comprehend the far-reaching power of suggestion, let me refer to the Introductory Lesson, in which the principle of telepathy is described. If you now understand and accept the principle of telepathy (the communication of thought from one mind to another without the aid of signs, symbols or sounds) as a reality, you of course understand why Enthusiasm is contagious, and why it influences all within its radius.

When your own mind is vibrating at a high rate, because it has been stimulated with Enthusiasm, that vibration registers in the minds of all within its radius, and especially in the minds of those with whom you come in close contact. When a public speaker 'senses' the feeling that his audience is 'en rapport' with him he merely recognises the fact that his own Enthusiasm has influenced the minds of his listeners until their minds are vibrating in harmony with his own.

When the salesman 'senses' the fact that the 'psychological' moment for closing a sale has arrived, he merely feels the effect of his own Enthusiasm as it influences the mind of his prospective buyer and places that mind 'en rapport' (in harmony) with his own.

The subject of suggestion constitutes so vitally an important part of this lesson, and of this entire course, that I will now proceed to describe the three mediums through which it usually operates; namely, what you say, what you do and what you think!

When you are enthusiastic over the goods you are selling or the services you are offering, or the speech you are delivering, your state of mind becomes obvious to all who hear you, by the tone of your voice. Whether you have ever thought of it in this way or n o t, it is the tone in which you make a statement, more than it is the statement itself, that carries conviction or fails to convince. No mere combination of words can ever take the place of a deep belief in a statement that is expressed with burning enthusiasm. Words are but devitalized sounds unless collared with feeling that is born of Enthusiasm.

Here the printed word fails me, for I can never express with mere type and paper the difference between words that fall from unemotional lips, without the fire of Enthusiasm back of them, and those which seem to pour forth from a heart that is bursting with eagerness for expression. The difference is there, however.

Thus, what you say, and the way in which you say it, conveys a meaning that may be just the opposite to what is intended. This accounts for many a failure by the salesman who presents his arguments in words which seem logical enough, but lack the colouring that can come only from enthusiasm that is born of sincerity and belief in the goods he is trying to sell. His, words said one thing, but the tone of his voice suggested something entirely different; therefore, no sale was made.

That which you say is an important factor in the operation of the principle of suggestion, but not nearly so important as that which you do. Your acts will count for more than your words, and woe unto you if the two fail to harmonize.

If a man preach the Golden Rule as a sound rule of conduct his words will fall upon deaf ears if he does not practice that which he preaches. The most effective sermon that any man can preach on the soundness of the Golden Rule is that which he p reaches, by suggestion, when he applies this rule in his relationships with his fellow men.

If a salesman of Ford automobiles drives up to his prospective purchaser in a Buick, or some other make of car, all the arguments he can present in behalf of the Ford will be without effect. Once I went into one of the offices of the Dictaphone Company to look at a dictaphone (dictating machine). The salesman in charge presented a logical argument as to the machine's merits, while the stenographer at his side was transcribing letters from a shorthand note-book. His arguments in favour of a dictating machine, as compared with the old method of dictating to a stenographer, did not impress me, because his actions were not in harmony with his words.

Your thoughts constitute the most important of the three ways in which you apply the principle of suggestion, for the reason that they control the tone of your words and, to some extent at least, your actions. If your thoughts and your actions and your words harmonize, you are bound to influence those with whom you come in contact, more or less toward your way of thinking.

We will now proceed to analyse the subject of suggestion and to show you exactly how to apply the principle upon which it operates. As we have already seen, suggestion differs from Auto-suggestion only in one way-we use it, consciously or unconsciously, when we influence others, while we use Auto-suggestion as a means of influencing ourselves.

Before you can influence another person through suggestion, that person's mind must be in a state of neutrality; that is, it must be open and receptive to your method of suggestion. Right here is where most salesmen fail-they try to make a sale before the mind of the prospective buyer has been rendered receptive or neutralized. This is such a vital point in this lesson that I feel impelled to dwell upon it until there can be no doubt that you understand the principle that I am describing.

When I say that the salesman must neutralize the mind of his prospective purchaser before a sale can be made I mean that the prospective purchaser's mind must be credulous. A state of confidence must have been established and it is obvious that there can be no set rule for either establishing confidence or neutralizing the mind to a state of openness. Here the ingenuity of the salesman must supply that which cannot be set down as a hard and fast rule.

I know a life insurance salesman who sells nothing but large policies, amounting to $100,000.00 and upward. Before this man even approaches the subject of insurance with a prospective client he familiarizes himself with the prospective client's complete history, including his education, his financial status, his eccentricities if he has any, his religious preferences and other data too numerous to be listed. Armed with this information, he manages to secure an introduction under conditions which permit him to know the Prospective client in a social as well as a business way. Nothing is said about the sale of life insurance during his first visit, nor his second, and sometimes he does not approach the subject of insurance until he has become very well acquainted with the prospective client.

All this time, however, he is not dissipating his efforts. He is taking advantage of these friendly visits for the purpose of neutralizing his prospective client's mind; that is, he is building up a relationship of confidence so that when the time comes for him to talk life insurance that which he says will fall upon ears that willingly listen.

Some years ago I wrote a book entitled How to Sell Your Services. Just before the manuscript went to the publisher, it occurred to me to request some of the well known men of the United States to write letters of endorsement to be published in the book. The printer was then waiting for the manuscript; therefore, I hurriedly wrote a letter to some eight or ten men, in which I briefly outlined exactly what I wanted, but the letter brought back no replies. I had failed to observe two important prerequisites for success-I had written the letter so hurriedly that I had failed to inject the spirit of enthusiasm into it, and, I had neglected so to word the letter that it had the effect of neutralizing the minds of those to whom it was sent; therefore, I had not paved the way for the application of the principle of suggestion.

After I discovered my mistake, I then wrote a letter that was based upon strict application of the principle of suggestion, and this letter not only brought back replies from all to whom it was sent, but many of the replies were masterpieces and served, far beyond my fondest hopes, as valuable supplements to the book. For the purpose of comparison, to show you how the principle of suggestion may be used in writing a letter, and what an important part enthusiasm plays in giving the written word 'flesh,' the two letters are here reproduced. It will not be necessary to indicate which letter failed, as that will be quite obvious:

My dear Mr. Ford:

I am just completing a manuscript for a new book entitled How to Sell Your Services. I anticipate the sale of several hundred thousand of these books and I believe those who purchase the book would welcome the opportunity of receiving a message from you as to the best method of marketing personal services.

Would you, therefore, be good enough to give me a few minutes of your time by writing a brief message to be published in my book?

This will be a big favour to me personally and I know it would be appreciated by the readers of the book.

Thanking you in advance for any consideration you may care to show me, I am,

> **Yours very truly,**
> **Hon. Thomas R. Marshall,**

Vice-President of the United States, Washington, D.C.

My dear Mr. Marshall:

Would you care for the opportunity to send a message of encouragement, and possibly a word of advice, to a few hundred thousand of your fellow men who have failed to make their mark in the world as successfully as you have done?

I have about completed a manuscript for a book to be entitled How to Sell Your Services. The main point made in the book is that service rendered is cause and the pay envelope is effect; and that the latter varies in proportion to the efficiency of the former.

The book would be incomplete without a few words of advice from a few men who, like yourself, have come up from the bottom to enviable positions in the world. Therefore, if you will write me of your views as to the most essential points to be borne in mind by those who are offering personal services for sale I will pass your message on through my book, which will insure its getting into hands where it will do a world of good for a class of earnest people who are struggling to find their places in the world's work.

I know you are a busy man, Mr. Marshall, but please bear in mind that by simply calling in your secretary and dictating a brief letter you will be sending forth an important message to possibly half a million people. In money this will not be worth to you the two cent stamp that you will place on the letter, but, if estimated from the viewpoint of the good it may do others who are less fortunate than yourself, it may be worth the difference between success and failure to many a worthy person who will read your message believe in it, and be guided by it.

Very cordially yours,

Now, let us analyse the two letters and find out why one failed in its mission while the other succeeded. This analysis should start with one of the most important fundamentals of salesmanship, namely motive. In the first letter it is obvious that the motive is entirely one of self-interest. The letter states exactly what is wanted, but the wording of it leaves a doubt as to w h y the request is made or whom it is intended, to benefit. Study the sentence in the second paragraph, 'This will be a big favour to me personally, etc.' Now it may seem to be a peculiar trait, but the truth is that most people will not grant favours just to please others. If I ask you to render a service that will benefit me, without bringing you some corresponding advantage, you will not show much enthusiasm in granting that favour; you may refuse altogether if you have a plausible excuse for refusing. But if I ask you to render a service that will benefit a third person, even though the service must be rendered through me; and if that service is of such a nature that it is likely to reflect credit on you, the chances are that you will render the service willingly.

We see this psychology demonstrated by the man who pitches a dime to the beggar on the street, or perhaps refuses even the dime, but willingly hands over a hundred or a thousand dollars to the charity worker who is begging in the name of others.

But the most damaging suggestion of all is contained in the last and most important paragraph of the letter, "Thanking you in advance for any consideration you may care to show me." This sentence strongly suggests that the writer of the letter anticipates a refusal of his request. It clearly indicates lack of enthusiasm. It paves the way for a refusal of the request. There is not one single word in the entire letter that places in the mind of a man to whom it is sent a satisfactory reason why he should comply with the request. On the other hand, he can clearly see that the object of the letter is to secure from him a letter of endorsement that will help sell the book. The most important selling argument-in fact, the only selling argument available in connection with this request, has been lost because it was not brought out and established as the real motive for making the request.

This argument was but faintly mentioned in the sentence, "I believe those who purchase the book would welcome the opportunity of receiving a message from you as to the best method of marketing personal services."

The opening paragraph of the letter violates an important fundamental of salesmanship because it clearly suggests that the object of the letter is to gain some advantage for its writer, and does not even hint at any corresponding advantage that may accrue to the person to whom it is sent. Instead of neutralizing the mind of the recipient of the letter, as it should do, it has just the opposite effect; it causes him to close his mind against all argument that follows; it puts him in a frame of mind that makes it easy for him to say no. It reminds me of a salesman-or, perhaps I should say, a man who wanted to be a salesman-who once approached me for the purpose of selling me a subscription to the Saturday Evening Post. As he held a copy of the magazine in front of me he suggested the answer I should make by this question:

"You wouldn't subscribe for the Post to help me out, would you?"

Of course I said no! He had made it easy for me to say no. There was no enthusiasm back of his words, and gloom and discouragement were written all over his face. He needed the commission he would have made on my subscription had I purchased; no doubt about that-but he suggested nothing that appealed to my self-interest motive, therefore he lost a sale. But the loss of this one sale was not the sad part of his misfortune; the sad part was that this same attitude was causing him to lose all other sales which he might have made had he changed his approach.

A few weeks later another subscription agent approached me. She was selling a combination of six magazines, one of which was the Saturday Evening Post, but how different was her approach. She glanced at my library table, on which she saw several magazines, then at my book shelves, and exclaimed with enthusiasm: "Oh! I see you are a lover of books and magazines."

I proudly pleaded guilty to the charge. Observe the word 'proudly,' for it has an important bearing on this incident. I laid down the manuscript that I was reading when this saleswoman came in, for I could see that she was a woman of intelligence. Just how I came to see this I will leave to your imagination. The important point is that I laid down the manuscript and actually felt myself wanting to hear what she had to say.

With the aid of eleven words, plus a pleasant smile, plus a tone of genuine enthusiasm, she had neutralized my mind sufficiently to make me want to hear her. She had performed her most difficult task, with those few words, because I had made up my mind when she was announced that I would keep my manuscript in my hands and thereby convey to her mind, as politely as I could, the fact that I was busy and did not wish to be detained.

Being a student of salesmanship and of suggestion, I carefully watched to see what her next move would be. She had a bundle of magazines under her arm and I expected she would unroll it and begin to urge me to purchase, but she didn't. You will recall that I said she was selling a combination of six magazines; not merely trying to sell them.

She walked over to my book shelves, pulled out a copy of Emerson's Essays, and for the next ten minutes she talked about Emerson's essay on Compensation so interestingly that I lost sight of the roll of magazines that she carried. (She was neutralizing my mind some more.)

Incidentally, she gave me a sufficient number of new ideas about Emerson's works to provide material for an excellent editorial.

Then she asked me which magazines I received regularly, and after I told her she smiled as she began to unroll her bundle of magazines and laid them on the table in front of me. She analysed her magazines one by one, and explained just why I should have each of them. The Saturday Evening Post would bring me the cleanest fiction; Literary Digest would bring me the news of the world in condensed form, such as a busy man like myself would demand; the American Magazine would bring me the latest biographies of the men who were leading in business and industry, and so on, until she had covered the entire list.

But I was not responding to her argument as freely as she thought I should have, so she slipped me this gentle suggestion:

"A man of your position is bound to be well informed and, if he isn't, it will show up in his own work!"

She spoke the truth! Her remark was both a compliment and a gentle reprimand. She made me feel somewhat sheepish because she had taken inventory of my reading matter-and six of the leading magazines were not on my list. (The six that she was selling.)

Then I began to 'slip' by asking her how much the six magazines would cost. She put on the finishing touches of a well presented sales talk by this tactful reply: "The cost? Why, the cost of the entire number is less than you receive for a single page of the typewritten manuscript that you had in your hands when I came in."

Again she spoke the truth. And how did she happen to guess so well what I was getting for my manuscript? The answer is, she didn't guess-she knew! She made it a part of her business to draw me out tactfully as to the nature of my work (which in no way made me angry). She became so deeply interested in the manuscript which I had laid down when she came in, that she actually induced me to talk about it. (I am not saying, of course, that this required any great amount of skill or coaxing, nor have I not said that it was my manuscript?) In my remarks about that manuscript, I suspect I admitted that I was receiving $250.00 for the fifteen pages; yes, I am sure I was careless enough to admit that I was being well paid for my work.

Perhaps she induced me to make the admission. At any rate, the information was valuable to her and she made effective use of it at the psychological moment. For all I know it was a part of her plan to observe carefully all that she saw and heard, with the object of finding out just what my weaknesses were and what I was most interested in discussing. Some salesmen take the time to do this; some do not. She was one of those who did.

Yes, she went away with my order for the six magazines; also my twelve dollars. But that was not all the benefit she derived from tactful suggestion plus enthusiasm; she got my consent to canvass my office, and before she left she had five other orders from my employees.

At no time during her stay did she leave the impression that I was favoring her by purchasing her magazines. Just to the contrary, she distinctly impressed me with the feeling that she was rendering me a favour. This was tactful suggestion.

Before we get away from this incident, I wish to make an admission-when she drew me into conversation she did it in such a way that I talked with enthusiasm. There were two reasons for this. She was one of them; and the other one was the fact that she managed to get me to talk about my own work! Of course I am not suggesting that you should be meddlesome enough to smile at my carelessness as you read this; or that you should gather from this incident the impression that this tactful saleswoman actually led me to talk of my own work for the purpose of neutralizing my mind so that I would listen to her, when she was ready to talk of her magazines, as patiently as she had listened to me. However, if you should be clever enough to draw a lesson from her method, there is no way for me to stop you from doing so.

As I have stated, when I talked I mixed enthusiasm with my conversation. Perhaps I caught the spirit of enthusiasm from this clever saleswoman, when she made that opening remark as she came into my study. Yes, I am sure this is where I caught it, and, I am just as sure that her enthusiasm was not a matter of accident. She had trained herself to look for something in her prospective purchaser's office, or his work, or his conversation, over which she could express Enthusiasm.

Remember, suggestion and Enthusiasm go hand in hand!

I can remember, as though it were yesterday, the feeling that came over me when that would-be salesman pushed that Saturday Evening Post in front of me, as he remarked:

"You wouldn't subscribe for the Post to help me out, would you?"

His words were chilled, they were lifeless; they lacked enthusiasm; they registered an impression in my mind, but that impression was one of coldness. I wanted to see the man go out at the door at which he had come in. Mind you, I am not naturally unsympathetic, but the tone of his voice, the look on his face, his general bearing suggested that he was there to ask a favour and not to offer one.

Suggestion is one of the most subtle and powerful principles of psychology. You are making use of it in all that you do and say and think, but, unless you understand the difference between negative suggestion and positive suggestion, you may be using it in such a way that it is bringing you defeat instead of success.

Science has established the fact that through the negative use of suggestion life may be extinguished. Some years ago, in France, a criminal was condemned to death, but before the time for his execution an experiment was performed on him which conclusively proved that through the principle of suggestion death, could be produced. The criminal was brought to the guillotine and his head was placed under the knife, after he had been blindfolded. A heavy, sharp edged plank was then dropped on his neck, producing a shock similar to that of a sharp edged knife. Warm water was then gently poured on his neck and allowed to trickle slowly down his spine, to imitate the flow of warm blood. In seven minutes the doctors pronounced the man dead. His imagination, through the principle of suggestion, had actually turned the sharp edged plank into a guillotine blade and stopped his heart from beating.

In the little town where I was raised, there lived an old lady who constantly complained that she feared death from cancer. During her childhood she had seen a woman who had cancer and the sight had so impressed itself upon her mind that she began to look for the symptoms of cancer in her own body. She was sure that every little ache and pain was the beginning of her long-looked-for symptom of cancer. I have seen her place her hand on her breast and have heard her exclaim, "Oh, I am sure I have a cancer growing here. I can feel it." When complaining of this imaginary disease, she always placed her hand on her left breast, where she believed the cancer was attacking her.

For more than twenty years she kept this up.

A few weeks ago she died-with cancer on her left breast! If suggestion will actually turn the edge of a plank into a guillotine blade and transform healthy body cells into parasites out of which cancer will develop, can you not imagine what it will do in destroying disease germs, if properly directed? Suggestion is the law through which mental healers work what appear to be miracles. I have personally witnessed the removal of parasitical growths known as warts, through the aid of suggestion, within forty-eight hours.

You-the reader of this lesson-can be sent to bed with imaginary sickness of the worst sort, in two hours' time or less, through the use of suggestion. If you should start down the street and three or four people in whom you had confidence should meet you and each exclaim that you look ill you would be ready for a doctor. This brings to mind an experience that I once had with a life insurance salesman. I had made application for a policy, but was undecided as to whether I would take ten or twenty thousand dollars. Meanwhile, the agent had sent me to the life insurance company's doctor to be examined. The following day I was called back for another examination. The second time the examination was more searching, and the doctor carried a worried look on his face. The third day I was called back again, and this time two consulting physicians were there to look me over. They gave me the most searching examination I had ever received or even heard of.

The next day the agent called on me and addressed me as follows:

"I do not wish to alarm you! but the doctors who examined you do not agree on your analysis. You have not yet decided whether you will take ten or twenty thousand dollars' worth of insurance, and I do not think it fair for me to give you a report on your medical examination until you make this decision, because if I did you might feel that I was urging you to take the larger amount"

Then I spoke up and said: "Well, I have already decided to take the full amount." True enough; I had decided to take the full twenty thousand dollar policy.

I decided the moment the agent planted the suggestion in my mind that perhaps I had some constitutional weakness that would make it hard for me to get as much insurance as I wanted.

'Very well,' said the agent, "now that you have decided I feel it my duty to tell you that two of the doctors believe you have the tubercular germ in your system, while the other two disagree with them." The trick had been turned. Clever suggestion had pushed me over the fence of indecision and we were all satisfied.

Where does enthusiasm come in, do you ask? Never mind, it 'came in' all right, but if you wish to know who brought it you will have to ask the life insurance agent and his four medical accomplices, for I am sure they must have had a hearty laugh at my expense. But the trick was all right. I needed the insurance anyway.

Of course, if you happen to be a life insurance agent you will not grab this idea and work stouten the next prospective client who is slow in making up his mind about taking a policy. Of course you will not!

A few months ago I received one of the most effective pieces of advertising I ever saw. It was a neat little book in which a clever automobile insurance salesman had reprinted press dispatches that he had gathered from all over the country, in which it was shown that sixty-five automobiles had been stolen in a single day. On the back page of the book was this highly suggestive statement:

"Your car may be the next one to go. Is it insured?"

At the bottom of the page was the salesman's name and address; also his telephone number. Before I had finished reading the first two pages of the book I called the salesman on the telephone and made inquiry about rates. He came right over to see me, and you know the remainder of the story.

Go back, now, to the two letters and let us analyse the second one, which brought the desired replies from all to whom it was sent. Study, carefully, the first paragraph and you will observe that it asks a question which can be answered in but one way. Compare this opening paragraph with that of the first letter, by asking yourself which of the two would have impressed you most favourably. This paragraph is worded as it is for a two-fold purpose; first, it is intended to serve the purpose of neutralizing the mind of the reader so he will read the remainder of the letter in an open-minded attitude; and, second, it asks a question which can be answered in but one way, for the purpose of committing the reader to a viewpoint which harmonizes with the nature of the service that he is to be requested to render in subsequent paragraphs of the letter.

In the second lesson of this course you observed that Andrew Carnegie refused to answer my question, when I asked him to what he attributed his success, until he had asked me to define the word success. He did this to avoid misunderstanding. The first paragraph of the letter we are analyzing is so worded that it states the object of the letter and at the same time practically forces the reader to accept that object as being sound and reasonable.

Any person who would answer the question asked in this paragraph of the letter under discussion, in the negative, would, by the same answer, convict himself on the charge of selfishness, and no man wants to face himself with a guilty conscience on such a charge. Just as the farmer first plows his ground, then fertilizes it, and perhaps harrows it and prepares it to receive the seed, in order that he may be sure of a crop, so does this paragraph fertilize the mind of the reader and prepare it for the seed which is to be placed there through the subtle suggestion that the paragraph contains.

Study, carefully, the second paragraph of the letter and you will observe that it carries a statement of fact which the reader can neither question nor deny! It provides him with no reason for argument because it is obviously based upon a sound fundamental. It takes him the second step of the psychological journey that leads straight toward compliance with the request that is carefully clothed and covered up in the third paragraph of the letter, but you will notice that the third paragraph begins by paying the reader a nice little compliment that was not designed to make him angry. "Therefore, if you will write me of your views as to the most essential points to be borne in mind by those who are offering personal services for sale," etc., Study the wording of this sentence, together with the setting in which it has been placed, and you will observe that it hardly appears to be a request at all, and certainly there is nothing about it to suggest that the writer of the letter is requesting a favour for his personal benefit. At most, it can be construed merely as a request for a favour for others.

Now study the closing paragraph and notice how tactfully concealed is the suggestion that if the reader should refuse the request he is placing himself in the awkward position of one who does not care enough about those who are less fortunate than himself to spend a two cent stamp and a few minutes of time for their benefit.

From start to finish the letter conveys its strongest impressions by mere suggestion, yet this suggestion is so carefully covered that it is not obvious except upon careful analysis of the entire letter.

The whole construction of the letter is such that if the reader lays it aside without complying with the request it makes he will have to reckon with his own conscience! This effect is intensified by the last sentence of the last paragraph and especially by the last thirteen words of that sentence, "who will read your message, believe in it, and be guided by it."

This letter brings the reader up with a bang and turns his own conscience into an ally of the writer; it corners him, just as a hunter might corner a rabbit by driving it into a carefully prepared net.

The best evidence that this analysis is correct is the fact that the letter brought replies from every person to whom it was sent, despite the fact that every one of these men was of the type that we speak of as being a man of affairs-the type that is generally supposed to be too busy to answer a letter of this nature. Not only did the letter bring the desired replies, but the men to whom it was sent replied in person, with the exception of the late Theodore Roosevelt, who replied under the signature of a secretary.

John Wanamaker and Frank A. Vanderlip wrote two of the finest letters I have ever read, each a mast ear piece that might well have adorned the pages of a more dignified volume than the one for which the letters were requested. Andrew Carnegie also wrote a letter that was well worth consideration by all who have personal services for sale. William Jennings Bryan wrote a fine letter, as did, also, the late

Lord Northcliffe. None of these men wrote merely to please me, for I was unknown to all of them, with the exception of four. They did not write to please me-they wrote to please themselves and to render a worthy service. Perhaps the wording of the letter had something to do with this, but, as to that, I make no point other than to state that all of these men whom I have mentioned, and most others of their type, are generally the most willing men to render service for others when they are properly approached.

I wish to take advantage of this appropriate opportunity to state that all of the really big men whom I have had the pleasure of knowing have been the most willing and courteous men of my acquaintance when it came to rendering service that was of benefit to others. Perhaps that was one reason why they were really big men.

The human mind is a marvellous piece of machinery!

One of its outstanding characteristics is noticed in the fact that all impressions which reach it, either through outside suggestion or Auto-suggestion, are recorded together in groups which harmonize in nature. The negative impressions are stored away, all in one portion of the brain, while the positive impressions are stored in another portion. When one of these impressions (or past experiences) is called into the conscious mind, through the principle of memory, there is a tendency to recall with it all others of a similar nature, just as the raising of one link of a chain brings up other links with it. For example, anything that causes a feeling of doubt to arise in a person's mind is sufficient to call forth all of his experiences which caused him to become doubtful. If a man is asked by a stranger to cash a check, immediately he remembers having cashed checks that were not good, or of having heard of others who did so. Through the law of association all similar emotions, experiences and sense impressions that reach the mind are filed away together, so that the recalling of one has a tendency to bring back to memory all the others.

To arouse a feeling of distrust in a person's mind has a tendency to bring to the surface every doubt-building experience that person ever had. For this reason successful salesmen endeavour to keep away from the discussion of subjects that may arouse the buyer's 'chain of doubt impressions' which he has stored away by reason of previous experiences. The successful salesman quickly learns that 'knocking' a competitor or a competing article may result in bringing to the buyer's mind certain negative emotions growing out of previous experiences which may make it impossible for the salesman to 'neutralize" the buyer's mind.

This principle applies to and controls every sense impression that is lodged in the human mind. Take the feeling of fear, for example; the moment we permit a single emotion that is related to fear to reach the conscious mind, it calls with it all of its unsavoury relations. A feeling of courage cannot claim the attention of the conscious mind while a feeling of fear is there. One or the other must dominate. They make poor room-mates because they do not harmonize in nature. Like attracts like. Every thought held in the conscious mind has a tendency to draw to it other thoughts of a similar nature. You see, therefore, that these feelings, thoughts and emotions growing out of past experiences, which claim the attention of the conscious mind, are backed by a regular army of supporting soldiers of a similar nature, that stand ready to aid them in their work.

Deliberately place in your own mind, through the principle of Auto-suggestion, the ambition to succeed through the aid of a definite chief aim, and notice how quickly all of your latent or undeveloped ability in the nature of past experiences will become stimulated and aroused to action in your behalf. Plant in a boy's mind, through the principle of suggestion, the ambition to become a successful lawyer or doctor or engineer or business man or financier, and if you plant that suggestion deeply enough, and keep it there, by repetition, it will begin to move that boy toward the achievement of the object of that ambition.

If you would plant a suggestion 'deeply,' mix it generously with enthusiasm; for enthusiasm is the fertilizer that will insure its rapid growth as well as its permanency.

When that kind-hearted old gentleman planted in my mind the suggestion that I was a 'bright boy' and that I could make my mark in the world if I would educate myself, it was not so much what he said, as it was the way in which he said it that made such a deep and lasting impression on my mind. It was the way in which he gripped my shoulders and the look of confidence in his eyes that drove his suggestion so deeply into my subconscious mind that it never gave me any peace until I commenced taking the steps that led to the fulfillment the suggestion.

This is a point that I would stress with all the power at my command. It is not so much what you say as it is the TONE and MANNER in which you say it that makes. a lasting impression.

It naturally follows, therefore, that sincerity of purpose, honesty and earnestness must be placed back of all that one says if one would make a lasting and favourable impression.

Whatever you successfully sell to others you must first sell to yourself!

Not long ago I was approached by an agent of the government of Mexico who sought my services as a writer of propaganda for the administration in charge at that time. His approach was about as follows:

"Whereas, Senior has a reputation as an exponent of the Golden Rule philosophy; and whereas, Señor is known throughout the United States as an independent who is not allied with any political faction, now, therefore, would Señor be gracious enough to come to Mexico, study the economic and political, affairs of that country, then return to the United States and write a series of articles to appear in the newspapers, recommending to the people of America the immediate recognition of Mexico by the government of the United States, etc."

For this service, I was offered more money than I shall, perhaps, ever possess during my entire life; but I refused the commission, and for a reason that will fail to impress anyone except those who understand the principle which makes it necessary for all who would influence others to remain on good terms with their own conscience.

I could not write convincingly of Mexico's cause for the reason that I did not believe in that cause; therefore, I could not have mixed sufficient enthusiasm with my writing to have made it effective, even though I had been willing to prostitute my talent and dip my pen into ink that I knew to be muddy.

I will not endeavour further to explain my philosophy on this incident for the reason that those who are far enough advanced in the study of Auto-suggestion will not need further explanation, while those who are not far enough advanced would not and could not understand.

No man can afford to express, through words or acts, that which is not in harmony with his own belief, and if he does so he must pay by the loss of his ability to influence others.

Please read, aloud, the foregoing paragraph! It is worth emphasizing by repetition, for lack of observation of the principle upon which it is based constitutes the rocks and reefs upon which many a man's definite chief aim dashes itself to pieces.

I do not believe that I can afford to try to deceive anyone, about anything, but I know that I cannot afford to try to deceive myself. To do so would destroy the power of my pen and render my words ineffective. It is only when I write with the fire of enthusiasm burning in my heart that my writing impresses others favourably; and it is only when I speak from a heart that is bursting with belief in my message, that I can move my audience to accept that message.

IS there not food for thought in the fact that no newspaper has ever published any account of 'Wild drinking parties' or other similar scandals in connection with the names of Edison, Ford, Rockefeller and most of the other really big fellows?

I would also have you read, aloud, the foregoing paragraph. Yes, I would have you commit it to memory. Even more than this, I would have you write it out and place it where it may serve as a daily reminder of a principle, nay, alawas immutable as the law of gravitation, without which you can never become a power in your chosen life-work.

There have been times, and many of them, when it appeared that if I stood by this principle it would mean starvation!

There have been times when my closest friends and business advisers have strongly urged me to shade my philosophy for the sake of gaining a needed advantage here and there, but somehow I have managed to cling to it, mainly, I suppose, for the reason that I have preferred peace and harmony in my own heart to the material gain that I might have had by a forced compromise with my conscience.

Strange as it may seem, my deliberations and conclusions on this subject of refusing to strangle my own conscience have seldom been based upon what is commonly called 'honesty.' That which I have done in the matter of refraining from writing or speaking anything that I did not believe has been solely a question of honour between my conscience and myself. I have tried to express that which my heart dictated because I have aimed to give my words 'flesh.' It might be said that my motive was based more upon self-interest than it was on a desire to be fair with others, although I have never desired to be unfair with others, so far as I am able to analyse myself.

No man can become a master salesman if he compromises with falsehood. Murder will out, and even though no one ever catches him red-handed in expressing that which he does not believe, his words will fail in the accomplishment of their purpose because he cannot give them 'flesh,' if they do not come from his heart, and if they are not mixed with genuine, unadulterated Enthusiasm.

I would also have you read, aloud, the foregoing paragraph, for it embraces a great law that you must understand and apply before you can become a person of influence in any undertaking.

In making these requests, for the sake of emphasis, I am not trying to take undue liberties with you. I am giving you full credit for being an adult, a thinker,: an intelligent person, yet I know how likely you are to skip over these vital laws without being sufficiently impressed by them to make them a part of your own workaday philosophy. I know your weakness because I know my own. It has required the better part of twenty-five years of ups and downs-mostly downs-to impress these basic truths upon my own mind so' that they influenced me. I have tried both them and their opposites; therefore, I can speak, not as one who merely believes in their soundness, but as one who knows.

And what do I mean by 'these truths'?

So that you cannot possibly misunderstand my meaning, and so that these words of warning cannot possibly convey an abstract meaning, I will state that by 'these truths' I mean this:

You cannot afford to suggest to another person, by word of mouth or by an act of yours, that which you do not believe.

Surely that is plain enough.

And, there as on you cannot afford to do so, is this:

If you compromise with your own conscience, it will not be long before you will have no conscience; for your conscience will fail to guide you, just as an alarm clock will fail to awaken you if you do not heed it.

Surely, that is plain enough, also.

And how do I happen to be an authority on this vital subject, do you ask?

I am an authority because I have experimented with the principle until I know how it works!

'But,' you may ask, 'how do I know that you are telling the truth?'

The answer is that you will know only by experimenting for yourself, and by observing others who faithfully apply this principle and those who do not apply it.

If my evidence needs backing, then consult any man whom you know to be a person who has 'tried to get by' without observing this principle, and if he will not or cannot give you the truth you can get it, nevertheless, by analyzing the man.

There is but one thing in the world that gives a man real and enduring power, and that is character! Reputation, bear in mind, is not character. Reputation is that which people are believed to be; character is that which people are! If you would be a person of great influence, then be a person of real character.

Character is the philosopher's lode-stone through which all who have it may turn the base metals of their life into pure gold. Without character you have nothing; you are nothing; and you can be nothing, except a pile of flesh and bone and hair, worth perhaps twenty-five dollars. Character is something that you cannot beg or steal or buy. You can get it only by building it; and you can build it by your own thoughts and deeds, and in no other way.

Through the aid of Auto-suggestion, any person can build a sound character, no matter what his past has been. As a fitting close for this lesson, I wish to emphasize the fact that all who have character have enthusiasm and personality sufficient to draw to them others who have character.

You will now be instructed as to how you shall proceed in developing enthusiasm, in the event that you do not already possess this rare quality.

The instructions will be simple, but you will be unfortunate if you discount their value on that account.

First: Complete the remaining lessons of this course, because other important instructions which are to be coordinated with this one will be found in subsequent lessons.

Second: If you have not already done so, write out your definite chief aim in clear, simple language, and follow this by writing out the plan through which you intend to transform your aim into reality.

Third: Read over the description of your definite chief aim each night, just before retiring, and as you read, see yourself (in your imagination) in full possession of the object of your aim. Do this with full faith in your ability to transform your definite chief aim into reality. Read aloud, with all the enthusiasm at your command, emphasizing every word. Repeat this reading until the small still voice within you tells you that your purpose will be realised. Sometimes you will feel the effects of this voice from within the first time you read your definite chief aim; while another times, you may have to read it a dozen or fifty times before the assurance comes, but do not stop until you feel it.

If you prefer to do so you may read your definite chief aim as a prayer.

The remainder of this lesson is for the person who has not yet learned the power of faith and who knows little or nothing of the principle of auto-suggestion.

To all who are in this class, I would recommend the reading of the seventh and eighth verses of the seventh chapter, and the twentieth verse of the seventeenth chapter of St. Matthew.

One of the greatest powers for good, upon the face of this earth, is faith. To this marvellous power may be traced miracles of the most astounding nature. It offers peace on earth to all who embrace it.

Faith involves a principle that is so far-reaching in its effect that no man can say what are its limitations, or if it has limitations. Write into the description of your definite chief aim a statement of the qualities that you intend to develop in yourself, and the station in life that you intend to attain, and have faith, as you read this description each night, that you can transform this purpose into reality.

Surely, you cannot miss the suggestion contained in this lesson.

To become successful you must be a person of action. Merely to 'know' is not sufficient. It is necessary both to know and do.

Enthusiasm is the mainspring of the mind which urges one to put knowledge into action.

Billy Sunday is the most successful evangelist this country has ever known. For the purpose of studying his technique and checking up on his psychological methods the author of this course went through three campaigns with Reverend Sunday.

His success is based very largely upon one word-

ENTHUSIASM!

By making effective use of the law of suggestion Billy Sunday conveys his own spirit of enthusiasm to the minds of his followers and they become influenced by it. He sells his sermons by the use of exactly the same sort of strategy employed by many Master Salesmen.

Enthusiasm is as essential to a salesman as water is to a duck!

All successful sales managers understand the psychology of enthusiasm and make use of it, in various ways, as a practical means of helping their men produce more sales.

Practically all sales organisations have get-together meetings at stated times, for the purpose of revitalizing the minds of all members of the sales force, and injecting the spirit of enthusiasm, which can be best done en masse, through group psychology.

Sales meetings might properly be called 'revival' meetings, because their purpose is to revive interest and arouse enthusiasm which will enable the salesman to take up the fight with renewed ambition and energy.

During his administration as Sales Manager of the National Cash Register Company Hugh Chalmers (who later became famous in the motor car industry) faced a most embarrassing situation which threatened to wipe out his position as well as that of thousands of salesmen under his direction.

The company was in financial difficulty. This fact had become known to the salesmen in the field and the effect of it was to cause them to lose their Enthusiasm. Sales began to dwindle until finally the conditions became so alarming that a general meeting of the sales organisation was called, to be held at the company's plant in Dayton, Ohio. Salesmen were called in from all over the country.

Mr. Chalmers presided over the meeting. He began by calling on several of his best salesmen to get on their feet and tell what was wrong out in the field that orders had fallen off. One by one they got up, as called, and each man had a most terrible tale of grief to unfold: Business conditions were bad, money was scarce, people were holding off buying until after Presidential election, etc. As the fifth man began to enumerate the difficulties which had kept him from making his usual quota of sales Mr. Chalmers jumped up on top of a table, held up his hands for silence, and said 'STOP! I order this convention to come to a close for ten minutes while I get my shoes shined.'

Then turning to a small collared boy who sat nearby he ordered the boy to bring his shoe-shine outfit and shine his shoes, right where he stood, on top of the table.

The salesmen in the audience were astounded! Some of them thought that Mr. Chalmers had suddenly lost his mind. They began to whisper among themselves. Meanwhile, the little collared boy shined first one and then the other shoe, taking plenty of time and doing a first-class job.

After the, job was finished Mr. Chalmers handed the boy a dime, then went ahead with his speech:

'I want each of you,' said he, 'to take a good look at this little collared boy. He has the concession for shoe-shining throughout our plant and offices. His predecessor was a white boy, considerably older than himself, and despite the fact that the company subsidized him with a salary of $5.00 a week he could not make a living in this plant, where thousands of people are employed.

"This little collared boy not only makes a good living, without any subsidy from the company, but he is actually saving money out of his earnings each week, working under the same conditions, in the same plant, for the same people.

"Now I wish to ask you a question: Whose fault was it that the white boy did not get more business? Was it his fault, or the fault of his buyers?"

In a mighty roar from the crowd the answer came back:

"IT WAS THE BOY'S FAULT, OF COURSE!" 'Just so,' replied Chalmers, "and now I want to tell you this, that you are selling Cash Registers in the same territory, to the same people, with exactly the same business conditions that existed a year ago, yet you are not producing the business that you were then. Now whose fault is that? Is it yours, or the buyer's?"

And again the answer came back with a roar:

"IT IS OUR FAULT, OF COURSE!"

"I am glad that you are frank to acknowledge your faults," Chalmers continued, "and I now wish to tell you what your trouble is: You have heard rumours about this company being in financial trouble and that has killed off your enthusiasm so that you are not making the effort that you formerly made. If you will go back into your territories with a definite promise to send in five orders each during the next thirty days this company will no longer be in financial difficulty, for that additional business will see us clear. Will you do it?"

They said they would, and they did!

That incident has gone down in the history of the National Cash Register Company under the name of Hugh Chalmers' Million Dollar Shoe Shine, for it is said that this turned the tide in the company's affairs and was worth millions of dollars.

Enthusiasm knows no defeat! The Sales Manager who knows how to send out an army of enthusiastic salespeople may set his own price on his services, and what is more important even than this, he can increase the earning capacity of every person under his direction; thus, his enthusiasm benefits not only himself but perhaps hundreds of others.

Enthusiasm is never a matter of chance. There are certain stimuli which produce enthusiasm, the most important of these being as follows:

1. Occupation in work which one loves best.
2. Environment where one comes in contact with others who are enthusiastic and optimistic.
3. Financial success.
4. Complete mastery and application, in one's daily work, of the Fifteen Laws of Success.
5. Good health.
6. Knowledge that one has served others in some helpful manner.
7. Good clothes, appropriate to the needs of one's occupation.

All of these seven sources of stimuli are self-explanatory with the exception of the last. The psychology of clothes is understood by very few people, and for this reason it will be here explained in detail. Clothes constitute the most important part of the embellishment which every person must have in order to feel self-reliant, hopeful and enthusiastic.

The Psychology of Good Clothes

When the good news came from the theatre of war, on November the eleventh, 1918, my worldly possessions amounted to but little more than they did the day I came into the world.

The war had destroyed my business and made it necessary for me to make a new start!

My wardrobe consisted of three well worn business suits and two uniforms which I no longer needed.

Knowing all too well that the world forms its first and most lasting impressions of a man by the clothes he wears, I lost no time in visiting my tailor.

Happily, my tailor had known me for many years, therefore he did not judge me entirely by the clothes I wore. If he had I would have been 'sunk. '

With less than a dollar in change in my pocket, I picked out the cloth for three of the most expensive suits I ever owned, and ordered that they be made up for me at once.

The three suits came to $375.00!

I shall never forget the remark made by the tailor as he took my measure. Glancing first at the three bolts of expensive cloth which I had selected, and then at me, he inquired:

'Dollar-a-year man, eh?'

ALL anyone really requires, as a capital on which to start a successful career, is a sound mind, a healthy body and a genuine desire to be of as much service as possible to as many people as possible.

'No,' said I, "if I had been fortunate enough to get on the dollar-a-year payroll I might now have enough money to pay for these suits."

The tailor looked at me with surprise. I don't think he got the joke.

One of the suits was a beautiful dark gray; one was a dark blue; the other was a light blue with a pin stripe.

Fortunately I was in good standing with my tailor, therefore he did not ask when I was going to pay for those expensive suits.

I knew that I could and would pay for them in due time, but could I have convinced him of that? This was the thought which was running through my mind, with hope against hope that the question would not be brought up.

I then visited my haberdasher, from whom I purchased three less expensive suits and a complete supply of the best shirts, collars, ties, hosiery and underwear that he carried.

My bill at the haberdasher's amounted to a little over $300.00.

With an air of prosperity I nonchalantly signed the charge ticket and tossed it back to the salesman, with instructions to deliver my purchase the following morning. The feeling of renewed self-reliance and success had begun to come over me, even before I had attired myself in my newly purchased outfit.

I was out of the war and $675.00 in debt, all in less than twenty-four hours.

The following day the first of the three suits ordered from the haberdasher was delivered. I put it on at once, stuffed a new silk handkerchief in the out-side pocket of my coat, shoved the $50.00 I had borrowed on my ring down into my pants pocket, and walked down Michigan Boulevard, in Chicago, feeling as rich as Rockefeller.

Every article of clothing I wore, from my underwear out, was of the very best. That it was not paid for was nobody's business except mine and my tailor's and my haberdasher's.

Every morning I dressed myself in an entirely new outfit, and walked down the same street, at precisely the same hour. That hour 'happened' to be the time when a certain wealthy publisher usually walked down, the same street, on his way to lunch.

I made it my business to speak to him each day, and occasionally I would stop for a minute's chat with him.

After this daily meeting had been going on for about a week I met this publisher one day, but decided I would see if he would let me get by without speaking.

Watching him from under my eyelashes I looked straight ahead, and started to pass him when he stopped and motioned me over to the edge of the sidewalk, placed his hand on my shoulder, looked me over from head to foot, and said: 'You look damned prosperous for a man who has just laid aside a uniform. Who makes your clothes?'

'Well,' said I, 'Wilkie & Sellery made this particular suit.'

He then wanted to know what sort of business I was engaged in. That 'airy' atmosphere of prosperity which I had been wearing, along with a new and different suit every day, had got the better of his curiosity. (I had hoped that it would.)

Flipping the ashes from my Havana perfecto, I said 'Oh, I am preparing the copy for a new magazine that I am going to publish.'

'A new magazine, eh?' he queried, 'and what are you going to call it?'

'It is to be named Hill's Golden Rule.'

'Don't forget,' said my publisher friend, "that I am in the business of printing and distributing magazines. Perhaps I can serve you, also."

That was the moment for which I had been waiting. I had that very moment, and almost the very spot of ground on which we stood, in mind when I was purchasing those new suits.

But, is it necessary to remind you, that conversation never would have taken place had this publisher observed me walking down that street from day to day, with a 'whipped-dog' look on my face, an unpressed suit on my back and a look of poverty in my eyes.

An appearance of prosperity attracts attention always, with no exceptions whatsoever. Moreover, a look of prosperity attracts 'favourable attention,' because the one dominating desire in every human heart is to be prosperous.

My publisher friend invited me to his club for lunch. Before the coffee and cigars had been served he had 'talked me out of' the contract for printing and distributing my magazine. I had even 'consented' to permit him to supply the capital, without any interest charge.

For the benefit of those who are not familiar with the publishing business may I not offer the information that considerable capital is required for launching a new nationally distributed magazine.

Capital, in such large amounts, is often hard to get, even with the best of security. The capital necessary for launching Hill's Golden Rule Magazine, which you may have read, was well above $30,000.00, and every cent of it was raised on a 'front' created mostly by good clothes. True, there may have been some ability back of those clothes, but many millions of men have ability who never have anything else, and who are never heard of outside of the limited community in which they live. This is a rather sad truth!

To some it may seem an unpardonable extravagance for one who was 'broke' to have gone in debt for $675.00 worth of clothes, but the psychology back of that investment more than justified it.

The appearance of prosperity not only made a favourable impression on those to whom I had to look for favours, but of more importance still was the effect that proper attire HAD ON ME.

I not only knew that correct clothes would impress others favourably, but I knew also that good clothes would give me an atmosphere of self-reliance, without which I could not hope to regain my lost fortunes.

I got my first training in the psychology of good clothes from my friend Edwin C. Barnes, who is a close business associate of Thomas A. Edison. Barnes afforded considerable amusement for the Edison staff when, some twenty-odd years ago, he rode into West Orange on a freight train (not being able to raise sufficient money for passenger fare) and announced at the Edison offices that he had come to enter into a partnership with Mr. Edison.

Nearly everybody around the Edison plant laughed at Barnes, except Edison himself. He saw something in the square jaw and determined face of young Barnes which most of the others did not see, despite the fact that the young man looked more like a tramp than he did a future partner of the greatest inventor on earth.

Barnes got his start, sweeping floors in the Edison offices!

That was all he sought-just a chance to get a toehold in the Edison organisation. From there on he made history that is well worth emulation by other young men who wish to make places for themselves.

Barnes has now retired from active business, even though he is still a comparatively young man, and spends most of his time at his two beautiful homes in Bradentown, Florida, and Damariscotta, Maine. He is a multimillionaire, prosperous and happy.

I first became acquainted with Barnes during the early days of his association with Edison, before he had 'arrived.'

In those days he had the largest and most expensive collection of clothes I had ever seen or heard of one man owning. His wardrobe consisted of thirty-one suits; one for each day of the month. He never wore the same suit two days in succession.

Moreover, all his suits were of the most expensive type. (Incidentally, his clothes were made by the same tailors who made those three suits for me.)

He wore socks which cost six dollars per pair.

There is a suitable reward for every virtue and appropriate punishment for every sin a man commits. Both the reward and the punishment are effects over which no man has control, as they come upon him voluntarily.

His shirts and other wearing apparel cost in similar proportion. His cravats were specially made, at a cost of from five to seven dollars and a half each.

One day, in a spirit of fun, I asked him to save some of his old suits which he did not need, for me.

He informed me that he hadn't a single suit which he did not need!

He then gave me a lesson on the psychology of clothes which is well worth remembering. 'I do not wear thirty-one suits of clothes,' said he, "entirely for the impression they make on other people; I do it mostly for the impression they have on me."

Barnes then told me of the day when he presented himself at the Edison plant, for a position. He said he had to walk around the plant a dozen times before he worked up enough courage to announce himself, because he knew that he looked more like a tramp than he did a desirable employee.

Barnes is said to be the most able salesman ever connected with the great inventor of West Orange. His entire fortune was made through his ability as a salesman, but he has often said that he never could have accomplished the results which have made him both wealthy and famous had it not been for his understanding of the psychology of clothes.

I have met many salesman in my time. During the past ten years I have personally trained and directed the efforts of more than 3,000 salespeople, both men and women, and I have observed that, without a single exception, the star producers were all people who understood and made good use of the psychology of clothes.

I have seen a few well dressed people who made no outstanding records as salesmen, but I have yet to see the first poorly dressed man who became a star producer in the field of selling.

I have studied the psychology of clothes for so long, and I have watched its effect on people in so many different walks of life, that I am fully convinced there is a close connection between clothes and success.

Personally I feel no need of thirty-one suits of clothes, but if my personality demanded a wardrobe of this size I would manage to get it, no matter how much it might cost.

To be well dressed a man should have at least ten suits of clothes. He should have a different suit for each of the seven days of the week, a full dress suit and a Tuxedo, for formal evening occasions, and a cutaway for formal afternoon occasions.

For summer wear he should have an assortment of at least four appropriate light suits, with blue coat and white flannel trousers for informal afternoon and evening occasions. If he plays golf he should have at least one golf suit.

This, of course, is for the man who is a notch or two above the 'mediocre' class. The man who is satisfied with mediocrity needs but few clothes.

It may be true, as a well known poet has said, that 'clothes do not make the man,' but no one can deny the fact that good clothes go a very long way toward giving him a favourable start.

A man's bank will generally loan him all the money he wants when he does not need it-when he is prosperous, but never go to your bank for a loan with a shabby-looking suiton your back and a look of poverty in your eyes, for if you do you'll get the gate.

Success attracts success! There is no escape from this great universal law; therefore, if you wish to attract success make sure that you look the part of success, whether your calling is that of day labourer or merchant prince.

For the benefit of the more 'dignified' students of this philosophy who may object to resorting to 'stunt' stimuli or 'trick clothing' as a means of achieving success, it may be profitably explained that practically every successful man on earth has discovered some form of stimulus through which he can and does drive himself on to greater effort.

It may be shocking to members of the Anti-Saloon League, but it is said to be true, nevertheless, that James Whitcomb Riley wrote his best poems when he was under the influence of alcohol. His stimulus was liquor. (The author wishes it distinctly understood that he does not recommend the use of alcoholic or narcotic stimuli, for any purpose whatsoever, as either will eventually destroy both body and mind of all who use them.) Under the influence of alcohol Riley became imaginative, enthusiastic and an entirely different person, according to close personal friends of his.

Edwin Barnes spurred himself into the necessary action to produce outstanding results, with the aid of good clothes.

Some men rise to great heights of achievement as the result of love for some woman. Connect this with the brief suggestion to the subject which was made in the Introductory Lesson and you will, if you are a person who knows the ways of men, be able to finish the discussion of this particular phase of enthusiasm stimulus without further comment by the author which might not be appropriate for the younger minds that will assimilate this philosophy.

Underworld characters who are engaged in the dangerous business of highway robbery, burglary, etc., generally 'dope' themselves for the occasion of their operations, with cocaine, morphine and other narcotics. Even in this there is a lesson which shows that practically all men need temporary or artificial stimuli to drive them to greater effort than that normally employed in the ordinary pursuits of life.

HEIGHTS OF ENDEAVOR ABOVE THE ORDINARY. One of the most successful writers in the world employs an orchestra of beautifully dressed young women who play for him while he writes. Seated in a room that has been artistically decorated to suit his own taste, under lights that have been collared, tinted and softened, these beautiful young ladies, dressed in handsome evening gowns, play his favourite music. To use his own words, "I become drunk with enthusiasm, under the influence of this environment, and rise to heights I never know or feel on other occasions. It is then that I do my work. The thoughts pour in on me as if they were dictated by an unseen and unknown power."

This author gets much of his inspiration from music and art. Once a week he spends at least an hour in an art museum, looking at the works of the masters.

On these occasions, again using his own words, "I get enough enthusiasm from one hour's visit in the museum of art to carry me for two days."

Edgar Allan Poe wrote 'The Raven' when, it is reported, he was more than half intoxicated. Oscar Wilde wrote his poems under the influence of a form of stimulus which cannot be appropriately mentioned in a course of this nature.

Henry Ford (so it is believed by this author, who admits that this is merely the author's opinion) got his real start as the result of his love for his charming life-companion. It was she who inspired him, gave him faith in himself, and kept him keyed up so that he carried on in the face of adversities which would have killed off a dozen ordinary men.

These incidents are cited as evidence that men of outstanding achievement have, by accident or design, discovered ways and means of stimulating themselves to a high state of enthusiasm.

Associate that which has been here stated with what was said concerning the law of the 'Master Mind,' in the Introductory Lesson, and you will have an entirely new conception of the modus operandi through which that law may be applied. You will also have a somewhat different understanding of the real purpose of "allied effort, in a spirit of perfect harmony," which constitutes the best known method of bringing into use the Law of the Master Mind.

Your employer does not control the sort of service you render. You control that, and it is the thing that makes or breaks you.

At this point it seems appropriate to call your attention to the manner in which the lessons of this course blend. You will observe that each lesson covers the subject intended to be covered, and in addition to this it overlaps and gives the student a better understanding of some other lesson or lessons of the course.

In the light of what has been said in this lesson, for example, the student will better understand the real purpose of the Law of the Master Mind; that purpose being, in the main, a practical method of stimulating the minds of all who participate in the group constituting the Master Mind.

Times too numerous to be here described this author has gone into conference with men whose faces showed the signs of care, who had the appearance of worry written all over them, only to see those same men straighten up their shoulders, tilt their chins at a higher angle, soften their faces with smiles of confidence, and get down to business with that sort of ENTHUSIASM which knows no defeat.

The change took place the moment harmony of purpose was established.

If a man goes about the affairs of life in the same day-in and day-out, prosaic, lackadaisical spirit, devoid of enthusiasm, he is doomed to failure. Nothing can save him until he changes his attitude and learns how to stimulate his mind and body to unusual heights of enthusiasm AT WILL!

The author is unwilling to leave this subject without having stated the principle here described in so many different ways that it is bound to be understood and also respected by the students of this course, who, all will remember, are men and women of all sorts of natures, experiences and degrees of intelligence. For this reason much repetition is essential.

Your business in life, you are reminded once again, is to achieve success!

With the stimulus you will experience from studying this philosophy, and with the aid of the ideas you will gather from it, plus the personal co-operation of the author who will give you an accurate inventory of your outstanding qualities, you should be able to create a DEFINITE PLAN that will lift you to great heights of achievement. However, there is no plan that can produce this desirable result without the aid* of some influence that will cause you to arouse yourself, in a spirit of enthusiasm, to where you will exert greater than the ordinary effort which you put into your daily occupation.

You are now ready for the lesson on Self-control! As you read that lesson you will observe that it has a vital bearing on this lesson, just as this lesson

has a direct connection with the preceding lessons on A Definite Chief Aim, self-confidence, Initiative and Leadership and Imagination.

The next lesson describes the Law which serves as the balance wheel of this entire philosophy.

The Seven Deadly Horsemen

An After-the-Lesson Visit With the Author

The 'seven horsemen' are labelled, in order shown, Intolerance, Greed, Revenge, Egotism, Suspicion, Jealously and ?

The worst enemy that any man has is the one that walks around under his own hat.

If you could see yourself as others see you the enemies that you harbour in your own personality might be discovered and thrown out. The Seven Enemies named in this essay are the commonest which ride millions of men and women to failure without being discovered. Weigh yourself carefully and find out how many of the Seven you are harbouring.

You see, in this picture, seven deadly warriors! From birth until death every human being must give battle to these enemies. Your success will be measured very largely by the way you manage your battle against these swift riders.

If these enemies rode openly, on real horses, they would not be dangerous, because they could be rounded up and put out of commission. But, they ride unseen, in the minds of men. So silently and subtly do they work that most people never recognise their presence.

Take inventory of yourself and find out how many of these seven horsemen you are harbouring.

In the foreground you will find the most dangerous and the commonest of the riders. You will be fortunate if you discover this enemy and protect yourself against it. This cruel warrior, INTOLERANCE, has killed more people, destroyed more friendships, brought more misery and suffering into the world and caused more wars than all of the other six horsemen that you see in this picture.

Until you master INTOLERANCE you will never become an accurate thinker. This enemy of mankind closes up the mind and pushes reason and logic and FACTS into the back-ground. If you find yourself hating those whose religious viewpoint is different from your own you may be sure that the most dangerous of the seven deadly horsemen still rides in your brain.

Next, in the picture, you will observe REVENGE and GREED!

These riders travel side by side. Where one is found the other is always close at hand. GREED warps and twists man's brain so that he wants to build a fence around the earth and keep everyone else on the outside of it. This is the enemy that drives man to accumulate millions upon top of millions of dollars which he does not need and can never use. This is the enemy that causes man to twist the screw until he has wrung the last drop of blood from his fellow man.

And, thanks to REVENGE which rides alongside of GREED, the unfortunate person who gives brain-room to these cruel twins is not satisfied to merely take away his fellow man's earthly belongings; he wants to destroy his reputation in the bargain.

"Revenge is a naked sword-
It has neither hilt nor guard.
Would'st thou wield this brand of the Lord:

Is thy grasp then firm and hard?
But the closer thy clutch of the blade,
The deadlier blow thou would'st deal,
Deeper wound in thy hand is made-
It is thy blood reddens the steel.
And when thou hast dealt the blow-
When the blade from thy hand has flown-
Instead of the heart of the foe
Thou may'st find it sheathed in thine own."

If you would know how deadly are ENVY and GREED, study the history of every man who has set out to become RULER OF THIS WORLD!

If you do not wish to undertake so ambitious a program of research, then study the people around YOU; those who have tried and those who are now trying to 'feather their own nests' at the cost of others. GREED and REVENGE stand at the crossroads of life, where they turn aside to failure and misery every person who would take the road that leads to success. It is a part of your business not to permit them to interfere with you when you approach one of these crossroads.

Both individuals and nations rapidly decline where GREED and ENVY ride in the minds of those who dominate. Take a look at Mexico and Spain if you wish to know what happens to the envious and the greedy.

Most important of all, take a look at YOURSELF and make sure that these two deadly enemies are not riding in your brain!——

Turn your—attention,—now,—to—two—more twins of destruction-EGOTISM and SUSPICION. Observe that they, also, ride side by side. There is no hope of success for the person who suffers either from too much self-love or lack of confidence in others.

Someone who likes to manipulate figures has estimated that the largest club in the world is the 'IT CAN'T BE DONE CLUB.' It is claimed that there are approximately ninety-nine million members of this club in the United States of America alone.

If you have no FAITH in other people you have not the seed of success in you. SUSPICION is a prolific germ. If permitted to get a start it rapidly multiplies itself until it leaves no room for FAITH.

Make no mistake about it-those who have all they want, including happiness and good health, have driven the seven horsemen out of their brains.

Come back to this essay a month from now, after you have had time to analyse yourself carefully. Read it again and it may bring you face to face with FACTS that will emancipate you from a horde of cruel enemies that now ride within your brain without your knowing it.

□

5

Self-Control

"You Can Do It if You Believe You Can!"

In the preceding lesson you learned of the value of enthusiasm. You also learned how to generate enthusiasm and how to transmit its influence to others, through the principle of suggestion.

You come, now, to the study of self-control, through which you may direct your Enthusiasm to constructive ends. Without self-control enthusiasm resembles the unharnessed lightning of an electrical storm-it may strike anywhere; it may destroy life and property.

Enthusiasm is the vital quality that arouses you to action, while self-control is the balance wheel that directs your action so that it will build up and not tear down.

To be a person who is well 'balanced,' you must be a person in whom enthusiasm and self-control are equalized. A survey which I have just completed of the 160,000 adult inmates of the penitentiaries of the United States discloses the startling fact that ninety-two per cent of these unfortunate men and women are in prison because they lacked the necessary self-control to direct their energies constructively.

Read the foregoing paragraph again; it is authentic, it is startling!

It is a fact that the majority of a man's grief's come about through lack of self-control. The holy scriptures are full of admonition in support of self-control. They even urge us to love our enemies and to forgive those who injure us. The law of non-resistance runs, like a golden cord, throughout the Bible.

Study the records of those whom the world calls great, and observe that every one of them possesses this quality of self-control!

For example, study the characteristics of our own immortal Lincoln. In the midst of his most trying hours he exercised patience, poise and self-control. These were some of the qualities which made him the great man that he was. He found disloyalty in some of the members of his cabinet; but, for the reason that this disloyalty was toward him, personally, and because those in whom he found it had qualities which made them valuable to his country, Lincoln exercised self-control and disregarded the objectionable qualities.

How many men do you know who have self-control to equal this?

In language more forceful than it was polished, Billy Sunday exclaimed from the pulpit: "There is something as rotten as hell about the man who is always trying to show some other fellow up!" I wonder if the 'devil' didn't yell, 'Amen, brother!' when Billy made that statement?

However, self-control becomes an important factor in this Reading Course on The Law of Success, not so much because lack of it works hardships on those who become its victims, as for the reason that those who do not exercise it suffer the loss of a great power which they need in their struggle for achievement of their definite chief aim.

If you neglect to exercise self- control, you are not only likely to injure others, but you are sure to injure yourself!

During the early part of my public career I discovered what havoc lack of self- control was playing in my life, and this discovery came about through a very commonplace incident. (I believe it not out of place here to digress by making the statement that most of the great truths of life are wrapped up in the ordinary, commonplace events of every-day life.)

This discovery taught me one of the most important lessons I have ever learned. It came about in this way:

One day, in the building in which I had my office, the janitor and I had a misunderstanding. This led to a most violent form of mutual dislike between us. As a means of showing his contempt for me, this janitor would switch off the electric lights of the building when he knew that I was there alone at work in my study. This happened on several occasions until I finally decided to 'strike back.' My opportunity came one Sunday when I came to my study to prepare an address that I had to deliver the following night. I had hardly seated myself at my desk when off went the lights.

I jumped to my feet and ran toward the basement of the building where I knew I would find the janitor.

When I arrived, I found him busily engaged, shoveling coal into the furnace, and whistling as though nothing unusual had happened.

Without ceremony I pitched into him, and for five minutes I hurled adjectives at him which were hotter than the fire that he was feeding. Finally, I ran out of words and had to slow down. Then he straightened himself up, looked back over his shoulder, and in a calm, smooth tone of voice that was full of poise and self-control, and with a smile on his face that reached from ear to ear, he said:

'Why, you-all's just a little bit excited this morning, isn't you?'

That remark cut as though it had been a stiletto 1 Imagine my feelings as I stood there before an illiterate man who could neither read nor write, but who, despite this handicap, had defeated me in a duel that had been fought on grounds-and with a weapon-of my own choice.

My conscience pointed an accusing finger at me. I knew that not only had I been defeated but, what was worse, I knew that I was the aggressor and that I was in the wrong, which only served to intensify my humiliation.

Not only did my conscience point an accusing finger at me, but it placed some very embarrassing thoughts in my mind; it mocked me and it tantalized me. There I stood, a boasted student of advanced psychology, an exponent of the Golden Rule philosophy, having at least a fair acquaintance with the works of Shakespeare, Socrates, Plato, Emerson and the Bible; while facing me stood a man who knew nothing of literature or of philosophy, but who had, despite this lack of knowledge, whipped me in a battle of words.

I turned and went back to my office as rapidly as I could go. There was nothing else for me to do. As I began to think the matter over I saw my mistake, but, true to nature, I was reluctant to do that which I knew must be done to right the wrong. I knew that I would have to apologize to that man before I could place myself at peace in my own heart, much less with him. Finally, I made up my mind to go back down to the basement and suffer this humility which I knew I had to undergo. The decision was not easily reached, nor did I reach it quickly.

I started down, but I walked more slowly than I had when I went down the first trip. I was trying to think how I would make the second approach so as to suffer the least humiliation possible.

When I got to the basement I called to the janitor to come over to the door. In a calm, kindly tone of voice he asked:

'What do you wish this time?'

I informed him that I had come back to apologize for the wrong I had done, if he would permit me to do so. Again that smile spread all over his face as he said:

'For the love of the Lord, you don't have to apologize. Nobody heard you except these four walls and you and me. I isn't going to tell it and I know you isn't going to tell it, so just forget it.'

And that remark hurt more than his first one, for he had not only expressed a willingness to forgive me, but he had actually indicated his willingness to help me cover the incident up, so it would not become known and do me an injury.

The man who actually knows just what he wants in life has already gone a long way toward attaining it.

But I walked over to him and took him by the hand. I shook with more than my hand-I shook with my heart-and as I walked back to my office I felt good for having summoned the courage with which to right the wrong I had done.

This is not the end of the story. It is only the beginning! Following this incident, I made a resolution that I would never again place myself in a position in which another man, whether he be an illiterate janitor or a man of letters, could humiliate me because I had lost my self-control.

Following that resolution, a remarkable change began to take place in me. My pen began to take on greater power. My spoken words began to carry greater weight. I began to make more friends and fewer enemies among men of my acquaintance. The incident marked one of the most important turning-points of my life. It taught me that no man can control others unless he first controls himself. It gave me a clear conception of the philosophy back of these words, "Whom the gods would destroy, they first make mad." It also gave me a clear conception of the law of non-resistance and helped me interpret many passages of the holy scriptures, bearing on the subject of this law, as I had never before interpreted them.

This incident placed in my hands the pass-key to a storehouse of knowledge that is illuminating and helpful in all that I do, and, later in life, when enemies sought to destroy me, it gave me a powerful weapon of defence that has never failed me.

Lack of self-control is the average salesman's most damaging weakness. The prospective buyer says something that the salesman does not wish to hear, and, if he has not this quality of self-control, he will 'strike back' with a counter remark that is fatal to his sale.

In one of the large department stores of Chicago I witnessed an incident that illustrated the importance of self-control. A long line of women were in front of the 'complaint' desk, telling their troubles and the store's faults to the young woman in charge. Some of the women were angry and unreasonable and some of them made very ugly remarks. The young woman at the desk received the disgruntled women without the slightest sign of resentment at their remarks. With a smile on her face she directed these women to the proper departments with such charming grace and poise that I marvelled at her self-control.

Standing just back of her was another young woman who was making notations on slips of paper and passing them in front of her, as the women in the line unburdened their troubles. These slips of paper contained the gist of what the women in the line were saying, minus the 'vitriolic colouring' and the anger.

The smiling young woman at the desk who was 'hearing' the complaints was stone deaf! Her assistant supplied her with all the necessary facts, though those slips of paper.

I was so impressed with the plan that I sought the manager of the store and interviewed him. He informed me that he had selected a deaf woman for one of the most trying and important positions in the store for the reason that he had not been able to find any other person with sufficient self-control to fill the place.

As I stood and watched that line of angry women, I observed what pleasant effect the smile of the young woman at the desk had upon them. They came before her growling like wolves and went away as meek and quiet as sheep. In fact some of them had 'sheepish' looks on their faces as they left, because the young woman's self-control had made them ashamed of themselves.

Ever since I witnessed that scene, I have thought of the poise and self-control of that young woman at the desk every time I felt myself becoming irritated at remarks which I did not like, and often I have thought that everybody should have a set of 'mental ear muffs' which they could slip over their ears at times. Personally, I have developed the habit of 'closing' my ears against much of the idle chatter such as I used to make it my business to resent. Life is too short and there is too much constructive work to be done to justify us in 'striking back' at everyone who says that which we do not wish to hear.

In the practice of law I have observed a very clever trick that trial lawyers use when they wish to get a statement of facts from a belligerent witness who answers questions with the proverbial 'I do not remember' or 'I do not know.' When everything else fails, they manage to make such a witness angry; and in this state of mind they cause him to lose his self-control and make statements that he would not have made had he kept a 'cool' head.

Most of us go through life with our 'weather eye' cast skyward in quest of trouble. We usually find that for which we are looking. In my travels I have been a student of men whom I have heard in 'Pullman car conversation,' and I have observed that practically nine out of every ten have so little self-control that they will 'invite' themselves into the discussion of almost any subject that may be brought up. But few men are contented to sit in a smoking compartment and listen to a conversation without joining in and 'airing' their views.

Once I was travelling from Albany to New York City. On the way down, the 'Smoking Car Club' started a conversation about the late Richard Croker, who was then chief of Tammany Hall. The discussion became loud and bitter. Everyone became angry except one old gentleman who was agitating the argument and taking a lively interest in it. He remained calm and seemed to enjoy all the mean things the others said about the 'Tiger' of Tammany Hall. Of course, I supposed that he was an enemy of the Tammany Chief, but he wasn't!

He was Richard Croker, himself!

This was one of his clever tricks through which he found out what people thought of him and what his enemies' plans were.

Whatever else Richard Croker might have been, he was a man of self- control. Perhaps that is one reason why he remained undisputed boss of Tammany Hall as long as he did. Men who control themselves usually boss the job, no matter what it may be.

Please read, again, the last sentence of the preceding paragraph, for it carries a subtle suggestion that might be of profit to you. This is a commonplace incident, but it is in just such incidents that the great truths of life are hidden-hidden because the settings are ordinary and commonplace.

Not long ago I accompanied my wife on a 'bargain hunting' bee. Our attention was attracted by a crowd of women who were elbowing each other out of the way in front of a petticoat counter at which 'bargains' were being offered. One lady who looked to be about forty-five years of age crawled on her hands and knees through the crowd and 'bobbed' up in front of a customer who had engaged the attention of the saleswoman ahead of her. In a loud, high-pitched tone of voice she demanded attention. The saleswoman was a diplomat who understood human nature; she also possessed self-control, for she smiled sweetly at the intruder and said: 'Yes, Miss ; I will be with you in a moment!'

The intruder calmed herself!

I do not know whether it was the 'Yes, Miss,' or the sweet tone in which it was said that modified her attitude; but it was one or the other; perhaps it was both. I do know, however, that the saleswoman was rewarded for her self-control by the sale of three petticoats, and the happy 'Miss "went away feeling much younger for the remark.

Roast turkey is a very popular dish, but overeating of it cost a friend of mine, who is in the printing business, a fifty thousand dollar order. It happened the day after Thanksgiving, when I called at his office for the purpose of introducing him to a prominent Russian who had come to the United States to publish a book. The Russian spoke broken English and it was therefore hard for him to make himself easily understood. During the interview he asked my printer friend a question which was mistaken as a reflection upon his ability as a printer. In an unguarded moment he countered with this remark:

No man can rise to fame and fortune without carrying others along with him. It simply cannot be done.

"The trouble with you Bolsheviks is that you look with suspicion on the remainder of the world just because of your own short-sightedness."

My 'Bolshevik' friend nudged me on the elbow and whispered:

"The gentleman seems to be sick. We shall call again, when he is feeling better."

But, he never called again. He placed his order with another printer, and I learned afterward that the profit on that order was more than $10,000.00!

Ten thousand dollars seems a high price to pay for a plate of turkey, but that is the price that it cost my printer friend; for he offered me an apology for his conduct on the ground that his turkey dinner had given him indigestion and therefore he had lost his self-control.

One of the largest chain store concerns in the world has adopted a unique, though effective, method of employing salespeople who have developed the essential quality of self-control which all successful salespeople must possess. This concern has in its employ a very clever woman who visits department stores and other places where salespeople are employed and selects certain ones whom she believes to possess tact and self-control; but, to be sure of her judgment, she approaches these salespeople and has them show her their wares. She asks all sorts of questions that are designed to try their patience. If they stand the test, they are offered better positions; if they fail in the test, they have merely allowed a good opportunity to pass by without knowing it.

No doubt all people who refuse or neglect to exercise self-control are literally turning opportunity after opportunity away without knowing it. One day I was standing at the glove counter of a large retail store talking to a young man who was employed there. He was telling me that he had been with the store four years, but on account of the 'short-sightedness' of the store, his services had not been appreciated and he was looking for another position. In the midst of this conversation a customer walked up to him and asked to see some hats. He paid no attention to the customer's inquiry until he had finished telling me his troubles, despite the fact that the customer was obviously becoming impatient. Finally, he returned to the customer and said: 'This isn't the hat department.' When the customer inquired as to where he might find that department the young man replied: "Ask the floor-walker over there; he will direct you."

For four years this young man had been standing on top of a fine opportunity but he did not know it. He could have made a friend of every person whom he served in that store and these friends could have made him one of the most valuable men in the store, because they would have come back to trade with him. 'Snappy' answers to inquiring customers do not bring them back.

One rainy afternoon an old lady walked into a Pittsburgh department store and wandered around in an aimless sort of way, very much in the manner that people who have no intention of buying often do. Most of the salespeople gave her the 'once over' and busied themselves by straightening the stock on their shelves so as to avoid being troubled by her. One of the young men saw her and made it his business to inquire politely if he might serve her. She informed him that she was only waiting for it to stop raining; that she did not wish to make any purchases. The young man assured her that she was welcome, and by engaging her in conversation made her feel that he had meant what he said. When she was ready to go he accompanied her to the street and raised her umbrella for her. She asked for his card and went on her way.

The incident had been forgotten by the young man when, one day, he was called into the office by the head of the firm and shown a letter from a lady who wanted a salesman to go to Scotland and take an order for the furnishings for a mansion.

That lady was Andrew Carnegie's mother; she was also the same woman whom the young man had so courteously escorted to the street many months previously.

In the letter, Mrs. Carnegie specified that this young man was the one whom she desired to be sent to take her order. That order amounted to an enormous sum, and the incident brought the young man an opportunity for advancement that he might never have had except for his courtesy to an old lady who did not look like a 'ready sale.'

Just as the great fundamental laws of life are wrapped up in the commonest sort of every-day experiences that most of us never notice, so are the real opportunities often hidden in the seemingly unimportant transactions of life.

Ask the next ten people whom you meet why they have not accomplished more in their respective lines of endeavour, and at least nine of them will tell you that opportunity does not seem to come around their w a y. Go a step further and analyse each of these nine accurately by observing their actions for one single day, and the chances are that you will find that every one of them is turning away the finest sort of opportunities every hour of the day.

One day I went to visit a friend who was associated with a Commercial School, in the capacity of solicitor. When I asked him how he was getting along he replied: "Rotten! I see a large number of people but I am not making enough sales to give me a good living. In fact my account with the school is overdrawn and I am thinking about changing positions as there is no opportunity here."

It happened that I was on my vacation and had ten days' time that I could use as I wished, so I challenged his remark that he had no opportunity by telling him that I could turn his position into $250.00 in a week's time and show him how to make it worth that every week thereafter. He looked at me in amazement and asked me not to joke with him over so serious a matter. When he was finally convinced that I was in earnest he ventured to inquire how I would perform the 'miracle.'

Then I asked him if he had ever heard of organised effort, to which he replied: 'What do you mean by organised effort?' I informed him that I had reference to the direction of his efforts in such a manner that he would enrol from five to ten students with the same amount of effort that he had been putting into the enrolment of one or of none. He said he was willing to be shown, so I gave him instructions to arrange for me to speak before the employees of one of the local department stores. He made the appointment and I delivered the address. In my talk I outlined a plan through which the employees could not only increase their ability so that they could earn more money in their present positions, but it also offered them an opportunity to prepare themselves for greater responsibilities and better positions. Following my talk, which of course was designed for that purpose, my friend enrolled eight of those employees for night courses in the Commercial School which he represented.

The following night he booked me for a similar address before the employees of a laundry, and following the address he enrolled three more students, two of them young women who worked over the washing machines at the hardest sort of labour.

Two days later he booked me for an address before the employees of one of the local banks, and following the address he enrolled four more students, making a total of fifteen students, and the entire time consumed was not more than six hours, including the time required for the delivery of the addresses and the enrolment of the students.

My friend's commission on the transactions was a little over four hundred dollars!

These places of employment were within fifteen minutes' walk of this man's place of business, but he had never thought of looking there for business. Neither had he ever thought of allying himself with a speaker who could assist him in 'group' selling. That man now owns a splendid Commercial School of his own, and I am informed that his net income last year was over $10,000.00.

'No opportunities' come your way? Perhaps they come but you do not see them. Perhaps you will see them in the future as you are preparing yourself, through the aid of this Reading Course on The Law of Success, so that you can recognise an opportunity when you see it. The sixth lesson of this course is on the subject of imagination, which was the chief factor that entered into the transaction that I have just related. Imagination, plus a Definite Plan, plus Self-confidence, plus Action, were the main factors that entered into this transaction. You now know how to use all of these, and before you shall have finished this lesson you will understand how to direct these factors through self-control.

Now let us examine the scope of meaning of the term self-control, as it is used in connection with this course, by describing the general conduct of a person who possesses it. A person with well-developed self-control does not indulge in hatred, envy, jealousy, fear, revenge, or any similar destructive emotions. A person with well-developed self-control does not go into ecstasies or become ungovernably enthusiastic over anything or anybody.

Greed and selfishness and self-approval beyond the point of accurate self-analysis and appreciation of one's actual merits, indicate lack of self-control in one of its most dangerous forms. Self-confidence is one of the important essentials of success, but when this faculty is developed beyond the point of reason it becomes very dangerous.

Self-sacrifice is a commendable quality, but when it is carried to extremes, it, also, becomes one of the dangerous forms of lack of self-control.

You owe it to yourself—not to permit your e motions to place your happiness in the keeping of another person. Love is essential for happiness, but the person who loves so deeply that his or her happiness is placed entirely in the hands of another, resembles the little lamb who crept into the den of the 'nice, gentle little wolf' and begged to be permitted to lie down and go to sleep, or the canary bird that persisted in playing with the cat's whiskers.

A person with well-developed self-control will not permit himself to be influenced by the cynic or the pessimist; nor will he permit another person to do his thinking for him.

A person with well-developed self-control will stimulate his imagination and his enthusiasm until they have produced action, but he will then control that action and not permit it to control him.

A person with well-developed self-control will never, under any circumstances, slander another person or seek revenge for any cause whatsoever.

A person with self-control will not hate those who do not agree with him; instead, he will endeavour to understand the reason for their disagreement, and profit by it.

We come, now, to a form of lack of self-control which causes more grief than all other forms combined; it is the habit of forming opinions before studying the facts. We will not analyse this particular form in detail, in this lesson, for the reason that it is fully covered in Lesson Eleven, on accurate thought, but the subject of self-control could not be covered without at least a passing reference to this common evil to which we are all more or less addicted.

No one has any right to form an opinion that is not based either upon that which he believes to be facts, or upon a reasonable hypothesis; yet, if you will observe yourself carefully, you will catch yourself forming opinions on nothing more substantial than your desire for a thing to be or not to be.

Another grievous form of lack of self-control is the 'spending' habit. I have reference, of course, to the habit of spending beyond one's needs. This habit has become so prevalent since the close of the world war that it is alarming. A well known economist has prophesied that three more generations will transform the United States from the richest country in the world to the poorest if the children are not taught the savings habit, as a part of their training in both the schools and the homes. On every hand, we see people buying automobiles on the instalment plan instead of buying homes. Within the last fifteen years the automobile 'fad' has become so popular that literally tens of thousands of people are mortgaging their futures to own cars.

A prominent scientist, who has a keen sense of humour, has prophesied that not only will this habit grow lean bank accounts, but, if persisted in, it will eventually grow babies whose legs will have become transformed into wheels.

This is a speed-mad, money-spending age in which we are living, and the uppermost thought in the minds of most of us is to live faster than our neighbours. Not long ago the general manager of a concern that employs 600 men and women became alarmed over the large number of his employees who were becoming involved with 'loan sharks,' and decided' to put an end to this evil. When he completed his investigation, he found that only nine per cent of his employees had savings accounts, and of the other ninety-one per cent who had no money ahead, seventy-five per cent were in debt in one form or another, some of them being hopelessly involved financially.

Of those who were in debt 210 owned automobiles.

We are creatures of imitation. We find it hard to resist the temptation to do that which we see others doing. If our neighbour buys a Buick, we must imitate him and if we cannot scrape together enough to make the first payment on a Buick we must, at least, have a Ford. Meanwhile, we take no heed of the morrow. The old-fashioned 'rainy-day nest egg' has become obsolete. We live from day to day. We buy our coal by the pound and our flour in five pound sacks, thereby paying a third more for it than it ought to cost, because it is distributed in small quantities.

Of course this warning does not apply to you!

It is intended only for those who are binding themselves in the chains of poverty by spending beyond their earning capacity, and who have not yet heard that there are definite laws which must be observed by all who would attain success.

The automobile is one of the modern wonders of the world, but it is more often a luxury than it is a necessity, and tens of thousands of people who are now 'stepping on the gas' at a lively pace are going to see some dangerous skidding when their 'rainy days' arrive.

It requires considerable self-control to use the street cars as a means of transportation when people all around us are driving automobiles, but all who exercise this self-control are practically sure to see the day when many who are now driving cars will be either riding the street cars or walking.

It was this modem tendency to spend the entire income which prompted Henry Ford to safe-guard his employees with certain restrictions when he established his famous $5.00 a day minimum wage scale.

Twenty years ago, if a boy wanted a wagon, he fashioned the wheels out of boards and had the pleasure of building it himself. Now, if a boy wants a wagon, he cries for it-and gets it!

Lack of self-control is being developed in the oncoming generations by their parents who have become victims of the spending habit. Three generations ago, practically any boy could mend his own shoes with the family cobbling outfit. Today the boy takes his shoes to the corner shoe-shop and pays $1.75 for heels and half soles, and this habit is by no means confined to the rich and well-to-do classes.

I repeat-the spending habit is turning America into a nation of paupers!

I am safe in assuming that you are struggling to attain success, for if you were not you would not be reading this course. Let me remind you, then, that a little savings account will attract many an opportunity to you that would not come your way without it. The size of the account is not so important as is the fact that you have established the savings habit, for this habit marks you as a person who exercises an important form of self-control.

The modem tendency of those who work for a salary is to spend it all. If a man who receives $3,000.00 a year and manages to get along on it fairly well, receives an increase of $1,000.00 a year, does he continue to live on $3,000.00 and place the increased portion of his income in the savings bank? No, not unless he is one of the few who have developed the savings habit. Then, what does he do with this additional $1,000.00? He trades in the old automobile and buys a more expensive one, and at the end of the year he is poorer on a $4,000.00 income than he was the previous year on a $3,000.00 income.

This is a 'modern, twentieth century model' American that I am describing, and you will be lucky if, upon close analysis, you do not find yourself to be one of this class.

Somewhere between the miser who hoards every penny he gets his hands on, in an old sock, and the man who spends every cent he can earn or borrow, there is a 'happy medium,' and if you enjoy life with reasonable assurance of average freedom and contentment, you must find this half-way point and adopt it as a part of your self-control program.

Self-discipline is the most essential factor in the development of personal power, because it enables you to control your appetite and your tendency to spend more than you earn and your habit of 'striking back' at those who offend you and the other destructive habits which cause you to dissipate your energies through non-productive effort that takes on forms too numerous to be catalogued in this lesson.

Very early in my public career I was shocked when I learned how many people there are who devote most of their energies to tearing down that which the builders construct. By some queer turn of the wheel of fate one of these destroyers crossed my path by making it his business to try to destroy my reputation.

Ask any wise man what he most desires and he will, more than likely, say 'more wisdom.'

At first, I was inclined to 'strike back' at him, but as I sat at my typewriter late one night, a thought came to me which changed my entire attitude toward this man. Removing the sheet of paper that was in my typewriter, I inserted another one on which I stated this thought, in these words:

You have a tremendous advantage over the man who does you an injury: you have it within your power to forgive him, while he has no such advantage over you.

As I finished writing those lines, I made up my mind that I had come to the point at which I had to decide upon a policy that would serve as a guide concerning my attitude toward those who criticize my work or try to destroy my reputation. I reached this decision by reasoning something after this fashion: Two courses of action were open to me. I could waste much of my time and energy in striking back at those who would try to destroy me, or I could devote this energy to furthering my life-work and let the result of that work serve as my sole answer to all who would criticize my efforts or question my motives. I decided upon the latter as being the better policy and adopted it.

'By their deeds you shall know them!'

If your deeds are constructive and you are at peace with yourself, in your own heart, you will not find it necessary to stop and explain your motives, for they will explain themselves.

The world soon forgets its destroyers. It builds its monuments to and bestows its honours upon none but its builders. Keep this fact in mind and you will more easily reconcile yourself to the policy of refusing to waste your energies by 'striking back' at those who offend you.

Every person who amounts to anything in this world comes to the point, sooner or later, at which he is forced to settle this question of policy toward his enemies, and if you want proof that it pays to exercise sufficient self-control to refrain from dissipating your vital energies by 'striking back' then study the records of all who have risen to high stations in life and observe how carefully they curbed this destructive habit.

It is a well known fact that no man ever reached a high station in life without opposition of a violent nature from jealous and envious enemies. The late President Warren G. Harding and ex-President Wilson and John H. Patterson of the National Cash Register Company and scores of others whom I could mention, were victims of this cruel tendency, of a certain type of depraved man, to destroy reputation. But these men wasted no time explaining or 'striking back' at their enemies. They exercised self-control.

I do not know but that these attacks on men who are in public life, cruel and unjust and untruthful as they often are, serve a good purpose. In my own case, I know that I made a discovery that was of great value to me, as a result of a series of bitter attacks which a contemporary journalist launched against me. I paid no attention to these attacks for four or five years, until finally they became so bold that I decided to override my policy and 'strike back' at my antagonist. I sat down at my typewriter and began to write. In all of my experience as a writer I do not believe I ever assembled such a collection of biting adjectives as those which I used on this occasion. The more I wrote, the more angry I became, until I had written all that I could think of on the subject. As the last line was finished, a strange feeling came over me-it was not a feeling of bitterness toward the man who had tried to injure me-it was a feeling of compassion, of sympathy, of forgiveness.

I had unconsciously psycho-analysed myself by releasing, over the keys of my typewriter, the repressed emotions of hate and resentment which I had been unintentionally gathering in my sub-conscious mind over a long period of years.

Now, if I find myself becoming very angry, I sit down at my typewriter and 'write it out of my system,' then throw away the manuscript, or file it away as an exhibit for my scrapbook to which I can refer back in the years to come-after the evolutionary processes have carried me still higher in the realm of understanding.

Repressed emotions, especially, the emotion of hatred, resemble a bomb that has been constructed of high explosives, and unless they are handled with as much understanding of their nature as an expert would handle a bomb, they are as dangerous. A bomb may be rendered harmless by explosion in an open field, or by disintegration in a bath of the proper sort. Also, a feeling of anger or hatred may be rendered harmless by giving expression to it in a manner that harmonizes with the principle of psycho-analysis.

Before you can achieve success in the higher and broader sense you must gain such thorough control over yourself that you will be a person of poise.

While others may side-track your ambitions not a few times, remember that discouragement most frequently comes from within.

You are the product of at least a million years of evolutionary change. For countless generations preceding you Nature has been tempering and refining the materials that have gone into your make-up. Step by step, she has removed from the generations that have preceded you the animal instincts and baser passions until she has produced, in you, the finest specimen of animal that lives. She has endowed you, through this slow evolutionary process, with reason and poise and 'balance' sufficient to enable you to control and do with yourself whatever you will.

No other animal has ever been endowed with such self-control as you possess. You have been endowed with the power to use the most highly organised form of energy known to man, that of thought. It is not improbable that thought is the closest connecting link there is between the material, physical things of this world and the world of Divinity.

You have not only the power to think but, what is a thousand times more important still, you have the power to control your thoughts and direct them to do your bidding!

We are coming, now, to the really important part of this lesson. Read slowly and meditatively! I approach this part of this lesson almost with fear and trembling, for it brings us face to face with a subject which but few men are qualified to discuss with reasonable intelligence.

I repeat, you have the power to control your thoughts and make them do your bidding!

Your brain may be likened to a dynamo, in this respect, that it generates or sets into motion the mysterious energy called thought. The stimuli that start your brain into action are of two sorts; one is Auto suggestion and the other is Suggestion. You can select the material out of which your thinking is produced, and that is Auto-suggestion (or self-suggestion). You can permit others to select the material out of which your thinking is produced and that is Suggestion. It is a humiliating fact that most thought is produced by the outside suggestions of others, and it is more humiliating, still, to have to admit that the majority of us accept this suggestion without either examining it or questioning its soundness. We read the daily papers as though every word were based upon fact. We are swayed by the gossip and idle chatter of others as though every word were true.

Thought is the only thing over which you have absolute control, yet, unless you are the proverbial exception, which is about one out of every ten thousand, you permit other people to enter the sacred mansion of your mind and there deposit, through suggestion, their troubles and woes, adversities and falsehoods, just as though you did not have the power to close the door and keep them out.

You have within your control the power to select the material that constitutes the dominating thoughts of your mind, and just as surely as you are reading these lines, those thoughts which dominate your mind will bring you success or failure, according to their nature.

The fact that thought is the only thing over which you have absolute control is, within itself, of most profound significance, as it strongly suggests that thought is your nearest approach to Divinity, on this earthly plane. This fact also carries another highly impressive suggestion; namely, that thought is your most important tool; the one with which you may shape your worldly destiny according to your own liking. Surely, Divine Providence did not make thought the sole power over which you have absolute control without associating with that power potentialities which, if understood and developed, would stagger the imagination.

Self-control is solely a matter of thought-control!

Please read the foregoing sentence aloud; read it thoughtfully and meditate over it before reading further, because it is, without doubt, the most important single sentence of this entire course.

You are studying this course, presumably because you are earnestly seeking truth and understanding sufficient to enable you to attain some high station in life.

You are searching for the magic key that will unlock the door to the source of power; and yet you have the key in your own hands, and you may make use of it the moment you learn to control your thoughts.

Place in your own mind, through the principle of Auto-suggestion, the positive, constructive thoughts which harmonize with your definite chief aim in life, and that mind will transform those thoughts into physical reality and hand them back to you, as a finished product.

This is thought-control!

When you deliberately choose the thoughts which dominate your mind and firmly refuse admittance to outside suggestion, you are exercising self-control in its highest and most efficient form. Man is the only living animal that can do this.

How many millions of years Nature has required in which to produce this animal no one knows, but every intelligent student of psychology knows that the dominating thoughts determine the actions and the nature of the animal.

The process through which one may think accurately is a subject that has been reserved for Lesson Eleven, of this course. The point we wish clearly to establish, in this lesson, is that thought, whether accurate or inaccurate, is the most highly organised functioning power of your mind; and that you are but the sum total of your dominating or most prominent thoughts.

If you would be a master salesman, whether of goods and wares or of personal services, you must exercise sufficient self-control to shutout all adverse arguments and suggestions. Most salesmen have so little self-control that they hear the prospective purchaser say 'no' even before he says it. Not a few salesmen hear this fatal word 'no' even before they come into the presence of their prospective purchaser. They have so little self- control that they actually suggest to themselves that their prospective purchaser will say 'no' when asked to purchase their wares.

How different is the man of self-control! He not only suggests to himself that his prospective purchaser will say 'yes,' but if the desired 'yes' is not forthcoming, he stays on the job until he breaks down the opposition and forces a 'yes.' If his prospective purchaser says 'no,' he does not hear it. If his prospective purchaser says 'no'-a second, and a third, and a fourth time-he does not hear it, for he is a man of self-control and he permits no suggestions to reach his mind except those which he desires to influence him.

The master salesman, whether he be engaged in selling merchandise, or personal services, or sermons, or public addresses, understands how to control his own thought s. Instead of being a person who accepts, with meek submission, the suggestions of others, he is a person who persuades others to accept his suggestions. By controlling himself and by placing only positive thoughts in his own mind, he thereby becomes a dominating personality, a master salesman.

This, too, is self-control!

A master salesman is one who takes the offensive, and never the defensive side of an argument, if argument arises.

Please read the foregoing sentence again!

If you are a master salesman you know that it is necessary for you to keep your prospective purchaser on the defensive, and you also know that it will be fatal to your sale if you permit him to place you on the defensive and keep you there. You may, and of course you will at times, be placed in a position in which you will have to assume the defensive side of the conversation for a time, but it is your business to exercise such perfect poise and self-control that you will change places with your prospective purchaser without his noticing that you have done so, by placing him back on the defensive.

This requires the most consummate skill and self-control!

Most salesmen sweep this vital point aside by becoming angry and trying to scare the prospective purchaser into submission, but the master salesman remains calm and serene, and usually comes out the winner.

People like to use their excess energy by 'chewing the rag.' Wm. Wrigley, Jr., capitalized this human trait by giving them a stick of Spearmint.

The word 'salesman' has reference to all people who try to persuade or convince others by logical argument or appeal to self-interest. We are all salesmen; or, at least, we should be, no matter what form of service we are rendering or what sort of goods we are offering.

The ability to negotiate with other people without friction and argument is the outstanding quality of all successful people. Observe those nearest you and notice how few there are who understand this art of tactful negotiation. Observe, also, how successful are the few who understand this art, despite the fact that they may have less education than those with whom they negotiate.

It is a knack that can be cultivated.

The art of successful negotiation grows out of patient and painstaking self-control. Notice how easily the successful salesman exercises self-control when he is handling a customer who is impatient. In his heart such a salesman may be boiling over, but you will see no evidence of it in his face or manner or words.

He has acquired the art of tactful negotiation!

A single frown of disapproval or a single word denoting impatience will often spoil a sale, and no one knows this better than the successful salesman. He makes it his business to control his feelings, and as a reward he sets his own salary mark and chooses his own position.

To watch a person who has acquired the art of successful negotiation is a liberal education, within itself. Watch the public speaker who has acquired this art; notice the firmness of his step as he mounts the platform; observe the firmness of his voice as he b e g ins to speak; study the expression on his face as he sweeps his audience with the mastery of his argument.

He has learned how to negotiate without friction.

Watch the physician who has acquired this art, as he walks into the sick room and greets his patient with a smile. His bearing, the tone of his voice, the look of assurance on his face, all mark him as one who has acquired the art of successful negotiation, and the patient begins to feel better the moment he enters the sick room.

Watch the foreman of the works who has acquired this art, and observe how his very presence spurs his men to greater effort and inspires them with confidence and enthusiasm.

Watch the lawyer who has acquired this art, and observe how he commands the respect and attention of the court, the jury and his fellow-practitioners. There is something about the tone of his voice, the posture of his body, and the expression on his face which causes his opponent to suffer by comparison. He not only knows his case, but he convinces the court and the jury that he knows, and as his reward he wins his cases and claims big retaining fees.

And all of this is predicated upon self-control!

And self-control is the result of thought-control!

Deliberately place in your own mind the sort of thoughts that you desire there, and keep out of your mind those thoughts which others place there through suggestion, and you will become a person of self-control.

This privilege of stimulating your mind with suggestions and thoughts of your own choosing is your prerogative power that Divine Providence gave you, and if you will exercise this holy right there is nothing within the bounds of reason that you cannot attain.

'Losing your temper,' and with it your case, or your argument, or your sale, marks you as one who has not yet familiarized himself with the fundamentals upon which self-control is based, and the chief one of these fundamentals is the privilege of choosing the thoughts that dominate the mind.

A student in one of my classes once asked how one went about controlling one's thoughts when in a state of intense anger, and I replied: 'In exactly the same way that you would change your manner and the tone of your voice if you were in a heated argument with a member of your family and heard the door bell ring, warning you that company was about to visit you. You would control yourself because you would desire to do so.'

If you have ever been in a similar predicament, where you found it necessary to cover up your real feelings and change the expression on your face quickly, you know how easily it can be done, and you also know that it can be done because one wants to do it!

Back of all achievement, back of all self-control, back of all thought control, is that magic something called DESIRE!

It is no misstatement of fact to say that you are limited only by the depth of your desires!

When your desires are strong enough you will appear to possess superhuman powers to achieve. No one has ever explained this strange phenomenon of the mind, and perhaps no one ever will explain it, but if you doubt that it exists you have but to experiment and be convinced.

If you were in a building that was on fire, and all the doors and windows were locked, the chances are that you would develop sufficient strength with which to break down the average door, because of your intense desire to free yourself.

If you desire to acquire the art of successful negotiation, as you undoubtedly will when you understand its significance in relation to your achievement of your definite chief aim, you will do so, providing your desire is intense enough.

Napoleon desired to become emperor of France and did rule. Lincoln desired to free the slaves, and he accomplished it. The French desired that 'they shall not pass,' at the beginning of the world war, and they didn't pass! Edison desired to produce light with electricity, and he produced it-although he was many years in doing so. Roosevelt desired to unite the Atlantic and Pacific oceans, through the Panama Canal, and he did it. Demosthenes desired to become a great public speaker, and despite the handicap of serious impediment of speech, he transformed his desire into reality. Helen Keller desired to speak, and despite the fact that she was deaf, dumb and blind, she now speaks. John H. Patterson desired to dominate in the production of cash registers, and he did it. Marshall Field desired to be the leading merchant of his time, and he did. Shakespeare desired to become a great playwright, and, despite the fact that he was only a poor itinerant actor, he made his desire come true. Billy Sunday desired to quit playing base-ball and become a master preacher, and he did. James J.

Hill desired to become an empire builder; and, despite the fact that he was only a poor telegraph operator, he transformed that desire into reality.

Don't say, 'It can't be done,' or that you are different from these and thousands of others who have achieved noteworthy success in every worthy calling. If you are 'different,' it is only in this respect: they desired the object of their achievement with more depth and intensity than you desire yours.

Plant in your mind the seed of a desire that is constructive by making the following your creed and the foundation of your code of ethics:

"I wish to be of service to my fellow men as I journey through life. To do this I have adopted this creed as a guide to be followed in dealing with my fellow-beings:

"To train myself so that never, under any circumstances, will I find fault with any person, no matter how much I may disagree with him or how inferior his work may be, as long as I know he is sincerely trying to do his best.

"To respect my country, my profession and myself. To be honest and fair with my fellow men, as I expect them to be honest and fair with me. To be a loyal citizen of my country. To speak of it with praise, and act always as a worthy custodian of its good name. To be a person whose name carries weight wherever it goes.

"To base my expectations of reward on a solid foundation of service rendered. To be willing to pay the price of success in honest effort. To look upon my work as an opportunity to be seized with joy and made the most of, and not as a painful drudgery to be reluctantly endured.

"To remember that success lies within myself-in my own brain. To expect difficulties and to force my way through them.

"To avoid procrastination in all its forms, and never, under any circumstances, put off until tomorrow any duty that should be performed today.

"Finally, to take a good grip on the joys of life, so I may be courteous to men, faithful to friends, true to God-a fragrance in the path I tread."

The energy which most people dissipate through lack of self-control would, if organised and used constructively, bring all the necessities and all the luxuries desired.

The time which many people devote to 'gossiping' aboutothers would, if controlled and directed constructively, be sufficient to attain the object of their definite chief aim (if they had such an aim).

All successful people grade high on self-control! All 'failures' grade low, generally zero, on this important law of human conduct.

Study the comparative analysis chart in the Introductory Lesson, and observe the self-control grading of Jesse James and Napoleon.

Study those around you and observe, with profit, that all the successful ones exercise self-control, while the 'failures' permit their THOUGHTS, WORDS and DEEDS to run wild!

One very common and very destructive form of lack of self-control is the habit of talking too much. People of wisdom, who know what they want and are Benton getting it, guard their conversation carefully.

There can be no gain from a volume of uninvited, uncontrolled, loosely spoken words.

It is nearly always more profitable to listen than it is to speak. A good listener may, once in a great while, hear something that will add to his stock of knowledge. It requires self-control to become a good listener, but the benefits to be gained are worth the effort.

"Taking the conversation away from another person" is a common form of lack of self-control which is not only discourteous, but it deprives those who do it of many valuable opportunities to learn from others.

After completing this lesson you should go back to the self-analysis chart, in the Introductory Lesson, and re-grade yourself on the Law of Self-control. Perhaps you may wish to reduce your former grading somewhat.

Self-control was one of the marked characteristics of all successful leaders whom I have analysed, in gathering material for this course. Luther Burbank said that, in his opinion, self-control was the most important of the Fifteen Laws of Success. During all his years of patient study and observation of the evolutionary processes of vegetable life he found it necessary to exercise the faculty of self-control, despite the fact that he was dealing with inanimate life.

John Burroughs, the naturalist, said practically the same thing; that self-control stood near the head of the list, in importance, of the Fifteen Laws of Success.

The man who exercises complete self-control cannot be permanently defeated, as Emerson has so well stated in his essay on Compensation, for the reason that obstacles and opposition have a way of melting away when confronted by the determined mind that is guided to a definite end with complete self-control.

Every wealthy man whom I have analysed (referring to those who have become wealthy through their own efforts) showed such positive evidence that self-control had been one of his strong points that I reached the conclusion that no man can hope to accumulate great wealth and keep it without exercising this necessary quality.

The saving of money requires the exercise of self-control of the highest order, as, I hope, has been made quite clear in the fourth lesson of this course.

I am indebted to Edward W. Bok for the following rather colorful description of the extent to which he found it necessary to exercise self-control before he achieved success and was crowned with fame as one of the great journalists of America:

Why I Believe in Poverty as the Richest Experience that Can Come to a Boy

I make my living trying to edit the Ladies' Home Journal. And because the public has been most generous in its acceptance of that periodical, a share of that success has logically come to me. Hence a number of my very good readers cherish an opinion that often I have been tempted to correct, a temptation to which I now yield. My correspondents express the conviction variously, but this extract from a letter is a fair sample:

"It is all very easy for you to preach economy to us when you do not know the necessity for it: To tell us how, as for example in my own case, we must live within my husband's income of eight hundred dollars a year, when you have never known what it is to live on less than thousands. Has it occurred to you, born with the proverbial silver spoon in your mouth, that theoretical writing is pretty cold and futile compared to the actual hand-to-mouth struggle that so many of us live, day by day and year in and year out-an experience that you know not of?"

"An experience that you know not of!"

Now, how far do the facts square with this statement?

Whether or not I was born with the proverbial silver spoon in my mouth, I cannot say. It is true that I was born of well-to-do parents. But when I was six years old my father lost all his means, and faced life at forty-five, in a strange country, without even necessaries. There are men and their wives who know what that means; for a man to try to 'come back' at forty-five, and in a strange country!

I had the handicap of not knowing one word of the English language. I went to a public school and learned what I could. And sparse morsels they were! The boys were cruel, as boys are. The teachers were impatient, as tired teachers are.

My father could not find his place in the world. My mother who had always had servants at her beck and call, faced the problems of housekeeping that she had never learned nor been taught. And there was no money.

So, after school hours, my brother and I went home, but not to play. After-school hours meant for us to help a mother who daily grew more frail under the burdens that she could not carry. Not for days, but for years, we two boys got up in the gray cold winter dawn when the beds feel so warm to growing boys, and we sifted the coal ashes of the day-before's fire for a stray lump or two of unburned coal, and with what we had or could find we made the fire and warmed up the room. Then we set the table for the scant breakfast, went to school, and directly after school we washed the dishes, swept and scrubbed the floors. Living in a three-family tenement, each third week meant that we scrubbed the entire three flights of stairs from the third story to the first, as well as the doorsteps and the sidewalk outside. The latter work was the hardest; for we did it on Saturdays, with the boys of the neighborhood looking on none too kindly, so we did it to the echo of the crack of the ball and baton the adjoining lot!

In the evening when the other boys could sit by the lamp or study their lessons, we two boys went out with a basket and picked up wood and coal in the adjoining lots, or went after the dozen or so pieces of coal left from the ton of coal put in that afternoon by one of the neighbours, with the spot hungrily fixed in mind by one of us during the day, hoping that the man who carried in the coal might not be too careful in picking up the stray lumps!

"An experience that you know not of!" Don't I? At ten years of age I got my first job, washing the windows of a baker's shop at fifty cents a week. In a week or two I was allowed to sell bread and cakes behind the counter after school hours for a dollar a week-handing out freshly baked cakes and warm, delicious-smelling bread, when scarcely a crumb had passed my mouth that day!

Then on Saturday mornings I served a route for a weekly paper, and sold my remaining stock on the street. It meant from sixty to seventy cents for that day's work.

I lived in Brooklyn, New York, and the chief means of transportation to Coney Island at that time was the horse car. Near where we lived the cars would stop to water the horses, the men would jump out and get a drink of water, but the women had no means of quenching their thirst. Seeing this lack I got a pail, filled it with water and a bit of ice, and, with a glass, jumped on each car on Saturday afternoon and all day Sunday, and sold my wares at a cent a glass. And when competition came, as it did very quickly when other boys saw that a Sunday's work meant two or three dollars, I squeezed a lemon or two in my pail, my liquid became 'lemonade' and my price two cents a glass, and Sunday meant five dollars to me.

Then, in turn, I became a reporter during the evenings, an office boy day-times, and learned stenography at midnight.

My correspondent says she supports her family of husband and child on eight hundred dollars a year, and says I have never known what that means. I supported a family of three on six dollars and twenty-five cents a week-less than one-half of her yearly income. When my brother and I, combined, brought in eight hundred dollars a year we felt rich!

I have for the first time gone into these details in print so that you may' know, at first hand, that the editor of the Ladies' Home journal is not a theorist when he writes or prints articles that seek to preach economy or that reflect a hand-to-hand struggle on a small or an invisible income. There is not a single step, not an inch, on the road of direct poverty that I do not know of or have not experienced. And, having experienced every thought, every feeling and every hardship that come to those who travel that road, I say today that I rejoice with every boy who is going through the same experience.

Nor am I discounting or forgetting one single pang of the keen hardships that such a struggle means. I would not today exchange my years of the keenest hardship that a boy can know or pass through for any single experience that could have come to me. I know what it means to earn-not a dollar, but to earn two cents. I know the value of money as I could have learned it or known it in no other way. I could have been trained for my life-work in no surer way. I could not have arrived at a truer understanding of what it means to face a day without a penny in hand, not a loaf of bread in the cupboard, not a piece of kindling wood for the fire-with nothing to eat, and then be a boy with the hunger of nine and ten, with a mother frail and discouraged!

"An experience that you know not of!" Don't I? And yet I rejoice in the experience, and I repeat:

I envy every boy who is in that condition and going through it. But-and here is the pivot of my strong belief in poverty as an undisguised blessing to a boy-I believe in poverty as a condition to experience, to go through, and then to get out of : not as a condition to stay in. 'That's all very well,' some will say; 'easy enough to say, but how can you get out of it?' No one can definitely tell another that. No one told me. No two persons can find the same way out. Each must find his way for himself. That depends on the boy. I was determined to get out of poverty, because my mother was not born in it, could not stand it and did not belong in it. This gave me the first essential: a purpose. Then I backed up the purpose with effort and willingness to work and to work at anything that came my way, no matter what it was, so long as it meant 'the way out.' I did not pick and choose; I took what came and did it in the best way I knew how; and when I didn't like what I was doing I still did it well while I was doing it, but I saw to it that I didn't do it any longer than I had to do it. I used every rung in the ladder as a rung to the one above. It meant effort, but out of the effort and the work came the experience; the up building, the development; the capacity to understand and sympathize; the greatest heritage that can come to a boy. And nothing in the world can give that to a boy, so that it will burn into him, as will poverty.

That is why I believe so strongly in poverty, the greatest blessing in the way of the deepest and fullest experience that can come to a boy. But, as I repeat: always as a condition to work out of, not to stay in.

Before you can develop the habit of perfect self-control you must understand the real need for this quality. Also, you must understand the advantages which self-control provides those who have learned how to exercise it.

By developing self-control you develop, also, other qualities that will add to your personal power.

Among other laws which are available to the person who exercises self-control is the Law of Retaliation.

You know what 'retaliate' means!

In the sense that we are using here it means to 'return like for like,' and not merely to avenge or to seek revenge, as is commonly meant by the use of this word.

If I do you an injury you retaliate at first opportunity. If I say unjust things about you, you will retaliate in kind, even in greater measure!

On the other hand, if I do you a favour you will reciprocate even in greater measure if possible.

Through the proper use of this law I can get you to do whatever I wish you to do. If I wish you to dislike me and to lend your influence toward damaging me, I can accomplish this result by inflicting upon you the sort of treatment that I want you to inflict upon me through retaliation.

If I wish your respect, your friendship and your co-operation I can get these by extending to you my friendship and co-operation.

On these statements I know that we are together. You can compare these statements with your own experience and you will see how beautifully they harmonize.

How often have you heard the remark, "What a wonderful personality that person has." How often have you met people whose personalities you coveted?

The man who attracts you to him through his pleasing personality is merely making use of the Law of Harmonious Attraction, or the Law of Retaliation, both of which, when analysed, mean that 'like attracts like.'

If you will study, understand and make intelligent use of the Law of Retaliation you will be an efficient and successful salesman. When you have mastered this simple law and learned how to use it you will have learned all that can be learned about salesmanship.

The first and probably the most important step to be taken in mastering this law is to cultivate complete self-control. You must learn to take all sorts of punishment and abuse without retaliating in kind. This self-control is a part of the price you must pay for mastery of the Law of Retaliation.

When an angry person starts in to vilify and abuse you, justly or unjustly, just remember that if you retaliate in a like manner you are being drawn down to that person's mental level, therefore that person is dominating you!

On the other hand, if you refuse to become angry, if you retain your self-composure and remain calm and serene you retain all your ordinary faculties through which to reason. You take the other fellow by surprise. You retaliate with a weapon with the use of which he is unfamiliar, consequently you easily dominate him.

Like attracts like! There's no denying this! Literally speaking, every person with whom you come in contact is a mental looking-glass in which you may see a perfect reflection of your own mental attitude.

As an example of direct application of the Law of Retaliation, let us cite an experience that I recently had with my two small boys, Napoleon Junior and James.

It is well worth remembering that the customer is the most important factor in any business. If you don't think so, try to get along without him for a while.

We were on our way to the park to feed the birds and squirrels. Napoleon junior had bought a bag of peanuts and James had bought a box of 'Crackerjack.' James took a notion to sample the peanuts. Without asking permission he reached over and made a grab for the bag. He missed and Napoleon junior 'retaliated' with his left fist which landed rather briskly on James' jaw.

I said to James: "Now, see here, son, you didn't go about getting those peanuts in the right manner. Let me show you how to get them." It all happened so quickly that I hadn't the slightest idea when I spoke what I was going to suggest to James, but I sparred for time to analyse the occurrence and work out a better way, if possible, than that adopted by him.

Then I thought of the experiments we had been making in connection with the Law of Retaliation, so I said to James: "Open your box of `Crackerjack' and offer your little brother some and see what happens." After considerable coaxing I persuaded him to do this. Then a remarkable thing happened-a happening out of which I learned my greatest lesson in salesmanship!

Before Napoleon would touch the 'Crackerjack' he insisted on pouring some of his peanuts into lames' overcoat pocket. He 'retaliated in kind!' out of this simple experiment with two small boys I learned more about the art of managing them than I could have learned in any other manner. Incidentally, my boys are beginning to learn how to manipulate this Law of Retaliation which saves them many a physical combat.

None of us have advanced far beyond Napoleon Junior and James as far as the operation and influence of the Law of Retaliation is concerned. We are all just grown-up children and easily influenced through this principle. The habit of 'retaliating in kind' is so universally practiced among us that we can properly call this habit the Law of Retaliation. If a person presents us with a gift we never feel satisfied until we have 'retaliated' with something as good or better than that which we received. If a person speaks well of us we increase our admiration for that person, and we 'retaliate' in return!

Through the principle of retaliation we can actually convert our enemies into loyal friends. If you have an enemy whom you wish to convert into a friend you can prove the truth of this statement if you will forget that dangerous millstone hanging around your neck, which we call 'pride' (stubbornness). Make a habit of speaking to this enemy with unusual cordiality. Go out of your way to favour him in every manner possible. He may seem immovable at first, but gradually he will give way to your influence and 'retaliate in kind!' The hottest coals of fire ever heaped upon the head of one who has wronged you are the coals of human kindness.

One morning in August, 1863, a young clergyman was called out of bed in a hotel at Lawrence, Kansas. The man who called him was one of Quantrill's guerrillas, and he wanted him to hurry downstairs and be shot. All over the border that morning people were being murdered. A band of raiders had ridden in early to perpetrate the Lawrence massacre.

The guerrilla who called the clergyman was impatient. The latter, when fully awake, was horrified by what he saw going on through his window. As he came downstairs the guerrilla demanded his watch and money, and then wanted to know if he was an abolitionist. The clergyman was trembling. But he decided that if he was to die then and there it would not be with a lie on his lips. So he said that he was, and followed up the admission with a remark that immediately turned the whole affair into another channel.

He and the guerrilla sat down on the porch, while people were being killed through the town, and had a long talk. It lasted until the raiders were ready to leave. When the clergyman's guerrilla mounted to join his confederates he was strictly on the defensive. He handed back the New Englander's valuables, apologized for disturbing him and asked to be thought well of.

That clergyman lived many years after the Lawrence massacre. What did he say to the guerrilla? What was there in his personality that led the latter to sit down and talk? What did they talk about?

'Are you a Yankee abolitionist?' the guerrilla had asked. 'Yes, I am,' was the reply, 'and you know very well that you ought to be ashamed of what you're doing'

This drew the matter directly to a moral issue. It brought the guerrilla up roundly. The clergyman was only a stripling beside this seasoned border ruffian. But he threw a burden of moral proof on to the raider, and in a moment the latter was trying to demonstrate that he might be a better fellow than circumstances would seem to indicate.

After waking this New Englander to kill him on account of his politics, he spent twenty minutes on the witness stand trying to prove an alibi. He went into his personal history at length. He explained matters from the time when he had been a tough little kid who wouldn't say his prayers, and became quite sentimental in recalling how one thing had led to another, and that to something worse, until-well, here he was, and 'a mighty bad business to be in, pardoner.' His last request in riding away was: "Now, pardoner, don't think too hard on me, will you?"

The New England clergyman made use of the Law of Retaliation, whether he knew it at that time or not. Imagine what would have happened had he come downstairs with a revolver in his hand and started to meet physical force with physical force!

But he didn't do this! He mastered the guerrilla because he fought him with a force that was unknown to the brigand.

Why is it that when once a man begins to make money the whole world seems to beat a pathway to his door?

Take any person that you know who enjoys financial success and he will tell you that he is being constantly sought, and that opportunities to make money are constantly being urged upon him!

"To him that hath shall be given, but to him that hath not shall be taken away even that which he hath"

This quotation from the Bible used to seem ridiculous to me, yet how true it is when reduced to its concrete meaning.

Yes, 'to him that hath shall be given!' If he 'hath' failure, lack of self-confidence, hatred or lack of self-control, to him shall these qualities be given in still greater abundance! But, if he 'hath' success, self-confidence, self-control, patience, persistence and determination, to him shall these qualities be increased!

Sometimes it may be necessary to meet force with force until we overpower our opponent or adversary, but while he is down is a splendid time to complete the 'retaliation' by taking him by the hand and showing him a better way to settle disputes.

Like attracts like! Germany sought to bathe her sword in human blood, in a ruthless escapade of conquest. As a result she has drawn the 'retaliation in kind' of most of the civilised world.

It is for you to decide what you want your fellow men to do and it is for you to get them to do it through the Law of Retaliation!

'The Divine Economy is automatic and very simple: we receive only that which we give.'

How true it is that 'we receive only that which we give'! It is not that which we wish for that comes back to us, but that which we give.

I implore you to make use of this law, not alone for material gain, but, better still, for the attainment of happiness and good-will toward men.

This, after all, is the only real success for which to strive.

SUMMARY

In this lesson we have learned a great principle-probably the most important major principle of psychology! We have learned that our thoughts and actions toward others resemble an electric magnet which attracts to us the same sort of thought and the same sort of action that we, ourselves, create.

We have learned that 'like attracts like,' whether in thought or in expression of thought through bodily action. We have learned that the human mind responds, in kind, to whatever thought impressions it receives. We have learned that the human mind resembles mother earth in that it will reproduce a crop of muscular action which corresponds, in kind, to the sensory impressions planted in it. We have learned that kindness begets kindness and unkindness and injustice beget unkindness and injustice.

We have learned that our actions toward others, whether of kindness or unkindness, justice or injustice, come back to us, even in a larger measure! We have learned that the human mind responds in kind, to all sensory impressions it receives, therefore we know what we must do to influence any desired action upon the part of another.

We have learned that 'pride' and 'stubbornness' must be brushed away before we can make use of the Law of Retaliation in a constructive way. We have not learned what the Law of Retaliation is, but we have learned how it works and what it will do; therefore, it only remains for us to make intelligent use of this great principle.

You are now ready to proceed with Lesson Nine, where you will find other laws which harmonize perfectly with those described in this lesson on Self-control.

It will require the strongest sort of self-control to enable the beginner to apply the major law of the next lesson, on the Habit of Doing More Than Paid For, but experience will show that the development of such control is more than justified by the results growing out of such discipline.

IF you are successful remember that somewhere, sometime, someone gave you a lifter an idea that started you in the right direction. Remember, also, that you are indebted to life until you help some less fortunate person, just as you were helped.

The Evolution of Transportation

An After-the-Lesson Visit With the Author

Nothing is permanent except change. Life resembles a great kaleidoscope before which Time is ever shifting, changing and rearranging both the stage setting and the players. New friends are constantly replacing the old. Everything is in a state of flux. In every heart is the seed of both rascality and justice. Every human being is both a criminal and a saint, depending upon the expediency of the moment as to which will assert itself. Honesty and dishonesty are largely matters of individual viewpoint. The weak and the strong, the rich and the poor, the ignorant and the well-informed are exchanging places continuously.

Know YOURSELF and you know the entire human race. There is but one real achievement, and that is the ability to THINK ACCURATELY. We move with the procession, or behind it, but we cannot stand still.

NOTHING is permanent except change!

In the picture above you see proof that the law of evolution is working out improvements in the methods of travel. Remember, as you study this picture, that all these changes took place first in the minds of men.

At the extreme left you see the first crude method of transportation. Man was not satisfied with this slow process. Those two little words 'not satisfied,' have been the starting point of all advancement. Think of them as you read this article.

Next, in the picture, you see the history of transportation step by step, as man's brain began to expand. It was a long step forward when man discovered how to hitch a bullock to a wagon and thereby escape the toil of pulling the load. That was practical utility. But, when the stage-coach was ushered into use that was both utility and style. Still man was 'not satisfied' and this dissatisfaction created the crude locomotive that you see in the picture.

Now all these methods of travel have been discarded except in certain uncivilised (or uncommercialized) parts of the world. The man drawing the cart, the bullock drawing the cart, the stage-coach and the crude locomotive all belong to ages that have passed.

At the right you see the transportation methods of the present. Compare them with those of the past and you may have a fair idea of the enormous expansion that has taken place in the brain and mind of man. Man now moves about more rapidly than in the past. From the first type of locomotive there has been evolved a powerful machine capable of hauling a hundred cars of freight, compared with the one small light car that could be drawn with the original. Automobiles that travel at the speed of seventy-five miles an hour are now as common as were the two-wheel carts in ages past. Moreover, they are within the means of all who want them.

And still man's mind was 'not satisfied.' Travel on the earth was too slow. Turning his eyes upward he watched the birds soaring high in the elements and became 'DETERMINED' to excel them. Study, also, the word 'determined,' for whatever man becomes determined to do man does! Within the brief period of fifteen years man has mastered the air and now travels in the airplane at the rate of a hundred and fifty miles an hour.

Not only has man made the air carry him at amazingly rapid speed, but he has harnessed the ether and made it carry his words all the way around the earth in the fractional part of a second.

We have been describing the PAST and the PRESENT!

At the bottom of the picture we may see the next step forward that man will take in methods of travel; a machine that will fly in the air, run on the ground and swim in the water, at the discretion of man.

The purpose of this essay and the picture at the top of the page is to provide food for THOUGHT!

Any influence that causes one to think causes one, also, to grow stronger mentally. Mind stimulants are essential for growth. From the days of the man-drawn cart to the present days of air mastery the only progress that any man has made has been the result of some influence that stimulated his mind to greater than normal action.

The two great major influences that cause the mind of man to grow are the urge of necessity and the urge of desire to create. Some minds develop only after they have undergone failure and defeat and other forms of punishment which arouse them to greater action. Other minds wither away and die under punishment, but grow to unbelievable heights when provided with the opportunity to use their imaginative forces in a creative way.

Study the picture of the evolution of transportation and you will observe one outstanding fact worth remembering, namely, that the whole story has been one of development and advancement that grew out of necessity. The entire period described in the picture as 'THE PAST' was one wherein the urge was that of necessity.

In the period described in the picture above as 'THE PRESENT' the urge has been a combination of both necessity and the desire to create. The period described as 'THE FUTURE' will be one in which the strong desire to create will be the sole urge that will drive man's mind on and on to heights as yet undreamed of.

It is a long distance from the days of the man-drawn cart to the present, when man has harnessed the lightning of the clouds and made it turn machinery that will perform as much service in a minute as ten thousand men could perform in a day. But, if the distance has been long the development of man's mind has been correspondingly great, and that development has been sufficient to eventually do the work of the world with machines operated by Nature's forces and not by man's muscles.

The evolutionary changes in the methods of transportation have created other problems for man's mind to solve. The automobile drove man to build better roads and more of them. The automobile and the speedy locomotive, combined, have created dangerous crossings which claim thousands of lives annually. Man's mind must now respond to the urge of 'necessity' and meet this emergency.

Keep this essay and remember this prophecy: Within five years every railroad crossing in the country will be amply protected against automobile accidents, and, the automobile, itself, will manipulate the system that will do the protecting; a system that will be fool-proof and effective; a system that will work whether the driver of the automobile is asleep or awake, drunk or sober.

Come, now, for a brief glimpse at the machinery of the imagination of man, as it works under the stimulant of desire to create.

Some imaginative man; perhaps some fellow who never did anything else of note and who will never do anything worthwhile again; will create a system of railroad crossing protection that will be operated by the weight of the passing automobile. Within the required distance from the crossing a platform similar to the platform of a large freight scale will cover an entire section of the roadway. As soon as an automobile mounts this platform the weight of the machine will lower a gate, ring a gong and flash a red light in front of the motorist. The gate will rise in one minute, allowing the motorist to pass over the track, thus forcing him to 'stop, look and listen.'

If you have a highly imaginative mind you may be the one who will create this system and collect the royalties from its sale.

To be practical the imaginative mind should be always on the alert for ways and means of diverting waste motion and power into useful channels. Most automobiles are far too heavy in comparison with the load they carry. This weight can be utilized by making it provide the motorist with railroad crossing protection.

Remember, the purpose of this essay is to give you merely the seed of suggestion; not the finished product of an invention ready to set up and render service. The value to you, of this suggestion, lies in the possibility of thought that you may devote to it, thereby developing and expanding your own mind.

Study yourself and find out to which of the two great major urges to action your mind responds most naturally-the urge of necessity or the desire to create. If you have children, study them and determine to which of these two motives they respond most naturally. Millions of children have had their imagination dwarfed and retarded by parents who removed as much as possible of the urge of necessity. By 'making it easy' for your child you may be depriving the world of a genius. Bear in mind the fact that most of the progress that man has made came as the result of bitter, biting NECESSITY!

You need no proof that methods of transportation have undergone a continuous process of evolution. So marked has the change been that the old one-lung type of automobile now provokes a laugh wherever it is found on the street.

The law of evolution is always and everywhere at work, changing, tearing down and rebuilding every material element on this earth and throughout the universe. Towns, cities and communities are undergoing constant change. Go back to the place where you lived twenty years ago and you will recognise neither the place nor the people. New faces will have made their appearance. The old faces will have changed. New buildings will have taken the place of the old. Everything will appear differently because everything will be different.

The human mind is also undergoing constant change. If this were not true we would never grow beyond the child-mind age. Every seven years the mind of a normal person becomes noticeably developed and expanded. It is during these periodical changes of the mind that bad habits may be left off and better habits cultivated. Fortunate for the human being that his mind is undergoing a continuous process of orderly change.

The mind that is driven by the urge of necessity, or out of love to create, develops more rapidly than does the mind that is never stimulated to greater action than that which is necessary for existence.

The imaginative faculty of the human mind is the greatest piece of machinery ever created out of it has come every man-made machine and every manmade object.

Back of the great industries and railroads and banking houses and commercial enterprises is the all-powerful force of IMAGINATION!

Force your mind to THINK! Proceed by combining old ideas into new plans. Every great invention and every outstanding business or industrial achievement that you can name is, in final analysis, but the application of a combination of plans and ideas that have been used before, in some other manner.

'Back of the beating hammer
By which the steel is wrought,

Back of the workshop's clamor
The seeker may find the Thought;
The thought that is ever Master
Of iron and steam and steel,
That rises above disaster
And tramples it under heel.
"The drudge may fret and tinker
Or labour with lusty blows,
But back of him stands the Thinker,
The clear-eyed man who knows;
For into each plow or saber,
Each piece and part and whole,
Must go the brains of labour,
Which gives the work a soul.
"Back of the motor's humming,
Back of the bells that ring,
Back of the hammer's drumming,
Back of the cranes that swing,
There is the Eye which scans them,
Watching through stress and strain,
There is the Mind which plans them–
Back of the brawn, the Brain.
"Might of the roaring boiler,
Force of the engine's thrust,
Strength of the sweating toiler,
Greatly in these we trust;
But back of them stands the schemer,
The Thinker who drives things through,
Back of the job-the Dreamer
Who's making the dream come true."

Six months or a year from now come back and read this essay again and you will observe how much more you will get from it than you did at first reading. TIME gives the law of evolution a chance to expand your mind so it can see and understand more.

☐

6

Accurate Thought

"You Can Do It if You Believe You Can!"

This is a tone and the same time the most important, the most interesting and the most difficult to present lesson of this entire course on The Law of Success.

It is important because it deals with a principle which runs through the entire course. It is interesting for the same reason. It is difficult to present for the reason that it will carry the average student far beyond the boundary line of his common experiences and into a realm of thought in which he is not accustomed to dwell.

Unless you study this lesson with an open mind, you will miss the very key-stone to the arch of this course, and without this stone you can never complete your Temple of Success.

This lesson will bring you a conception of thought which may carry you far above the level to which you have risen by the evolutionary processes to which you have been subjected in the past; and, for this reason, you should not be disappointed if, at first reading, you do not fully understand it. Most of us disbelieve that which we cannot understand, and it is with knowledge of this human tendency in mind that I caution you against closing your mind if you do not grasp all that is in this lesson at the first reading.

For thousands of years men made ships of wood, and of nothing else. They used wood because they believed that it was the only substance that would float; but that was because they had not yet advanced far enough in their thinking process to understand the truth that steel will float, and that it is far superior to wood for the building of ships. They did not know that anything could float which was lighter than the amount of water is displaced, and until they learned of this great truth they went on making ships of wood.

Until some twenty-five years ago, most men thought that only the birds could fly, but now we know that man can not only equal the flying of the birds, but he can excel it.

Men did not know, until quite recently, that the great open void known as the air is more alive and more sensitive than anything that is on the earth. They did not know that the spoken word would travel through the ether with the speed of a flash of lightning, without the aid of wires. How could they know this when their minds had not been unfolded sufficiently to enable them to grasp it? The purpose of this lesson is to aid you in so unfolding and expanding your mind that you will be able to think with accuracy, for this enfoldment will open to you a door that leads to all the power you will need in completing your Temple of Success.

All through the preceding lessons of this course you observed that we have dealt with principles which any one could easily grasp and apply. You will also observe that these principles have been so presented that they lead to success as measured by material wealth. This seemed necessary for the reason that to most people the word success and the word money are synonymous terms. Obviously, the previous lessons of this course were intended for those who look upon worldly things and material wealth as being all that there is to success.

Presenting the matter in another way, I was conscious of the fact that the majority of the students of this course would feel disappointed if I pointed out to them a roadway to success that leads through other than the doorways of business, and finance, and industry; for it is a matter of common knowledge that most men want success that is spelled SUCCESS!

Very well-let those who are satisfied with this standard of success have it; but some there are who will want to go higher up the ladder, in search of success which is measured in other than material standards, and it is for their benefit in particular that this and the subsequent lessons of this course are intended.

Accurate thought involves two fundamentals which all who indulge in it must observe. First, to think accurately you must separate facts from mere information. There is much 'information' available to you that is not based upon facts. Second, you must separate facts into two classes; namely, the important and the unimportant, or, the relevant and the irrelevant.

Only by so doing can you think clearly.

All facts which you can use in the attainment of your definite chief aim are important and relevant; all that you cannot use are unimportant and irrelevant. It is mainly the neglect of some to make this distinction which accounts for the chasm which separates so widely people who appear to have equal ability, and who have had equal opportunity. Without going outside of your own circle of acquaintances you can point to one or more persons who have had no greater opportunity than you have had, and who appear to have no more, and perhaps less, ability than you, who are achieving far greater success.

And you wonder why!

Search diligently and you will discover that all such people have acquired the habit of combining and using the important facts which affect their line of work. Far from working harder than you, they are perhaps working less and with greater ease. By virtue of their having learned the secret of separating the important facts from the unimportant, they have provided themselves with a sort of fulcrum and lever with which they can move with their little fingers loads that you cannot budge with the entire weight of your body.

The person who forms the habit of directing his attention to the important facts out of which he is constructing his Temple of Success, thereby provides himself with a power which may be likened to a trip-hammer which strikes a ten-ton blow as compared to a tack-hammer which strikes a one-pound blow!

If these similes appear to be elementary you must keep in mind the fact that some of the students of this course have not yet developed the capacity to think in more complicated terms, and to try to force them to do so would be the equivalent of leaving them hopelessly behind.

That you may understand the importance of distinguishing between facts and mere information, study that type of man who is guided entirely by that which he hears; the type who is influenced by all the 'whisperings of the winds of gossip'; that accepts, without analysis, all that he reads in the newspapers and judges others by what their enemies and competitors and contemporaries say about them.

Search your circle of acquaintances and pick out one of this type as an example to keep before your mind while we are on this subject. Observe that this man usually begins his conversation with some such term as this-'I see by the papers,' or 'they say. "The accurate thinker knows that the newspapers are not always accurate in their reports, and he also knows that what 'they say' usually carries more falsehood than truth. If you have not risen above the 'I see by the papers,' and the "they say" class, you have still far to go before you become an accurate thinker. Of course, much truth and many facts travel in the guise of idle gossip and newspaper reports; but the accurate thinker will not accept as such all that he sees and hears.

This is a point which I feel impelled to emphasize, for the reason that it constitutes the rocks and reefs on which so many people flounder and go down to defeat in a bottomless ocean of false conclusions.

In the realm of legal procedure, there is a principle which is called the law of evidence; and the object of this law is to get at the facts. Any judge can proceed with justice to all concerned, if he has the facts upon which to base his judgment, but he may play havoc with innocent people if he circumvents the law of evidence and reaches a conclusion or judgment that is based upon hears ay information.

The law of Evidence varies according to the subject and circumstances with which it is used, but you will not go far wrong if, in the absence of that which you know to be facts, you form your judgments on the hypothesis that only that part of the evidence before you which furthers your own interests without working any hardship on others is based upon facts.

This is a crucial and important point in this lesson; therefore, I wish to be sure that you do not pass it by lightly. Many a man mistakes, knowingly or otherwise, expediency for fact; doing a thing, or refraining from doing it, for the sole reason that his action furthers his own interest without consideration as to whether it interferes with the rights of others.

No matter how regrettable, it is true that most thinking of today, far from being accurate, is based upon the sole foundation of expediency. It is amazing to the more advanced student of accurate thought, how many people there are who are 'honest' when it is profitable to them, but find myriads of facts (?) to justify themselves in following a dishonest course when that course seems to be more profitable or advantageous.

No doubt you know people who are like that.

The accurate thinker adopts a standard by which he guides himself, and he follows that standard at all time s, whether it works always to his immediate advantage, or carries him, now and then, through the fields of disadvantage (as it undoubtedly will).

The accurate thinker deals with facts, regardless of how they affect his own interests, for he knows that ultimately this policy will bring him out on top, in full possession of the object of his definite chief aim in life. He understands the soundness of the philosophy that the old philosopher, Croesus, had in mind when he said:

"There is a wheel on which the affairs of men revolve, and its mechanism is such that it prevents any man from being always fortunate."

The accurate thinker has but one standard by which he conducts himself, in his intercourse with his fellow men, and that standard is observed by him as faithfully when it brings him temporary disadvantage as it is when it brings him outstanding advantage; for, being an accurate thinker, he knows that, by the law of averages, he will more than regain at some future time that which he loses by applying his standard to his own temporary detriment.

You might as well begin to prepare yourself to understand that it requires the staunchest and most unshakable character to become an accurate thinker, for you can see that this is where the reasoning of this lesson is leading.

There is a certain amount of temporary penalty attached to accurate thinking ; there is no denying this fact; but, while this is true, it is also true that the compensating reward, in the aggregate, is so overwhelmingly greater that you will gladly pay this penalty.

In searching for facts it is often necessary to gather them through the sole source of knowledge and experience of others. It then becomes necessary to examine carefully both the evidence submitted and the person from whom the evidence comes; and when the evidence is of such a nature that it affects the interest of the witness who is giving it, there will be reason to scrutinize it all the more carefully, as witnesses who have an interest in the evidence that they are submitting often yield to the temptation to color and pervert it to protect that interest.

If one man slanders another, his remarks should be accepted, if of any weight at all, with at least a grain of the proverbial salt of caution; for it is a common human tendency for men to find nothing but evil in those whom they do not like. The man who has attained to the degree of accurate thinking that enables him to speak of his enemy without exaggerating his faults, and minimizing his virtues, is the exception and not the rule.

Some very able men have not yet risen above this vulgar and self-destructive habit of belittling their enemies, competitors and contemporaries. I wish to bring this common tendency to your attention with all possible emphasis, because it is a tendency that is fatal to accurate thinking.

Before you can become an accurate thinker, you must understand and make allowance for the fact that the moment a man or a woman begins to assume leadership in any walk of life, the slanderers begin to circulate 'rumours' and subtle whisperings reflecting upon his or her character.

No matter how fine one's character is or what service he may be engaged in rendering to the world, he cannot escape the notice of those misguided people who delight in destroy in g instead of building. Lincoln's political enemies circulated the report that he lived with a collared woman. Washington's political enemies circulated a similar report concerning him. Since both Lincoln and Washington were southern men, this report was undoubtedly regarded by those who circulated it as being atone and the same time the most fitting and degrading one they could imagine.

But we do not have to go back to our first President to find evidence of this slanderous nature with which men are gifted, for they went a step further, in paying their tributes to the late President Harding, and circulated the report that he had negro blood in his veins.

When Woodrow Wilson came back from Paris with what he believed to be a sound plan for abolishing war and settling international disputes, all except the accurate thinker might have been led to believe, by the reports of the 'they say' chorus, that he was a combination of Nero and Judas Iscariot. The little politicians, and the cheap politicians, and the 'interest-paid' politicians, and the plain ignorant who did not thinking of their own, all joined in one mighty chorus for the purpose of destroying the one and only man in the history of the world who offered a plan for abolishing war.

The slanderers killed both Harding and Wilson-murdered them with vicious lies. They did the same to Lincoln, only in a somewhat more spectacular manner, by inciting a fanatic to hasten his death with a bullet.

Statesmanship and politics are not the only fields in which the accurate thinker must be on guard against the 'they say' chorus. The moment a man begins to make himself felt in the field of industry or business, this chorus becomes active. If a man makes a better mouse-trap than his neighbour, the world will make a beaten path to his door; no doubt about that; and in the gang that will trail along will be those who come, not to commend, but to condemn and to destroy his reputation. The late John H. Patterson, president of the National Cash Register Company, is a notable example of what may happen to a man who builds a better cash register than that of his neighbour; yet, in the mind of the accurate thinker, there is not one scintilla of evidence to support the vicious reports that Mr. Patterson's competitors circulated about him.

As for Wilson and Harding, we may only judge how posterity will view them by observing how it has immortalized the names of Lincoln and Washington. Truth, alone, endures. All else must pass on with time.

The object of these references is not to eulogize those who stand in no particular need of eulogy; but, it is to direct your attention to the fact that 'they say' evidence is always subject to the closest scrutiny; and all the more so when it is of a negative or destructive nature. No harm can come from accepting, as fact, hearsay evidence that is constructive; but its opposite, if accepted at all, should be subjected to the closest inspection possible under the available means of applying the law of evidence.

As an accurate thinker,it is both your privilege—and—your—duty—to avail yourself—of—facts,—even—though you must go out of your way to get them. If you permit yourself to be swayed to and fro by all manner of information that comes to your attention, you will never become an accurate thinker ; and if you do not think accurately, you cannot be sure of attaining the object of your definite chief aim in life.

Many a man has gone down to defeat because, due to his prejudice and hatred, he underestimated the virtues of his enemies or competitors. The eyes of the accurate thinker see facts-not the delusions of prejudice, hate and envy.

An accurate thinker must be something of a good sportsman-in that he is fair enough (with himself at least) to look for virtues as well as faults in other people, for it is not without reason to suppose that all men have some of each of these qualities.

'I do not believe that I can afford to deceive others-I know I cannot afford to deceive myself!'

This must be the motto of the accurate thinker.

With the supposition that these 'hints' are sufficient to impress upon your mind the importance of searching for facts until you are reasonably sure that you have found them, we will take up the question of organising, classifying and using these facts.

Look, once more, in the circle of your own acquaintances and find a person who appears to accomplish more with less effort than do any of his associates. Study this man and you observe that he is a strategist in that he has learned how to arrange facts so that he brings to his aid the Law of Increasing Returns which we described in a previous lesson.

The man who k n o w s that he is working with facts goes at his task with a feeling of self- confidence which enables him to refrain from temporizing, hesitating or waiting to make sure of his ground. He knows in advance what the outcome of his efforts will be; therefore, he moves more rapidly and accomplishes more than does the man who must 'feel his way' because he is not sure that he is working with facts.

The man who has learned of the advantages of searching for facts as the foundation of his thinking has gone a very long way toward the development of accurate thinking, but the man who has learned how to separate facts into the important and the unimportant has gone still further. The latter may be compared to the man who uses a trip-hammer, and thereby accomplishes atone blow more than the former, who uses a tack-hammer, can accomplish with ten thousand blows.

Let us analyse, briefly, a few men who have made it their business to deal with the important or relevant facts pertaining to their life-work.

If it were not for the fact that this course is being adapted to the practical needs of men and women of the present workaday world, we would go back to the great men of the past-Plato, Aristotle, Epictetus, Socrates, Solomon, Moses and Christ-and direct attention to their habit of dealing with facts. However, we can find examples nearer our own generation that will serve our purpose to better advantage at this particular point.

Inasmuch as this is an age in which money is looked upon as being the most concrete proof of success, let us study a man who has accumulated almost as much of it as has any other man in the history of the world-John D. Rockefeller.

Mr. Rockefeller has one quality that stands out, like a shining star, above all of his other qualities; it is his habit of dealing only with the relevant facts pertaining to his life-work. As a very young man (and a very poor young man, at that) Mr. Rockefeller adopted, as his definite chief aim, the accumulation of great wealth. It is not my purpose, nor is it of any particular advantage, to enter into Mr. Rockefeller's method of accumulating his fortune other than to observe that his most pronounced quality was that of insisting on facts as the basis of his business philosophy. Some there are who say that Mr. Rockefeller was not always fair with his competitors. That may or may not be true (as accurate thinkers we will leave the point undisturbed), but no one (not even his competitors) ever accused Mr. Rockefeller of forming 'snap-judgments' or of underestimating the strength of his competitors. He not only recognised facts that affected his business, wherever and whenever he found them, but he made it his business to search for them until he was sure he had found them.

Thomas A. Edison is another example of a man who has attained to greatness through the organisation, classification and use of relevant facts. Mr. Edison works with natural laws as his chief aids; therefore, he must be sure of his facts before he can harness those laws. Every time you press a button and switch on an electric light, remember that it was Mr. Edison's capacity for organising relevant facts which made this possible.

Every time you hear a phonograph, remember that Mr. Edison is the man who made it a reality, through his persistent habit of dealing with relevant facts.

Every time you see a moving picture, remember that it was born of Mr. Edison's habit of dealing with important and relevant facts.

In the field of science relevant facts are the tools with which men and women work. Mere information, or hearsay evidence, is of no value to Mr. Edison; yet he might have wasted his life working with it, as millions of other people are doing.

Hearsay evidence could never have produced the incandescent electric light, the phonograph or the moving picture, and if it had, the phenomenon would have been an 'accident.' In this lesson we are trying to prepare the student to avoid 'accidents.'

The question now arises as to what constitutes an important and relevant fact.

The answer depends entirely upon what constitutes your definite chief aim in life, for an important and relevant fact is any fact which you can use, without interfering with the rights of others, in the attainment of that purpose.

All other facts, as far as you are concerned, are superfluous and of minor importance at most.

However, you can work just as hard in organising, classifying and using unimportant and irrelevant facts as you can in dealing with their opposites, but you will not accomplish as much.

Up to this point we have been discussing only one factor of accurate thought, that which is based upon deductive reasoning. Perhaps this is the point at which some of the students of this course will have to think along lines with which they are not familiar, for we come, now, to the discussion of thought which does much more than gather, organise and combine facts.

Let us call this creative thought!

That you may understand why it is called creative thought it is necessary briefly to study the process of evolution through which the thinking man has been created.

Thinking man has been a long time on the road of evolution, and he has travelled a very long way. In the words of judge T. Troward (in Bible Mystery and Bible Meaning), 'Perfected man is the apex of the Evolutionary Pyramid, and this by a necessary sequence.'

Let us trace thinking man through the five evolutionary steps through which we believe he has travelled, beginning with the very lowest; namely-

1. The Mineral Period. Here we find life in its lowest form, lying motionless and inert; a mass of mineral substances, with no power to move.

2. Then comes the Vegetable Period. Here we find life in a more active form, with intelligence sufficient to gather food, grow and reproduce, but still unable to move from its fixed moorings.

3. Then comes the Animal Period. Here we find life in a still higher and more intelligent form, with ability to move from place to place.—

4. Then comes the Human or Thinking Man Period, where we find life in its highest known form; the highest,—because man can think, and because thought is the highest known form of organised energy. In the realm of thought man knows no limitations. He can send his thoughts to the stars with the quickness of a flash of lightning. He can gather facts and assemble them in new and varying combinations. He can create hypotheses and translate them into physical reality, through thought. He can reason both inductively and deductively.

5. Then comes the Spiritual Period. On this plane the lower forms of life, described in the previously mentioned four periods, converge and become infinitude in nature. At this point thinking man has unfolded, expanded and grown until he has projected his thinking ability into infinite intelligence. As yet, thinking man is but an infant in this fifth period, for he has not learned how to appropriate to his own use this infinite intelligence called Spirit. Moreover, with a few rare exceptions, man has not yet recognised thought as the connecting link which gives him access to the power of infinite intelligence. These exceptions have been such men as Moses, Solomon, Christ, Plato, Aristotle, Socrates, Confucius and a comparatively small number of others of their type. Since their time we have had many who partly uncovered this great truth; yet the truth, itself, is as available now as it was then.

To make use of creative thought, one must work very largely on faith, which is the chief reason why more of us do not indulge in this sort of thought. The most ignorant of the race can think in terms of deductive reasoning, in connection with matters of a purely physical and material nature, but to go a step higher and think in terms of infinite intelligence is another question. The average man is totally at sea the moment he gets beyond that which he can comprehend with the aid of his five physical senses of seeing, hearing, feeling, smelling and tasting. Infinite intelligence works through none of these agencies and we cannot invoke its aid through any of them.

How, then, may one appropriate the power of infinite intelligence? is but a natural question.

And the answer is:

Through creative thought!

To make clear the exact manner in which this is done I will now call your attention to some of the preceding lessons of this course through which you have been prepared to understand the meaning of creative thought.

In the second lesson, and to some extent in practically every other lesson that followed it, up to this one, you have observed the frequent introduction of the term 'auto-suggestion.' (Suggestion that you make to yourself.) We now come back to that term again, because Auto-suggestion is the telegraph line, so to speak, over which you may register in your subconscious mind a description or plan of that which you wish to create or acquire in physical form.

It is a process you can easily learn to use.

The sub-conscious mind is the intermediary between the conscious thinking mind and infinite intelligence, and you can invoke the aid of infinite intelligence only through the medium of the sub-conscious mind, by giving it clear instructions as to what you want. Here you become familiar with the psychological reason for a definite chief aim.

If you have not already seen the importance of creating a definite chief aim as the object of your life-work, you will undoubtedly do so before this lesson shall have been mastered.

Knowing, from my own experience as a beginner in the study of this and related subjects, how little I understood such terms as 'Sub-conscious Mind' and 'auto-suggestion' and 'Creative Thought,' I have taken the liberty, throughout this course, of describing these terms through every conceivable simile and illustration, with the object of making their meaning and the method of their application so clear that no student of this course can possibly fail to understand. This accounts for the repetition of terms which you will observe throughout the course, and at the same time serves as an apology to those students who have already advanced far enough to grasp the meaning of much that the beginner will not understand at first reading.

The sub-conscious mind has one outstanding characteristic to which I will now direct your attention; namely, it records the suggestions which you send it through Auto-suggestion, and invokes the aid of infinite intelligence in translating these suggestions into their natural physical form, through natural means which are in no way out of the ordinary. If is important that you understand the foregoing sentence, for, if you fail to understand it, you are likely to fail, also, to understand the importance of the very foundation upon which this entire course is built-that foundation being the principle of infinite intelligence, which may be reached and appropriated at will through aid of the law of the 'Master Mind' described in the Introductory Lesson.

Study carefully, thoughtfully and with meditation, the entire preceding paragraph.

The sub-conscious mind has another outstanding characteristic-it accepts and acts upon all suggestions that reach it, whether they are constructive or destructive, and whether they come from the outside or from your own conscious mind.

You can see, therefore, how essential it is for you to observe the law of evidence and carefully follow the principles laid down in the beginning of this lesson, in the selection of that which you will pass on to your sub-conscious mind through Auto-suggestion. You can see why one must search diligently for facts, and why one cannot afford to lend a receptive ear to the slanderer and the scandalmonger-for to do so is the equivalent of feeding the sub-conscious mind with food that is poison and ruinous to creative thought.

The sub-conscious mind may be likened to the sensitive plate of a camera on which the picture of any object placed before the camera will be recorded. The plate of the camera does not choose the sort of picture to be recorded on it, it records anything which reaches it through the lens. The conscious mind may be likened to the shutter which shuts off the light from the sensitized plate, permitting nothing to reach the plate for record except that which the operator wishes to reach it. The lens of the camera may be likened to Auto-suggestion, for it is the medium which carries the image of the object to be registered, to the sensitized plate of the camera. And infinite intelligence may be likened to the one who develops the sensitized plate, after a picture has been recorded on it, thus bringing the picture into physical reality.

The ordinary camera is a splendid instrument with which to compare the whole process of creative thought. First comes the selection of the object to be exposed before the camera. This represents one's definite chief aim in life. Then comes the actual operation of recording a clear outline of that purpose, through the lens of Auto-suggestion, on the sensitized plate of the sub-conscious mind. Here infinite intelligence steps in and develops the outline of that purpose in a physical form appropriate to the nature of the purpose. The part which you must play is clear!

You select the picture to be recorded (definite chief aim). Then you fix your conscious mind upon this purpose with such intensity that it communicates with the sub-conscious mind, through Auto-suggestion, and registers that picture. You then begin to watch for and to expect manifestations of physical realisation of the subject of that picture.

Bear in mind the fact that you do not sit down and wait, nor do you go to bed and sleep, with the expectation of awaking to find that infinite intelligence has showered you with the object of your definite chief aim. You go right ahead, in the usual way, doing your daily work in accordance with the instructions laid down in Lesson Nine of this course, with full faith and confidence that natural ways and means for the attainment of the object of your definite purpose will open to you at the proper time and in a suitable manner.

The way may not open suddenly, from the first step to the last, but it may open one step at a time. Therefore, when you are conscious of an opportunity to take the first step, take it without hesitation, and do the same when the second, and the third, and all subsequent steps, essential for the attainment of the object of your definite chief aim, are manifested to you.

Infinite intelligence will not build you a home and deliver that home to you, ready to enter; but infinite intelligence will open the way and provide the necessary means with which you may build your own house.

Infinite intelligence will not command the cashier of your bank to place a definite sum of money to your credit, just because you suggested this to your subconscious mind; but infinite intelligence will open to you the way in which you may earn or borrow that money and place it to your own credit.

Infinite intelligence will not throw out the present incumbent of the White House and make you President in his place; but infinite intelligence would most likely proceed, under the proper circumstances, to influence you to prepare yourself to fill that position with credit and then help you to attain it through the regular method of procedure.

Do not rely upon the performance of miracles for the attainment of the object of your definite chief aim; rely upon the power of infinite intelligence to guide you, through natural channels, and with the aid of natural laws, for its attainment. Do not expect infinite intelligence to bring to you the object of your definite chief aim; instead, expect infinite intelligence to direct you toward that object.

As a beginner, do not expect infinite intelligence to move quickly in your behalf; but, as you become m o re adept in the use of the principle of Auto-suggestion, and as you develop the faith and understanding required for its quick realisation, you can create a definite chief aim and witness its immediate translation into physical reality. You did not walk the first time you tried, but now, as an adult (an adept at walking), you walk without effort. You also look down at the little child as it wobbles around, trying to walk, and laugh at its efforts. As a beginner in the use of creative thought, you may be compared to the little child who is learning to take its first step.

I have the best of reasons for knowing that this comparison is accurate, but I will not state them. I will let you find out your own reason, in your own way.

Keep in mind, always, the principle of evolution through the operation of which everything physical is eternally reaching upward and trying to complete the cycle between finite and infinite intelligences.

Man, himself, is the highest and most noteworthy example of the working of the principle of evolution. First, we find him down in the minerals of the earth, where there is life but no intelligence. Next, we find him raised, through the growth of vegetation (evolution), to a much higher form of life, where he enjoys sufficient intelligence to feed himself. Next, we find him functioning in the animal period, where he has a comparatively high degree of intelligence, with ability to move around from place to place. Lastly, we find him risen above the lower species of the animal kingdom, to where he functions as a thinking entity, with ability to appropriate and use infinite intelligence.

Observe that he did not reach this high state all atone bound. He climbed-step by step, perhaps through many reincarnations.

Keep this in mind and you will understand why you cannot reasonably expect infinite intelligence to circumvent the natural laws and turn man into the storehouse of all knowledge and all power until he has prepared himself to use this knowledge and power with higher than finite intelligence.

If you want a fair example of what may happen to a man who suddenly comes into control of power, study some newly-rich or someone who has inherited a fortune. Money-power in the hands of John D. Rockefeller is not only in safe hands, but it is in hands where it is serving mankind throughout the world, blotting out ignorance, destroying contagious disease and serving in a thousand other ways of which the average individual knows nothing.

But place John D. Rockefeller's fortune in the hands of some young lad who has not yet finished high school and you might have another story to tell, the details of which your own imagination and your knowledge of human nature will supply.

I will have more to say on this subject in Lesson Fourteen.

If you have ever done any farming, you understand that certain preparations are necessary before a crop can be produced from the ground. You know, of course, that grain will not grow in the woods, that it requires sunshine and rain for its growth. Likewise, you understand that the farmer must plow the soil and properly plant the grain.

After all this has been done, he then wait son Nature to do her share of the work; and she does it in due time, without outside help.

This is a perfect simile which illustrates the method through which one may attain the object of one's definite chief aim. First comes the preparing of the soil to receive the seed, which is represented by faith and infinite intelligence and understanding of the principle of Auto-suggestion and the sub-conscious mind through which the seed of a definite purpose may be planted. Then comes a period of waiting and working for the realisation of the object of that purpose. During this period, there must be continuous, intensified faith, which serves as the sunshine and the rain, without which the seed will wither and die in the ground. Then comes realisation, harvest-time.

And a wonderful harvest can be brought forth.

I am fully conscious of the fact that much of that which I am stating will not be understood by the beginner, at the first reading, for I have in mind my own experiences at the start. However, as the evolutionary process carries on its work (and it will do so; make no mistake about this) all the principles described in this and in all other lessons of this course, will become as familiar to you as did the multiplication table after you had mastered it; and, what is of greater importance still, these principles will work with the same unvarying certainty as does the principle of multiplication.

Each lesson of this course has provided you with definite instructions to follow. The instructions have been simplified as far as possible, so anyone can understand them. Nothing has been left to the student except to follow the instructions and supply the faith in their soundness without which they would be useless.

In this lesson you are dealing with four major factors to which I would again direct your attention with the request that you familiarize yourself with them. They are: auto-suggestion, the Sub-conscious Mind, Creative Thought and Infinite Intelligence.

These are the four roadways over which you must travel in your upward climb in quest of knowledge. Observe that you control three of these. Observe, also-and this is especially emphasized-that upon the manner in which you traverse these three roadways will depend the time and place at which they will converge into the fourth, or infinite intelligence.

You understand what is meant by the terms Auto suggestion and Sub-conscious Mind. Let us make sure that you understand, also, what is meant by the term Creative Thought. This means thought of a positive, non-destructive, creative nature. The object of Lesson Eight, on Self-control, was to prepare you to understand and successfully apply the principle of Creative Thought. If you have not mastered that lesson you are not ready to make use of Creative Thought in the attainment of your definite chief aim.

Let me repeat a simile already used by saying that your sub-conscious mind is the field or the soil in which you sow the seed of your definite chief aim. Creative Thought is the instrument with which you keep that soil fertilized and conditioned to awaken that seed into growth and maturity. Your subconscious mind will not germinate the seed of your definite chief aim nor will infinite intelligence translate that purpose into physical reality if you fill your mind with hatred, and envy, and jealousy, and selfishness and greed. These negative or destructive thoughts are the weeds which will choke out the seed of your definite purpose.

Creative thought pre-supposes that you will keep your mind in a state of expectancy of attainment of the object of your definite chief aim; that you will have full faith and confidence in its attainment in due course and in due order.

If this lesson does that which it was intended to do, it will bring you a fuller and deeper realisation of the third lesson of this course, on Self-confidence. As you begin to learn how to plant the seed of your desires in the fertile soil of your sub-conscious mind, and how to fertilize that seed until it springs into life and action, you will then have reason, indeed, to believe in yourself.

And, after you have reached this point in the process of your evolution, you will have sufficient knowledge of the real source from which you are drawing your power, to give full credit to infinite intelligence for all that you had previously credited to your self-confidence.

Auto-suggestion is a powerful weapon with which one may rise to heights of great achievement, when it is used constructively. Used in a negative manner, however, it may destroy all possibility of success, and if so used continuously it will actually destroy health.

Careful comparison of the experiences of leading physicians and psychiatrists disclosed the startling information that approximately seventy-five per cent of those who are ill are suffering from hypochondria, which is a morbid state of mind causing useless anxiety about one's health.

Stated in plain language, the hypochondriac is a person who believes he or she is suffering with some sort of imaginary disease, and often these unfortunates believe they have every disease of which they ever heard the name.

Hypochondriacally conditions are generally super-induced by auto-intoxication, or poisoning through failure of the intestinal system to throw off the waste matter. The person who suffers with such a toxic condition is not only unable to think with accuracy, but suffers from all sorts of perverted, destructive, illusory thoughts. Many sick people have tonsils removed, or teeth pulled, or the appendix taken out, when their trouble could have been removed with an internal bath and a bottle of Citrate of Magnesia (with due apologies to my friends, the physicians, one of the leading of whom gave me this information).

Hypochondria is the beginning of most cases of insanity!

Dr. Henry R. Rose is authority for the following typical example of the power of auto-suggestion:

"If my wife dies I will not believe there is a God' His wife was ill with pneumonia, and this is the way he greeted me when I reached his home. She had sent for me because the doctor had told her she could not recover. (Most doctors know better than to make a statement such as this in the presence of a patient.) She had called her husband and two sons to her bedside and bidden them good-by. Then she asked that I, her minister, be sent for. I found the husband in the front room sobbing and the sons doing their best to brace her up. When I went into her room she was breathing with difficulty, and the trained nurse told me she was very low.

"I soon found that Mrs. N_ had sent for me to look after her two sons after she was gone. Then I said to her: 'You mustn't give up. YOU ARE NOT GOING TO DIE! You have always been a strong and healthy woman and I do not believe God wants you to die and leave your boys to me or anyone else.'

"I talked to her along this line and then read the 103d Psalm and made a prayer in which I prepared her to get well rather than to enter eternity. I told her to put her faith in God and throw her mind and will against every thought of dying. Then I left her, saying, 'I will come again after the church service, and I will then find you much better.'

"This was on Sunday morning. I called that afternoon. Her husband met me with a smile. He said that the moment I had gone his wife called him and the boys into the room and said: 'Dr. Rose says that I am not going to die; that I am going to get well, and I am.'

"She did get well. But what did it? Two things Auto-suggestion, super induced by the suggestion I had given her, and faith on her part. I came just in the nick of time, and so great was her faith in me that I was able to inspire faith in herself. It was that faith that tipped the scales and brought her through the pneumonia. No medicine can cure pneumonia. The physicians admit that. There are cases of pneumonia, perhaps, that nothing can cure. We all sadly agree to that, but there are times, as in this case, when the mind, if worked upon and worked with in just the right way, will turn the tide. While there is life there is hope; but hope must rule supreme and do the good that hope was intended to do.

"Here is another remarkable case showing the power of the human mind when used constructively. A physician asked me to see Mrs. H_. He said there was nothing organically wrong with her, but she just wouldn't eat. Having made up her mind that she could not retain anything on her stomach, she had quit eating, and was slowly starving herself to death. I went to see her and found, first, that she had no religious belief. She had lost her faith in God. I also found that she had no confidence in her power to retain food. My first effort was to restore her faith in the Almighty and to get her to believe that He was with her and would give her power. Then I told her that she could eat anything she wanted. True, her confidence in me was great and my statement impressed her. She began to eat from that day! She was out of her bed in three days, for the first time in weeks. She is a normal, healthy and happy woman today.

"What did it? The same forces as those described in the preceding case; outside suggestion (which she accepted in faith and applied, through self-suggestion) and inward confidence.

"There are times when the mind is sick and it makes the body sick. At such times it needs a stronger mind to heal it by giving it direction and especially by giving it confidence and faith in itself. This is called suggestion. It is transmitting your confidence and power to another, and with such force as to make the other believe as you wish and do as you will. It need not be hypnotism. You can get wonderful results with the patient wide awake and perfectly rational. The patient must believe in you and you must understand the workings of the human mind in order to meet the arguments and questions of the patient. Each one of us can be a healer of this sort and thus help our fellow men.

"It is the duty of every person to read some of the best books on the forces of the human mind and learn what amazing things the mind can do to keep people well and happy. We see the terrible things that wrong thinking does to people, even going to such lengths as to make them positively insane. It is high time we found out the good things the mind can do, not only to cure mental disorders, but physical diseases as well"

You should delve deeper into this subject.

I do not say the mind can cure everything. There is no reliable evidence that certain forms of cancer have been cured by thinking or faith or any mental or religious process. If you would be cured of cancer you must take it at the very beginning and treat it surgically. There is no other way, and it would be criminal to suggest that there is. But the mind can do much with so many types of human indisposition and disease that we ought to rely upon it more often than we do.

Napoleon, during his campaign in Egypt, went among his soldiers who were dying by the hundreds of the black plague. He touched one of them and lifted a second, to inspire the others not to be afraid, for the awful disease seemed to spread as much by the aid of the imagination as in any other way. Goethe tells us that he himself went where there was malignant fever and never contracted it because he put forth his will. These giants among men knew something WE ARE SLOWLY BEGINNING TO FIND OUT-the power of Auto-suggestion! This means the influence we have upon ourselves by believing we cannot catch a disease or be sick. There is something about the operation of the automatic or sub-conscious mind by which it rises above disease germs and bids defiance to them when we resolve not to let the thought of them frighten us, or when we go in and out among the sick, even the contagiously sick, without thinking anything about it.

"Imagination will kill a cat," so runs the old adage. It certainly will kill a man, or, on the other hand, it will help him rise to heights of achievement of the most astounding nature, providing he uses it as the basis of self-confidence. There are authentic cases on record of men having actually died because they imagined they were cut by a knife across the jugular vein, when in reality a piece of ice was used and water was allowed to drip so they could hear it and imagine their blood was running out. They had been blindfolded before the experiment was begun. No matter how well you may be when you start for work in the morning, if everyone you meet should say to you, "How will you look; you should see a doctor," it will not be long before you begin to feel ill, and if this keeps up a few hours you will arrive at home in the evening as limp as a rag and ready for a doctor. Such is the power of the imagination or Auto-suggestion.

The imaginative faculty of the human mind is a marvellous piece of mental machinery, but it may, and usually does, play queer tricks on us unless we keep constantly on guard and control it.

If you allow your imagination to 'expect the worst' it will play havoc with you. Young medical students not infrequently become frightened and believe they have every disease on the medical calendar, as the result of medical lectures and class-room discussions of the various diseases.

As has been stated, hypochondria may often be super induced by toxic poisoning, through improper elimination of the waste matter of the body; also, it may be brought on by false alarm, through improper use of the imagination. In other words, the hypochondriacally condition may have as its cause a real physical basis, or it may arise entirely as the result of allowing the imagination to run wild.

Physicians are pretty well agreed upon this point! Dr. Schofield describes the case of a woman who had a tumour. They placed her on the operating table and gave her anaesthetics, when lo! the tumour immediately disappeared, and no operation was necessary. But when she came back to consciousness the tumour returned. The physician then learned that she had been living with a relative who had a real tumour, and that her imagination was so vivid that she had imagined this one upon herself. She was placed on the operating table again, given anaesthetics and then she was strapped around the middle so that the tumour could not artificially return. When she revived she was told that a successful operation had been performed but that it would be necessary to wear the bandage for several days. She believed the doctor, and when the bandage was finally removed the tumour did not return. No operation whatever had been performed. She had simply relieved her sub-conscious mind of the thought that she had a tumour and her imagination had nothing to work upon save the idea of health, and, as she had never really been sick, of course she remained normal.

The mind may be cured of imaginary ills in exactly the same manner that it became diseased with those ills, by Auto-suggestion. The best time to work on a faulty imagination is at night, just as you are ready to go to sleep, for then the automatic or sub-conscious mind has everything its own way, and the thoughts or suggestions you give it just as your conscious or 'day' mind is about to go off duty will be taken up and worked on during the night.

This may seem impossible, but you can easily test the principle by the following procedure: You wish to get up at seven o'clock tomorrow morning, or at some hour other than your regular time to awaken. Say to yourself, as you are about ready to go to sleep, 'I must arise at seven o'clock tomorrow without fail.' Repeat this several times, at the same time impressing the fact upon your mind that you must actually arise at the precise moment mentioned. Turn this thought over to your sub-conscious mind with absolute confidence that you will awaken at seven o'clock, and when that hour arrives your sub-conscious mind will awaken you. This test has been successfully made hundreds of times. The sub-conscious mind will awaken you, at any hour you demand, just as if someone came to your bed and tapped you on the shoulder. But you must give the command in no uncertain or indefinite terms. Likewise, the sub-conscious mind may be given any other sort of orders and it will carry them out as readily as it will awaken you at a given hour. For example, give the command, as you are about to go to sleep each night, for your sub-conscious mind to develop self-confidence, courage, initiative or any other quality, and it will do your bidding.

If the imagination of man can create imaginary ills and send one to bed with those ills, it can also, and just as easily, remove the cause of those ills.

Man is a combination of chemical equivalents the value of which is said to be about twenty-six dollars, with the exception, of course, of that stupendous power called the human mind.

In the aggregate the mind seems to be a complicated machine, but in reality; as far as the manner in which it may be used is concerned, it is the nearest thing to perpetual motion that is known. It works automatically when we are asleep; it works both automatically and in conjunction with the will, or voluntary section, when we are awake.

The mind is deserving of the minutes possible analysis in this lesson because the mind is the energy with which all thinking is done. To learn how to THINK ACCURATELY, the teaching of which is the sole object of this lesson, one must thoroughly understand:

First: That the mind can be controlled, guided and directed to creative, constructive ends.

Second: That the mind can be directed to destructive ends, and, that it may, voluntarily, tear down and destroy unless it is with plan and deliberation controlled and directed constructively.

Third: That the mind has power over every cell of the body, and can be made to cause every cell to do its intended work perfectly, or it may, through neglect or wrong direction, destroy the normal functionary purposes of any or all cells.

Fourth: That all achievement of man is the result of thought, the part which his physical body plays being of secondary importance, and in many instances of no importance whatsoever except as a housing place for the mind.

Fifth: That the greatest of all achievements, whether in literature, art, finance, industry, commerce, transportation, religion, politics or scientific discoveries, are usually the results of ideas conceived in one man's brain but ACTUALLY TRANSFORMED INTO REALITY BY OTHER MEN, through the combined use of their minds and bodies. (Meaning that the conception of an idea is of greater importance than the transformation of that idea into more material form, because relatively few men can conceive useful ideas, while there are hundreds of millions who can develop an idea and give it material form after it has been conceived.)

Sixth: The majority of all thoughts conceived in the minds of men are not ACCURATE, being more in the nature of 'opinions' or 'snap-judgments.'

When Alexander the Great sighed because he had no more worlds (as he believed) that could be conquered he was in a frame of mind similar to that of the present-day 'Alexander's' of science, industry, invention, etc., whose 'accurate thoughts' have conquered the air and the sea, explored practically every square mile of the little earth on which we live, and wrested from Nature thousands of 'secrets' which, a few generations ago, would have been set down as 'miracles' of the most astounding and imponderable sort.

In all this discovery and mastery of mere physical substances is it not strange, indeed, that we have practically neglected and overlooked the most marvellous of all powers, the human mind!

All scientific men who have made a study of the human mind readily agree on this-that the surface has not yet been scratched in the study of the wonderful power which lies dormant in the mind of man, waiting, as the oak tree sleeps in the acorn, to be aroused and put to work. Those who have expressed themselves on the subject are of the opinion that the next great cycle of discovery lies in the realm of the human mind.

The possible nature of these discoveries has been suggested, in many different ways, in practically every lesson of this course, particularly in this and the following lessons of the course.

If these suggestions appear to lead the student of this philosophy into deeper water than he or she is accustomed to, bear in mind the fact that the student has the privilege of stopping at any depth desired, until ready, through thought and study, to go further.

The author of this course has found it necessary to take the lead, and to keep far enough ahead, as it were, to induce the student to go at least a few paces ahead of the normal average range of human thought.

It is not expected that any beginner will, at first, try to assimilate and put into use all that has been included in this philosophy. But, if the net result of the course is nothing more than to sow the seed of constructive thought in the mind of the student the author's work will have been completed. Time, plus the student's own desire for knowledge, will do the rest.

This is an appropriate place to state frankly that many of the suggestions passed on through this course would, if literally followed, lead the student far beyond the necessary bounds and present needs of what is ordinarily called business philosophy. Stated differently, this course goes more deeply into the functioning processes of the human mind than is necessary as far as the use of this philosophy as a means of achieving business or financial success is concerned.

However, it is presumed that many students of this course will wish to go more deeply into the study of mind power than may be required for purely material achievement, and the author has had in mind these students throughout the labour of organising and writing this course.

Summary of Principles Involved In Accurate Thinking

We have discovered that the body of man is not singular, but plural-that it consists of billions on top of billions of living, intelligent, individual cells which carry on a very definite, well organised work of building, developing and maintaining the human body.

We have discovered that these cells are directed, in their respective duties, by the sub-conscious or automatic action of the mind; that the subconscious section of the mind can be, to a very large extent, controlled and directed by the conscious or voluntary section of the mind.

We have found that any idea or thought which is held in the mind, through repetition, has a tendency to direct the physical body to transform such thought or idea into its material equivalent. We have found that any order that is PROPERLY given to the subconscious section of the mind (through the law of Auto-suggestion) will be carried out unless it is sidetracked or countermanded by another and stronger order. We have found that the sub-conscious mind does not question the source from which it receives orders, nor the soundness of those orders, but it will proceed to direct the muscular system of the body to carry out any order it receives.

This explains the necessity for guarding closely the environment from which we receive suggestions, and by which we are subtly and quietly influenced at times and in ways of which we do not take cognizance through the conscious mind.

We have found that every movement of the human body is controlled by either the conscious or the subconscious section of the mind; that not a muscle can be moved until an order has been sent out by one or the other of these two sections of the mind, for the movement.

When this principle is thoroughly understood we understand, also, the powerful effect of any idea or thought which we create through the faculty of IMAGINATION and hold in the conscious mind until the sub-conscious section of the mind has time to take over that thought and begin the work of transforming it into its material counterpart. When we understand the principle through which any idea is first placed in the conscious mind, and held there until the subconscious section of the mind picks it up and appropriates it, we have a practical working knowledge of the Law of Concentration, covered by next lesson (and, it might be added, we have also a thorough understanding of the reason why the Law of Concentration is necessarily a part of this philosophy).

When we understand this working relationship between the imagination, the conscious mind and the sub-conscious section of the mind, we can see that the very first step in the achievement of any definite chief aim is to create a definite picture of that which is desired. This picture is then placed in the conscious mind, through the Law of Concentration, and held there (through the formulas described in next lesson) until the sub-conscious section of the mind picks it up and translates it into its ultimate and desired form.

Surely this principle has been made clear. It has been stated and restated, over and over, not only for the purpose of thoroughly describing it, but, of greater importance, to impress upon the mind of the student the part it plays in all human achievement.

The Value of Adopting A Chief Aim

This lesson on Accurate Thought not only describes the real purpose of a definite chief aim, but it explains in simple terms the principles through which such an aim or purpose may be realised. We first create the objective toward which we are striving, through the imaginative faculty of the mind, then transfer an outline of this objective to paper by writing out a definite statement of it in the nature of a definite chief aim. By daily reference to this written statement the idea or thing aimed for is taken up by the conscious mind and handed over to the sub-conscious mind, which, in turn, directs the energies of the body to transform the desire into material form.

Desire

Strong, deeply rooted desire is the starting point of all achievement. Just as the electron is the last unit of matter discernible to the scientist, DESIRE is the seed of all achievement; the starting place, back of which there is nothing, or at least there is nothing of which we have any knowledge.

A definite chief aim, which is only another name for DESIRE, would be meaningless unless based upon a deeply seated, strong desire for the object of the chief aim. Many people 'wish' for many things, but a wish is not the equivalent of a strong DESIRE, and therefore wishes are of little or no value unless they are crystallized into the more definite form of DESIRE.

It is believed by men who have devoted years of research to the subject, that all energy and matter throughout the universe respond to and are controlled by the Law of Attraction which causes elements and forces of a similar nature to gather around certain centres of attraction. It is through the operation of this same universal Law of Attraction that constant, deeply seated, strong DESIRE attracts the physical equivalent or counter part of the thing desired, or the means of securing it.

We have learned, then, if this hypothesis is correct, that all cycles of human achievement work somewhat after this fashion: First, we picture in our conscious minds, through a definite chief aim (based upon a strong desire), some objective; we then focus our conscious mind upon this objective, by constant thought of it and belief in its attainment, until the subconscious section of the mind takes up the picture or outline of this objective and impels us to take the necessary physical action to transform that picture into reality.

Suggestion and Auto-Suggestion

Through this and other lessons of The Law of Success course the student has learned that sense impressions arising out of one's environment, or from statements or actions of other people, are called suggestions, while sense impressions that we place in our own minds are placed there by self-suggestion, or Auto suggestion.

All suggestions coming from others, or from environment, influence us only after we have accepted them and passed them on to the sub-conscious mind, through the principle of Auto-suggestion, thus it is seen that suggestion becomes, and must become, Auto suggestion before it influences the mind of the one receiving it.

Stated in another way, no one may influence another without the consent of the one influenced, as the influencing is done through one's own power of Auto-suggestion.

The conscious mind stands, during the hours when one is awake, as a sentinel, guarding the sub-conscious mind and warding off all suggestions which try to reach it from the outside, until those suggestions have been examined by the conscious mind, passed upon and accepted. This is Nature's way of safeguarding the human being against intruders who would otherwise take control of any mind desired at will.

It is a wise arrangement.

The value of auto-suggestion in accomplishing the object of your definite chief aim.

One of the greatest uses to which one may direct the power of auto-suggestion is that of making it help accomplish the object of one's definite chief aim in life.

The procedure through which this may be accomplished is very simple. While the exact formula has been stated in Lesson Two, and referred to in many other lessons of the course, the principle upon which it is based will be here, again, described, viz.:

Write out a clear, concise statement of that which you intend to accomplish, as your definite chief aim, covering a period of, let us say, the next five years. Make at least two copies of your statement, one to be placed where you can read it several times a day, while you are at work, and the other to be placed in the room where you sleep, where it can be read several times each evening before you go to sleep and just after you arise in the morning.

The suggestive influence of this procedure (impractical though it may seem) will soon impress the object of your definite chief aim on your sub-conscious mind and, as if by a stroke of magic, you will begin to observe events taking place which will lead you nearer and nearer the attainment of that object.

From the very day that you reach a definite decision in your own mind as to the precise thing, condition or position in life that you deeply desire, you will observe, if you read books, newspapers and magazines, that important news items and other data bearing on the object of your definite chief aim will begin to come to your attention; you will observe, also, that opportunities will begin to come to you that will, if embraced, lead you nearer and nearer the coveted goal of your desire. No one knows better than the author of this course how impossible and impractical this may seem to the person who is not informed on the subject of mind operation; however, this is not an age favourable to the doubter or the sceptic, and the best thing for any person to do is to experiment with this principle until its practicality has been established.

To the present generation it may seem that there are no more worlds to conquer in the field of mechanical invention, but every thinker (even those who are not accurate thinkers) will concede that we are just entering a new era of evolution, experiment and analysis as far as the powers of the human mind are concerned.

The word 'impossible' means less now than ever before in the history of the human race. There are some who have actually removed this word from their vocabularies, believing that man can do anything he can imagine and BELIEVE HE CAN DO!

We have learned, for sure, that the universe is made up of two substances: matter and energy. Through patient scientific research we have discovered what we believe to be good evidence that everything that is or ever has been in the way of matter, when analysed to the finest point, can be traced back to the electron, which is nothing but a form of energy. On the other hand, every material thing that man has created began in the form of energy, through the seed of an idea that was released through the imaginative faculty of the human mind. In other words, the beginning of every material thing is energy and the ending of it is energy.

All matter obeys the command of one form or another of energy. The highest known form of energy is that which functions as the human mind. The human mind, therefore, is the sole directing force of everything man creates, and what he may create with: this force in the future, as compared with that which he has created with it in the past, will make his past achievements seem petty and small.

We do not have to wait for future discoveries in connection with the powers of the human mind for evidence that the mind is the greatest force known to mankind. We know, now, that any idea, aim or purpose that is fixed in the mind and held there with a will to achieve or attain its physical or material equivalent, puts into motion powers that cannot be conquered.

Buxton said: 'The longer I live the more certain I am that the great difference between men, between the feeble and the powerful, the great and the insignificant, is energy-invincible determination-a purpose once fixed, and then death or victory. That quality will do anything that can be done in this world-and no talents, no circumstances, no opportunities will make a two-legged creature a man without it.'

Donald G. Mitchell has well said: 'Resolve is what makes a man manifest. Not puny resolve; not crude determinations; not errant purposes-but that strong and indefatigable will which treads down difficulties and danger, as a boy treads down the heaving frost-lands of winter, which kindles his eye and brain with proud pulse beat toward the unattainable. WILL MAKES MEN GIANTS!'

The great Disraeli said: "I have brought myself, by long meditation, to the conviction that a human being with a settled purpose must accomplish it, and that nothing can resist a will which will stake even existence upon its fulfilment."

Sir John Simpson said: "A passionate DESIRE and an unwearied will can perform impossibilities, or what may seem to be such to the cold, timid and feeble."

And John Foster adds his testimony when he says: "It is wonderful how even the casualties of life seem to bow to a spirit that will not bow to them, and yield to sub serve a design which they may, in their first apparent tendency, threaten to frustrate. When a firm, decisive spirit is recognised, it is curious to see how the space clears around a man and leaves him room and freedom."

Abraham Lincoln said of General Grant: "The great thing about Grant is his cool persistency of purpose. He is not easily excited, and he has got the grip of a bull-dog. When he once gets his teeth in, nothing can shake him off."

It seems appropriate to state here that a strong desire, to be transformed into reality, must be backed with persistency until it is taken over by the subconscious mind. It is not enough to feel very deeply the desire for achievement of a definite chief aim, for a few hours or a few days, and then forget all about that desire. The desire must be placed in the mind and held there, with PERSISTENCE THAT KNOWS NO DEFEAT, until the automatic or sub-conscious mind takes it over. Up to this point you must stand back of the desire and push it; beyond this point the desire will stand back of you and push you on to achievement.

Persistence may be compared to the dropping of water which finally wears away the hardest stone. When the final chapter of your life shall have been completed it will be found that your persistence, or lack of this sterling quality, played an important part in either your success or your failure.

This author watched the Tunney-Dempsey fight, in Chicago. He also studied the psychology leading up to and surrounding their previous bout. Two things helped Tunney defeat Dempsey, on both occasions, despite the fact that Dempsey is the stronger of the two men, and, as many believe, the better fighter.

And these two things, which spelled Dempsey's doom, were, first, his own lack of self-confidence-the fear that Tunney might defeat him; and, second, Tunny's complete self-reliance and his belief that he would whip Dempsey.

Tunney stepped into the ring, with his chin in the air, an atmosphere of self-assurance and certainty written in his every movement. Dempsey walked in, with a sort of uncertain stride, eying Tunney in a manner that plainly queried, "I wonder what you'll do to me?"

Dempsey was whipped, in his own mind, before he entered the ring. Press agents and propagandists had done the trick, thanks to the superior thinking ability of his opponent, Tunney.

And so the story goes, from the lowest and most brutal of occupations, prize-fighting, on up to the highest and most commendable professions. Success is won by the man who understands how to use his power of thought.

Throughout this course much stress has been laid upon the importance of environment and habit out of which grow the stimuli that put the 'wheels' of the human mind into operation. Fortunate is the person who has found how to arouse or stimulate his or her mind so that the powers of that mind will function constructively, as they may be made to do when placed back of any strong, deeply seated desire.

Accurate thinking is thinking that makes intelligent use of all the powers of the human mind, and does not stop with the mere examination, classification and arranging of ideas. Accurate thought creates ideas and it may be made to transform these ideas into their most profitable, constructive form.

The student will perhaps be better prepared to analyse, without a feeling of scepticism and doubt, the principles laid down in this lesson if the fact is kept in mind that the conclusions and hypotheses here enumerated are not solely those of the author. I have had the benefit of close co-operation from some of the leading investigators in the field of mental phenomena, and conclusions reached, as stated in this entire course, are those of many different minds.

In the lesson on Concentration, you will be further instructed in the method of applying the principle of Auto-suggestion. In fact, throughout the course, the principle of gradual enfoldment has been followed, paralleling that of the principle of evolution as nearly as possible. The first lesson laid the foundation for the second, and the second prepared the way for the third, and so on. I have tried to build this course just as Nature builds a man-by a series of steps each of which lifts the student just another step higher and nearer the apex of the pyramid which the course, as a whole, represents.

The purpose in building this course in the manner outlined is one that cannot be described in words, but that purpose will become obvious and clear to you as soon as you shall have mastered the course, for its mastery will open to you a source of knowledge which cannot be impacted by one man to another, but is attainable only by educing, drawing out and expanding, from within one's own mind. The reason this knowledge cannot be impacted by one to another is the same as that which makes it impossible for one person to describe colors to a blind person who has never seen colors.

The knowledge of which I write became obvious to me only after I had diligently and faithfully followed the instructions which I have laid down in this course for your guidance and enlightenment; therefore, I speak from experience when I say that there are no illustrations, similes or words with which to describe this knowledge adequately. It can only be imparted from within.

With this vague 'hint' as to the reward which awaits all who earnestly and intelligently search for the hidden passageway to knowledge to which I refer, we will now discuss that phase of accurate thought which will take you as high as you can go-except through the discovery and use of the secret passageway to which I have alluded.

Thoughts are things!

It is the belief of many that every completed thought starts an unending vibration with which the one who releases it will have to contend at a later time; that man, himself, is but the physical reflection of thought that was put into motion by infinite intelligence.

"And the Word was made flesh, and dwelt among us, (and we beheld his glory, the glory as of the only begotten of the Father,) full of grace and truth."

The only hope held out to mankind in the entire Bible is of a reward which may be attained in no way except by constructive thought. This is a startling statement, but if you are even an elementary student and interpreter of the Bible you understand that it is a true statement.

If the Bible is plain on any one point above all others, it is on the fact that thought is the beginning of all things of a material nature.

At the beginning of every lesson of this course you will observe this motto:

"You can do it if you BELIEVE you can!"

This sentence is based upon a great truth which is practically the major premise of the entire Bible teaching. Observe the emphasis which is placed upon the word BELIEVE. Back of this word 'believe' lies the power with which you can vitalize and give life to the suggestions that you pass on to your sub-conscious mind, through the principle of Auto-suggestion, with the aid of the law of the Master Mind. Do not miss this point. You cannot afford to miss it, as it is the very beginning, the middle and the end of all the power you will ever have.

All thought is creative! However, not all thought is constructive or positive. If you think thoughts of misery and poverty and see no way to avoid these conditions, then your thoughts will create those very conditions and curse you with them. But reverse the order, and think thoughts of a positive, expectant nature and your thoughts will create those conditions.

Thought magnetizes your entire personality and attracts to you the outward, physical things that harmonize with the nature of your thoughts. This has been made clear in practically every lesson preceding this one, yet it is repeated here, and will be repeated many times more in the lessons that follow. The reason for this constant repetition is that nearly all beginners in the study of mind operation overlook the importance of this fundamental and eternal truth.

When you plant a definite chief aim in your subconscious mind you must fertilize it with full belief that infinite intelligence will step in and mature that purpose into reality in exact accordance with the nature of the purpose. Anything short of such belief will bring you disappointment.

When you suggest a definite chief aim which embodies some definite desire, in your sub-conscious mind, you must accompany it with such faith and belief in the ultimate realisation of that purpose that you can actually see yourself in possession of the object of the purpose. Conduct yourself in the exact manner in which you would if you were already in possession of the object of your definite purpose, from the moment you suggest it to your sub-conscious mind.

Do not question; do not wonder if the principles of Auto-suggestion will work; do not doubt, but believe!

Surely this point has been sufficiently emphasized to impress upon your mind its importance.

Positive belief in the attainment of your definite purpose is the very germ with which you fertilize the 'egg of your thought' and if you fail to give it this fertilization, you might as well expect an unfertilized hen-egg to produce a chicken as to expect the attainment of the object of your definite chief aim.

You never can tell what a thought will do
In bringing you hate or love;
For thoughts are things, and their airy wings
Are swifter than a carrier dove.
They follow the law of the universe,-
Each thought creates its kind,
And they speed o'er the track to bring you back
Whatever went out from your mind.

Thoughts are things! This is a great truth which, when you understand it, will bring you as close to the door of that secret passage-way to knowledge, previously mentioned, as is possible for another person to bring you. When you grasp this fundamental truth you will soon find that door and open it.

The power to think as you wish to think is the only power over which you have absolute control.

Please read and study the foregoing sentence until you grasp its meaning. If it is within your power to control your thoughts the responsibility then rests upon you as to whether your thoughts will be of the positive or the negative type, which brings to mind one of the world's most famous poems:

Out of the night that covers me,
Black as the pit from pole to pole,
I thank whatever gods may be
For my unconquerable soul.
In the fell clutch of circumstance
I have not winced or cried aloud.
Under the bludgeoning of chance
My head is bloody, but unbowed.

Beyond this place of wrath and tears
Looms but the horror of the shade,
And yet the menace of the years
Finds, and shall find, me unafraid.
It matters not how strait the gate,
How charged with punishments the scroll,
I am the master of my fate,
I am the captain of my soul.

—**Henley**

Henley did not write this poem until after he had discovered the door to that secret passage-way which I have mentioned.

You are the 'master of your fate' and the 'captain of your soul,' by reason of the fact that you control your own thoughts, and, with the aid of your thoughts, you may create whatever you desire.

As we approach the close of this lesson, let us pull aside the curtain that hangs over the gateway called death and take a look into the Great Beyond. Behold a world peopled with beings who function without the aid of physical bodies. Look closely and, whether for weal or for woe, observe that you look at a world peopled with beings of your own creation, which correspond exactly to the nature of your own thoughts as you expressed them before death. There they are, the children of your own heart and mind, patterned after the image of your own thoughts.

Those which were born of your hatred and envy and jealousy and selfishness and injustice toward your fellow men will not make very desirable neighbours, but you must live with them just the same, for they are your children and you cannot turn them out.

You will be unfortunate, indeed, if you find there no children which were born of love, and justice, and truth, and kindness toward others.

In the light of this allegorical suggestion, the subject of accurate thought takes on a new and a much more important aspect, doesn't it?

If there is a possibility that every thought you release during this life will step out, in the form of a living being, to greet you after death, then you need no further reason for guarding all your thoughts more carefully than you would guard the food that you feed your physical body.

I refer to this suggestion as 'allegorical' for a reason that you will understand only after you shall have passed through the door of that secret passage-way to knowledge that I have heretofore mentioned.

To ask me how I know these things, before you pass through that door, would be as useless as it would be for a man who has never seen with his physical eyes to ask me what the color red looks like.

I am not urging you to accept this viewpoint. I am not even arguing its soundness. I am merely fulfilling my duty and discharging my responsibility by giving you the suggestion. You must carry it out to a point at which you can accept or reject it, in your own way,, and of your own volition.

The term 'accurate thought' as used in this lesson refers to thought which is of your own creation. Thought that comes to you from others, through either suggestion or direct statement, is not accurate thought within the meaning and purpose of this lesson, although it may be thought that is based upon facts.

I have now carried you to the apex of the pyramid of this lesson on accurate thought. I can take you no further. However, you have not gone the entire distance; you have but started. From here on you must be your own guide, but, if you have not wholly missed the great truth upon which the lesson is founded, yarn will not have difficulty in finding your own way.

Let me caution you, however, not to become discourage if the fundamental truth of this lesson does not dawn upon you at first reading. It may require weeks or even months of meditation for you to comprehend fully this truth, but it is worth working for.

The principles laid down in the beginning of this lesson you can easily understand and accept, because they are of the most elementary nature. However, as you began to follow the chain of thought along toward the close of the lesson, you perhaps found yourself being carried into waters too deep for you to fathom.

Perhaps I can throw one final ray of light on the subject by reminding you that the sound of every voice, and of every note of music, and of every other nature that is being released at the time you are reading these lines is floating through the ether right where you are. To hear these sounds you need but the aid of a modern radio outfit. Without this equipment as a supplement to your own sense of hearing you are powerless to hear these sounds.

Had this same statement been made twenty years ago, you would have believed the one who made it to be insane or a fool. But you now accept the statement without question, because you know it is true.

Thought is a much higher and more perfectly organised form of energy than is mere sound; therefore, it is not beyond the bounds of reason to suppose that every thought now being released and every thought that has ever been released is also in the ether (or somewhere else) and may be interpreted by those who have the equipment with which to do it.

And, whats or to fequipment is necessary? you ask.

That will be answered when you shall have passed through the door that leads to the secret passage-way to knowledge. It cannot be answered before. The passage-way can be reached only through the medium of you r own thoughts. This is one reason why all the great philosophers of the past admonished man to know himself. 'Know thyself' is and has been the cry of the ages. The life of Christ was one uninterrupted promise of hope and possibility based entirely upon the knowledge which all may discover who search within their own beings.

One of the unanswerable mysteries of God's work is the fact that this great discovery is always self-discovery. The truth for which man is eternally searching is wrapped up in his own being; therefore, it is fruitless to search far afield in the wilderness of life or in the hearts of other men to find it. To do so brings you no nearer that which you are seeking, but takes you further away from it.

And, it may be-who knows but you?-that even now, as you finish this lesson, you are nearer the door that leads to the secret passage-way to knowledge than you have ever been before.

With your mastery of this lesson will come a fuller understanding of the principle referred to in the Introductory Lesson as the 'Master Mind.' Surely you now understand the reason for friendly co-operative alliance between two or more people. This alliance 'steps up' the minds of those who participate in it, and permits them to contact their thought-power with infinite intelligence.

With this statement the entire Introductory Lesson should have a new meaning for you. This lesson has familiarized you with the main reason why you should make use of the law of the Master Mind by showing you the height to which this law may be made to carry all who understand and use it.

By this time you should understand why a few men have risen to great heights of power and fortune, while others all around them remained in poverty and want. If you do not now understand the cause for this, you will by the time you master the remaining lessons of this course.

Do not become discouraged if complete understanding of these principles does not follow your first reading of this lesson. This is the one lesson of the entire course which cannot be fully assimilated by the beginner through one reading. It will give up its rich treasures of knowledge only through thought, reflection and meditation. For this reason you are instructed to read this lesson at least four times, at intervals of one week apart.

You are also instructed to read, again, the Introductory Lesson, that you may more accurately and definitely understand the law of the Master Mind and the relationship between this law and the subjects covered by this lesson on accurate thought.

The Master Mind is the principle through which you may become an accurate thinker!

Is not this statement both plain and significant?

FAILURE : An after-the-lesson visit with the author.

The great Success Lessons that can be learned from reverses.

An all-wise providence has arranged the affairs of mankind so that every person who comes into the age of reason must bear the cross of FAILURE in one form or another.

You see, in the picture at the top of this page, the heaviest and most cruel of all the crosses, POVERTY!

Hundreds of millions of people living on this earth today find it necessary to struggle under the burden of this cross in order to enjoy the three bare necessities of life, a place to sleep, something to eat and clothes to wear.

Carrying the cross of POVERTY is no joke!

But, it seems significant that the greatest and most successful men and women who ever lived found it necessary to carry this cross before they 'arrived.'

FAILURE is generally accepted as a curse. But few people ever understand that failure is a curse only when it is accepted as such. But few ever learn the truth that FAILURE is seldom permanent.

Go back over your own experiences for a few years and you will see that your failures generally turned out to be blessings in disguise. Failure teaches men lessons which they would never learn without it. Moreover, it teaches in a language that is universal. Among the great lessons taught by failure is that of HUMILITY.

No man may become great without feeling himself humble and insignificant when compared to the world about him and the stars above him and the harmony with which Nature does her work.

For every rich man's son who becomes a useful, constructive worker in behalf of humanity, there are ninety-nine others rendering useful service who come up through POVERTY and misery. This seems more than a coincidence!

Most people who believe themselves to be failures are not failures at all. Most conditions which people look upon as failure are nothing more than temporary defeat.

If you pity yourself and feel that you are a failure, think how much worse off you would be if you had to change places with others who have real cause for complaint.

In the city of Chicago lives a beautiful young woman. Her eyes are a light blue. Her complexion is extremely fair. She has a sweet charming voice. She is educated and cultured. Three days after graduating in one of the colleges of the East she discovered that she had negro blood in her veins.

The man to whom she was engaged refused to marry her. The negroes do not want her and the whites will not associate with her. During the remainder of her life she must bear the brand of permanent FAILURE.

Remember, this is PERMANENT failure!

As this essay is being written news comes of a beautiful girl baby who was born to an unwed girl and taken into an orphanage, there to be brought up mechanically, without ever knowing the influence of a mother's love. All through life this unfortunate child must bear the brunt of another's mistake which can never be corrected.

How fortunate are YOU, no matter what may be your imaginary failures, that you are not this child.

If you have a strong body and a sound mind you have much for which you ought to be thankful. Millions of people all about you have no such blessings.

Careful analysis of one hundred men and women whom the world has accepted as being 'great' shows that they were compelled to undergo hardship and temporary defeat and failure such as you probably have never known and never will know.

Woodrow Wilson went to his grave altogether too soon, the victim of cruel slander and disappointment, believing, no doubt, that he was a FAILURE. TIME, the great miracle worker that rights all wrongs and turns failure into success, will place the name of Woodrow Wilson at the top of the page of the really great.

Few now living have the vision to see that out of Wilson's 'FAILURE' will come, eventually, such a powerful demand for universal peace that war will be an impossibility.

Lincoln died without knowing that his 'FAILURE' gave sound foundation to the greatest nation on this earth.

Columbus died, a prisoner in chains, without ever knowing that his 'FAILURE' meant the discovery of the great nation which Lincoln and Wilson helped to preserve, with their 'FAILURES.'

Do not use the word FAILURE carelessly. Remember, carrying a burdensome cross temporarily is not FAILURE. If you have the real seed of success within you, a little adversity and temporary defeat will only serve to nature that seed and cause it to burst forth into maturity.

When Divine Intelligence wants a great man or woman to render some needed service in the world, the fortunate one is tested out through some form of FAILURE. If you are undergoing what you believe to be failure, have patience; you may be passing through your testing time.

No capable executive would select, as his lieutenants, those whom he had not tested for reliability, loyalty, perseverance and other essential qualities.

Responsibility, and all that goes with it in the way of remuneration, always gravitates to the person who will not accept temporary defeat as permanent failure.

"The test of a man is the fight he makes,

The grit that he daily shows;

The way he stands on his feet and takes

Fate's numerous bumps and blows,
A coward can smile when there's naught to fear,
When nothing his progress bars;
But it takes a man to stand up and cheer
While some other fellow stars.
"It isn't the victory, after all,
But the fight that a brother makes;
The man who, driven against the wall,
Still stands up erect and takes
The blows of fate with his head held high:
Bleeding, and bruised, and pale,
Is the man who'll win in the by and by,
For he isn't afraid to fail.
"It's the bumps you get, and the jolts you get,
And the shocks that your courage stands,
The hours of sorrow and vain regret,
The prize that escapes your hands,
That test your mettle and prove your worth;
It isn't the blows you deal,
But the blows you take on the good old earth,
That show if your stuff is real. "

Failure often places one in a position where unusual effort must be forthcoming. Many a man has wrung victory from defeat, fighting with his back to the wall, where he could not retreat.

Caesar had long wished to conquer the British. He quietly sailed his soldier-laden ships to the British island, unloaded his troops and supplies, then gave the order to burn all the ships. Calling his soldiers about him he said: 'Now it is win or perish. We have no choice.'

They won! Men usually win when they make up their minds to do so.

Burn your bridges behind you and observe how well you work when you know that you have no retreat.

A street car conductor got a leave of absence while he tried out a position in a great mercantile business. "If I do not succeed in holding my new position," he remarked to a friend, "I can always come back to the old job."

At the end of the month he was back, completely cured of all ambition to do anything except work on a street car. Had he resigned instead of asking for a leave of absence he might have made good in the new job.

The Thirteen—Club—movement,——which is now spreading over the entire country, was born as the result of a shocking disappointment experienced by its founder. That shock was sufficient to open the mind to a broader and more comprehensive view of the needs of the age, and this discovery led to the creation of one of the most outstanding influences of this generation.

The Fifteen Laws of Success, upon which this course is based, grew out of twenty years of hardship and poverty and failure such as rarely come to one person in an entire lifetime.

Surely those of you who have followed this series of lessons from the beginning must have read between the lines and back of them a story of struggle which has meant self-discipline and self-discovery such as never would have been known without this hardship.

Study the roadway of life, in the picture at the beginning of this essay, and observe that everyone who travels that road carries a cross. Remember, as you take inventory of your own burdens, that Nature's richest gifts go to those who meet FAILURE without flinching or whining.

Nature's ways are not easily understood. If they were, no one could be tested for great responsibility, with FAILURE!

"When Nature wants to make a man,
And shake a man,
And wake a man;
When Nature wants to make a man
To do the Future's will;
When she tries with all her skill
And she yearns with all her soul
To create him large and whole ...
With what cunning she prepares him!
How she goads and never spares him!
How she whets him, and she frets him,
And in poverty begets him....
How she often disappoints
How she often anoints,
With what wisdom she will hide him,
Never minding what betide him

Though his genius sob with slighting
And his pride may not forget!
Bids him struggle harder yet.
Makes him lonely
So that only
God's high messages shall reach him, So that she may surely teach him
What the Hierarchy planned.
Though he may not understand
Gives him passions to command.
How remorselessly she spurs him
With terrific ardour stirs him
When she poignantly prefers him!
Lo, the crisis! Lo, the shout
That must call the leader out.
When the people need salvation
Doth he come to lead the nation....
Then doth Nature show her plan
When the world has found-A MAN!"

There is no FAILURE. That which looks to be failure is usually nothing but temporary defeat. Make sure that you do not accept it as PERMANENT!

□

7

Concentration

"You Can Do It if You Believe You Can!"

This lesson occupies a key-stone position in this course, for the reason that the psychological law upon which it is based is of vital importance to every other lesson of the course.

Let us define the word concentration, as it is here used, as follows:

"Concentration is the act of focusing the mind upon a given desire until ways and means for its realisation have been worked out and successfully put into operation."

Two important laws enter into the act of concentrating the mind on a given desire. One is the law of Auto-suggestion and the other is the law of habit. The former having been fully described in a previous lesson of this course, we will now briefly describe the law of habit.

Habit grows out of environment-out of doing the same thing in the same way over and over again-out of repetition-out of thinking the same thoughts over and over-and, when once formed, it resembles a cement block that has hardened in the meld-in that it is hard to break.

Habit is the basis of all memory training, a fact which you may easily demonstrate in remembering the name of a person whom you have just met, by repeating that name over and over until you have fixed it permanently and plainly in your mind.

"The force of education is so great that we may meld the minds and manners of the young into whatever shape we please and give the impressions of such habits as shall ever afterwards remain."
—Atter bury.

Except on rare occasions when the mind rises above environment, the human mind draws the material out of which thought is created, from the surrounding environment, and habit crystallizes this thought into a: permanent fixture and stores it away in the subconscious mind where it becomes a vital part of our personality which silently influences our actions, forms our prejudices and our biases, and controls our opinions.

A great philosopher had in mind the power of habit when he said: 'We first endure, then pity, and finally embrace,' in speaking of the manner in which honest men come to indulge in crime.

Habit may be likened to the grooves on a phonograph record, while the mind may be likened to the needle point that fits into that groove. When any habit has been well formed (by repetition of thought or action) the mind attaches itself to and follows that habit as closely as the phonograph needle follows the groove in the wax record, no matter what may be the nature of that habit.

We begin to see, therefore, the importance of selecting our environment with the greatest of care, because environment is the mental feeding ground out of which the food that goes into our minds is extracted.

Environment very largely supplies the food and materials out of which we create thought, and h a bit crystallizes these into permanency. You of course understand that 'environment' is the sum total of sources through which you are influenced by and through the aid of the five senses of seeing, hearing, smelling, tasting and feeling.

"Habit is force which is generally recognised by the average thinking person, but which is commonly viewed in its adverse aspect to the exclusion of its favourable phase. It has been well said that all men are 'the creatures of habit,' and that 'habit is a cable; we weave a thread of it each day and it becomes so strong that we cannot break it.'

"If it be true that habit becomes a cruel tyrant, ruling and compelling men against their will, desire, and inclination-and this is true in many cases-the question naturally arises in the thinking mind whether this mighty force cannot be harnessed and controlled in the service of men, just as have other forces of Nature. If this result can be accomplished, then man may master habit and set it to work, instead of being a slave to it and serving it faithfully though comp linings. And the modern psychologists tell us in no uncertain tones that habit may certainly be thus mastered, harnessed and set to work, instead of being allowed to dominate one's actions and character. And thousands of people have applied this new knowledge and have turned the force of habit into new channels, and have compelled it to work their machinery of action, instead of being allowed to run to waste, or else permitted to sweep away the structures that men have erected with care and expense, or to destroy fertile mental fields.

"A habit is a 'mental path' over which our actions have travelled for some time, each passing making the path a little deeper and a little wider. If you have to walk over a field or through a forest, you know how natural it is for you to choose the clearest path in preference to the less worn ones, and greatly in preference to stepping out across the field or through the woods and making a new path. And the line of mental action is precisely the same. It is movement along the lines of least resistance-passage over the well-worn path. Habits are created by repetition and are formed in accordance to a natural law, observable in all animate things and some would say in inanimate things as well. As an instance of the latter, it is pointed out that a piece of paper once folded in a certain way will fold along the same lines the next time. And all users of sewing machines, or other delicate pieces of machinery, know that as a machine or instrument is once 'broken in' so will it tend to run thereafter. The same law is also observable in the case of musical instruments. Clothing or gloves form into creases according to the person using them, and these creases once formed will always be in effect, notwithstanding repeated pressings. Rivers and streams of water cut their courses through the land, and thereafter flow along the habit-course. The law is in operation everywhere.

"These illustrations will help you to form the idea of the nature of habit, and will aid you in forming new mental paths-new mental creases. And-remember this always-the best (and one might say the only) way in which old habits may be removed is to form new habits to counteract and replace the undesirable ones. Form new mental paths over which to travel, and the old ones will soon become less distinct and in time will practically fill up from disuse. Every time you travel over the path of the desirable mental habit, you make the path deeper and wider, and make it so much easier to travel it thereafter. This mental path-making is a very important thing, and I cannot urge upon you too strongly the injunction to start to work making the desirable mental paths over which you wish to travel. Practice, practice, practice-be a good path-maker."

The following are the rules of procedure through which you may form the habits you desire:

First: At the beginning of the formation of a new habit put force and enthusiasm into your expression. Feel what you think. Remember that you are taking the first steps toward making the new mental path; that it is much harder at first than it will be afterwards. Make the path as clear and as deep as you can, at the beginning, so that you can readily see it the next time you wish to follow it.

Second: Keep your attention firmly concentrated on the new path-building, and keep your mind away from the old paths, lest you incline toward them. Forget all about the old paths, and concern yourself only with the new ones that you are building to order.

Third: Travel over your newly made paths as often as possible. Make opportunities for doing so, without waiting for them to arise through luck or chance. The oftener you go over the new paths the sooner will they become well worn and easily travelled. Create plans for passing over these new habit-paths, at the very start.

Fourth: Resist the temptation to travel over the older, easier paths that you have been using in the past. Every time you resist a temptation, the stronger do you become, and the easier will it be for you to do so the next time. But every time you yield to the temptation, the easier does it become to yield again, and the more difficult it becomes to resist the next time. You will have a fight on at the start, and this is the critical time. Prove—your—determination, persistency and will-power—now,—at the very beginning.

Fifth: Be sure that you have mapped out the right path, as your definite chief aim, and then go ahead without fear and without allowing yourself to doubt. "Place your hand upon the plow, and look not backward." Select your goal, then make good, deep, wide mental paths leading straight to it.

As you have already observed, there is a close relationship between habit and Auto-suggestion (self-suggestion). Through habit, an act repeatedly performed in the same manner has a tendency to become Permanent, and eventually we come to perform the act automatically or unconsciously. In playing a piano, for example, the artist can play a familiar piece while his or her conscious mind is on some other subject.

Auto-suggestion is the tool with which we dig a mental path; Concentration is the hand that holds that tool; and Habit is the map or blueprint which the mental path follows. An idea or desire, to be transformed into terms of action or physical reality, must be held in the conscious mind faithfully and persistently until habit begins to give it permanent form.

Let us turn our attention, now, to environment. As we have already seen, we absorb the material for thought from our surrounding environment. The term 'environment' covers a very broad field. It consists of the books we read, the people with whom we associate, the community in which we live, the nature of the work in which we are engaged, the country or nation in which we reside, the clothes we wear, the songs we sing, and, most important of all, the religious and intellectual training we receive prior to the age of fourteen years.

The purpose of analyzing the subject of environment is to show its direct relationship to the personality we are developing, and the importance of so guarding it that its influence will give us the materials out of which we may attain our definite chief aim in life.

The mind feeds upon that which we supply it, or that which is forced upon it, through our environment; therefore, let us selector environment, as far as possible, with the object of supplying the mind with suitable material out of which to carry on its work of attaining our definite chief aim.

If your environment is not to your liking, change it!

The first step is to create in your own mind an exact, clear and well rounded out picture of the environment in which you believe you could best attain your definite chief aim, and then concentrate your mind upon this picture until you transform it into reality.

In Lesson Two, of this course, you learned that the first step you must take, in the accomplishment of any desire, is to create in your mind a dear, well defined picture of that which you intend to accomplish. This is the first principle to be observed in your plans for the achievement of success, and if you fail or neglect to observe it, you cannot succeed, except by chance.

Your daily associates constitute one of the most important and influential parts of your environment, and may work for your progress or your retrogression, according to the nature of those associates. As far as possible, you should select as your most intimate daily associates those who are in sympathy with your aims and ideals-especially those represented by your definite chief aim-and whose mental attitude inspires you with enthusiasm, self-confidence, determination and ambition.

Remember that every word spoken within your hearing, every sight that reaches your eyes, and every sense impression that you receive through any of the five senses, influences your thought as surely as the sun rises in the east and sets in the west. This being true, can you not see the importance of controlling, as far as possible, the environment in which you live and work? Can you not see the importance of reading books that deal with subjects which are directly related to your definite chief aim? Can you not see the importance of talking with people who are in sympathy with your aims, and, who will encourage you and spur you on toward their attainment?

We are living in what—we call a 'twentieth century civilisation.' The leading scientists of the world are agreed that Nature has been millions of years in creating, through the process of evolution, our present civilised environment.

How many hundreds of centuries the so-called Indians had lived upon the North American continent, without any appreciable advance toward modem civilisation, as we understand it, we have no way of ascertaining. Their environment was the wilderness, and they made no attempt whatsoever to change or improve that environment; the change took place only after new races from afar came over and forced upon them the environment of progressive civilisation in, which we are living today.

Observe what has happened within the short period of three centuries. Hunting grounds have been transformed into great cities, and the Indian has taken on education and culture, in many instances, that equal the accomplishment of his white brothers. (In Lesson Fifteen, we discuss the effects of environment from a worldwide viewpoint, and describe, in detail, the principal of social heredity which is the chief source through which the effects of environment may be imposed upon the minds of the young.)

The clothes you wear influence you; therefore, they constitute a part of your environment. Soiled or shabby clothes depress you and lower your self-confidence, while clean clothes, of an appropriate style, have just the opposite effect.

It is a well known fact that an observant person can accurately analyse a man by seeing his work-bench, desk or other place of employment. A well organised desk indicates a well organised brain. Show me the merchant's stock of goods and I will tell you whether he has an organised or disorganised brain, as there is a close relationship between one's mental attitude and one's physical environment.

The effects of environment so vitally influence those who work in factories, stores and offices, that employers are gradually realizing the importance of creating an environment that inspires and encourages the workers.

One unusually progressive laundryman, in the city of Chicago, has plainly outdone his competitors, by installing in his work-room a player-piano, in charge of a neatly dressed young woman who keeps it going during the working hours. His laundrywomen are dressed in white uniforms, and there is no evidence about the place that work is drudgery. Through the aid of this pleasant environment, this laundryman turns out more work, earns more profits, and pays better wages than his competitors can pay.

This brings us to an appropriate place at which to describe the method through which you may apply the principles directly and indirectly related to the subject of concentration.

Let us call this method the-MAGIC KEY TO SUCCESS!

In presenting you with this 'Magic Key' let me first explain that it is no invention or discovery of mine.

It is the same key that is used, in one form or another, by the followers of New Thought and all other sects which are founded upon the positive philosophy of optimism.

This Magic Key constitutes an irresistible power which all who will may use.

The person who receives no pay for his services except that which comes in the pay envelope is underpaid, no matter how much money that envelope may contain.

It win unlock the door to riches! It will unlock the door to fame!

And, in many instances, it will unlock the door to physical health.

It will unlock the door to education and let you into the storehouse of all your latent ability. It will act as a pass-key to any position in life for which you are fitted.

Through the aid of this Magic Key we have unlocked the secret doors to all of the world's great inventions.

Through its magic powers all of our great geniuses of the past have been developed.

Suppose you are a labourer, in a menial position, and desire a better place in life. The Magic Key will help you attain it! Through its use Carnegie, Rockefeller, Hill, Harriman, Morgan and scores of others of their type have accumulated vast fortunes of material wealth.

It will unlock prison doors and turn human derelicts into useful, trustworthy human beings. It will turn failure into success and misery into happiness.

You ask-'What is this Magic Key?'

And I answer with one word-concentration! Now let me define Concentration in the sense that it is here used. First, I wish it to be clearly understood that I have no reference to occultism, although I will admit that all the scientists of the world have failed to explain the strange phenomena produced through the aid of c o n centration.

Concentration, in the sense in which it is here used, means the ability, through fixed habit and practice, to keep your mind on one subject until you have thoroughly familiarized yourself with that subject and mastered it. It means the ability to control your attention and focusiton a given problem until you have solved it.

It means the ability to throw off the effects of habits which you wish to discard, and the power to build new habits that are more to your liking. It means complete self-mastery.

Stating it in another way, concentration is the ability to think as you wish to think; the ability to control your thoughts and direct them to a definite end; and the ability to organise your knowledge into a plan of action that is sound and workable.

You can readily see that in concentrating your mind upon your definite chief aim in life, you must cover many closely related subjects which blend into each other and complete the main subject upon which you are concentrating.

Ambition and desire are the chief factors which enter into the act of successful concentration. Without these factors the Magic Key is useless, and the main reason why so few people make use of this key is that most people lack ambition, and desire nothing in particular.

Desire whatever you may, and if your desire is within reason and if it is strong enough the Magic Key of concentration will help you attain it. There are learned men of science who would have us believe that the wonderful power of prayer operates through the principle of concentration on the attainment of a deeply seated desire.

Nothing was ever created by a human being which was not first created in the imagination, through desire, and then transformed into reality through concentration.

Now, let us put the Magic Key to a test, through the aid of a definite formula.

First, you must put your foot on the neck of scepticism and doubt! No unbeliever ever enjoyed the benefits of this Magic Key. You must believe in the test that you are about to make.

We will assume that you have thought something about becoming a successful writer, or a powerful public speaker, or a successful business executive, or an able financier. We will take public speaking as the subject of this test, but remember that you must follow instructions to the letter.

Take a plain sheet of paper, ordinary letter size, and write on it the following:

I am going to become a powerful public speaker because this will enable me to render the world useful service that is needed-and because it will yield me a financial return that will provide me with the necessary material things of life.

I will concentrate my mind upon this desire for ten minutes daily, just before retiring at night and just after arising in the morning, for the purpose of determining just how I shall proceed to transform it into reality.

I know that I can become a powerful and magnetic speaker, therefore I will permit nothing to interfere with my doing so.

(Signed..............)

Sign this pledge, then proceed to do as you have pledged your word that you would do. Keep it up until the desired results have been realised.

Now, when you come to do your concentrating, this is the way to go about it: Look ahead one, three, five or even ten years, and see yourself as the most powerful speaker of your time. See, in your imagination, an appropriate income. See yourself in your own home that you have purchased with the proceeds from your efforts as a speaker or lecturer. See yourself in possession of a nice bank account as a reserve for old age. See yourself as a person of influence, due to your great ability as a public speaker. See yourself engaged in a life-calling in which you will not fear the loss of your position.

Paint this picture clearly, through the powers of your imagination, and lo! it will soon become transformed—into—a beautiful picture of deeply seated desire. Use—this—desire as the chief object of your Concentration and observe what happens.

You now have the secret of the Magic Key!

Do not underestimate the power of the Magic Key because it did not come to you clothed in mysticism, or because it is described in language which all who will may understand. All great truths are simple in final analysis, and easily understood; if they are not they are not great truths.

Use this Magic Key with intelligence, and only for the attainment of worthy ends, and it will bring you enduring happiness and success. Forget the mistakes you have made and the failures you-have experienced. Quit living in the past, for do you not know that your yesterdays never return? Start all over again, if your previous efforts have not turned out well, and make the next five or ten years tell a story of success that will satisfy your most lofty ambitions.

Make a name for yourself and render the world a great service, through ambition, desire and concentrated effort!

You can do it if you BELIEVE you can!

Thus endeth the Magic Key.

The presence of any idea or thought in your consciousness tends to produce an 'associated' feeling and to urge you to appropriate or corresponding action. Hold a deeply seated desire in your consciousness, through the principle of concentration, and if you do it with full faith in its realisation your act attracts to your aid powers which the entire scientific world has failed to understand or explain with a reasonable hypothesis.

When you become familiar with the powers of concentration you will then understand the reason for choosing a definite chief aim as the first step in the attainment of enduring success.

Concentrate your mind upon the attainment of the object of a deeply seated desire and very soon you will become a lode-stone that attracts, through the aid of forces which no man can explain, the necessary material counterparts of that desire, a statement of fact which paves the way for the description of a principle which constitutes the most important part of this lesson, if not, in fact, the most important part of the entire course, viz.:

When two or more people ally themselves, in a spirit of perfect harmony, for the purpose of attaining a definite end,—if that alliance is faithfully observed by all of whom it is composed, the alliance brings, to each of those of whom it is composed, power that is superhuman and seemingly irresistible in nature.

Back of the foregoing statement is a law, the nature of which science has not yet determined, and it is this law that I have had in mind in connection with my repeated statements concerning the power of organised effort which you will notice throughout this course.

In chemistry we learn that two or more elements may be so compounded that the result is something entirely different in nature, from any of the individual elements. For example, ordinary water, known in chemistry under the formula of H_2O, is a compound consisting of two atoms of hydrogen and one atom of oxygen, but water is neither hydrogen nor oxygen. This 'marrying' of elements creates an entirely different substance from that of either of its component parts.

The same law through which this transformation of physical elements takes place may be responsible for the seemingly superhuman powers resulting from the alliance of two or more people, in a perfect state of harmony and understanding, for the attainment of a given end.

This world, and all matter of which the other planets consist, is made up of electrons (an electron being the smallest known analyzable unit of matter, and resembling, in nature, what we call electricity, or a form of energy). On the other hand, thought, and that which we call the 'mind,' is also a form of energy; in fact it is the highest form of energy known.

Thought, in other words, is organised energy, and it is not improbable that thought is exactly the same sort of energy as that which we generate with an electric dynamo, although of a much more highly organised form.

Now, if all matter, in final analysis, consists of groups of electrons, which are nothing more than a form of energy which we call electricity, and if the mind is nothing but a form of highly organised electricity, do you not see how it is possible that the laws which affect matter may also govern the mind?

And if combining two or more elements of matter, in the proper proportion and under the right conditions, will produce something entirely different from those original elements (as in the case of H_2O), do you not see how it is possible so to combine the energy of two or more minds that the result will be a sort of composite mind that is totally different from the individual minds of which it consists?

You have undoubtedly noticed the manner in which; you are influenced while in the presence of other people. Some people inspire you with optimism and enthusiasm. Their very presence seems to stimulate your own mind to greater action, and, this not only 'seems' to be true, but it is true. You have noticed that the presence of others had a tendency to lower your vitality and depress you; a tendency which I can assure you was very real!

What, do you imagine, could be the cause of these changes that come over us when we come within a certain range of other people, unless it is the change resulting from the blending or combining of their minds with our own, through the operation of a law that is not very well understood, but resembles (if, in fact, it is not the same law) the law through which the combining of two atoms of hydrogen and one atom of oxygen produces water.

I have no scientific basis for this hypothesis, but I have given it many years of serious thought and always I come to the conclusion that it is at least a sound hypothesis, although I have no possible way, as yet, of reducing it to a provable hypothesis.

You need no proof, however, that the presence of some people inspires you, while the presence of others depresses you, as you know this to be a fact. Now it stands to reason that the person who inspires you and arouses your mind to a state of greater activity gives you more power to achieve, while the person whose presence depresses you and lowers your vitality, or causes you to dissipate it in useless, disorganised thought, has just the opposite effect on you. You can understand this much without the aid of a hypothesis and without further proof than that which you have experienced time after time.

Come back, now, to the original statement that: "When two or more people ally themselves, in a spirit of perfect harmony, for the purpose of attaining a definite end, if that alliance is faithfully observed by all of whom it is composed, the alliance brings, to each of those of whom it is composed, power that is superhuman and seemingly irresistible in nature."

Study, closely, the emphasized part of the foregoing statement, for there you will find the 'mental formula' which, if not faithfully observed, destroys the effect of the whole.

One atom of hydrogen combined with one atom of oxygen will not produce water, nor will an alliance in name only, that is not accompanied by 'a spirit of perfect harmony' (between those forming the alliance), produce "power that is superhuman and seemingly irresistible in nature."

I have in mind a family of mountain-folk who, for more than six generations, have lived in the mountainous section of Kentucky. Generation after generation of this family came and went without any noticeable improvement of a mental nature, each generation following in the footsteps of its ancestors. They made their living from the soil, and as far as they knew, or cared, the universe consisted of a little spoof territory known as Letcher County. They married strictly in their own 'set,' and in their own community.

Finally, one of the members of this family strayed away from the flock, so to speak, and married a well educated and highly cultured woman from the neighbour-state of Virginia. This woman was one of those types of ambitious people who had learned that the universe extended beyond the border line of Letcher County, and covered, at least, the whole of the southern states. She had heard of chemistry, and of botany, and of biology, and of pathology, and of psychology, and of many other subjects that were of importance in the field of education. When her children began to come along to the age of understanding, she talked to them of these subjects; and they, in turn, began to show a keen interest in them.

One of her children is now the president of a great educational institution, where most of these subjects, and many others of equal importance, are taught. Another one of them is a prominent lawyer, while still another is a successful physician.

Her husband (thanks to the influence of her mind) is a well known dental surgeon, and the first of his family, for six generations, to break away from the traditions by which the family had been bound.

The blending of her mind with his gave him the needed stimulus to spur him on and inspired him with ambition such as he would never have known without her influence.

For many years I have been studying the biographies of those whom the world calls great, and it seems to me more than a mere coincidence that in every instance where the facts were available the person who was really responsible for the greatness was in the background, behind the scenes, and seldom heard of by the hero-worshiping public. Not infrequently is this 'hidden power' a patient little wife who has inspired her husband and urged him on to great achievement, as was true in the case I have just described.

Henry Ford is one of the modem miracles of this age, and I doubt that this country, or any other, ever produced an industrial genius of his equal. If the facts were known (and perhaps they are known) they might trace the cause of Mr. Ford's phenomenal achievements to a woman of whom the public hears but little-his wife!

We read of Ford's achievements and of his enormous income and imagine him to be blessed with matchless ability; and he is-ability of which the world would never have heard had it not been for the modifying influence of his wife, who has co-operated with him, during all the years of his struggle, 'in a spirit of perfect harmony, for the purpose of attaining a definite end.'

I have in mind another genius who is well known to the entire civilised world, Thomas A. Edison. His inventions are so well known that they need not be named. Every time you press a button and turn on an electric light, or hear a phonograph playing, you should think of Edison, for it was he who perfected both the incandescent light and the modem phonograph. Every time you see a moving picture you should think of Edison, for it was his genius, more than that of any other person, who made this great enterprise possible.

But, as in the case of Henry Ford, back of Mr. Edison stands one of the most remarkable women in America-his wife! No one outside of the Edison family, and perhaps a very few intimate personal friends of theirs, knows to what extent her influence has made Edison's achievements possible. Mrs. Edison once told me that Mr. Edison's outstanding quality, the one which, above all others, was his greatest asset, was that of-concentration!

When Mr. Edison starts a line of experiment or research or investigation; he never 'lets go' until he either finds that for which he is looking or exhausts every possible effort to do so.

Back of Mr. Edison stand two great powers; one is concentration and the other is Mrs. Edison!

Night after night Mr. Edison has worked with such enthusiasm that he required but three or four hours of sleep. (Observe what was said about the sustaining effects of enthusiasm in Lesson Seven of this course.)

Plant a tiny apple seed in the right sort of soil, at the right time of the year, and gradually it will burst forth into a tiny sprig, and then it will expand and grow into an apple tree. That tree does not come from the soil, nor does it come from the elements of the air, but from both of these sources, and the man has not yet lived who could explain the law that attracts from the air and the soil the combination of cells of which that apple tree consists.

The tree does not come out of the tiny apple seed, but, that seed is the beginning of the tree.

When two or more people ally themselves, "in a spirit of perfect harmony, for the purpose of attaining a definite end," the end, itself, or the desire back of that end, may be likened to the apple seed, and the blending of the forces of energy of the two or more minds may be likened to the air and the soil out of which come the elements that form the material objects of that desire.

The power back of the attraction and combination of these forces of the mind can no more be explained than can the power back of the combination of elements out of which an apple tree 'grows.'

But the all-important thing is that an apple tree will 'grow' from a seed thus properly planted, an great achievement will follow the systematic blending of two or more minds with a definite object in view.

In Lesson Thirteen you will see this principle of allied effort carried to proportions which almost stagger the imagination of all who have not trained themselves to think in terms of organised thought!

This course, itself, is a very concrete illustration of the principle underlying that which we have termed organised effort, but you will observe that it requires the entire sixteen lessons to complete the description of this principle. Omit a single one of the sixteen lessons and the omission would affect the whole as the removal of one link would affect the whole of a chain.

As I have already stated in many different ways, and for the purpose of emphasis, I now repeat: there is a well founded hypothesis that when one concentrates one's mind upon a given subject, facts of a nature that is closely related to that subject will 'pour' in from every conceivable source. The theory is that a deeply seated desire, when once planted in the right sort of 'mental soil,' serves as a centre of attraction or magnet that attracts to it everything that harmonizes with the nature of the desire.

Dr. Elmer Gates, of Washington, D.C., is perhaps one of the most competent psychologists in the world. He is recognised both in the field of psychology and in other directly and indirectly related fields of science, throughout the world, as being a man of the highest scientific standing.

Come with me, for a moment, and study his methods!

After Dr. Gates has followed a line of investigation as far as possible through the usual channels of research, and has availed himself of all the recorded facts at his command, on a given subject, he then takes a pencil and a tablet and 'sits' for further information, by concentrating his mind on that subject until thoughts related to it begin to FLOW IN UPON HIM. He writes down these thoughts, as they come (from he knows not where). He told me that many of his most important discoveries came through this method. It was more than twenty years ago that I first talked with Dr. Gates on this subject. Since that time, through the discovery of the radio principle, we have been provided with a reasonable hypothesis through which to explain the results of these 'sittings,' viz.:

The ether, as we have discovered through the modern radio apparatus, is in a constant state of agitation. Sound waves are floating through the ether at all times, but these waves cannot be detected, beyond a short distance from their source, except by the aid of properly attuned instruments.

Now, it seems reasonable to suppose that thought, being the most highly organised form of energy known, is constantly sending waves through the ether, but these waves, like those of sound, can only be detected and correctly interpreted by a properly attuned mind.

There is no doubt that when Dr. Gates sat down in a room and placed himself in a quiet, passive state of mind, the dominating thoughts in his mind served as a magnetic force that attracted the related or similar thought waves of others as they passed through the ether about him.

Taking the hypothesis just a step further, it has occurred to me many times since the discovery of the modern radio principle, that every thought that has ever been released in organised form, from the mind of any human being, is still in existence in the form of a wave in the ether, and is constantly passing around and around in a great endless circle; that the act of concentrating one's mind upon a given subject with intensity sends out thought waves which reach and blend with those of a related or similar nature, thereby establishing a direct line of communication between the one doing the concentrating and the thoughts of a similar nature which have been previously set into motion.

Going still a step further, may it not be possible for one so to attune his mind and harmonize the rate of vibration of thought with the rate of vibration of the ether that all knowledge that has been accumulated through the organised thoughts of the past is available?

With these hypotheses in mind, go back to Lesson Two, of this course, and study Carnegie's description of the 'Master Mind' through which he accumulated his great fortune.

When Carnegie formed an alliance between more than a score of carefully selected minds, he created, by that means of compounding mind power, one of the strongest industrial forces that the world has ever witnessed. With a few notable (and very disastrous) exceptions, the men constituting the 'Master Mind' which Carnegie created thought and acted as one!

And, that 'Master Mind' (composed of many individual minds) was concentrated upon a single purpose, the nature of which is familiar to everyone who knew Mr. Carnegie; particularly those who were competing with him in the steel business.

If you have followed Henry Ford's record, even slightly, you undoubtedly have observed that concentrated effort has been one of the outstanding features of his career. Nearly thirty years ago he adopted a policy of standardisation as to the general type of automobile that he would build, and he consistently maintained that policy until the change in public demand forced him, in 1927, to change it.

A few years ago, I met the former chief engineer of the Ford plant, and he told me of an incident that happened during the early stages of Mr. Ford's automobile experience which very clearly points to concentrated effort as being one of his prominent fundamentals of economic philosophy.

On this occasion the engineers of the Ford plant had gathered in the engineering office for the purpose of discussing a proposed change in the design of the rear axle construction of the Ford automobile. Mr. Ford stood around and listened to the discussion until each man had his 'say,' then he walked over to the table, tapped the drawing of the proposed axle with his finger, and said:

"Now listen! the axle we are using does the work for which it was intended, and does it well, and there's going to be no more change in that axle!"

He turned and walked away, and from that day until this the rear axle construction of the Ford automobile has remained substantially the same. It is not improbable that Mr. Ford's success in building and marketing automobiles has been due, very largely, to his policy of consistently concentrating his efforts back of one plan, with but one definite purpose in mind at a time.

A few years ago I read Edward Bok's book, The Man From Maine, which is the biography of his father-in-law, Mr. Cyrus H. K. Curtis, the owner of the Saturday Evening Post, the Ladies' Home journal, and several other publications. All through the book I noticed that the outstanding feature of Mr. Curtis' philosophy was that of concentration of effort back of a definite purpose.

During the early days of his ownership of the Saturday Evening Post, when he was pouring money into a losing venture by the hundreds of thousands of dollars, it required concentrated effort that was backed by courage such as but few men possess, to enable him to 'carry on.'

Read The Man From Maine. It is a splendid lesson on the subject of concentration, and supports, to the smallest detail, the fundamentals upon which this lesson is based.

The Saturday Evening Post is now one of the most profitable magazines in the world, but its name would have been long since forgotten had not Mr. Curtis concentrated his attention and his fortune on the one definite purpose of making it a great magazine.

We have seen what an important part environment and habit play in connection with the subject of concentration. We shall now discuss, briefly, a third subject which is no less related to the subject of concentration than are the other two, namely, memory.

The principles through which an accurate, unfaltering memory may be trained are few, and comparatively simple; viz.:

1. Retention: The receiving of a sense impression through one or more of the five senses, and the recording of this impression, in orderly fashion, in the mind. This process may be likened to the recording of s picture on the sensitized plate of a camera or Kodak.

2. Recall :The reviving or recalling into the conscious mind of those sense impressions which have been recorded in the sub-conscious mind. This process may be compared to the act of going through a card index and pulling out a card on which information had been previously recorded.

3. Recognition : The ability to recognise a sense impression when it is called into the conscious mind, and to identify it as being a duplicate of the original impression, and to associate it with the original source from which it came when it was first recorded. This process enables us to distinguish between 'memory' and 'imagination.'

These are the three principles that enter into the act of remembering. Now let us make application of these principles and determine how to use them effectively, which may be done as follows:

First: When you wish to be sure of your ability to recall a sense impression, such as a name, date or place, be sure to make the impression vivid by concentrating your attention upon it to the finest detail. An effective way to do this is to repeat, several times, that which you wish to remember. Just as a photographer must give an 'exposure' proper time to record itself on the sensitized plate of the camera, so must we give the subconscious mind time to record properly and clearly any sense impression that we wish to be able to recall with readiness.

Second: Associate that which you wish to remember with some other object, name, place or date with which you are quite familiar, and which you can easily recall when you wish, as, for example, the name of your home town, your close friend, the date of your birth, etc., for your mind will then file away the sense impression that you wish to be able to recall, with the one that you can easily recall, so that when bringing forth one into the conscious mind it brings, also, the other one with it.

Third: Repeat that which you wish to remember, a number of times, at the same time concentrating your mind upon it, just as you would fix your mind on a certain hour at which you wished to arise in the morning, which, as you know, insures your awakening at that precise hour. The common failing of not being able to remember the names of other people, which most of us have, is due entirely to the fact that we do not properly record the name in the first place. When you are introduced to a person whose name you wish to be able to recall at will, repeat that name four or five times, first making sure that you understood the name correctly. If the name is similar to that of some person whom you know well, associate the two names together, thinking of both as you repeat the name of the one whose name you wish to be able to recall.

If someone gives you a letter to be mailed, look at the letter, then increase its size, in your imagination, and see it hanging over a letter-box. Fix in your mind a letter approximately the size of a door, and associate it with a letter box, and you will observe that the first letter box you pass on the street will cause you to recall that big, odd-looking letter, which you have in your pocket.

Suppose that you were introduced to a lady whose name was Elizabeth Shearer, and you wished to be able to recall her name at will. As you repeat her name associate with it a large pair of scissors, say ten feet in length, and Queen Elizabeth, and you will observe that the recalling of either the large pair of scissors or the name of Queen Elizabeth will help you recall, also, the name of Elizabeth Shearer.

If you wish to be able to remember the name of Lloyd Keith, just repeat the name several times and associate with it the name of Lloyd George and Keith's Theatre, either of which you can easily recall at will.

The law of association is the most important feature of a well trained memory, yet it is a very simple law. All you have to do to make use of it is to record the name of that which you wish to remember with the name of that which you can readily remember, and the recalling of one brings with it the other.

Nearly ten years ago a friend gave me his residence telephone number, in Milwaukee, Wisconsin, and although I did not write it down I remember it today as well as I did the day he gave it to me. This is the way that I recorded it:

The number and exchange were Lake view 2651. At the time he gave me the number we were standing at the railroad station, in sight of Lake Michigan; therefore, I used the lake as an associated object with which to file the name of the telephone exchange. It so happened that the telephone number was made up of the age of my brother, who was 26, and my father, who was 51, therefore I associated their names with the number, thus insuring its recall. To recall the telephone exchange and number, therefore, I had only to think of Lake Michigan, my brother and my father.

An acquaintance of mine found himself to be suffering from what is ordinarily called a 'wandering mind.' He was becoming 'absent-minded' and unable to remember. Let him tell you, in his own words which follow, how he overcame this handicap:

"I am fifty years old. For a decade I have been a department manager in a large factory. At first my duties were easy, then the firm had a rapid expansion of business which gave me added responsibilities. Several of the young men in my department developed unusual energy and ability-at least one of them had his eye on my job.

"I had reached the age in life when a man likes to be comfortable and, having been with the company a long time, I felt that I could safely settle back into an easy berth. The effect of this mental attitude was well nigh disastrous to my position.

"About two years ago I noticed that my power of Concentration was weakening and my duties were becoming irksome. I neglected my correspondence until I looked with dread upon the formidable pile of letters; reports accumulated and subordinates were inconvenienced by the delay. I sat at my desk with my mind wandering elsewhere.

"Other circumstances showed plainly that my mind was not on my work; I forgot to attend an important meeting of the officers of the company. One of the clerks under me caught a bad mistake made in an estimate on 'a carload of goods, and, of course, saw to it that the manager learned of the incident.

"I was thoroughly alarmed at the situation! and asked for a week's vacation to think things over. I was determined to resign, or find the trouble and remedy it. A few days of earnest introspection at an out-of-the-way mountain resort convinced me that I was suffering from a plain case of mind wandering. I was lacking in concentration; my physical and mental activities at the desk had become desultory. I was careless and shiftless and neglectful-all because my mind was not alertly on the job. When I had diagnosed my case with satisfaction to myself I next sought the remedy. I needed a complete new set off working habits, and I made a resolve to acquire them.

"With paper and pencil I outlined a schedule to cover the working day: first, the morning mail; then, the orders to be filled; dictation; conference with subordinates and miscellaneous duties; ending with a clean desk before I left.

"'How is habit formed?' I asked myself mentally. 'By repetition,' came back the answer. 'But I have been doing these things over and over thousands of times,' the other fellow in me protested. 'True, but not in orderly concentrated fashion,' replied the echo.

"I returned to the office with mind in leash, but restless, and placed my new working schedule in force at once. I performed the same duties with the same zest and as nearly as possible at the same time every day. When my mind started to slip away I quickly brought it back.

"From a mental stimulus, created by will-power, I progressed in habit building. Day after day, I practiced concentration of thought. When I found repetition becoming comfortable, then I knew that I had won."

Your ability to train your memory, or to develop any desired habit, is a matter, solely, of being able to fix your attention on a given subject until the outline of that subject has been thoroughly impressed upon the 'sensitized plate' of your mind.

Concentration, itself, is nothing but a matter of control of the attention!

You will observe that by reading a line of print with which you are not familiar, and which you have never seen before, and then closing your eyes, you can see that line as plainly as though you were looking at it on the printed page. In reality, you are 'looking at it,' not on the printed page, button the sensitized plate of your own mind. If you try this experiment and it does not work the first time it is because you did not concentrate your attention on the line closely enough! Repeat the performance a few times and finally you will succeed.

If you wish to memorize poetry, for example, you can do so very quickly by training yourself to fix your attention on the lines so closely that you can shut your eyes and see them in your mind as plainly as you see them on the printed page.

So important is this subject of control of attention that I feel impelled to emphasize it in such a way that you will not pass it by lightly. I have reserved reference to this important subject until the last, as a climax to this lesson, for the reason that I consider it, by far, the most important part of the lesson.

The astounding results experienced by those who make a practice of 'crystal-gazing' are due, entirely, to their ability to fix attention upon a given subject for an unbroken period far beyond the ordinary.

Crystal-gazing is nothing but concentrated attention!

I have already hinted at that which I will now state as my belief, namely, that it is possible, through the aid of concentrated attention, for one so to attune one's mind to the vibration of the ether that all the secrets in the world of unfathomed and uncharted mental phenomena may become as open books which may be read at will.

What a thought this is to ponder over!

I am of the opinion, and not without substantial evidence to support me, that it is possible for one to develop the ability of fixing the attention so highly that one may 'tune in' and understand that which is in the mind of any person. But this is not all, nor is it the most important part of a hypothesis at which I have arrived after many years of careful research, for I am satisfied that one may just as easily go a step further and 'tune in' on the universal mind in which all knowledge is stored where it may be appropriated by all who master the art of coming after it.

To a highly orthodox mind these statements may seem very irrational; but, to the student (and, so far, there are but few people in the world who are more than mere students, of an elementary grade, of this subject) who has studied this subject with any appreciable degree of understanding, these hypotheses seem not only possible, but absolutely probable.

But put the hypothesis to a test of your own!

You can select no better subject upon which to try an experiment than that which you have selected as your definite chief aim in life.

Memorize your definite chief aim so you can repeat it without looking at the written page, then make a practice of fixing your attention on it at least twice a day, proceeding as follows:

Go into some quiet place where you will not be disturbed; sit down and completely relax your mind and your body; then close your eyes and place your fingers in your ears, thereby excluding the ordinary sound waves and all of the light waves. In that position repeat your definite chief aim in life, and as you do so see yourself, in your imagination, in full possession of the object of that aim. If a part of your aim is the accumulation of money, as it undoubtedly is, then see yourself in possession of that money. If a part of the object of your definite aim is the ownership of a home, then see a picture of that home, in your imagination, just as you expect to see it in reality. If a part of your definite aim is to become a powerful and influential public speaker, then see yourself before an enormous audience, and feel yourself playing upon the emotions of that audience as a great violinist would play upon the strings of the violin.

As you approach the end of this lesson, there are two things which you might do, viz.

First: You might begin, now, to cultivate the ability to fix attention, at will, on a given subject, with a feeling that this ability, when fully developed, would bring you the object of your definite chief aim in life; or,

Second: You might tilt your nose in the air and with the smile of a cynic say to yourself-'Bosh' and thereby mark yourself a fool!

Take your choice!

This lesson was not written as an argument, nor as the subject of a debate. It is your privilege to accept it, in whole or in part, or reject it, just as you please.

But at this place I wish to state, however, that this is not an age of cynicism or doubt. An age that has conquered the air above us and the sea beneath us, that has enabled us to harness the air and turn it into a messenger that will carry the sound of our voice half-way around the earth in the fractional part of a second, certainly is not an age that lends encouragement to the 'doubting Thomases' or the "I-don't-believe-it Joneses."

The human family has passed through the 'Stone Age' and the 'Iron Age' and the 'Steel Age,' and unless I have greatly misinterpreted the trend of the times it is now entering the 'Mind Power Age,' which will eclipse, in stupendous achievement, all the other 'ages' combined.

Learn to fix your attention on a given subject, at will, for whatever length of time you choose, and you will have learned the secret passage-way to power and plenty!

This is concentration!

You will understand, from this lesson, that the object of forming an alliance between two or more people, and thereby creating a 'Master Mind,' is to apply the Law of Concentration more effectively than it could be applied through the efforts of but one person.

The principle referred to as the 'Master Mind' is nothing more nor less than group concentration of mind power upon the attainment of a definite objector end. Greater power comes through group mind concentration because of the 'stepping up' process Produced through the reaction of one mind upon another or others.

PERSUASION VS. FORCE

Success, as has been stated in dozens of different ways throughout this course, is very largely a matter of tactful and harmonious negotiation with other people. Generally speaking, the man who understands how to 'get people to do things' he wants done may succeed in any calling.

As a fitting climax for this lesson, on the Law of Concentration, we shall describe the principles through which men are influenced; through which cooperation is gained; through which antagonism is eliminated and friendliness developed.

Force sometimes gets what appear to be satisfactory results, but force, alone, never has built and never can build enduring success.

The world war has done more than anything which has happened in the history of the world to show us the futility of force as a means of influencing the human mind. Without going into details or recounting the instances which could be cited, we all know that force was the foundation upon which German philosophy has been built during the past forty years. The doctrine that might makes right was given a worldwide trial and it failed.

The human body can be imprisoned or controlled by physical force, but it is not so with the human mind. No man on earth can control the mind of a normal, healthy person if that person chooses to exercise his God-given right to control his own mind. The majority of people do not exercise this right. They go through the world, thanks to our faulty educational system, without having discovered the strength which lies dormant in their own minds. Now and then something happens, more in the nature of an accident than anything else, which awakens a person and causes him to discover where his real strength lies and how to use it in the development of industry or one of the professions. Result: a genius is born!

There is a given point at which the human mind stops rising or exploring unless something out of the daily routine happens to 'push' it over this obstacle. In some minds this point is very low and in others it is very high. In still others it varies between low and high. The individual who discovers a way to stimulate his mind artificially, arouse it and cause it to go beyond this average stopping point frequently, is sure to be rewarded with fame and fortune if his efforts are of a constructive nature.

The educator who discovers a way to stimulate any mind and cause it to rise above this average stopping point without any bad reactionary effects, will confer a blessing on the human race second to none in the history of the world. We, of course, do not have reference to physical stimulants or narcotics. These will always arouse the mind for a time, but eventually they ruin it entirely. We have reference to a purely mental stimulant, such as that which comes through intense interest, desire, enthusiasm, love, etc., the factors out of which a 'Master Mind' may be developed.

The person who makes this discovery will do much toward solving the crime problem. You can do almost anything with a person when you learn how to influence his mind. The mind may be likened to a great field. It is a very fertile field which always produces a crop after the kind of seed which is sown in it. The problem, then, is to learn how to select the right sort of seed and how to sow that seed so that it takes root and grows quickly. We are sowing seed in our minds daily, hourly, nay, every second, but we are doing it promiscuously and more or less unconsciously. We must learn to do it after a carefully prepared p l a n, according to a well laid out design! Haphazardly sown seed in the human mind brings back a haphazard crop! There is no escape from this result.

History is full of notable cases of men who have been transformed from law-abiding, peaceful, constructive citizens to roving, vicious criminals. We also have thousands of cases wherein men of the low, vicious, so-called criminal type have been transformed into constructive, law-abiding citizens. In every one of these cases the transformation of the human being took place in the mind of the man. He created in his own mind, for one reason or another, a picture of what, he desired and then proceeded to transform that picture into reality. As a matter of fact, if a picture of; any environment, condition or thing be pictured in the human mind and if the mind be focused or concentrated on that picture long enough and persistently enough, and backed up with a strong desire for the thing pictured, it is but a short step from the picture, to the realisation of it in physical or mental form.

The world war brought out many startling tendencies of the human mind which corroborate the work which the psychologist has carried on in his research into the workings of the mind. The following account of a rough, uncouth, unschooled, undisciplined young mountaineer is an excellent case in point:

Fought for His Religion; Now Great War Hero

Rotarians Plan to Present Farm to Arvin York, Unlettered Tennessee Squirrel Hunter BY GEORGEWDIXON

How Arvin Cullom York, an unlettered Tennessee squirrel hunter, became the foremost hero of the American Expeditionary Forces in France, forms a romantic chapter in the history of the world war.

York is a native of Fen tress County. He was born and reared among the hardy mountaineers of the Tennessee woods. There is not even a railroad in Fen tress County. During his earlier years he was reputed to be a desperate character. He was what was known as a gunman. He was a dead shot with a revolver, and his prowess with the rifle was known far and wide among the plain people of the Tennessee hills.

One day a religious organisation pitched its tent in the community in which York and his parents lived. It was a strange sect that came to the mountains looking for converts, but the methods of the evangels of the new cult were full of fire and emotionalism. They denounced the sinner, the vile character and the man who took advantage of his neighbour. They pointed to the religion of the Master as an example that all should follow.

Alvin Gets Religion

Alvin Cullom York startled his neighbours one night by flinging himself down at the mourners' bench. Old men stirred in their seats and women craned their necks, as York wrestled with his sins in the shadows of the Tennessee mountains.

York became an ardent apostle of the new religion. He became an exhorter, a leader in the religious life of the community and, although his marksmanship was as deadly as ever, no one feared him who walked in the path of righteousness.

When the news of the war reached that remote section of Tennessee and the mountaineers were told that they were going to be 'conscripted,' York grew sullen and disagreeable. He didn't believe in killing human beings, even in war. His Bible taught him, 'Thou shalt not kill.' To his mind this was literal and final. He was branded as a 'conscientious objector.'

The draft officers anticipated trouble. They knew that his mind was made up, and they would have to reach him in some manner other than by threats of punishment.

War in a Holy Cause

They went to York with a Bible and showed him that the war was in a holy cause-the cause of liberty and human freedom. They pointed out that men like himself were called upon by the Higher Powers to make the world free; to protect innocent women and children from violation; to make life worth living for the poor and oppressed; to overcome the 'beast' pictured in the Scriptures, and to make the world free for the development of Christian ideals and Christian manhood and womanhood. It was a fight between the hosts of righteousness and the hordes of Satan. The devil was trying to conquer the world through his chosen agents, the Kaiser and his generals.

York's eyes blazed with a fierce light. His big hands closed like a vise. His strong jaws snapped. 'The Kaiser,' he hissed between his teeth, "the beast! the destroyer of women and children! I'll show him where he belongs if I ever get within gunshot of him!"

He caressed his rifle, kissed his mother good-by and told her he would see her again when the Kaiser had been put out of business.

He went to the training camp and drilled with scrupulous care and strict obedience to orders.

His skill at target practice attracted attention. His comrades were puzzled at his high scores. They had not reckoned that a backwoods squirrel hunter would make fine material for a sniper in the front-line trenches.

York's part in the war is now history. General Pershing has designated him as the foremost individual hero of the war. He won every decoration, including the Congressional Medal, the Croix de Guerre, the Legion of Honour. He faced the Germans without fear of death. He was fighting to vindicate his religion, for the sanctity of the home; the love of women and children; the preservation of the ideals of Christianity and the liberties of the poor and oppressed. Fear was not in his code or his vocabulary. His cod daring electrified more than a million men and set the world to talking about this strange, unlettered hero from the hills of Tennessee.

Here we have a case of a young mountaineer who, had he been approached from just a slightly different angle, undoubtedly would have resisted conscription and, likely as not, would have become so embittered toward his country that he would have become an outlaw, looking for an opportunity to strike back at the first chance.

Those who approached him knew something of the principles through which the human mind works. They knew how to manage young York by first overcoming the resistance that he had worked up in his own mind. This is the very point at which thousands of men, through improper understanding of these principles, are arbitrarily classed as criminals and treated as dangerous, vicious people. Through suggestion these people could have been handled as effectively as young York was handled, and developed into useful, productive human beings.

In your search for ways and means of understanding and manipulating your own mind so you can persuade it to create that which you desire in life, let us remind you that, without a single exception, anything which irritates you and arouses you to anger, hatred, dislike, or cynicism, is destructive and very bad for you.

You can never get the maximum or even a fair average of constructive action out of your mind until you have learned to control it and keep it from becoming stimulated through anger or fear!

These two negatives, anger and fear, are positively destructive to your mind, and as long as you allow them to remain you can be sure of results which are unsatisfactory and away below what you are capable of producing.

In our discussion of environment and habit we learned that the individual mind is amenable to the suggestions of environment;

that the minds of the individuals of a crowd blend with one another conforming to the suggestion of the prevailing influence of the leader or dominating figure. Mr. J.A. Fisk gives us an interesting account of the influence of mental suggestion in the revival meeting, which bears out the statement that the crowd mind blends into one, as follows:

Mental Suggestion In the Revival

Modern psychology has firmly established the fact that the greater part of the phenomena of the religious 'revival' are psychical rather than spiritual in their nature, and abnormally psychical at that. The leading authorities recognise the fact that the mental excitement attendant upon the emotional appeals of the 'revivalist' must be classified with the phenomena, of hypnotic suggestion rather than with that of true, religious experience. And those who have made a close study of the subject believe that instead of such excitement tending to elevate the mind and exalt the spirit of the individual, it serves to weaken and degrade the mind and prostitute the spirit by dragging it in the mud of abnormal psychic frenzy and emotional excess. In fact, by some careful observers, familiar with the respective phenomena, the religious 'revival' meeting is classed with the public hypnotic 'entertainment' as a typical example of psychic intoxication and hysterical excess.

David Starr Jordan, chancellor emeritus of Leland Stanford University, says: "Whisky, cocaine and alcohol bring temporary insanity, and so does a revival of religion." The late Professor William James, of Harvard University, the eminent psychologist, says: "Religious revivalism is more dangerous to the life of society than drunkenness."

It should be unnecessary to state that in this lesson the term 'revival' is used in the narrower signification indicating the typical religious emotional excitement known by the term in question, and is not intended to apply to the older and respected religious experience designated by the same term, which was so highly revered among the Puritans, Lutherans and others in the past. A standard reference work speaks of the general subject of the 'revival' as follows:

"Revivals occur in all religions. When one takes place a large number of persons who have been comparatively dead or indifferent to spiritual considerations simultaneously or in quick succession become alive to their importance, alter spiritually and morally, and act with exceeding zeal in converting others to their views. A Mohammedan revival takes the form of a return to the strict doctrines of the Koran, and a desire to propagate them by the sword. A Christian minority living in the place is in danger of being massacred by the revivalists. Pentecostal effusion of the Holy Spirit produced a revival within the infant church, followed by numerous conversions from outside. Revivals, though not called by that name, occurred at intervals from apostolic times till the Reformation, the revivalists being sometimes so unsympathetically treated that they left the church and formed sects, while, in other cases, and notably in those of the founders of the monastic orders, they were retained and acted on the church as a whole. The spiritual impulse which led to the Reformation, and the antagonistic one which produced or attended the rise of the Society of Jesus, were both revivalist. It is, however, to sudden increase of spiritual activity within the Protestant churches that the term 'revival' is chiefly confined. The enterprise of the Wesleys and Whitefield in this country and England from 1738 onward was thoroughly revivalist.... Since then, various revivals have from time to time occurred, and nearly all denominations aim at their production. The means adopted are prayer for the Holy Spirit, meetings continued night after night, often to a late hour, stirring addresses, chiefly from revivalist laymen, and after-meetings to deal with those impressed. Ultimately it has been found that some of those apparently converted have been steadfast, others have fallen back, while deadness proportioned to the previous excitement temporarily prevails. Sometimes excitable persons at revival meetings utter piercing cries, or even fall prostrate.

"These morbid manifestations are now discouraged, and have in consequence become more rare."

In order to understand the principle of the operation of mental suggestion in the revival meeting, we must first understand something of what is known as the psychology of the crowd. Psychologists are aware that the psychology of a crowd, considered as a whole, differs materially from that of the separate individuals composing that crowd. There is a crowd of separate individuals, and a composite crowd in which the emotional natures of the units seem to blend and fuse. The change from the first-named crowd to the second arises from the influence of earnest attention, or deep emotional appeals or common interest. When this change occurs the crowd becomes a composite individual, the degree of whose intelligence and emotional control is but little above that of its weakest member. This fact, startling as it may appear to the average reader, is well known and is admitted by the leading psychologists of the day; and many important essays and books have been written thereupon. The predominant characteristics of this 'composite-mindedness' of a crowd are the evidences of extreme suggestibility, response to appeals of emotion, vivid imagination, and action arising from imitation-all of which are mental traits universally manifested by primitive man. In short, the crowd manifests atavism, or reversion to early racial traits.

Dials, in his Psychology of the Aggregate Mind of an Audience, holds that the mind of an assemblage listening to a powerful speaker undergoes a curious process called 'fusion,' by which the individuals in the audience, losing their personal traits for the time being, to a greater or less degree, are reduced, as it were, to a single individual, whose characteristics are those of an impulsive youth of twenty, imbued in general with high ideals, but sacking in reasoning. Power and will Tarde, the French psychologist, advances similar views.

Professor Joseph Jastrow, in his Fact and Fable in Psychology, says:

"In the production of this state of mind a factor as yet unmentioned plays a leading role, the power of mental contagion. Error, like truth, flourishes in crowds. At the heart of sympathy each finds a home...

No form of contagion is so insidious in its outset, so difficult to check in its advance, so certain to leave g e r m s that may at any moment reveal their pernicious power, as a mental contagion-the contagion of fear, of panic, of fanaticism, of lawlessness, of superstition, of error. In brief, we must add to the many factors which contribute to deception, the recognised lowering of critical ability, of the power of accurate observation, indeed, of rationality, which merely being one of a crowd induces. The conjurer finds it easy to perform to a large audience, because, among other reasons, it is easier to arouse their admiration and sympathy, easier to make them forget themselves and enter into the uncritical spirit of wonderland. It would seem that in some respects the critical tone of an assembly, like the strength of a chain, is that of its weakest member."

Professor Le Bon, in his The Crowd, says:

"The sentiments and ideas of all the persons in the gathering take one and the same direction, and their conscious personality vanishes. A collective mind is formed, doubtless transitory, by presenting very clearly marked characteristics. The gathering has become what, in the absence of a better expression, I will call an organised crowd, or, if the term be considered preferable, a psychological crowd. It forms a single being, and is subjected to the law of the mental unity of crowds....The most striking peculiarity presented by a psychological crowd is the following: Whoever be the individuals that compose it, however like or unlike be their mode of life, their occupation, their character, or their intelligence, the fact that they have been transformed into a crowd puts them in Possession of a sort of collective mind which makes them feel, think and act in a manner quite different from that in which each individual of them would feel, think and act were he in a state of isolation. There are certain ideas and feelings which do not come into being, or do not transform themselves into acts, except in the case of the individuals forming a crowd....In crowds it is stupidity and not mother wit that is accumulated. In the collective mind the intellectual aptitudes of the individuals, and in consequence their individuality, is weakened....The most careful observations seem to prove that an individual immerged for some length of time in a crowd in action soon finds himself in a special state, which most resembles the state of fascination in which the hypnotized individual finds himself....The conscious personality has entirely vanished, will and discernment are lost. All feelings and thoughts are bent in the direction determined by the hypnotizer....Under the influence of a suggestion he will undertake the accomplishment of certain acts with irresistible impetuosity. This impetuosity is the more irresistible in the case of crowds, from the fact that, the suggestion being the same for all the individuals of the crowd, it gains in strength by reciprocity. Moreover, by the mere fact that he forms part of an organised crowd, a man descends several rungs in the ladder of civilisation. Isolated, he may be a cultured individual; in a crowd, he is a barbarian-that is, a creature acting by instinct. He possesses the spontaneity, the violence, the ferocity, and also the enthusiasm and heroism of primitive beings, whom he further tends to resemble by the facility with which he allows himself to be induced to commit acts contrary to his most obvious interests and his best known habits. An individual in a crowd is a grain of sand a m id other grains of sand, which the wind stirs up at will."

Professor Davenport, in his Primitive Traits in Religious Revivals, says:

"The mind of the crowd is strangely like that of primitive man. Most of the people in it may be far from primitive in emotion, in thought, in character; nevertheless, the result tends always to be the same. Stimulation immediately begets action. Reason is in abeyance. The cool, rational speaker has little chance beside the skilful emotional orator. The crowd thinks in images, and speech must take this form to be accessible to it. The images are not connected by any natural bond, and they take each other's place like the slides of a magic lantern. It follows from this, of course, that appeals to the imagination have paramount influence....The crowd is united and governed by emotion rather than by reason. Emotion is the natural bond, for men differ much less in this respect than in intellect. It is also true that in a crowd of a thousand men the amount of emotion actually generated and existing is far greater than the sum which might conceivably be obtained by adding together the emotions of the individuals taken by themselves. The explanation of this is that the attention of the crowd is always directed either by the circumstances of the occasion or by the speaker to certain common ideas-as 'salvation' in religious gatherings....and every individual in the gathering is stirred with emotion, not only because the idea or the shibboleth stirs him, but also because he is conscious that every other individual in the gathering believes in the idea or the shibboleth, and is stirred by it, too.

SOME men are successful as long as someone else stands back of them and encourages them, and some men are successful in spite of Hell!

Take your choice.

And this enormously increases the volume of his own emotion and consequently the total volume of emotion in the crowd. As in the case of the primitive mind, imagination has unlocked the floodgates of emotion, which on occasion may become wild enthusiasm or demoniac frenzy."

The student of suggestion will see that not only are the emotional members of a revival audience subject to the effect of the 'composite-mindedness' arising from the 'psychology of the crowd' and are thereby weakened in resistive power, but that they are also brought under the influence of two other very potent forms of mental suggestion. Added to the powerful suggestion of authority exercised by the revivalist, which is exerted to its fullest along lines very similar to that of the professional hypnotist, is the suggestion of imitation exerted upon each individual by the combined force of the balance of the crowd.

As Durkheim observed in his psychological investigations, the average individual is 'intimidated by the mass' of the crowd around him, or before him, and experiences that peculiar psychological influence exerted by the mere number of people as against his individual self. Not only does the suggestible person find it easy to respond to the authoritative suggestions of the preacher and the exhortations of his helpers, but he is also brought under the direct fire of the imitative suggestions of those on all sides who are experiencing emotional activities and who are manifesting them outwardly. Not only does the voice of the shepherd urge forward, but the tinkle of the bellwether's bell is also heard, and the imitative tendency of the flock, which causes one sheep to jump because one ahead of him does so (and so on until the last sheep has jumped), needs but the force of the example of a leader to start into motion the entire flock. This is not an exaggeration-human beings, in times of panic, fright, or deep emotion of any kind, manifest the imitative tendency of the sheep, and the tendency of cattle and horses to 'stampede' under imitation.

To the student experienced in the experimental work of the psychological laboratory there is the very closest analogy observed in the respective phenomena of the revival and hypnotic suggestion. In both cases the attention and interest is attracted by the unusual procedure; the element of mystery and awe is induced by words and actions calculated to inspire them; the senses are tired by monotonous talk in an impressive and authoritative tone; and finally the suggestions are projected in a commanding, suggestive manner familiar to all students of hypnotic suggestion. The subjects in both cases are prepared for the final suggestions and commands, by previously given minor suggestions, such as: 'Stand up,' or 'Look this way,' etc., in the case of the hypnotist; and by: 'All those who think so-and-so, stand up,' and 'All who are willing to become better, stand up,' etc., in the case of the revivalist. The impressionable subjects are thus accustomed to obedience to suggestion by easy stages.

And, finally, the commanding suggestion: 'Come right up-right up-this way-right up-come, I say, come, come, COME! 'etc., which takes the impressed ones right off their feet and rushes them to the front, are, almost precisely the same in the hypnotic experiment or séance, on the one hand, and the sensational revival, on the other. Every good revivalist would make a good hypnotic operator, and every good hypnotic operator would make a good revivalist if his mind were turned in that direction.

In the revival, the person giving the suggestions has the advantage of breaking down the resistance of his audience by arousing their sentiments and emotions. Tales depicting the influence of mother, home and heaven; songs like 'Tell Mother, I'll Be There'; and personal appeals to the revered associations of one's past and early life tend to reduce one to the state of emotional response, and render him most susceptible to strong, repeated suggestions along the same line. Young people and hysterical women are especially susceptible to this form of emotional suggestion. Their feelings are stirred, and the will is influenced by the preaching, the songs, and the personal appeals of the co-workers of the revivalist.

The most sacred sentimental memories are reawakened for the moment and old conditions of mind are rein sured. 'Where Is My Wandering Boy Tonight?' Brings forth tears to many a one to whom the memory of the mother is sacred, and the preaching that the mother is dwelling in a state of bliss beyond the skies, from which the unconverted child is cutoff unless he professes faith, serves to move many to action for the time being. The element of fear is also invoked in the revival-not so much as formerly, it is true, but still to a considerable extent and more subtly. The fear of a sudden death in an unconverted condition is held over the audience, and, "Why not now-why not tonight ? "is asked him, accompanied by the hymn; "Oh, Why Do You Wait, Dear Brother?" As Davenport says:

"It is well known that the employment of symbolic images immensely increases the emotion of an audience. The vocabulary of revivals abounds in them-the cross, the crown, the angel band, hell, heaven. Now vivid imagination and strong feeling and belief are states of mind favourable to suggestion as well as to impulsive action. It is also true that the influence of a crowd largely in sympathy with the ideas suggested is thoroughly coercive or initiative upon the individual sinner. There is considerable professed conversion which results in the beginning from little more than this form of social pressure, and which may never develop beyond it. Finally, the inhibition of all extraneous ideas is encouraged in revival assemblies both by prayer and speech. There is, therefore, extreme sensitiveness to suggestion. When to these conditions of negative consciousness on the part of an audience there has been added a conductor of the meetings who has a high hypnotic potential, such as Wesley or Finney, or who is only a thoroughly persuasive and magnetic personality, such as Whitefield, there may easily be an influence exerted upon certain individuals of a crowd which closely approaches the abnormal or thoroughly hypnotic. When this point is not reached there is still a great amount of highly acute though normal suggestibility to be reckoned with."

The persons who show signs of being influenced are then 'laboured with' by either the revivalist or his co-workers. They are urged to surrender their will, and 'Leave it all to the Lord.' They are told to 'Give yourself to God, now, right now, this minute'; or to 'Only believe now, and you shall be saved'; or 'Won't you give yourself to Jesus?' etc. They are exhorted and prayed with; arms are placed around their shoulders, and every art of emotional persuasive suggestion is used to make the sinner 'give up.'

Star buck in his The Psychology of Religion relates a number of instances of the experiences of converted persons at revivals. One person wrote as follows:

"My will seemed wholly at the mercy of others, particularly of the revivalist M_. There was absolutely no intellectual element. It was pure feeling. There followed a period of ecstasy. I was benton doing good and was eloquent in appealing to others. The state of moral exaltation did not continue. It was followed by a complete relapse from orthodox religion."

Davenport has the following to say in reply to the claim that the old methods of influencing converts at a revival have passed away with the crude theology of the past:

"I lay particular stress upon this matter here, because, while the employment of irrational fear in revivals has largely passed away, the employment of the hypnotic method has not passed away. There has rather been a recrudescence and a conscious strengthening of it because the old prop of terror is gone. And it cannot be too vigorously emphasized that such a force is not a 'spiritual' force in any high and clear sense at all, but is rather uncanny and psychic and obscure. And the method itself needs to be greatly refined before it can ever be of any spiritual benefit whatever. It is thoroughly primitive and belongs with the animal and instinctive means of fascination. In this bald, crude form, the feline employs it upon the helpless bird and the Indian medicine-man upon the ghost-dance votary. When used, as it has often been, upon little children who are naturally highly suggestible, it has no justification whatever and is mentally and morally injurious in the highest degree. I do not see how violent emotional throes and the use of suggestion in its crude forms can be made serviceable even in the cases of hardened sinners, and certainly with large classes of the population the employment of this means is nothing but psychological malpractice. We guard with intelligent care against quackery in physiological obstetrics. It would be well if a sterner training and prohibition hedged about the spiritual obstetrician, whose function it is to guide the far more delicate process of the new birth."

Some who favour the methods of the revival, but who also recognise the fact that mental suggestion plays a most important part in the phenomena thereof, hold that the objections similar to those here advanced are not valid against the methods of the revival, inasmuch as mental suggestion, as is well known, may be used for good purposes as well as bad-for the benefit and uplifting of people as well as in the opposite direction. This being admitted, these good folks argue that mental suggestion in the revival is a legitimate method or "weapon of attack upon the stronghold of the devil." But this argument is found to be defective when examined in its effects and consequences. In the first place, it would seem to identify the emotional, neurotic and hysterical mental states induced by revival methods with the spiritual uplift and moral regeneration which is the accompaniment of true religious experience. It seeks to place the counterfeit on a par with the genuine-the baleful glare of the rays of the psychic moon with the invigo rating and animating rays of the spiritual sun. It seeks to raise the hypnotic phase to that of the 'spiritual-mindedness' of man. To those who are familiar with the two classes of phenomena, there is a difference as wide as that between the poles existing between them.

As a straw showing how the wind of the best modern religious thought is blowing, we submit the following, from the volume entitled

Religion and Miracle, from the pen of Rev. Dr. George A. Gordon, pastor emeritus of the New Old South Church of Boston:

"For this end professional revivalism, with its organisations, its staff of reporters who make the figures suit the hopes of good men, the system of advertisements, and the exclusion or suppression of all sound critical comment, the appeals to emotion and the use of means which have no visible connection with grace and cannot by any possibility lead to glory, is utterly inadequate. The world waits for the vision, the passion, the simplicity and the stem truthfulness of the Hebrew prophet; it awaits the imperial breadth and moral energy of the Christian apostle to the nations; it awaits the teacher who, like Christ, shall carry his doctrine in a great mind and a great character."

While there have undoubtedly been many instances of persons attracted originally by the emotional excitement of the revival, and afterwards leading worthy religious lives in accordance with the higher spiritual nature, still in too many cases the revival has exerted but a temporary effect for good upon the persons yielding to the excitement, and after the stress has passed has resulted in creating an indifference and even an aversion for true religious feeling. The reaction is often equal to the original action. The consequences of 'backsliding' are well known in all churches, after a spirited revival. In others there is merely awakened a susceptibility to emotional excitement, which causes the individual to undergo repeated stages of 'conversion' at each revival, and a subsequent 'backsliding' after the influence of the meeting is withdrawn.

Moreover, it is a fact known to psychologists that persons who have given way to the emotional excitement and excesses of the typical revival are rendered afterwards far more suggestible and open to 'isms,' fads and false religions than before. The people flocking to the support of the various pseudo-religious adventurers and impostors of the age are generally found to be the same people who were previously the most ardent and excitable converts of the revival. The ranks of the 'Messiahs,' 'Elijahs' and 'Prophets of the Dawn,' who have appeared in great numbers in this country and England during the past fifty years, have been recruited almost exclusively from those who have previously 'experienced' the revival fervour in the orthodox churches. It is the old story of the training of the hypnotic subject. Especially harmful is this form of emotional intoxication among young people and women. It must be remembered that the period of adolescence is one in which the mental nature of the individual is undergoing great changes. It is a period noted for peculiar development of the emotional nature, the sex nature, and the religious nature. The existing conditions at this period render the psychic debauchery of the revival, séance or hypnotic exhibition particularly harmful. Excessive emotional excitement, coupled with mystery, fear and awe, at this period of life, often results in morbid and abnormal conditions arising in after life. As Davenport well says: "It is no time for the shock of fear or the agony of remorse. The only result of such misguided religious zeal is likely to be a strengthening in many cases of those tendencies, especially in females, toward morbidity and hysteria, toward darkness and doubt."

There are other facts connected with the close relation existing between abnormal religious excitement and the undue arousing of the sexual nature, which are well known to all students of the subject, but which cannot be spoken of here. As a hint, however, the following, from Davenport, will serve its purpose: "... At the age of puberty there is an organic process at work which pushes into activity at nearly the same time the sexual and the spiritual. There is no proof, however, of the causation of the latter by the former. But it does appear to be true that the two are closely associated at the point in the physical process where they branch in different directions, that at that critical period any radical excitation of the one has its influence upon the other."

A careful consideration of this important statement will serve to explain many things that have sorely perplexed many good people in the past, in connection with revival excitement in a town, camp meetings, etc. This apparent influence of the devil, which so worried our forefathers, is seen to be but the operation of natural psychological and physiological laws. To understand it is to have the remedy at hand."

But what do the authorities say of the revival of the future-the new revival-the real revival? Let Professor Davenport speak for the critics-he is well adapted for the task. He says:

"There will be, I believe, far less use of the revival meeting as a crass coercive instrument for overriding the will and overwhelming the reason of the individual man. The influence of public religious gatherings will be more indirect, more unobtrusive. It will be recognised that hypnotization and forced choices weaken the soul, and there will be no attempt to press to decision in so great a matter under the spell of excitement and contagion and suggestion....

The converts may be few. They may be many. They will be measured, not by the capacity of the preacher for administrative hypnotism, but rather by the capacity for unselfish friendship of every Christian man and woman. But of this I think we may be confident-the days of religious effervescence and passion unrestraint are dying. The days of intelligent, undemonstrative and self-sacrificing piety are dawning. To do justly, to love mercy, to walk humbly with God-these remain the cardinal tests of the divine in man.

Religious experience is an evolution. We go on from the rudimentary and the primitive to the rational and the spiritual. And, believe Paul, the mature fruit of the Spirit is not the subliminal uprush, the lapse of inhibition, but rational love, joy, peace, long-suffering, kindness,—goodness, faithfulness, meekness-self control."

The Law of Concentration is one of the major principles which must be understood and applied intelligently by all who would successfully experiment with the principle described in this course as the 'Master Mind.'

The foregoing comments, by leading authorities of the world, will give you a better understanding of the Law of Concentration as it is often used by those who wish to 'blend' or 'fuse' the minds of a crowd so they will function as a single mind.

You are now ready for the lesson on Co-operation, which will take you further into the methods of applying the psychological laws upon which this philosophy of success is based.

□□□